We hope you enjoy thi~~~ ~~~ ~~~ Please return ~~~
renew it by the due da~~~

You can renew it at w~~~ ~~~ or
by using our free libra~~~

D0866084

Otherwise you can phone 0344 800 8020 -
please have your library card and PIN ready.

You can sign up for email reminders too.

Christina Courtenay is an award-winning author of historical romance and time slip (dual time) stories. She started writing so that she could be a stay-at-home mum to her two daughters, but didn't get published until daughter number one left home aged twenty-one, so that didn't quite go to plan! Since then, however, she's made up for it by having eleven novels published and winning the RNA's Romantic Novel of the Year Award for Best Historical Romantic Novel twice with *Highland Storms* (2012) and *The Gilded Fan* (2014).

Christina is half Swedish and grew up in that country. She has also lived in Japan and Switzerland, but is now based in Herefordshire, close to the Welsh border. She's a keen amateur genealogist and loves history and archaeology (the armchair variety).

To find out more, visit **christinacourtenay.com**, find her on Facebook /**Christinacourtenayauthor** or follow her on Twitter **@PiaCCourtenay**.

By Christina Courtenay

Trade Winds
Highland Storms
Monsoon Mists
The Scarlet Kimono
The Gilded Fan
The Jade Lioness
The Silent Touch of Shadows
The Secret Kiss of Darkness
The Soft Whisper of Dreams
The Velvet Cloak of Moonlight
Echoes of the Runes

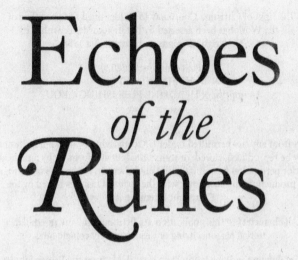

Echoes
of the
Runes

CHRISTINA COURTENAY

REVIEW

First published in 2020
by HEADLINE REVIEW
An imprint of HEADLINE PUBLISHING GROUP

5

Cataloguing in Publication Data is available from the British Library

ISBN 978 1 4722 6826 6

Typeset in Minion Pro by Avon DataSet Ltd, Bidford-on-Avon, Warwickshire

Printed and bound in Great Britain by Clays Ltd, Elcograf S.p.A.

HEADLINE PUBLISHING GROUP
An Hachette UK Company
Carmelite House
50 Victoria Embankment
London EC4Y 0DZ

www.headline.co.uk
www.hachette.co.uk

*To my wonderful mother
Birgitta Tapper
with all my love*

Prologue

On the outermost tip of the peninsula, she waited and watched through the lonely hours of dawn, scanning the water as far as the eye could see for a glimpse of the familiar snake's-head carving at the prow of his ship.

He would come back, she knew it. The runes had told her so, and Old Tyra said they were never wrong. It might not be in this life, but in the next, and although that possibility made her sad, her distress was temporary when she thought of spending eternity with the man she loved.

He would come back.

And she would be waiting.

Chapter One

Sweden, February 2000

One single Viking ring, displayed against a background of blue velvet, shouldn't even have merited a second glance from Mia Maddox. She handled such items on a daily basis as part of her job. And yet, at the sight of this one, she stopped and gasped out loud, barely registering the impressive two-kilo neck torque in the next glass case.

No, it can't be.

The basement of the Historical Museum in Stockholm definitely deserved its name – The Gold Room – as it contained unimaginable amounts of treasure trove. The ring she was staring at, by no means even the largest or finest in the collection, was nothing special. Merely a stylised snake, a common motif for the period in the same type of design as many other items here. It was hand-made and should have been unique, but Mia knew for a fact that it wasn't – because she was wearing an identical ring on her right index finger.

She felt light-headed for a moment, and imagined she heard a susurration echoing around the vault, as if the little serpent itself had just slithered round the perimeter and hissed, its soft scales

3

brushing the stone floor. The fine hairs on her arms and the back of her neck stood up, and she shivered.

'I don't believe it,' she murmured.

Frowning slightly, she looked from one ring to the other, holding up her hand to compare every detail. There was no difference, as far as she could see, other than the size – hers was definitely smaller, in circumference at least. Still, they could have been cast from the same mould, so alike were they. Another shiver went through her.

It was uncanny.

She caught movement out of the corner of her eye and realised someone had been watching her, but whoever it was had ducked out of sight. Probably another tourist, wondering why she was talking to herself. Self-consciously, she stuffed her hand in her pocket while still staring at the exhibits. She blinked several times, as if that would change things, but the rings remained the same. If she hadn't known better, she would have said that their little snake faces had looked pleased to see one another, but that thought was just too bizarre for words. Shaking her head, she tore herself away and headed for the exit. She would have to make enquiries at the information desk to solve this mystery.

The Gold Room was underneath the museum, in a specially excavated vault. Shallow stairs, dark and dimly lit, led back up to the entrance hall. The walls here were painted with Viking motifs in rusty red and ochre, and several enormous rune stones guarded the top and bottom of the staircase. Mia had studied them with interest earlier, but now she was lost in thought and hardly spared her surroundings a glance. As she reached the halfway landing, a man appeared out of nowhere and blocked her way, making her jump.

'Excuse me, but could you come with me for a moment,

please?' he said in Swedish, staring straight at her, his blue eyes intense under a deep frown.

Mia came to an abrupt halt. 'Sorry? Are you talking to me?' She understood him perfectly, being half Swedish herself, but didn't know why he'd be addressing her. She glanced around, but she was the only person on the stairs at that moment and his gaze was firmly fixed on her.

'Yes, I'd like to ask you a few questions, if you don't mind. It concerns your ring.' He glanced at the golden serpent that encircled her finger and she fancied she could feel its coils gripping her more firmly, defiantly hanging on for dear life, as if this man posed a threat to it. But that was just ridiculous. What the hell was the matter with her? She wasn't normally this fanciful.

'M-my ring?' Unconsciously she made a fist to conceal it, but that was futile, as he'd obviously seen it already. And once seen, it wasn't easily forgotten. The reptile had a head at either end of its body, which was curious to say the least. Beautifully shaped, it was covered in tiny decorations consisting of lines and swirls all along its back. Whenever she moved her hand, the pure gold glinted. Eighteen carat? Maybe even twenty-four. For a brief moment now she thought the snake's eyes glittered with . . . what? Excitement? Anger?

She shook her head again. The snake was an inanimate object; it had no expression whatsoever.

'That's right, your ring,' the man said, bringing her back from her strange thoughts. Mia noticed that his accent was Norwegian and wondered what he was doing in Sweden's capital. More to the point, what authority did he have here, challenging her like this?

'And who are you?' she asked. She knew she sounded curt, perhaps even rude, but he had disconcerted her with his sudden appearance.

He pointed to an identity card that hung round his neck. 'Haakon Berger, one of the archaeologists based here.'

'Oh, right.' How stupid not to have noticed the ID, which was right in front of her nose. He must think her a complete idiot. 'Well, I . . .' Panic assailed her, as if she had been caught doing something illegal, but she quashed it. This was ridiculous. She had a right to visit the museum just like anyone else, and the fact that her ring happened to look exactly like one of the exhibits she'd just seen was mere coincidence. Wasn't it?

She'd been going in search of some answers herself. Perhaps this man could provide them. 'OK, fine,' she conceded. 'Lead on then, but I don't have much time, so you'll have to make it quick.'

He nodded and began to mount the remaining steps up to ground-floor level, taking them two at a time. Mia followed at a slower pace, belatedly registering his appearance properly. About her own age – late twenties, early thirties – tall and athletic-looking, with a shock of white-blond hair that stood up as if gelled in place, he could have been an advertisement for pure Viking genes. She had noted that his blue eyes were set in a sharply angled face with a very straight nose and high cheekbones, and with that uncompromising mouth he resembled nothing so much as a Norse god bent on vengeance. She shivered yet again. His anger had seemed directed at her. Why would that be?

The reception area was quiet when they reached it. Two guards stood next to the information desk, talking in hushed voices. Berger nodded to them, as if he knew them well, but didn't pause. He strode across the hall, Mia trailing behind. The huge space was lofty and modern, with enormous windows overlooking a courtyard quadrangle. In front of her was the obligatory gift shop, and in one corner was a door leading to an exhibition about Vikings, which she had wanted to visit. She resented the fact that because of this man there might not be enough time for that now.

'This way,' Berger said, and entered a door marked *Private* set in the far wall. Inside was another staircase, this one much steeper, and they climbed it in silence. As before, he was much faster than her and had to wait at the top, holding open a door that led into a corridor. Mia could hear the hum of voices from somewhere nearby, but there was no time to listen as the archaeologist ushered her into one of the first rooms on the right. It was nothing more than an untidy alcove really, with bits of paper strewn everywhere and old artefacts in boxes and bubble wrap. She wondered how he could work in such a mess.

He removed some items from a chair. 'Please, sit down.'

Mia did as she was asked, then waited as he took the room's only other chair, behind a cluttered desk. He crossed his arms over his chest and regarded her thoughtfully.

'May I ask your name? And do you have any ID with you?'

'Myfanwy Maddox, but I'm usually known as Mia.' Her name was none of his business, but she had no reason to conceal it either. She took out her wallet and handed him her English driver's licence. He gave it a cursory glance before passing it back.

'You're not Swedish, then?' He looked surprised, but she was used to this, since most people took her for a native.

'Half. I'm British, but I have a Swedish mother. I'm visiting her at the moment.' That wasn't quite true, but he didn't need to know that.

'I see. I take it you come here a lot?'

'Yes, but I don't see what that has to do with anything.' Mia frowned at him, but he ignored this and ploughed on.

'Miss Maddox, are you aware that any ancient finds have to be reported to the relevant authorities here in Sweden?' His Norwegian accent was more pronounced now, and she wondered briefly why he was working here in Stockholm instead of in his home country.

'Yes, of course I am. As a matter of fact, I—'

He didn't allow her to finish. 'When you dig up an ancient artefact, you have to take it to the nearest museum or council, where someone will tell you whether you have found anything of interest or not. If you have, they will add the item to the register of antiquities, and then possibly they'll make an appointment to view the site where it was found. In certain cases, you may be allowed to keep your find, but mostly you'll be recompensed and the item placed in a museum.'

'Yes, yes, I know all that, but—'

He interrupted once more. 'Under *no* circumstances are you allowed to keep the item for yourself if it's valuable. That is a crime.' He emphasised the last word while he glanced at her ring, and Mia followed his gaze, again suppressing the urge to hide the snake.

'Is that what you're accusing me of, Mr Berger?' she demanded, tired of being harangued. 'You think I've dug up this ring and kept it without telling anyone?'

He nodded. 'Judging by the length of time you stood in front of the display case downstairs, it can't have escaped your notice that there is a ring exactly like it in the museum's collection. As far as I'm aware, no permission has been granted to any jewellery company to make replicas of it, although I know a few of the others have been copied. That must mean that yours is as old as the one kept here. May I see it, please?'

He held out an imperious hand and Mia felt obliged to remove the gold snake and pass it across to him. It was an almost physical wrench. That ring was her last link to her beloved grandmother, who had died only a week ago. She couldn't bear to part with it now, and she could have sworn the serpent was

8

just as unwilling to leave her, since it took her a moment to wriggle it off her finger.

He received it reverently, turning it this way and that so the gold glimmered in the light from the small window. After a while, he hunted in his desk drawers until he came up with a magnifying glass, then studied the ring some more. At length, he looked up again and regarded her with a solemn expression.

'Viking. Ninth century, probably the middle to later part. An exact replica of the one downstairs, or as near as makes no difference. I happened to be looking at it only the other day. Now, I should very much like to know where you found it. Wherever it was, I'm afraid you can't keep it. It belongs to the state.'

Mia took a deep breath to contain the anger swirling inside her. How dare he treat her like a thief? She was nothing of the sort, and she knew as much about the subject as he did. Staring him straight in the eyes, she prepared herself for a fight.

'Now that's where you're wrong. And I can prove it.'

Chapter Two

'What do you mean, you can prove it? I'm an expert on Viking artefacts and you can't fool me into believing that ring is a fake. I can tell the difference, you know. It's my job.'

Haakon Berger glared at the woman, whose clear grey eyes were shooting sparks of anger at him, like sunlight glinting off ice. She looked seriously offended, her long, curly dark hair bouncing as she tossed her head, but he crossed his arms over his chest and waited. He knew that ring was over a thousand years old and it belonged in a museum. End of story.

She raised her chin. 'I'm not going to try and bamboozle you in any way. I know as well as you do that it's not a fake. As a matter of fact, I work at the British Museum in London, in the department that specialises in exactly this era. It's part of my job to be able to identify Viking artefacts too.'

He felt his frown deepen. 'Is that how you came by it then, as part of an English collection?' Although if that was the case, she still shouldn't be walking around wearing it, let alone taking it to Sweden illegally.

Mia shook her head. 'No, my Swedish grandmother gave it to me a few days ago, just before she passed away, in fact. It's been in her family for donkey's years, a family heirloom I suppose you could call it.'

'So someone in your family found it? Then it's still treasure trove, even if it was years ago.' He sent her a look of triumph, but she held his gaze with her own, not backing down.

'I doubt it. You see, there's no proof that it was found anywhere. It's mentioned in a will dated sixteen hundred and something, so it could have been handed down through the generations long before that. It might not have been buried in the earth at all, and you can't prove that it was.'

Haakon gave her another hard stare, wishing he could see through her and into her brain in order to check whether she was lying or not. It sounded plausible, but he had to make sure. 'And you can show me that will?' he asked curtly.

'Yes, when the lawyers finish sorting out my grandmother's effects. She told me I was to inherit most of her possessions, so I assume it will be with her papers. No doubt that will take a while, though.'

He took a moment to digest this information, then relaxed his expression a little. If she had proof that the ring was an heirloom, there was nothing he could do. But damn, he'd love to acquire it for the museum. Having a pair – a his and hers, if he wasn't mistaken, judging by their sizes – was extremely rare, if not unheard of. Not to mention exciting. He looked at Mia Maddox again. 'Do you know where your grandmother's family came from? Was there a farm or other property in particular?'

'No, but she said the land her summer cottage is built on had been in the family for a long time. That's on the southern shore of Lake Mälaren.'

'Really? The other ring was found near that lake. I wonder if they were originally a pair, or whether a goldsmith in that area just happened to make two that he sold to different buyers?' For some reason he was sure they were a pair, but he didn't want to tell her that, as it was just a gut instinct.

'I don't suppose we'll ever know.'

And what were the odds of both of them turning up in the twenty-first century? Pretty slim, actually, but it had happened.

Haakon studied the ring through the magnifying glass again. 'There's an inscription on yours. Runes. It looks like it could be E and R, and the last letter might be an I, but it's not clear. The other ring, if I remember correctly, has A and U written on the inside, and possibly an R at the end.'

Mia shrugged. 'So no similarities. That doesn't tell you anything.'

'Still, I'd like to examine the two together. Would you consider leaving your ring here for a day or two?' The thought of reuniting them made his heart rate kick up a notch, but Mia shook her head.

'No, I'm sorry, I can't let it out of my sight. I swore to Gran that I would keep it safe. If you want to examine it, you'll have to do so with me in the room, and right now, I simply don't have time. The funeral is tomorrow, and after that I have to return to London, to my job.'

Frustration coursed through him, but he didn't protest. 'Could you at least give me your contact details, then perhaps we could arrange for you to come in at some future date? And if at all possible, I'd like to have a look at that property you mentioned. There might be clues in the terrain as to whether it could have been a Viking settlement or burial ground. If that ring really was handed down through the generations, it's plausible that your family stayed in the same area. And if it was found – albeit centuries ago – it could have been there.'

'I suppose.' He pushed a pen and a notepad towards her, and she scribbled something before fishing a business card out of her purse. She tore off the piece of paper and handed it to him together with the card. 'Here. I'm at work most days, so it's easier if you contact me there. And this is where the cottage is. You can drive out and have a look if you want. Just go in through the gate; it's not locked. Obviously you can't get into the house itself, but then there wouldn't be anything of interest there anyway.'

He glanced at what she'd written, and at her card, which appeared to be genuine. *Mia Maddox, Conservator, Department of Prehistory & Europe, British Museum.* That made her a colleague, and therefore, hopefully, more trustworthy. 'Thank you, I might do that.' *Correction – I will definitely do that, and soon.* He looked up, feeling slightly awkward now. 'I'm sorry if I sounded a bit harsh earlier. I just get so frustrated with all these amateur archaeologists out there with their metal detectors. They have no idea what damage they're doing, making our job impossible when they dig things up without recording anything. Context, you know?'

Mia nodded. 'I know, it's the same in England, or so my colleagues tell me. I don't do much fieldwork myself. I promise you I'm not one of them, though. I'm on your side.'

He smiled. 'I'm glad to hear it.' And he was starting to believe that, at least.

She smiled back, relaxing at last, and Haakon felt a shiver of awareness slither through him. Those sparkling grey eyes, that tiny tip-tilted nose with its sprinkling of freckles, not to mention the glorious hair . . . she was lovely, and the sight of her affected him on an almost visceral level, something he'd never experienced before. He stood up abruptly, uncomfortable yet at the same time wanting her to stay a bit longer, but she got to her feet as well and grabbed her bag.

'Goodbye, Mr Berger,' she said firmly, and left the room before he could think of any way of continuing the conversation.

13

But it didn't matter, because he was sure they would meet again.

For now, he was going to have another look at the ring downstairs.

Birch Thorpe, or *Björketorp* in Swedish, was what the Swedes called a summer cottage – a small house by a lake, specifically built for living in only during the brief Nordic summer months.

As Mia stood at the back of her grandmother's house the following day, leaning her forehead against the cold glass panes of the nearest window, she breathed in the musty smell of neglect. Although Granny Elin had in fact lived here all year round, no one had been in the cottage for some time now, not since Elin had been taken ill. She'd been in hospital for over two months, which meant her home was in desperate need of cleaning and airing out. Sadly, that would have to wait, since Mia had to return to England that afternoon, and the Lord only knew when she'd be able to come back and see to everything.

The lake was visible to the left and right of a small peninsula that jutted out straight in front of her. It pointed like a finger towards an uninhabited island not too far from the shore, which was partly covered in fir trees and pine, with rocky outcrops next to the water. On this bleak day in February, the view was monochrome and dull, a stark contrast to the glorious riot of colours she was used to seeing every summer when she visited. There had been snow on the ground until recently, but it was thawing at the moment and lay in dirty, slushy piles in the garden and the field beyond. There was still some ice on the lake, but only hugging the shoreline; further out, the water was open, and angry waves lapped at the edges of the frozen parts.

Birch Thorpe was situated to the west of Stockholm, on the southern shore of Lake Mälaren, which wasn't strictly speaking a lake at all. Rather, it was an inlet of the Baltic Sea, stretching narrow tentacles deep into the countryside. In Viking times it had contained saltwater, but at some point after the twelfth century, the land around it rose until water began to flow out to sea instead of in, washing away the salt and transforming Mälaren into a freshwater area. It formed a huge natural network of channels and waterways connecting inland Sweden with the coastal regions and all-important trade routes.

In the old days, Mia knew, rich Swedes would have fled the large cities for their country properties during the hotter months of the year. Sometime in the late nineteenth and early twentieth centuries, the middle classes had begun to copy this exodus, although on a smaller scale. Thus, tiny wooden houses, usually without running water or any other amenities, began to crop up around the numerous Swedish lakes, and the traditional summer cottage was born.

With literally a hundred thousand lakes dotted all over the country, there was no shortage of land to be had for this purpose, but when Elin's family had followed suit, they apparently already owned the land needed.

'Mum, didn't Gran say her family had farmed in this area for generations?'

Her mother, Gunilla, was sitting in an antique rocking chair to her left, restlessly swinging it back and forth. 'What? How should I know? You were the one always listening to her stories, not me. Although come to think of it, I do remember visiting some cousins at a nearby farm a couple of times when I was little. I think they sold up in the late seventies, though.'

Interesting. Gran had never mentioned them, and Mia hadn't bothered to verify anything as fact, but she was now determined to check the records at the earliest opportunity. If nothing else, she wanted to prove to Berger that she hadn't been lying.

The house itself was a two-storey timbered building with a large glassed-in veranda at the back – a sort of early version of a conservatory – facing the lake. The ground floor was divided into two halves: a large kitchen to the left and a sitting room to the right, with a steep staircase rising in between them. The second floor contained two bedrooms with dormer windows and sloping ceilings, built under the eaves of the roof to utilise every inch of space, and a tiny bathroom in the middle.

Mia sighed and, still staring straight ahead, tackled the elephant in the room. 'She should have given the house to you. I live too far away to spend enough time here. Do you want me to sign over the deeds?'

'Heavens, no! Far be it from me to take something she obviously didn't want me to have.'

Mia heard the hurt in her mother's voice. '*Mamma . . .*' she began, using the Swedish version of the word on purpose because she knew that Gunilla liked it and she hoped it might placate her.

'No. I know you think I'm being childish, but your grandmother made it clear to me that you were to have Birch Thorpe. I had to sign a document renouncing my claim on the estate in your favour, since children automatically inherit half in this country. I don't deserve it, because she considered me a bad mother. And daughter, for that matter.'

'That's not true. She was always there for you.'

That wasn't strictly the truth either, although Mia kept that thought to herself. Gunilla had gone through a rough patch in her late twenties, becoming an alcoholic and having to give up custody of Mia to her then husband. And although Elin had done her best to help by having Mia to stay every summer, the old lady hadn't been very patient with her daughter. In Elin's opinion, Gunilla lacked willpower and ought simply to have pulled herself together. She never saw that her daughter first needed to eliminate the deep unhappiness that had caused her to turn to drink in the first place.

'No, she wasn't. She just paid for things and waited for me to sort myself out.'

'Well maybe that was what you needed,' Mia dared to suggest. 'If she had cosseted you, would you have made the effort to stop drinking and make a new life for yourself?'

'Of course I would, and a lot faster too,' Gunilla replied, sounding irritated, but Mia didn't believe her. Still, it was all water under the bridge now. Gunilla had a new husband and two young sons to keep her on the straight and narrow. She seemed happy with her life, most of the time. Except when she met up with Mia and the old feelings of guilt were stirred up. It was silly, because Mia didn't bear any grudges.

She sighed again, not wanting to get into an argument. 'Well, it's madness, giving me this. I told Gran that. How am I supposed to find the time to come over here and keep an eye on the place? I've got my work to do in England, and Charles won't want to spend every holiday here. Although he has nothing against Sweden as such, he loves travelling to different places.'

She tried to imagine her English fiancé spending his summers here, the way she herself had always done, and failed. He'd been here once, but it wasn't a successful visit. The shabby decor and somewhat primitive conditions, along with the whole living-in-tune-with-nature thing that Gran had going on, made him seem like a fish out of water. Charles was a city boy, a Londoner born and bred, and asking him to do something like put a worm on a hook to go fishing stumped him. For Mia's sake he'd tried to fit in, but she could tell he was supremely uncomfortable the whole time, and she'd visited on her own from then on.

For some reason she suddenly pictured Haakon Berger here. No doubt he'd be in his element – worms wouldn't faze him, and as an archaeologist he'd be used to roughing it. She remembered his face as he'd smiled at her yesterday, taking her by surprise. It had totally transformed his features, so much so that she'd nearly gasped. With the stern expression gone, she'd seen a dangerously attractive man, but not one she ought to have noticed. She had a fiancé, and besides, Berger wasn't her type. Men with looks like his were usually only too aware of their charm, and insufferable as a result. She'd fallen for that before and it hadn't ended well.

Best not to go back and see him, she decided. He'd probably forgotten all about her ring by now anyway. Or if he hadn't, she'd send him copies of the old wills once she received them. No need for any further contact between them at all.

'You could rent it out, you know?' Gunilla's words broke into her thoughts. 'Lots of Germans come over in the summer. I bet they'd pay huge sums to stay in a cottage like this. Or you could employ someone to look after it. She left you enough money to do that.'

'I don't think that's what she meant me to use it for.' Mia felt the hopelessness of it all settle like a heavy weight in her stomach. Gran had wanted her to continue to spend her summers in Sweden, but she wasn't a child any more and it just wasn't possible. She had a life in England. *I'm more English than Swedish, aren't I?*

She stared at the island again. So many happy memories of summer picnics, rowing out there with Gran and sitting on a blanket eating cake while listening to the old lady's stories.

'This place is special,' Elin had told her. 'Magical. It's belonged to our family for hundreds of years and it must stay that way. My father made me promise, and one day it will be up to you to keep it safe.'

'Safe from what?'

'Intruders.' Gran had looked serious. 'There are people who want to build on islands like this, but it should remain unspoilt.'

She'd swept an arm around. 'Can you imagine ruining this beautiful setting by cutting down the trees? It would be sacrilege.'

Mia didn't know what that word meant at the time, but she got the message. The island had to be protected. And she'd sworn to Gran that she would do her best, but how was she supposed to keep that promise now?

'So what are you going to do?' Gunilla asked, as if sensing Mia's turmoil.

'I don't know. I'll have to think about it. Could you possibly keep an eye on it for me until the spring at least? Maybe get a cleaning lady in every now and then – I'll pay, of course. I really don't want to rush into anything.'

'OK, fine, but you'd better make your mind up quickly. I don't have time to traipse out here every week. The place reminds me too much of my mother.'

Mia regarded her sadly. The hurt ran deep, she could see that. The rift between her mother and grandmother had never been healed, and it made her unhappy to think that it never would be now.

Gran was gone, and all that was left was Birch Thorpe. How could she possibly sell it? And yet how could she keep it?

Chapter Three

Haakon pushed open the rickety gate and closed it carefully behind him. It looked as though it could do with some new hinges; at least one of them was hanging off just one screw. The fence around the property also needed attention, some of it leaning at a precarious angle. No doubt the heavy snowdrifts earlier in the year had weighed it down, and someone would have to prop the fence posts up again during the spring. Mia? He smiled at the thought. She hadn't looked strong enough for such hard work.

A small sign told him he was definitely in the right place – *Björketorp* – and he walked across the garden, squelching through the slushy piles of snow that hadn't yet disappeared. He hated this time of year – neither proper winter nor full-on spring – when everything looked dull and dirty. The tufts of grass sticking up in between the snow heaps were yellowish and sickly-looking. He longed for spring, when everything would go back to vibrant green, but it would be a while yet.

Would Mia return then? And could he persuade her to come to the museum so he could study her ring some more?

'Oh, why does it matter?' he said out loud, exasperated at himself. He had loads of other work to be getting on with. This one ring was insignificant, way down on the list. And yet he couldn't let it go. The image of Mia smiling at him was still clear in his mind, refusing to let him forget.

At the back of the house, the lawn sloped gently towards the lake. He went to the shore first, checking the lie of the land from there upwards. A shimmer of excitement shot through him.

'Perfect,' he muttered.

Turning back to the water, he saw a small bay with a jetty, protected by a promontory, and a little island further out. A natural harbour, it would have been big enough for a Viking ship and a couple of rowing boats for sure, and he could visualise a much larger jetty sticking out into the water. Tethered to the end of it would be a *knarr*, perhaps, the type of vessel used for trading – they were usually short and broad, with high sides, the keel not too deep in the water. Or maybe a *karv*, a more versatile ship that was handy both for trading or as a warship. He narrowed his eyes and pictured the scene in his mind. Sail furled at the bottom of the mast in readiness, warriors boarding, stowing their sea chests under the narrow benches and hanging colourful shields along the railing, picking up their oars, cursing and laughing . . . It would have been a magnificent sight. Exciting.

Behind him and to the right of the house the land rose higher. It seemed to form a small plateau that would have been just right for a settlement – far enough from the water and with a view over the surrounding countryside. Trees grew up there now, but they would have come later, after the settlement was abandoned perhaps. Again Haakon imagined the scene – a huge longhouse in the centre with lots of smaller buildings around it, smoke drifting out of the thatched or turf roofs, and people scurrying around while performing their daily tasks . . .

He shook his head. It was almost too real, and for a moment there he'd thought he could smell the woodsmoke, hear the high-pitched voices of children and the sounds of daily activity. His imagination was working overtime today.

Glancing down at his right hand, guilt assailed him as a glint of gold flashed in the pale winter sun. He'd 'borrowed' the Viking ring from the museum for the day, a highly irregular thing to do. *No, be honest – it's totally against the rules. Technically you're a thief.* He made a fist and shoved his hand back into his pocket. What had possessed him? He'd taken it out of the display case, filling in a form to say he was studying it for a project he was working on, but that wasn't true at all. He'd just had this feeling that he ought to bring it here. No, he *had* to bring it.

Back to the place it had come from?

It certainly felt like it, but he had no proof of that whatsoever. Just gut instinct, and right now it was telling him to go up that hill to look for clues.

With long strides, he set off.

Irish Sea, AD 869

Haukr Erlendrsson was angry.

So angry, in fact, that he thought he might almost qualify as a berserker. Several weeks in an open boat, sailing all the way from Svíariki and across the North Sea, had not cooled his temper. Neither had the efforts of his friends and companions on the journey, nor copious amounts of ale. Being buffeted by rough seas and howling winds only added to his frustration, and the burning fury inside him refused to be quenched.

And it was all his wife's fault.

It had started with a question . . .

'Did they not have any nice silver jewellery for sale this time?'

Instead of finishing her evening meal like everyone else, Ragnhild had been fiddling with the string of amber beads he'd just bought her on his recent trading journey to Heiðabýr and, along the way, the island of Gotland.

Haukr looked from her to the necklace and back again. 'You already have silver rings aplenty. I thought that necklace was more beautiful. Did you not see the little seed trapped inside the largest bead?' It fascinated him, and he'd paid a goodly sum for it once the seller showed him that amazing feature.

Ragnhild shrugged. 'It's well enough. A mere trinket, though.'

'Trinket? I'll have you know it cost more than the arm ring I brought you last time.'

Her eyebrows went up. 'You surprise me, *bóndi*.' But she didn't look impressed.

An uncomfortable silence ensued while Haukr simmered quietly. Her unspoken words were clear – he'd not brought her a good enough gift. Silver and shiny objects were what she coveted. But he wasn't a king and she a queen. Although well connected and known as a jarl, he was really just a prosperous farmer who gave her what he could afford. If it wasn't to her liking . . .

Ragnhild suddenly turned to the man seated on her left, and elbowed him to get his attention. 'What did you bring back for your wife, Steinn?'

'What? From the journey?' Steinn looked confused. 'A silver ring. Why?'

It was clear he'd not been listening to their conversation. Ragnhild turned to Haukr with a small smile of triumph. 'See? Even Steinn knows how to please a woman.'

Haukr glared at her. 'I thought that was what I was doing. Most wives would be very happy with such a necklace. Obviously I'll have to bring you something better next time.'

'Why wait a whole year? And there's no guarantee the harvests will be as good. I hear tell there are still rich pickings abroad for those who go a-viking. My brothers were talking about going soon. Perhaps you could join them?'

There was a challenge in her blue eyes, but Haukr ignored it. 'We have no need to plunder.' He swept a hand out to indicate everything set out on the trestle tables before them. 'Do we not have plenty? No one goes hungry here.' He was proud of that. They were doing better and better each year, and lived well. 'Besides, you have five brothers, with only one settlement between them once your father dies. It makes sense that at least some of them will have to seek their luck elsewhere.'

Ragnhild snorted. 'We have food, yes, but nothing to show our status. You have the biggest landholding in this area, your father was related to the king, and yet we have no wealth on display.' She narrowed her eyes at him. 'Are you a coward that you do not go a-viking like everyone else?'

She had chosen – whether on purpose he'd never know – a moment when there was a lull in the conversations around them, and her voice was loud enough for every man in his hall to hear. Every single one. The challenge was clear, and there was a collective intake of breath before a hush descended as they all waited to hear his reply.

Ragnhild folded her arms and a small smile played on her lips. She was normally a beautiful sight, but in that moment all he wanted was to wring her neck. She'd backed him into a corner and she knew it.

She pressed home her advantage, pulling the amber necklace over her head and putting it on the table. 'Beads. No gold, no silver. Go out and plunder, I say. Bring me back something worthy of our status. And some more thralls wouldn't go amiss either. Fifteen at the very least. The ones you purchased are lazy and good for nothing, and we need to clear more land. How will we ever grow richer otherwise?'

And then she had the gall to turn her back on him, rise from the table and walk away, as if she had dismissed him, given him his marching orders. Haukr was almost incoherent with rage. It was a most unusual state for him, as hardly anything ever riled him, but he knew well enough that once an idea entered Ragnhild's head, he'd never hear the end of it until she'd had her way. He could ignore her, but as she'd called his manhood and courage into question in front of all and sundry, he now had no choice but to prove himself to everyone. It went against the grain, it surely did, but he couldn't see any other way.

So, still simmering with fury, he'd gathered his men and left the very next day, even though it was really too late in the year for such ventures. It would serve the woman right if none of them came back at all. Although perhaps that was what she was hoping for . . .

His anger still boiled like a bubbling cauldron in his veins, and he felt totally unlike himself. Normally he would never even contemplate taking anything that he hadn't honestly paid for. Or at least he hadn't done since he was young and hot-headed and had gone raiding with his father and uncle one summer. Normally he would never fight anyone he had no grudge against. But he was not himself, and he was about to do just that.

Chapter Four

'Where on earth have you been? I thought you said you'd be back in time for dinner. I'd booked us a table at Quentin's.'

'Nice to see you too, Charles. And the funeral went as well as can be expected of these things, thanks for asking.' Mia dropped her heavy bag on the floor with a thump and turned to divest herself of coat and boots. Nothing had gone as planned on the journey back from Stockholm, and she was not in the mood for any complaints from her fiancé.

'Sorry, I didn't mean . . . Of course I'm happy to see you, babe. And I'm sorry I couldn't be there with you, but work is manic at the moment, you know.' Charles came forward, arms outstretched, and she went into his embrace, waiting for the familiar feeling of safety and happiness to envelop her.

It didn't.

Slightly puzzled, she stepped away from him before he had time to kiss her, and headed for the fridge, telling herself she was just tired and still struggling to come to terms with her grief. Soon everything would be back to normal.

Their flat in Canary Wharf was tiny – the front door opened straight into the living room, which was open-plan with a kitchen-ette at one end. A cramped bedroom, a bathroom and the balcony completed their domain, but Mia knew they were lucky to have even this, and she loved it. Buying property in London was incredibly expensive, and a lot of people their age still flat-shared, something she'd hated. Charles often grumbled about the lack of space and the fact that they weren't living in west London. Recently he'd become obsessed with climbing the property ladder and buying something in what he called 'one of the posh areas', but Mia couldn't see the point. A large chunk of their wages already disappeared each month to pay the mortgage, and until such time as they decided to have children, they didn't need anything bigger.

'The plane was late taking off, then we were circling for ages over Heathrow,' she explained as he trailed after her. 'I honestly thought we were going to run out of fuel before they allowed us to land, and I was so grateful I hadn't eaten anything because it was like being on a roller coaster. Is there anything to eat here? I'm starving now.' She pulled open the fridge and stood looking at its meagre contents. Apparently Charles hadn't done any shopping at all since she'd left, except to buy milk and bread, but he'd probably been eating out with his friends and colleagues so there had been no need for anything else.

'Only sandwiches, I guess. As I said, I was going to take you out, but it's too late now.' He leaned on the counter, his hands in his pockets. 'Hey, maybe we can celebrate your homecoming tomorrow instead? I've missed you.'

'Sure, I'd like that.' She glanced at him while rooting around in the fridge drawer for something to put on the bread, and felt guilty for being grumpy. He looked so crestfallen, the lovely surprise of a posh restaurant meal spoiled by her lateness. Not his fault. Well, not anyone's really, just one of those things. 'You know I'm happy to go to Quentin's any time,' she added.

His expression cleared and he leaned over to give her a kiss.

'Excellent! I'll email them to rebook.' And as far as he was concerned, everything was sorted.

Mia wasn't so sure.

He was still the same man she'd said goodbye to a week ago – his boyish features as gorgeous as ever – but for some reason she wasn't feeling the usual pull of attraction, and that disturbed her. What was wrong with her? She loved him.

She'd met him at a fund-raising event at the museum, three years earlier. She was newly employed there then and still reeling from the loss of her dad, and Charles had just landed his dream job at a big accountancy firm. He was great fun to be with, reminding her of an enthusiastic Labrador puppy, all bouncy and happy, and he'd cheered her up. His high spirits were infectious; she'd been carried along on a wave of enthusiasm for life that helped her through her grief. It was just what she needed at the time.

Of average height, but solidly built, with hazel eyes, Charles was charming and good-looking. His dark hair hung in a floppy fringe across his forehead in that endearing, Hugh Grant fashion, and he'd flirted with her outrageously until she agreed to meet him for a drink the next day. Things had happened swiftly after that, and when Mia's then flatmate decided to move out, Charles moved in. Soon afterwards, they bought the flat in Canary Wharf.

And they'd been very happy living together – were still happy – so why did she have this feeling that something had changed? She tried to shake off the unease. She was just exhausted, that was all.

'So how did it go, really? Your mum being difficult?' Charles asked when they were both seated on the sofa in front of the TV, Mia with a plate of sandwiches, a bag of crisps and a glass of milk. She had a childish enthusiasm for 'the white stuff', as the adverts called it, which she'd never outgrown. It was a Swedish thing, as most people there had milk with their meals. Charles nursed a can of beer instead, wrinkling his nose at her choice of beverage while trying to steal some of her crisps.

Mia shrugged. 'Like I said, as well as could be expected. The same as all funerals, I guess. Not exactly a happy occasion, is it?'

'No, but what about afterwards? You said you were seeing a solicitor. Did the old lady leave you anything like you thought she would?'

'Oh, that. Yes, as a matter of fact, she left me everything, except for five thousand pounds each to my half-brothers. My mother wasn't exactly over the moon about that, as you can imagine, although to be fair Gran had always said that was what she was planning to do.'

'Everything? That's wonderful! It means we can put our plans into action much sooner than we—'

'Hold on a minute.' Mia held up a hand to stop him. 'I didn't inherit a fortune, you know. According to the solicitor, there's only about ten thousand pounds once all the expenses have been paid, and that might be needed for the upkeep of the property.'

'Yes, but as soon as you sell the house, there will be quite a little nest egg, won't there?' Charles caught her frown of annoyance. 'What? The will didn't stipulate that you have to go and live there or something, did it? You know I could never give up my job here, I told you before. And Swedish is a language for people with elastic tongues, not normal guys like me.'

'Charles, please stop jumping to conclusions. The will didn't say anything of the sort, but all the same, I think I want to keep the cottage for at least a few years. It's what Gran would have wanted, you know.' She hadn't actually decided this until now, but as she said the words out loud, it felt right.

'Keep it? But it's going to cost you a fortune, and for what? A week now and again by a Swedish lake.'

'I might be able to rent it out.' Although she didn't really want to, and couldn't visualise strangers tramping through Gran's home, using her things, sleeping in her bed . . .

'Honestly, wouldn't it be better to sell up and put some of the money aside? Then you can rent a cottage yourself just as easily, if that's what you want.'

Mia took a deep breath. He didn't understand her strong attachment to Birch Thorpe or the fact that it felt like her last link with her grandmother. To him, it was just a house.

She didn't want to rent just any old cottage. If she was going to Sweden, it had to be to Gran's place. It was her second home. Perhaps her true home. The rational part of her knew Charles was right – it would be silly to hang on to it – but the emotional part was winning at the moment. This was *her* inheritance, and as they weren't married yet, she had a right to decide what to do about it, but she needed time. Time to grieve, time to think. And she really was very tired from the journey, and not in the mood for an argument.

'Please, could we talk about this some other time? It's been a long day and you know what a strain I find it, spending time with my mother. I've had enough strife for one day.'

'Yes, but in my opinion there really isn't anything to talk about, surely? I was looking on the internet only yesterday, and those lakeside properties near Stockholm go for amazing amounts of money. One and a half to two million *kronor*. That's what – a hundred and fifty, two hundred thousand pounds? If we sell it and this, we could definitely afford a flat in west London. Maybe even in Kensington.'

'You checked out the cottage's value already? Without knowing whether it was going to be mine and without asking me if I was selling it?' For some reason this made Mia incredibly angry, although a little voice inside her head told her she was overreacting. She ignored it. 'You had no right to assume that I would want to part with it so soon. Gran's hardly even cold in her grave!'

He held up his hands as if to ward off her anger. 'Whoa, I'm sorry! I was only thinking of our future.' He took one of her hands and stroked it with his fingers. 'I know I'm impatient, but it's because I want to move our relationship to the next level. Instead of waiting a couple more years, we could buy a much nicer place in a matter of months if you sell up. Then we could set the date for the wedding and get everything organised. Isn't that what we've been waiting for? What you want?'

'I don't see what us buying a flat in west London has to do with whether we get married or not.'

'It would be a proper home for us, more fitting. Somewhere special to start our married lives. Not like this . . . this hovel.' He swept a hand out to indicate their tiny living room.

But Mia wasn't buying it. Living in a better area was *his* idea. He was climbing the corporate ladder in one of the biggest accountancy firms in the City, and everything seemed to be about status with him these days. Brand-name clothing, nice watches, flashy company car . . . The truth was, he was ashamed of where they lived, which was ridiculous, but then a lot of his workmates came from affluent backgrounds, so he felt he had a lot of catching up to do.

She swallowed the sharp retort that rose to her lips. Charles was right in a way. She was being selfish, but everything inside her screamed out in protest. Gran hadn't bequeathed her Birch Thorpe in order to give them a leg up the property ladder – it was a legacy to remind Mia that part of her belonged in Scandinavia. Sweden was in her blood, no matter how English she felt.

Elin had been almost obsessive about her Nordic heritage,

especially the Vikings she claimed to be descended from. Ever since Mia's childhood, her grandmother had been telling her stories of great heroes, of journeys far and wide, of plunder and mayhem. They were exciting tales, the kind that stuck in your mind for ever after, with larger-than-life characters and deeds. It was an amazing thought, that Mia belonged to such a nation, if only partly.

'You should be proud to be the descendant of such people,' Elin had told her over and over again, and Mia was, although this conflicted with her equal pride in the Welsh and English ancestors on her father's side, whose praises were sung every time she visited his family.

She sighed now and rose to take her plate to the sink. This flat was shabby and run-down, as well as claustrophobic, but it was all they could afford at the moment unless she sold Birch Thorpe, and she simply couldn't do that. Not yet.

'Let's discuss this tomorrow, I'm off to bed.' She yawned.

'Hmm, bed sounds like a great idea.' Charles's eyes lit up and he tried to reach for her as she passed him on the way to the bathroom. Mia stifled another spurt of irritation and side-stepped him.

'Sorry, Charles, just to sleep,' she said firmly. 'I told you, I've had a long day.'

'Come on, haven't you missed me even a little?' The look he sent her was full of hurt, in turn filling her with remorse.

'Of course I have, but I don't have the energy for the sort of homecoming you're obviously expecting. Maybe tomorrow, OK? Can we just cuddle and go to sleep together? I've missed having you next to me.'

But her olive branch wasn't enough. Charles muttered something about a programme he didn't want to miss. He switched the TV on, louder than was necessary, and Mia sighed. She really was too tired to deal with this. What on earth was the matter with her? She'd so been looking forward to coming home.

She locked herself in the bathroom, where she closed her eyes for a moment and leaned against the door. For some reason an image of Haakon Berger entered her mind again, contrasting strongly with her last view of Charles, angrily channel-hopping. She felt sure that Berger would never behave like that. Then guilt flooded her at this disloyal thought. She didn't know the Norwegian guy from Adam and had no idea how he would or wouldn't behave. Charles was her fiancé and he was entitled to expect a little more enthusiasm from her after such a long absence, surely? But she simply couldn't summon it.

As she lay in bed, thoughts of Birch Thorpe chasing endlessly round her skull, she was sure she hadn't heard the last of Charles's plans for the cottage. She would have to steel herself, as she had a feeling the coming weeks would be very trying.

The last thing her mind registered before sleep claimed her was the feel of the little golden snake wrapped snugly around her finger, as if giving her a reassuring squeeze . . .

Wales, AD 869

In the largest dwelling house at the centre of the village, Ceridwen, sister of Cadoc, the *uchelwr* – the highest-ranking man in the area – knew nothing of what was happening until a large hand was placed over her mouth, waking her from a deep slumber. Her heart stopped mid beat and her eyes flew open, but since her attacker had his back towards the faint light from the smouldering hearth, all she could see was the outline of someone large and menacing.

Stifling a scream, she became paralysed with fear, and panic assailed her when she found that she could only take shallow breaths through her nose. It wasn't enough; she needed more air, else she would faint. Although a part of her knew it was futile, she began to fight him, trying to escape the pressure of that hand, even going so far as to bite it. Her puny efforts were greeted with an impatient sigh, and the man caught both her arms with his free hand and pulled them up over her head as he dragged her out of bed.

Ceri did her best to calm her breathing, but her lungs refused to obey. Sheer terror had her in its grip and she found it impossible to keep her thoughts from imagining the worst. What did he want with her? Actually, she knew that only too well. She'd heard of raids by the Norsemen – who hadn't? – but as far as she knew they had never ventured this far inland, and the people of the village had always felt safe. So safe, in fact, that her brother had gone off to visit a kinsman, leaving only half his men behind with the women, children and old warriors. Ceri cursed inwardly. How could he have been so stupid?

To her surprise, the man let go of her and stepped back. He said something in his own language, and at first she was too busy pulling in huge lungfuls of air to pay attention. When at last her breathing steadied, his words penetrated her befuddled brain and began to make sense. After her mother died young, Ceri had been raised with the help of a Norsewoman – one of her uncles had unexpectedly brought back a wife from Dyflin after a trading expedition across the sea – and she had learned Eydis's language at the same time as her own. The Norseman's speech was only slightly different, his dialect unfamiliar.

'Your valuables,' he hissed again, gesturing at the bracelets she was wearing.

'That is all you want?' She replied in his tongue and drew in another shaky breath when he sent her a swift look of surprise. She wished she'd kept quiet. Now that he knew she could understand him, there was no saying what he'd demand.

'No, but it will do for a start. Hurry now, fetch everything hidden away in here or I'll have to make a thorough search, and you wouldn't like that.'

Her stomach was tied in knots as her brain stuck on that one word – no. He wanted something other than precious things, and there was only one thing she could think of. 'No!' It emerged as a hoarse whisper, even though she hadn't meant to utter it, and she saw his brows come down in a scowl.

'You defy me, woman?' He took a step closer, and Ceri stumbled backwards. He really was enormous – both tall and broad of shoulder – and it made her feel vulnerable and insignificant.

'N-no. I meant only . . .' Turning round, she fumbled in a small kist under one of the benches that circled the walls and pulled out some of her brother's most treasured possessions – a gold torque, a silver chalice, a foreign casket set with precious stones, and a handful of other bits and pieces. She also pulled off her own arm rings, one gold and six silver. 'Here, t-take it all, but please, I beg of you, don't . . .' She broke off, unable to put into words that which she feared so.

'And that?' He pointed at her right hand, and Ceri glanced at the ring she was wearing on the middle finger and slowly shook her head.

'I . . . I'm sorry, it . . . doesn't come off. It's stuck. Has been for months . . .' She knew she was babbling and shut her mouth with an effort. Her words were true, but why should he believe her? The beautiful ring made out of twisted strands of gold was probably just the sort of thing he was after, and it sounded like a pitiful excuse even to her. Would he cut her finger off in order to possess it? She shuddered at the thought.

To her amazement, he didn't insist. 'Very well, perhaps later,' he said, and turned his back on her. He began to stuff the other precious items into a sack at random, as if he didn't much care what they were. Some part of Ceri's brain suddenly registered the fact that he wasn't paying attention to her, and she grabbed her chance. Moving silently and slowly, she retrieved a bow from under a nearby bench, quickly nocked an arrow and aimed it straight at his heart. Her movement made him swing his gaze back in her direction, and he froze, momentarily taken off guard, and stared at her. If the situation had not been so serious, she would have laughed at his incredulous expression. As it was, she hissed at him instead.

'Come one step closer and I'll shoot. Take your loot and get out, Norseman!'

A slow smile spread over his features and a chuckle escaped him. The sound sent a shiver down Ceri's spine, and although he was much better-looking now he'd stopped scowling, somehow she found him even more dangerous when he wasn't angry. 'Put your toy down,' he said. 'I don't normally hurt women, but . . .'

'I mean it – leave!' she insisted. 'You have what you came for.' She prayed he couldn't see that her hand was not as steady as it ought to be, but he merely shook his head at her as if she was a foolish child.

'Not quite. I admire your spirit, but . . .' He dropped the sack to the ground, and for a short moment Ceri's eyes strayed from her target to the goods she'd had to give him. It was all the time he needed. The next thing she knew, a small knife was flying through the air, hitting her with unerring accuracy. It only grazed her shoulder, but that was enough to make her drop the bow. Before she could move so much as a muscle, he had her in a bear grip, her arms pinned to her sides. She was so close she could smell the tang of seawater from his clothing and feel the coarse wool of his tunic against her skin. 'I told you.' He shook his head. 'Women! You're all the same. Never listen.'

The panic she'd been holding at bay could no longer be contained, and she began to fight him as one demented, kicking, biting, clawing, hitting, anywhere and everywhere. This was it. This was the moment she had dreaded, when she had to submit to him in every way, but she refused to do it without a fight. Throughout the frenzied attack, he stood immobile, as if waiting for her to finish, and finally she collapsed against him with a sob, exhausted. 'Damn you! Damn you to *hell.*'

'And where is that then? Nowhere nice, I take it. Sounds very much like the place where the goddess of death, Hel, resides.' Another chuckle rumbled through his chest, and this time she felt it as well, since her cheek was virtually squashed against the front of his clothing.

Just when she thought the situation couldn't deteriorate any further, a hacking cough sounded from the farthest bench, and a small voice called her name. 'Ceri, please . . . need water . . .'

The man's eyes flew to the pale face that had appeared from under a mountain of pelts, then narrowed as he looked down on her. 'Your son?'

'N-no, nephew.' And she probably shouldn't have told him that either.

Abruptly he let her go and gave her a gentle push in the direction of the boy, who was now emerging, still calling her name. 'See to him,' the man said quietly, 'but quickly, then we have to go.'

'G-go?' Ceri hesitated, but he shooed her away.

'If you want him to live, give him whatever it is he's asking for, then come with me without a struggle.'

Her life and her . . . whatever he wanted of her, for the life of her brother's son. Squaring her shoulders, Ceri accepted her fate without hesitation. So be it. For little Bryn's sake she would put up with anything. He was as dear to her as if he'd been her own. It could have been worse; the man could have killed them both already, or he could be threatening to take the sick boy captive too. But why, oh why, could Bryn not have stayed asleep just a few moments longer?

While she bustled about filling a beaker with water from a bucket by the door, she asked quietly, 'Who are you?'

'I am called Haukr *inn hvíti*.'

The white hawk, she translated in her mind, and it was an apt name. His hair was blonder than any she'd ever seen on an adult, a thick fringe of it hanging down almost as far as his eyes, and his nose, although straight and proud, did give him a predatory air.

'Why are you doing this? Why can't your people leave us alone?'

An irritated expression crossed his features and his scowl returned. Ceri feared that she had gone too far, but when he answered, it seemed her question hadn't been the cause of his annoyance. 'You must ask my wife that when you meet her.' With that cryptic utterance, he picked up the sack once more, then turned for the door. 'I'll await you outside. You will hurry, or the boy dies.'

Ceri blinked at the doorway as he disappeared into the night, then she turned to Bryn and whispered urgently, 'Remember that, *cariad*; the man's name is Haukr *inn hvíti*. Can you repeat it for me?'

'Haukr *inn hvíti*,' the child replied. 'Why do I have to remember that?'

'Because I have to go on a journey with him and your father will want to know where I've gone. Tell him . . . tell him I'm fine, but I'll be waiting for him to come and bring me home. Understand?'

'Yes, but who will look after me?' Bryn's tone was querulous, his little body still racked by fever and the painful cough. Ceri didn't want to leave him, but she knew she must hurry or the boy wouldn't live to see the next day.

'I'll find someone, don't worry. Now be a good boy and remember me in your prayers. God willing, I'll see you soon.' She bent to place a swift kiss on his brow, then hurried towards the door.

The White Hawk was waiting, and the sooner they left, the better.

Chapter Five

'What's up with you then? You look like death warmed up.'

Mia looked up and caught sight of her colleague, Alun Emrys, coming towards her across the road. He fell into step beside her as she made her way down Great Russell Street to the British Museum. The enormous classical building with its distinctive columns and pediments emerged on their left, behind the iron railings that flanked the gates. As always, it gave Mia a sense of awe, its sheer size breathtaking and beautiful at the same time.

'That's not funny, Alun. I've just come back from my gran's funeral.'

'Have you?' Alun's smile disappeared. 'Oh shit, no one told me. Sorry, didn't mean to be insensitive.' He looked suitably contrite, and Mia couldn't help but smile at him. Small and wiry, with a shock of curly black hair and twinkling green eyes, he lived in his own little world most of the time, that of ancient manuscripts and Celtic folklore. The world of the *Mabinogion* and other such stories was more real to him than the present, and he didn't pay much attention to what was going on around him.

'It's OK, I forgive you. Actually, I was mostly grumpy because I'm running late. And also I didn't sleep well. Had some really weird dreams last night – about some big Viking guy abducting me!'

Alun spluttered with laughter. 'That'll teach you to stop watching those *Thor* films over and over.'

Mia bumped his arm with her fist but didn't defend herself, because he was right. She should know better than to watch films that bore little resemblance to actual Vikings or their myths. 'Whatever. You're late too – what's your excuse?'

'Overslept. And some days it just takes for ever, doesn't it?'

'Don't I know it!'

The commute to work was a pain – depending on which route she took, there were at least two Tube changes – but it could have been worse and she'd become used to it after a while. She spent most of the journey reading, and the time passed quickly, but some days, like today, there were delays and she ended up rushing. As she'd emerged from the newly refurbished Tottenham Court Road station, the dismal weather hadn't helped – rain, rain and more rain. It dampened her spirits, never mind her clothes. *If you lived in west London, the journey would be much shorter*, a little voice in her head needled her. It was true, but she didn't want to think about that right now.

The walk to the British Museum from the station was short, but by the time she and Alun reached the side entrance, her shoes were already soaked through. At least in Sweden they still had some snow and everyone wore sensible footwear. She decided to wear wellies tomorrow – it was quite fashionable with skirts at the moment, wasn't it?

'So what's been happening here while I've been gone?' It had only been just over a week, but it felt like months.

'In your department?' Alun shrugged. 'As far as I know, just the usual, that's to say nothing very exciting. No earth-shattering new finds brought in, no spectacular archaeological sites unearthed, just boring old cataloguing and cleaning of artefacts.'

'Suits me fine. I feel the need for some routine tasks that I can do without having to think too much.'

'That bloody, was it? The funeral, I mean, not your dream.' Alun looked at her with sympathy in his eyes, and Mia couldn't help but contrast this to Charles's insensitivity. Her fiancé didn't seem to understand how much her grandmother's death had affected her. All that talk about her inheritance – couldn't he see that it was premature? But as he'd said, he *was* only thinking of their future, and perhaps that was what she ought to be concentrating on as well. Only it really was too soon . . .

'To tell you the truth, I'm glad it's over with. Not just because funerals are so godawful, but because it means I don't have to see my mother for a while. We simply don't get on. It was such a relief to have a different life to return to here in London. Now I just want to get back to normal.'

Alun nodded. 'Yeah, I think I know what you mean. My folks and I don't exactly get on either.' He looked glum for a moment, then grinned suddenly. 'So you up for a celebratory pint at lunchtime then?'

'What's there to celebrate?'

'The start of the rest of our lives, of course.'

Mia smiled again. 'Sounds like a great idea. You're on.'

Mia had been back at the museum for over a week and had managed to immerse herself in her work and suppress all thoughts of her grandmother and Sweden. For a museum conservator there was never any shortage of items to assess, restore and catalogue. As always, the satisfaction she derived from returning long-lost artefacts to something resembling their former glory worked its magic on her and calmed her spirit. It was painstaking work, but well worth the effort as layers of dirt disappeared, revealing bronze, silver and sometimes gold. Even humbler items – what Charles called 'boring bits of old pots' – fascinated Mia. There was a special kind of joy in finding potsherds that clearly fitted together like pieces of a puzzle, and then glueing them to form part of a whole. She never tired of her job, and the long hours flew by.

She was kept busy with other things too – meetings about future exhibitions and displays that needed rearranging and so on – but it was all exciting and took her mind off everything else.

In Sweden, the lawyers were busy sorting things out, but so far she hadn't heard from them, and the longer it stayed that way, the better as far as she was concerned. Charles hadn't let up in his campaign to persuade her to sell Birch Thorpe, although he'd toned it down a bit and was only giving her subtle hints at the moment, but for now she was able to say quite truthfully that it wasn't hers yet. Time enough to think about selling later. It saved her from having to have the monumental row she knew was coming when she told him her final decision – that she just couldn't sell it. At least, not yet.

She was in the middle of cleaning a bronze harness buckle dating from the mid seventh century. It was covered in hardened soil and she used a microscope so she could see every millimetre of its surface. After applying a solvent to make the dirt softer, she was painstakingly extracting the soil using a natural thorn held in a pin vice. Thorns were perfect for the job – sharp and pointy enough to reach into any crevice, yet soft and natural so as not to hurt even gold objects in any way. Amazing that nature provided something better than science really, but there it was.

Just as she reached for a tiny brush to get rid of the bits of dirt she had loosened, the phone rang and absently, her mind still on the intricate work, she picked it up.

'Mia Maddox.'

'Miss Maddox, do you speak Swedish?' a male voice enquired with a very strong Scandinavian accent.

'Yes, I do,' she replied in his language, and almost heard a sigh of relief down the line.

'Good, good. I'm sorry to bother you, but my name is Lars Mattsson. Professor Mattsson, to be exact, and I'm calling from the Historical Museum in Stockholm.'

'Oh, right.' He had Mia's full attention now. She had thought him a lawyer and was expecting lots of legal jargon, but this sounded more interesting.

'My colleague Haakon Berger and I went out to look at your property. Birch Thorpe, is it? Anyway, it's rather an exciting place, an ideal site for a Viking settlement in our opinion, although at the moment there is still too much snow to be sure. We did find a couple of potsherds, where the snow had melted recently, forming a little brook. I was wondering if there was any chance you would give us permission to do a dig there this summer? Well, after we carry out some further checks once the snow is gone.'

'A dig? On my property?' Mia was stunned. She had never expected anything to come of Berger's visit to Birch Thorpe; hadn't even thought he would actually bother. The thought of him being there, walking around was . . . disturbing somehow. She had no idea why. 'Well, I don't know . . . Ideal in what way?'

'There's the natural harbour for one thing, with the peninsula jutting out protectively to form a little bay, and then there's its proximity to Birka. You know about Birka, I take it? The ancient trading centre on an island in Lake Mälaren?'

'Yes, of course.' It had been a significant place in the ninth and tenth centuries, with people coming from far and near to exchange goods.

'The cottage is built too near the lake, which wouldn't have been suitable for a Viking settlement. But we noticed that over to the right of the property, if you're looking up from the shore, the land is much higher and forms a plateau; that would have been a good place to build a longhouse. There are also one or two anomalies around it. And as I said, a couple of potsherds. We would definitely want to return later on in the spring to look a bit more, but I just thought I'd contact you now to see if you would be amenable. No point us doing anything otherwise. The paperwork involved would be exhausting.'

Mia suddenly had butterflies dancing in her stomach. The thought of a dig on her land – and she sincerely hoped the lawyers would be finished by then so it really was hers – was exciting. Gran would have been so pleased, especially since it concerned Vikings.

'Yes, I don't see why not.' She tried not to sound too eager. 'But there's one condition. I don't know if Mr Berger told you that I work at the British Museum? I'm a conservator here, in the Department of Prehistory and Europe – that includes the Viking period. So if you don't mind, I'd very much like to be a part of this if you go ahead with it. In fact, I'd insist on being co-director of the project.'

'Do you have experience of that sort of thing, if you don't mind me asking?' He sounded sceptical and she couldn't blame him.

Mia crossed her fingers childishly. 'I do. I've been part of quite a few digs.' And she had, only she'd been there as a student volunteer, many years ago, not in charge of anything. These days she didn't have time to volunteer, but she doubted things had changed much.

'Then of course you must be a part of it. I can quite see that you'd want to be there – I certainly would if it was mine. It'll be very exciting. As I said, this is only a preliminary query, though.

As always, we're short of funds and manpower, so who knows if we can actually put together a team? I'm sure you know how it is; it must be the same in England. These things are never a top priority with the government; we have to be grateful for what we can get.'

'You wouldn't need to pay me, obviously. I'd be responsible for my own food, lodging and expenses, if that would help.' It would mean having to use some of the money Gran had left her, but Mia felt sure the old lady would have approved of her spending the inheritance in this way.

'That would be marvellous! I tell you what, leave it with me and I'll see what I can do. We've got plenty of time before the summer, and we wouldn't start before June anyway.'

'Great. That gives me time to apply for leave of absence too, if necessary.'

'Good, good. Well, I hope to see you in the summer then. If you give me your email address, I'll keep in touch.'

'Yes, let me know as soon as possible, please.' Mia gave him her contact details and hung up, excitement building inside her. It seemed as if fate had taken a hand in this matter once more. Now all she had to do was tell Charles . . . or perhaps not. Best to wait until she knew whether the dig was going ahead or not.

She knew this was effectively burying her head in the sand, but she was still so raw emotionally, she couldn't face any conflict. It would have to wait.

Ceri sat huddled with her back against the hull of the sleek Viking ship, alternately worrying about her own fate and wondering whether Bryn was going to recover from his illness. The hacking cough and high fever had lasted far longer than she would have liked, and without constant ministration there was no saying what could happen. She clenched her fists in anger and frustration. Why did this have to happen now? She felt so helpless. While being hustled down to the river, she had managed to shout an order to Rhedyn, one of the older village women who was of no interest to the raiders. She fervently hoped the woman was capable of looking after the little boy properly. If not . . . well, the alternative didn't bear thinking about.

They were out on the open sea now and Ceri was very glad she had grabbed a plaid blanket to wrap around herself before leaving her brother's house. She'd been sleeping in nothing but her undergown, and the thin linen wouldn't have been much protection against the elements. Her feet were bare too, and she tried to tuck them underneath her legs. There was a chilly breeze, and saltwater droplets sprayed them at regular intervals as the ship's bow cut through the water with surprising smoothness. The clinker-built hull shook intermittently with the impact of the waves, but seemed supple enough to adapt to any conditions. And so far, the motion had been slight, not causing her any undue discomfort.

Two men had hoisted the big square sail by using some sort of pulley system, while two others hung on to ropes to keep the sail steady until it could be tied in place. Once up, it billowed out in the wind and the ship fairly skipped along the surface of the waves with amazing speed. From time to time, the planking at the bottom of the vessel quivered, but it seemed sturdy nonetheless.

When the sun began to rise, she could make out the tired faces of her captors in the grey morning light. There were no more than twelve of them, but for the most part they were all big, muscular men, and she could see how, with a bit of stealth, they'd been able to overpower everyone in the village. For ages the ship had floated silently down the river, its currents propelling them without the need for rowing, but later the men had put their backs into the hard work. No doubt they had wanted to make sure they were as far away from the coast as possible before anyone came in pursuit of them.

'You were right, Haukr, about the rich pickings in Bretland, especially further inland. It took much longer to get here, but it was well worth the effort. Was it in Heiðabýr you heard about this area?'

Ceri looked up at the speaker, a man sitting near the back. He had an old scar across one eyebrow, making him look permanently surprised, and he shot a grin at his leader, who was standing only a few feet away from where Ceri sat. To her surprise, Haukr the White only grunted in reply. He was steering, his white-blond hair flying out behind him in the breeze, his intense blue gaze fixed firmly towards the front, but the expression on his face was anything but triumphant. Ceri would have expected him to be jubilant, congratulating his men on a job well done, but there had been nothing but silence since the start of the journey. Strange. Glancing furtively at the other men, she saw that most of them wore a look of satisfaction, but no one else ventured to address their leader.

What was wrong with the man? Suddenly angry, some devil prompted Ceri to goad him.

'What's the matter, high and mighty one? Did we not provide you with enough spoils?' she sneered.

He blinked, as if his thoughts had been far away, and focused on her with a small frown. 'What are you prattling about, woman?'

'You're not gloating over your bounty as you should, nor shouting for joy. Were you perhaps hoping for more?'

'I had more than enough possessions already.' He shook his head. 'There was no need for any plunder at all, if you ask me, but certain people are never happy with what they do have.'

Another cryptic statement. So puzzled was she by his reply that Ceri stopped trying to annoy him. There was something here that wasn't right, and until she knew what it was, perhaps she should tread carefully, the way his men appeared to be doing. Haukr the White didn't strike her as being like other men, and she determined to find out the cause of his dissatisfaction, and soon.

Her survival, and that of the rest of the captives, might depend on it.

Chapter Six

'So I've come across this story, written down in the twelfth century, but probably passed down through many generations before that . . .'

Mia wasn't really listening as Alun described his latest find in an old manuscript that had been buried inside the wall of a former monastery somewhere near the Welsh Marches. He was forever coming up with such tales, and to her they were just that – fairy tales. But Alun's mission in life was to prove that the people in those stories had actually existed. He believed they were real, even King Arthur of the Round Table, but Mia doubted he'd ever find enough evidence for any of his theories.

'. . . and the manuscript had a much older inscription that'd been scraped off, but it showed up when we used infrared reflectography. It seems to be about this Welsh woman stolen away in the night by some mythical bird of prey – a *hebog* – and held for ransom . . .'

Normally she enjoyed listening to his lovely Welsh accent, as it reminded her of her dad, but today she had other things on her mind and tuned out again. Professor Mattsson had just been in touch to say that he had been given the go-ahead for the dig. He said he'd been out to Birch Thorpe a couple of times, and after a recent spell of warmer weather, he'd found more evidence of Viking occupation.

'I brought some of my university students – did I tell you I teach part-time? – and we did a bit of field walking,' he'd told her. 'Well, not proper field walking, obviously, as there's no actual ploughed area, but I'm sure you know what I mean. In your garden.'

Mia did. A group of people would have checked the ground of her property in a methodical way, looking for fragments of things. Anything that could have archaeological meaning.

'And what did you find?'

'More potsherds, a broken loom weight, a fishing hook made of bone, that kind of thing. All Viking or possibly slightly later.'

'Interesting. I guess I should have had a look around myself, but it never occurred to me, to be honest. It's always just been my gran's summer cottage, not a potential dig site.'

Mattsson laughed. 'Understandable. But I have a good feeling about this. I really hope it's going to yield some even better finds this summer.'

Mia hoped so too, because if it didn't, she'd be jeopardising her relationship with Charles for nothing.

'Are you listening to me?' Alun's voice cut into her thoughts.

'Huh? Oh, I'm sorry. I've been a bit . . . preoccupied. Please, tell me again. I promise I'll pay attention.'

'Nah, it can wait. Come on – what's bothering you then? You were miles away.'

Mia sighed. 'I don't really want to burden you with my problems.' She and Alun were good mates, but this was personal. They'd become friends when he discovered that she spoke passable Welsh – learned from her dad – but that didn't mean she could dump her issues with Charles on him.

He bumped her with his shoulder. 'I said spill. Is Charlie boy being an arse? Want me to come and sort him out for you?'

Mia laughed. The very idea was ludicrous – small, nerdy Alun versus sturdy rugby-playing Charles. That could only have one outcome, and it definitely wouldn't help her predicament. 'No, he's not. It's me, really.'

'What, you're being an arse? I find that hard to believe.' Alun chuckled as she sent him a mock-glare.

'OK, I'll tell you my dilemma if you promise to keep it to yourself.'

'When don't I? I'm the proverbial clam, me.' And he was, Mia knew that. So she told him about inheriting Birch Thorpe, and Charles wanting her to sell it; about the ring and Professor Mattsson – she left out Berger's involvement as it had been minimal – and the talk she'd had with her boss that morning.

'She said it was OK for me to take three months' unpaid leave, but Charles is going to hit the roof. I mean, I'll be in Sweden for weeks on end, and then there's the whole issue about me not wanting to sell up . . .' She trailed off and took a large swig of her white wine spritzer. 'I . . . I just don't know how to tell him.'

'Hmm, I can see why.' Alun stared into his beer and chewed his lip. 'Tough one. I guess the best way is to come right out with it.' He sent her a doubtful look. 'You have already decided, right? I mean, it's not up for negotiation?'

'No, I don't think it is.' Mia sighed and glanced at her ring. Ever since that meeting with Berger, it was as if the little snake was trying to lure her back to Sweden. She dreamed constantly about Birch Thorpe and Vikings and ships and . . . It was completely ridiculous, but she just knew she *had* to do this. 'Look, I know it sounds selfish and I should have discussed it with him first, but it all feels so . . . right. Like it's meant to be. Do you believe in fate? That's what this is. Urðr, the Vikings called it.'

Alun nodded. 'Yeah, for sure. OK, well, if it's your fate, go for it!'

'Just like that?'

'Yep.'

Maybe it really was that simple.

❧

At midday, the captives were all given a piece of flatbread and some salted dried meat and bits of dried cod, the same fare as the crew. The bread was flavoursome and the meat palatable, though the fish was a bit smelly and took a lot of chewing. To wash it down, a jug of water was passed round, and although Ceri noticed that the oarsmen were given ale instead, this didn't disturb her. They had, after all, been working hard, and she was relieved to be given anything to eat at all. She had thought at first that perhaps the prisoners would be starved into submission.

Not that she expected any of her fellow thralls to give their new masters much trouble. About half were young women, all terrified and in awe of the captors. The rest were boys in their early to mid teens, none strong enough to even contemplate opposing the will of the Norsemen, despite their simmering resentment, which manifested itself in sullen looks and furtive glowering. As for herself, she wasn't foolhardy enough to think she could escape her fate. Even had she been a strong enough swimmer to jump overboard and head for the coast, she felt sure that someone – Haukr himself even – would have jumped in after her. No, she would have to wait and pray that her brother set out on their trail, and fast.

If only Bryn remembered her captor's name.

The wind picked up soon after their meal and the huge sail was stretched to its limits. Most of the men fell asleep almost instantly, although Haukr made sure a few stayed awake and on guard, while he continued to steer. Ceri couldn't rest, however, and sat staring into the unknown, wondering what her life would be like from now on. Would he be a kind master or a cruel one? What manner of place were they going to? Judging by the sun, they were travelling in a northerly direction, and she had heard that the lands up there were wild and cold. She shivered.

Please, oh Lord, protect me as I know that only you can, she prayed silently. Deliver me from these Norsemen and send my brother swiftly to our rescue. Amen.

When it was almost dark, they made landfall on a small, barren island, which consisted mainly of rocks. Some of the men began to prepare a meal over an open fire, while others herded their new thralls into the lea of a large rock.

'Stay there and don't move,' they were ordered, and none had the strength to protest. They all sank down on to the ground, shivering from the cold and most of them wet through from the salty sea spray.

'Cover yourselves.' A gruff man deposited a pile of blankets next to them. 'Haukr's orders.'

Ceri made do with her own blanket, even though it was a bit damp, while the others scrambled to supplement their meagre clothing – most wore only their undergowns or shirts, taken by surprise during the night just like her – and made themselves comfortable. At least they were out of the wind and on dry land, something most of them were extremely grateful for. The relentlessly roiling sea had eventually made even Haukr's supple ship rise and fall; many of the villagers had been extremely ill, and although Ceri had so far escaped with only minor queasiness, she too was happy to sit on the firm ground. She closed her eyes and let her mind drift . . .

'Here, eat this.'

She looked up to see Haukr himself holding out a bowl and another piece of dry bread to her, and she shot to her feet in surprise.

'What? I . . . Thank you, but should I not be waiting on you?' She couldn't keep a note of sarcasm from creeping into her voice.

'Time enough for that later.' He smiled at her, a gentle smile that changed his stern expression into something quite beautiful. In that moment, he looked to her like one of the angels described by the village priest – all golden and shiny, with eyes as blue as heaven itself. She shook her head in confusion.

'I do not understand you,' she muttered, and sank down with her food, her legs suddenly too tired to hold her upright.

'You don't need to. Just know this – there is nothing to fear if you do as you're told and keep a still tongue in your head.'

As he strode away to sit by the fire with his men, she prayed that he was speaking the truth.

Haakon woke with a start as something hurtled into his stomach. Still half asleep, he reached for his sword to defend himself, only to realise that he didn't own one, he wasn't a Viking, and he was lying on the sofa in his living room, not at the bottom of a longship.

'What the . . . ? Linnea?'

He blinked, and the mischievous face of his six-year-old daughter came into focus. She giggled and poked him in the midriff. 'You were asleep. You lied. You said you were watching football, but you're not, so can I watch cartoons instead? Please, Daddy, please?'

'Go for it.'

He sat up and dry-washed his face. God, he was so tired. Looking after Linnea on his own was exhausting. Not because she was a difficult child, but because he felt he ought to do things with her and not let her just sit in front of the TV or some stupid Nintendo game the whole time.

He knew he was overcompensating. His ex, Sofia, was a very easy-going mother and not big on discipline or supervision of their child. There was no denying she was a self-centred woman who preferred to concentrate on enjoying life rather than being a strict parent. Her selfishness and spending habits were some of the reasons he'd divorced her. Clearly, if Linnea was playing computer games, she wasn't hassling Sofia, which suited both of them well. Not so Haakon – in fact, it bugged the hell out of him.

'How is she ever going to take school and homework seriously if you just let her do whatever she feels like all the time? How's she going to cope with real life?' he'd asked Sofia when, yet again, he'd found his daughter in her PJs in front of a screen, rather than packed and ready for her fortnightly weekend with her father. 'Is this what she does all day?'

'Oh, come on, chill, Haakon! She's still little; she deserves to have fun before all the serious stuff starts. What's the big deal?' Sofia had shrugged off his concerns, but further questioning of Linnea made Haakon realise that his ex-wife wasn't thinking about their child's needs at all, only her own.

'Mummy is always busy with her friends and she's hardly ever home,' Linnea informed him. 'She doesn't have time to take me to the park like you do, but she buys me lots of new games so I don't get bored. Do you want to see? I have this great one with unicorns . . .'

Haakon didn't. Instead he'd taken her to a big playground in the nearby park and then they'd gone cycling. He'd taught her last year and she was very good at it now, able to cycle a couple of kilometres without stopping or complaining. But the thing with kids was that they didn't stop talking, not for a second, or so it seemed. And the constant barrage of questions wore him out. Still, someone had to teach Linnea that life wasn't all about games consoles, and it seemed that job was his alone.

His mobile buzzed on the table and he picked it up.

Can you keep Linnea for a couple more days? Have to go out of town so am off work tomorrow. S

Haakon glared at the screen. This seemed to be happening more and more, and although he had nothing against spending extra time with Linnea – quite the opposite – he couldn't just take unplanned leave whenever he felt like it. Finding a child-minder at short notice was nigh on impossible too, but Sofia didn't seem to take this into consideration. The truth was, she never really planned much at all when it came to her own life, so she didn't think about how her actions affected other people's lives either.

Sofia had a job in an upmarket clothing boutique in Stockholm Old Town, but because it was owned by her mother, she got away with taking an awful lot of time off. She was part of a jet-setting crowd of multimillionaire friends who thought nothing of flying to Paris for the weekend if the mood took them. With rich parents, she'd never had to worry about money, and even when married to Haakon, she had continued to rely on her father to supply the extra cash her husband couldn't possibly provide on his salary. At first, her capricious, fun-loving nature had seemed like a breath of fresh air, and Haakon had loved her spontaneity, but it soon started to grate on him. There were times when he needed to be organised and plan ahead, but that became impossible.

He began to realise that Sofia wasn't interested in standing on her own two feet, and as long as she had 'dear Daddy' to bankroll her, she didn't need to. Haakon had been brought up to be independent and not rely on anyone other than himself, so this attitude was anathema to him, and eventually he'd had enough. Unfortunately, by that time Sofia had become pregnant – accidentally, of course – and Haakon had tried to save their marriage for the child's sake. He'd hoped that being a mother would make his wife more mature and responsible, but he'd soon been disappointed, and there was no going back after that.

Just for one day, he messaged back now. *I'm travelling to Lund on Tuesday so you'll have to pick her up from school then.* H

Just in case, he'd have a word with the mother of Linnea's best friend. She'd been great on previous occasions and often helped out in emergencies. But it shouldn't have to be this way. Why couldn't Sofia put Linnea first? Or even think about Haakon occasionally?

Angry now, he stood up and stalked to the kitchen to make some coffee. The custody agreement only allowed him to have his daughter every second weekend, but he ought to fight Sofia for full-time custody – she was clearly not able to look after their child properly. And yet, what did he have to offer? He worked crazy hours sometimes, so Linnea would be shunted from pillar to post and left with other people a lot if she was with him. That was why he'd agreed to her being with her mother most of the time, and everyone had assured him that was best for the child. But what if the mother wasn't taking her role seriously?

At least at the moment he made sure his weekends with Linnea were a work-free zone, and they spent quality time together. But damn, he wanted to protect her from Sofia's careless parenting. And he wanted her safe, with him, all the time.

Haukr watched the tiny woman he'd captured. She sat quietly, contemplating the vast sea and the coastal areas they passed, but

she didn't complain. So far she'd not been sick, and for some reason he was absurdly pleased about that. He didn't want her suffering because of him.

Which was a completely ridiculous thought.

Of course she was suffering. She was his captive, at his mercy and probably terrified out of her wits, although she didn't show it. He admired the stubborn tilt to her chin, the flashing silver eyes, and the way she answered him without fear. No, she might be small, but she had spirit. And he respected that.

The moment he'd set eyes on her, he'd known he was going to bring her home with him, but there was no way he could make her a thrall. No, she was high-born, valuable, and someone would be willing to pay a ransom for her, he was sure. In the meantime . . .

In the meantime, he would have to protect her, from himself and every other man around, no doubt. Because there was something incredibly appealing about her – those beautiful eyes ringed with thick dark lashes, that glorious hair with its endless curls tumbling to her waist, and her small but neat figure. She would be enough to tempt even the gods themselves. Or those saints the Christians talked about – yes, he'd listened to the foreigners talking about Jesus, but he didn't see the need to add yet another god to those he worshipped – and he was definitely not a saint.

As he'd just proved by going a-viking.

The trolls take Ragnhild!

What was the matter with the woman? Why could she not be content with what they had? Be happy?

It hadn't always been thus.

Their first year together had been good – they'd laughed and loved, worked hard to increase the size of the settlement and improve conditions for everyone who lived there, and they seemed to share the same dreams and goals. They'd succeeded in becoming more prosperous, but then misfortune struck and their first child – a little boy – died after only a few days. Ragnhild was inconsolable, but Haukr accepted it as fate and told her they were young, they would have many more children.

Offerings were made to the gods and they tried again, but everything changed after she bore a second child, a girl this time. It was a difficult birth and Haukr had been as sympathetic and supportive as he could while she healed, but there were other factors involved – things he couldn't influence. And the experience changed Ragnhild into a harsh, bad-tempered harpy.

He bitterly regretted marrying her now. She might still have a lovely exterior, but she wasn't the same woman. Not at all. Now her tongue was sharper than his battleaxe, and he had yet to find a way of silencing her. If she had an opinion, she voiced it, caring nothing for his displeasure. She didn't fear his wrath, because she had five brothers who would avenge the slightest damage done to her, and she knew it. Besides, one didn't hit women – that was not allowed for an honourable man.

All he wanted was for her to be content – was that really too much to ask?

He glanced again at his captive. Ragnhild could learn a lot about stoic acceptance from the Celtic woman. The lady Ceridwen might have great spirit, but he would bet anything she'd never be intentionally cruel and grasping, no matter what.

Chapter Seven

'So what do you think? You've got to love those high ceilings, right? Gives such a sense of space, as the estate agent said.'

They were standing in the living room of a one-bedroom flat in South Kensington, and Charles's eyes were sparkling with enthusiasm. This was where he wanted to be, Mia could tell, and she was the person who could help make his dream come true. Only she wasn't going to, and she felt terrible about that. Her stomach was churning and she clenched her fists inside the pockets of her coat.

'It's no bigger than our current flat,' she commented, keeping her voice down even though the estate agent had tactfully gone outside to give them time to discuss their options. 'In fact, it's smaller because it doesn't have a balcony. Plus it's on the third floor with no lift. Not exactly convenient.'

Charles frowned. 'It's the location that counts, Mia. Just think how much faster it will be for you to get to work. We're only a few minutes away from Gloucester Road Tube station here.'

'For you it will take longer.'

'It's fine, I don't mind. You're the one always complaining about the commute.'

Mia took a deep breath. This was the fourth property they'd

viewed and Charles had been determined to like them all. She had to admit she loved the period details – cornicing, high ceilings, big windows and even a small Victorian fireplace in this one – but the flat *was* smaller and there was no storage space whatsoever. And either way, it didn't matter because they weren't buying it.

'Look, can we just forget about this for now, please? I told you, I'm not ready to sell Birch Thorpe yet and I don't want to view any more properties.'

Charles grabbed her hand, staring into her eyes as if he was trying to force his own thoughts into her brain. 'Are you seriously telling me you'd rather hang on to that old cottage than live here?' He indicated their surroundings. 'This is classy, the kind of place we can have dinner parties and friends over for Sunday lunch. The lawyers will be done soon and then you'll—'

'They're already done. They've finished and the cottage is all mine.'

Mia had known about this for days, but she'd been waiting for the right moment to tell him because she also had to raise the subject of the dig. Only there *was* no right moment, so she just had to get it over with, as Alun had said. This was it.

The weeks had passed and she still couldn't bring herself to even contemplate selling the cottage. It was simply too soon. She knew Charles would think she was being unreasonable, but she needed time to grieve for her grandmother, and helping out on the dig would give her that. Then afterwards she might feel ready to let go of both the grief and the property.

'What?' He stared at her, then her words sank in and his face lit up. 'It's all done? Finally!'

She didn't smile back. 'Yes, but . . . it doesn't change anything. In fact, I would like to spend the whole summer in Sweden. At Birch Thorpe.'

'Huh?' She had his full attention now, and his smile faltered. 'How can you do that? Have you been sacked?'

She shook her head. 'Nothing that drastic, don't worry. It's just that I've asked if it would be possible to have some time off, a leave of absence for about three months, starting on the first of June. My boss said it would be OK if I want to go ahead.'

He stared at her with his mouth open for a moment, then scowled. 'But . . . what about our summer plans? Weren't we going to book a couple of weeks in Italy? Or are you going to work on the cottage first to make it more saleable?' His expression lightened considerably at that possibility. 'Actually, that's probably not a bad idea.'

'No, although I might do a spot of painting if I feel like it. And definitely some cleaning and a clear-out. The thing is . . .' She swallowed hard. 'A professor from the Historical Museum in Stockholm has been in touch with me and they want to do a dig on my property. They think it might be an old Viking settlement and they seem very excited about the whole thing. I said they could only do it if I was part of the team. I'd like to help out so I can keep an eye on them, make sure they don't do too much damage, you know. But that would mean staying there the whole summer, and obviously I couldn't have that much holiday, so . . .'

'But . . . you can't just go off for months on end! What about your job? Are you sure they'll keep it open for you? And you'll have to live off your savings. That means even less money for our future home. Christ, Mia, what's got into you?' Colour was mounting in his cheeks and Mia could tell he was ready to explode. She hurried to calm him down, trying out a reassuring smile.

'It's all right. I told you, I've already spoken to my boss and she's agreed to give me unpaid leave for three months on condition that I write a report on the dig for her. You know how interested she is in the Vikings, and she's going to pay me for the time I spend on that. Also, anything of value that's found on the site I might be given some money for by the Swedish state – it will be treasure trove. Who knows, there might be a hoard of gold or something.'

She glanced at her snake ring. The thought of finding more items like that was beyond exciting, but realistically the chances were slim. Still, you never knew. She tried to keep her smile in place, but Charles's expression was still dark and her spirits plummeted when the implications sank in further and his eyes narrowed. 'Three months. You want to be in Sweden for three whole months? What about us? And don't I get a holiday?'

'Italy will have to wait, I'm afraid. It could be a great honeymoon destination for next year, though, don't you think? Where would be more romantic than Venice, Rome and Florence?'

But he wasn't buying it. 'So I'm not to see you all summer? And you've decided all this without even talking it over with me?'

Mia cringed. She should have mentioned it earlier, but she just hadn't known how to. 'I *am* talking to you about it now. And don't be silly. You can come over and stay any time you want, of course, and I can come back for a weekend now and again. It's only a short flight, two and a half hours max. It takes us longer to visit your parents in Devon, you know. And it's so relaxing and peaceful at Birch Thorpe, remember?'

'No, it's not. I only said that to please your granny. It was bloody freezing and I got bitten to death by mosquitoes. Besides, it won't be so peaceful with a garden full of archaeologists, now will it?'

He had a point, and Mia had run out of steam anyway. She fiddled with the snake ring and wondered how she could smooth things over with him. She was suddenly struck by the thought that she wasn't sure she *wanted* to. She was tired of being the diplomat. Tired of feeling guilty for wanting to keep her inheritance. He'd been impossible for weeks now, nagging her about selling the cottage and now finally taking her to see properties in Fulham and Kensington that she didn't really want to look at, hoping to persuade her that way. Perhaps some time apart from each other would be a good thing.

'I'm sorry, Charles, but this is something I'd really, really like to do. Please try to understand – it's just too soon for me to sell Gran's cottage. It still has so many memories for me, and if there's going to be a dig there, how can I not be a part of it? It's massively exciting! I mean, come on, I'm an archaeologist – well, conservator, but still; what could be more fun for someone like me than finding something amazing on my own property?'

Charles glared at her. 'OK, sure, I get that, but you've not said a word about this before. Instead, you've been stringing me along, letting me get all excited about buying a new place and—'

She cut him off. 'I didn't! I tried to tell you not to start looking yet, but you just went ahead and dragged me along. I said I needed more time. You weren't listening.'

'I thought if I showed you some great flats you'd get over your reluctance to sell that crappy old cottage faster.'

Mia gritted her teeth. 'That "crappy old cottage", as you put it, means a lot to me. It was the only place I felt truly happy while growing up. It's not just an asset, disposable, forgettable. I'm sorry if you don't like the idea of me spending the summer in Sweden, but this is a once-in-a-lifetime chance and I can't pass it up. If you don't want to holiday there, you can always go somewhere with your mates. You were so jealous of their "carefree" holiday last year, as I recall.'

She'd been furious that he had wanted to go on an 18–30 holiday with his friends while she was tied up with work. Everyone knew those were only an excuse for getting drunk and sleeping around, even though he swore he wasn't hankering after the latter and only wanted to have some fun. Now, she found herself almost wanting him to go. It was bizarre.

'Fine, maybe I will then.' Charles's expression was grim. 'Let's get out of here. And you can tell the estate agent we're not interested in this . . .' he flung his hand out to encompass their surroundings, 'fantastic property. You'd rather live in a boring modern shoebox in Canary bloody Wharf.'

He stalked out and, stifling a sigh, Mia followed more slowly. That had gone well. Not.

❧

The days and nights passed in an endless blur of water and rugged coastline. Ceri heard the Norsemen discussing their route, and gathered that they were to sail round the northern part of the mainland, past some islands they called Orkneyjar and then across a huge expanse of sea until they came upon the land of the Danes. From there, they would stay close to the coast and go through a channel into another sea, which would lead them to their homeland. It seemed frighteningly far to Ceri, but she tried not to think too much about the vast distance that would separate her from her brother and all she knew.

To protect their captives from the chilly weather and sea spray, a tent was erected in the middle of the ship.

'Stay inside and you should be warm enough,' Haukr ordered. Ceri and her fellow villagers were only too happy to comply. From time to time some of Haukr's men joined them, but at least one of them was always awake and on guard, which meant there was no point trying to overpower the ones that slept. Not that Ceri or the others had the strength for such a thing in any case. Most of them were still feeling the effects of the rolling sea on their stomachs, and those that were getting over it were faint and listless, not to mention numb with cold.

'Only a couple of days now,' one man called gleefully to another, who'd been complaining of the monotonous diet. 'Then there will be feasting the like of which you've seldom seen, my friend.'

'*Já*, I reckon you're right at that. We're bringing enough loot to pay for a hundred feasts, if not more.'

The satisfaction in the man's voice made Ceri feel slightly nauseous. It was partly her people's wealth that would be paying for the feasting, her and her fellow thralls' misfortune the cause of celebration. No doubt they would be pressed into service, filling cups of ale and cooking endless meals. It was a lowering thought.

Not that she was afraid of hard work. She had always done her fair share, and after her brother's wife had died in childbirth the previous year, she'd taken over the running of his household until such time as she was wed herself. This was different, however, since she would no longer be mistress in her own home. She would have to do other people's bidding, whether she wanted to or not, and she had no doubt the thralls would be given the most boring and mundane tasks, like milling flour, without receiving any thanks for their efforts. They might even be beaten.

She sighed.

She should have been married by now, happily settled in another village with a husband and children of her own. But God obviously had other plans for her, as first her intended had died of a sudden fever just before the wedding, so that Cadoc had to start searching for another suitable man for her, and now this . . . Her future had been snatched away from her twice, looming bleak and endless in a foreign land. It didn't seem fair, but then the priest was always telling them about the sufferings of Jesus Christ and how he had borne everything without complaint and with dignity. Ceri resolved to do the same.

'What ails you, woman?' The voice of Haukr startled her out of her deep reverie.

'Nothing, apart from wishing that I was free and back home. Far away from you.'

'Perhaps one day you will be again.'

'Yes, when I'm old and worn out, no doubt,' she sneered.

He chuckled. 'I'm sure you'll be ransomed long before then.'

'Ransomed? You are planning to send word to our relatives?' Her spirits rose at this piece of welcome news. If there was an end in sight, she could bear this ordeal with much more fortitude, she felt sure.

But he dashed some of her hopes. 'Just yours. I doubt anyone can afford to pay for the others.'

'My brother would. Please, ask him at least. What have you got to lose? I'm sure you could acquire thralls elsewhere with the ransom money.'

'Why would I want to go to the trouble of doing that? Makes no sense when I have these already.' He waved a hand in the direction of her fellow captives.

Ceri threw caution to the wind, momentarily forgetting her earlier resolve as fury and frustration got the better of her. 'Argh! You're impossible! And why did you have to raid our village at all? What gives you the right to just come and take what you want?'

He looked away and muttered something.

'What was that? You don't have an answer? Ha! Thought so.'

'I do not have to justify myself to you. I am but following in the footsteps of others. There is nothing unusual about my actions, and I'm sure you've been raided before.'

'No, actually, we've been lucky. Until now.' Ceri glared at him, trying to put as much venom into her expression as she could, but he just shrugged.

'Everyone's luck runs out at some point.' And with that, he moved away, effectively ending their conversation. Ceri hoped that he would at least think about what she had said, and she prayed that her brother really would be willing to pay for everyone. Although how he was to do so now, when the Norsemen had taken all his valuables, she had no idea.

With another sigh, she stared out to sea, blinking away the tears that threatened. She would *not* cry; it would gain her nothing. God would help her and her fellow thralls; she must hold on to that thought. And in the meantime, perhaps she would do better not to antagonise their captors.

Chapter Eight

It was icy cold in the cottage when Mia woke up the day after her arrival, not to mention damp. She burrowed under the eiderdown cover, reluctant to venture so much as a toe outside its comforting warmth. She knew she should have lit the old wood-burning stove downstairs last night, since its chimney went past her bedroom on the way to the roof and gave off quite a lot of heat, but she had simply been too tired. Now she was paying the price.

It didn't help that she'd been dreaming she was out on the open sea in a Viking ship, with blustery winds hurling saltwater showers at her every so often. She remembered huddling into a woollen blanket, scratchy and a bit smelly, but giving her blessed warmth. She'd burrowed her nose inside its edges, pulling it over her head and fastening it with some sort of pin, then woken up when a particularly large wave jolted the ship.

'Crazy,' she muttered. She'd never been on a Viking ship in her life, obviously. Not even a reconstructed one, although she'd love to try sometime. It was probably the musty smell of the cottage that had invaded her dreams – she really needed to air it out.

There was a bathrobe hanging on the back of the door, and eventually she steeled herself against the cold and made a dash to retrieve the old garment. She jumped up and down while trying to put it on, which didn't make the manoeuvre any faster, and finally managed to wrap it round herself and tie the belt. After dragging on a pair of thick socks, she went downstairs and lit the stove, warming her hands on the welcome flames until the room began to heat up.

It was ridiculous really, early June and still so cold, but the cottage would warm up soon, and once the sun was out, that would help too. Back in England she'd been sweltering in her office; she should be grateful for the reprieve. She shut the little door of the wood burner and turned to the one luxury her grandmother had allowed herself: the fridge. Before she could retrieve anything from its confines, however, there was a knock on the front door.

She glanced at her watch – it was only 7.30 a.m. With a frown, she went to peek out the window and saw a battered Jeep parked in the lane outside the fence. On her doorstep stood a tall man with his back to her. He looked vaguely familiar, but she couldn't see who it was from where she was standing. Should she open the door?

'Who is it?' she called out in Swedish through the thick wood, deciding that it was probably prudent to be cautious. After all, she was alone practically in the middle of the forest, although she knew there were other cottages not too far away.

'I'm here for the dig. Professor Mattsson sent me,' came the muffled reply, in Norwegian-accented Swedish. Her heart beat faster. Surely it couldn't be . . . ?

'Mr Berger!' She opened the door and took a step back as she stared up into his face. He was taller than she remembered, and big too, although in the nicest possible way. Broad shoulders and muscular arms strained against a faded T-shirt with the name of some heavy metal rock band emblazoned across the top, and his scruffy jeans clung tightly to strong thighs. There was a jagged tear over one knee, which she found unaccountably sexy, and she glimpsed the tanned skin underneath. He didn't appear to feel the cold, as his hoodie was tied loosely round his waist.

She scanned his face, which was tanned a light golden brown that contrasted greatly with his shock of white-blond hair. It was as unruly as before and looked almost as if he had tried to cut it himself, standing straight up in uneven tufts on the top of his head. The amazingly blue eyes showed a flicker of amusement while he gave her attire a sweeping glance. Mia suddenly remembered what she was wearing and felt herself blush to the roots of her hair.

'Haakon is fine.' She must have looked blank, because he elaborated. 'My name? You don't have to be so formal.'

'Oh, right. Um, where's the professor then?' She pulled the edges of the bathrobe together and crossed her arms to keep it in place. Mattsson hadn't mentioned that Berger – Haakon – was to join his team for the dig, so to find him on her doorstep was a bit of a shock, to say the least.

'He's not coming. I'm afraid he had a heart attack last week, poor guy. He's put me in charge instead.'

'Good grief, is he all right?' Concern for the man she'd never met, but whose kindness had shone through in their telephone conversations, overrode everything else in her mind for a moment.

'Yes, he'll recover, but the doctors have ordered complete rest. Not that I think he'll obey, but still . . .'

'I see.' She tried to digest the fact that she wouldn't be dealing with the nice elderly professor all summer, but would instead have to work with this man who disturbed her inner peace just by looking at her. *Bloody hell.*

'He said he was supposed to be staying with you and that I could have his room. Do you mind? Or should I just use my tent?'

'Room? Oh!' Mia had offered the professor the second bedroom

72

for the summer. She wasn't sure she wanted to extend the same courtesy to Ber— Haakon, but it would seem churlish to refuse.

'You do have a room ready, I take it?' Haakon looked as if he doubted this, and for some reason that made Mia mad as hell.

'I only just arrived myself last night, so I haven't had time to organise things properly yet,' she replied waspishly. 'I wasn't actually expecting anyone quite this early.'

'We always start at eight a.m. sharp. It's good to make use of as much daylight as possible. And you did agree to the first of June as the starting date.'

Jeez, he was abrupt. She knew Scandinavians didn't exchange pleasantries the way English people did, and could often seem curt to others when they got straight to the point, but this guy was verging on rudeness. 'Of course, but . . .'

'If you show me to my room and give me the sheets, I can make the bed myself.'

Mia took a deep breath and almost told him she would have expected that anyway. She wasn't his slave. Something made her bite her tongue, however, and instead she said, 'Can you give me a minute? If you wouldn't mind waiting down here?' She indicated the kitchen, and he nodded.

'Sure.'

Without another word, she turned and sprinted up the narrow staircase and into the room that used to be Granny Elin's. In her mind's eye, she could still see Gran standing by the window looking out over the lake and the island in the distance. It was her favourite view and they had shared many a quiet moment contemplating the beauty of the nature all around them. The lake was usually as smooth as a mirror in the early mornings, reflecting the sunlight with a thousand glittering prisms. From this window you could only see glimpses of it through the many birch and spruce trees, their various greens contrasting beautifully with each other. It was as if this view made time stand still, and it was easy to imagine people a thousand years ago staring in awe at the same thing.

'Just think,' Elin used to say, 'some Viking chieftain stood at the door to his hall, surveying this very scene. I bet it hasn't changed at all.'

Mia shook her head slightly and tried to concentrate on the present. The room had been stripped of all Gran's belongings apart from the furniture. Mia had asked her mother to shove everything into boxes and store these in her garage until such time as Mia felt able to sort through them properly. It was too soon, the pain too raw. But she had to get used to this, and the Norwegian guy was waiting. She opened the window to try and get some air into the room.

'OK, you can come up now,' she called down the stairs, while looking in the old cupboard on the landing that contained Gran's sheets.

When she turned around, Haakon was standing next to her, his head almost reaching the low ceiling. She took a step back and held out the sheets, then pointed at Gran's room.

'This was to be the professor's,' she said to her guest, and realised that it must look very meagre to him. 'I'm sorry, it's not much. You might prefer that tent after all.'

He glanced quickly round, then shrugged. 'It's fine. I'm getting too old for camping. This will be a lot drier than a tent, and possibly warmer too.'

'Don't be too sure of that,' Mia muttered. How old was he exactly? She had reckoned late twenties to early thirties the first time they'd met, but it was hard to tell.

'What was that?'

'Nothing. I was just wondering, are you a professor too?'

'Not yet, but I have a PhD. I specialise in Viking artefacts and inscriptions, but I can't bear to be cooped up indoors all year, so I usually spend my summers on various digs. I've worked with Professor Mattsson for the last five years.'

He gave her a look as if to say, *There, is that enough credentials for you?* and Mia decided he was an infuriating man. She needed a cup of tea and some decent clothes before dealing with him further.

'Right, well, I'd better see about getting dressed then.'

'Sure. Thanks for these.' He indicated the sheets. 'I haven't slept in anything like this since my granny died.'

Mia wasn't sure if he was mocking her or not. 'Oh, they are hand-made, and *my* gran made the lace.' They were the old-fashioned kind of sheets, with lace borders and an embroidered monogram. Most people these days wouldn't even know how to make up a bed with them, as they looked like two single sheets with a blanket or bolster on top. And you had to put the top sheet upside down in order to get the monogram to show properly. She regretted giving them to him now.

He held up a hand and smiled. 'No, no, I figured that. It was a compliment, honest. It just took me back, is all.'

'Right. OK. Um, is everyone else turning up this early as well?'

'Yep. Should be here any moment. First site meeting is in fifteen minutes, so you'd better hurry if you want to join us.'

She fled into her own room before she said something rude to him. It was way too early in the morning to cope with someone so abrupt.

'Seven women and eight skinny boys? Was that all you could find? Honestly, it was hardly worth the journey, was it? And couldn't you have taken some that were dressed properly? Now we'll have to clothe them, I suppose.'

Ceri looked up from where she was standing with the other captives by a long jetty, and saw a tall, striking woman striding down the path that led to the shore of the lake from a cluster of dwellings set on top of a hill. A strong chin jutted imperiously, as did a sharp nose, while the wide mouth was pursed. Long blonde hair had been tied in a knot at the nape of her neck, with the end flowing loosely down her back and swinging as she walked. A headscarf covered most of it, as befitted a married woman.

The sun glinted off two enormous bronze disc brooches that fastened the straps of her red ankle-length apron gown – or *smokkr*, as it was called – above each breast. The gown was partly made of silk panels that also shimmered in the light, and there were exquisitely woven decorative borders around the hem. A necklace of amber beads was strung between the brooches, while a bunch of keys and a small pouch hung off a chain connected to one of them, jingling melodiously. Ceri saw that the woman wore a blue tunic gown under the *smokkr*, its three-quarter-length sleeves also decorated with woven bands. At the top and bottom, a beautifully pleated white linen undergown, or *serk*, peeped out.

'Did you expect us to carry out an ambush in broad daylight? Of course they're only half dressed – they were dragged out of their beds! And you said you wanted fifteen thralls, so fifteen is what I brought you, wife. If you wanted more, you should have told me.' Haukr had come up behind Ceri and the others, and she saw him glaring at the blonde woman, who frowned back, her dark blue eyes shooting daggers.

So this was Haukr's wife. Ceri tried to make herself inconspicuous as the lady was obviously in a bad mood. The woman crossed her arms under her impressive bosom and adopted a belligerent stance.

'I don't recall mentioning a fixed number. I thought you would take as many as you could find.'

'Well that's where you're wrong. We don't need any more than that. How would we house them and feed them, Ragnhild?'

The woman rolled her eyes. 'We could have sold some, of course. Besides, we've lost a couple while you've been away.'

Ceri saw Haukr narrow his eyes. 'How? What happened to them?'

'A sickness carried them off, that's all. It was lucky no one else caught it.'

'Hmm. You're sure they were given their full rations of food, as I ordered?'

'Of course. Although starving once in a while never hurt anyone.'

'So you say. How anyone is to work on an empty stomach is beyond me . . .'

Ceri gathered that Haukr and his wife were not on the best of terms and sincerely hoped this wasn't going to cause problems for herself and the others. The lady Ragnhild seemed bad-tempered and demanding, and already Ceri could see that she would be difficult to please, if not impossible. She didn't like the sound of thralls starving, but stifled an inward sigh since there was nothing she could do about it.

'Well, don't just stand there; bring everything up to the hall. I assume you have brought something other than thralls? You'll have to spread it out so you can divide the spoils. I'll have the trestles put up.'

As Ragnhild marched back up the hill, Ceri heard Haukr mutter sarcastically, 'Oh, so you're sharing, are you? How unusual . . .'

He looked up and caught her amused glance, which she didn't have time to hide, and her heart lodged in her throat at the thought that she'd be reprimanded for laughing at her superiors. To her surprise, however, he grinned back and winked at her, before turning to issue orders to his men. Ceri felt her cheeks heat up. Haukr the White didn't act like any master she'd ever heard of, and she felt thoroughly confused.

She shook her head and stumbled off with the others when they were told to go up the hill. Living in this household was going to be very strange indeed.

Chapter Nine

Haakon put his bag on the floor and looked around, wondering if this was really such a good idea after all. He hadn't thought about the fact that he'd be in such close proximity to Ms Maddox – Mia. The cottage was tiny, especially the bedrooms and, if his quick glance was anything to go by, the bathroom too. They'd have to share that and the kitchen, and since he didn't much relish the idea of spending hot summer evenings cooped up here directly under the roof, he'd be trespassing on her territory in the evenings too.

Perhaps he should just go home and get a tent after all.

But like he'd said, this would be so much more comfortable, dry and warm with – he presumed – running water. They'd have to manage somehow. He set about making the bed. The room smelled as if it hadn't been used in months, but he knew most summer cottages were left shut up over winter and it would only be a matter of time before the fresh air improved things. He shook the blankets out of the open window and then banged the two pillows together as well. They weren't dusty, so there must have been some sort of bedspread covering them. He spotted it hanging over the back of a low chair in the corner of the room – white and floral, the old-fashioned home-crocheted kind.

God, that took him back.

He'd often stayed with his Swedish grandparents – his mother was from a county further south of here – and his granny had had the exact same taste in home furnishings. She was long gone, but the memories were flooding back to him now: sleeping in sheets like these, crisply ironed, helping to get the summer house habitable and the rowing boat into the lake. Meals on the terrace in the sunshine, lazy days swimming or fishing with his grandpa. Idyllic. Would this summer be the same?

But he had a job to do; he wasn't here for a vacation. There wouldn't be any lazing around. Instead he'd be spending long hours on his hands and knees – and he was going to love every minute. He always did.

Excitement fizzed through his veins. He couldn't wait to get started, and he had a good feeling about this place – it called to him somehow.

He really hoped he and Mia would get on well so that he could enjoy his down time just as much.

※

The hall was a huge rectangular building with double doors at one end that led first into a small entrance room. The main living area was accessed through a wide doorway set in a partition wall, which only reached two-thirds of the way up to the ceiling, leaving a gap at the top. The huge room beyond had a raised central hearth and wide benches built all along the walls. It was perhaps eight to ten long paces wide, and the roof, supported by heavy beams, was the height of at least three men in the centre, which gave a sense of spaciousness. The underside of the thatch that covered it was clearly visible, laid neatly on top of rows of horizontal supports. Tiny square openings in the outside walls added some light and air, as did the doors at either end of the room, but the atmosphere inside was still a bit smoky and gloomy, which took some getting used to. It was well made, though, good workmanship, a dwelling that would last a long time, and Haukr was proud of it. He'd even done some of the carvings on the posts himself.

As he entered right behind Ceridwen, he watched to see her reaction to her surroundings. He was pleased when an expression of awe appeared on her face.

'You like my humble abode?' he asked jokingly. It was humble by some standards, but definitely larger than the average.

She glanced at him and quickly masked her admiration, then commented in a sarcastic voice, 'Indeed. You are to be commended – it is much bigger than any of the dwellings I've ever been in. It must be so nice to inherit something like this from your forefathers.'

'My men and I raised this some ten summers ago. The previous hall was old and rotten – *that* was my inheritance,' Haukr informed her, and looked at it again with satisfaction. His father had let his domains go to rack and ruin – he'd cared for nothing but ale, women and picking fights with his men – but since his death, Haukr had made sweeping changes. The building and its roof were sturdy and watertight, no gaps anywhere to let in draughts or moisture. Even in winter it was a comfortable place to be, a refuge from the fierce weather of these northern lands. There was space for everyone who had a right to sleep in the hall, with some storage chests for personal belongings. At the far end of the building a couple of smaller rooms were partitioned off, one of which contained baskets and chests with tools and provisions. The walls were hung with colourful woven cloths that gave the long room a welcoming, warm appearance, as did the blankets and furs of various colours and shades that covered the benches.

'Huh.' Ceridwen crossed her arms over her chest, but he'd taken the wind out of her sails and she said no more.

Some women were in the process of putting up trestle tables, and there was a general air of happiness with much chattering and laughter. He smiled – it was wonderful to be home.

Well, most of the time.

He stifled a sigh as he caught sight of Ragnhild, who was haranguing some poor unfortunate soul who had dropped a pitcher of ale on the floor and was attempting unsuccessfully to mop up the mess.

Haukr ignored this commotion and directed his men to empty their sacks and chests on to the tables. A hush fell on the room as just about every item of any value from Ceridwen's village clanged and clattered on to the smooth boards, as well as a large collection of other objects. Haukr had known one place would never contain enough treasure to make their journey worthwhile, unless it belonged to a king. He and his men had therefore raided several other settlements first, including a small Christian enclave, without taking any captives. They'd saved that for last, as he didn't want to risk anyone hearing their approach, and there was always the possibility a captive could break free and call out a warning.

There were gasps of surprise and even Ragnhild stopped in the middle of a sentence to gape at the glimmering hoard. It was an impressive sight: coins, arm rings, torcs, rings, as well as silver items from the Christian church. These included a beautiful chalice set with semi-precious stones, several silver plates and some sort of jewelled clasp torn off a holy book.

'Well,' she said, coming to stand next to him with her hands on her hips, 'I see you found *something* of value then. Not as much as I had hoped, but I suppose it will do until next year.'

Haukr almost choked. 'Next year? If you think I'm going

a-viking again, you are sorely mistaken, woman. We have more than enough here to last a lifetime.'

'Hmm, well, we can discuss that in the spring.'

He gritted his teeth but didn't reply. There would be no discussion, or if there was, he'd make certain it was held in private where his wife couldn't cast doubt on his bravery in front of all and sundry. For now, he asked his men to be seated, apart from two, Thorald and Steinn, who helped him to divide the spoils into piles of gold, silver and other precious items, thus making it easier to share out. Whenever the piles were uneven, the men just cut bracelets, necklaces or other metallic objects into pieces, with no regard for the beauty of the craftsmanship. At one point he saw Ceridwen wince; presumably these items were precious to her, but it couldn't be helped. This was how most trading was done – the metal was weighed and valued, and the object itself was of no significance.

Once this was done, Haukr personally began to hand out portions of equal size to his men, keeping one for himself that was no larger than the others. Out of the corner of his eye he saw Ragnhild frown at this, but the woman held her tongue until he was finished. Then she pounced.

'Why are you not taking a larger share for yourself? As the jarl it is your right.'

Haukr swept out a hand to indicate the pile of treasure he had claimed for his own. 'Is this not enough for you? Most people would be grateful for such a hoard.' It was the truth: their share was more than adequate. He knew that a lot of jarls would have taken a much bigger portion and doled it out piecemeal to the men over the course of several years to keep them loyal, but that wasn't his way.

Ragnhild fingered some of the items, holding up a particularly lovely neck ring of beaten gold that he remembered as coming from the house Ceridwen lived in. Was it hers? Or her brother's wife's, perhaps? He couldn't help but feel for her, as she would now have to watch someone else wear it. 'This is nice, I suppose,' Ragnhild commented, 'but why should your men have an equal share? You're their leader.'

'And I did no more than *my* fair share of the looting, so why should I have more than them? Everyone played his part.'

'It's still not right,' Ragnhild insisted. 'I demand that you ask them to pay you a tenth of their gains, in lieu of their board and lodging here. We provide them with their food and a roof over their heads after all, and—'

He interrupted. 'Food they have helped to grow and buildings they've helped raise. Everyone here works hard. No, I will do no such thing.' He clenched his fists under the table and managed to keep his temper in check. He had always been slow to anger and knew it was better to stay calm. The few times he did lose it, it was usually fairly spectacular; an explosion of wrath to put the fear of the gods into most people.

'But—'

On the other hand, the time had obviously come to put his foot down. 'Enough, *víf*!' He fixed Ragnhild with an angry glare. 'You nagged me about going a-viking, attempting to shame me in front of my men, you nagged me about what to bring back, you nagged me about what *not* to bring back, and now you have the nerve to complain when I give you a treasure fit for a queen? Are you mad, woman? By Odin, I have a mind to send you off a-viking by yourself so you can fetch what you want!'

Haukr was conscious of the fact that his voice had risen by degrees, and he was now roaring so loudly that everyone else in the room had fallen silent. Everyone except a small girl of about five or six, standing not far from Ceridwen, who was staring at him with huge eyes, making strange keening noises to herself. It was obvious that she was terrified of his fury but unable to properly express it. He groaned inwardly. She was the last child in the settlement he wanted to scare.

To his relief, he saw Ceridwen act instinctively and bend down to lift the child into her arms. She averted the girl's face so she wouldn't see Haukr's angry expression, then rocked her slightly and stroked her back with a soothing motion while murmuring to her. The little one didn't look as if she understood a word – she never did – but nevertheless buried her face in Ceridwen's shoulder and made more weird noises.

Haukr turned away from the sight. It shouldn't be Ceridwen soothing the child. It should be . . . He saw Ragnhild stalk out of the hall and into one of the rooms at the far end, their bedchamber. 'Some leader you are,' she shot over her shoulder. 'Who's going to respect a man who treats everyone as an equal? You're the one who's mad.' And with that, she disappeared behind the door curtain, swishing it angrily into place behind her.

Haukr was sorely tempted to go after her and beat the living daylights out of her, but obviously he couldn't, because she was a woman. An honourable man would never hit his wife, but by all the gods, she tried his patience. Instead he took some deep breaths and ordered everyone else to be about their business. The spoils quickly disappeared into coffers and kists of various sizes, and his men hurried outside. Haukr himself pushed his share of loot back into a sack and dumped it just inside the curtain to the back room, without looking in. Then he turned and, catching sight of Ceridwen and the little girl again, felt his expression soften. He walked over to put his hand on the child's head.

'Jorun *mín*.' The little one jumped and stared at him, her gaze still wary, while he in turn looked at Ceridwen. 'Did I scare her? That wasn't my intention. Perhaps you could take her over to Old Tyra and find her something to eat to distract her? She's . . . she's not like other children.' He swallowed hard.

'Old Tyra?' Ceridwen asked.

'Oh, I was forgetting, you won't know anyone yet. Aase!' he yelled, and an elderly serving woman hurried over. 'This woman is to look after Jorun for the afternoon. Could you introduce her to Old Tyra, please?' He lifted his eyebrows at Ceridwen. 'If you don't mind? I can see you are fond of children.'

'Very well.' The words were grudging, but he could tell she was relieved to be given such a relatively easy task. She had obviously been expecting far worse.

'Thank you. Take good care of her.'

He knew she would, even without him asking.

Chapter Ten

When Mia came down, dressed warmly in sweater and jeans with an extra fleece on top, she found that a large tent had already been erected in her front garden and there were several more cars parked in the lane. Various individuals were making their way towards the tent, so she followed them and saw that it contained a table and folding chairs for at least ten people. Although still vaguely annoyed with her guest, she had to concede that he was extremely efficient.

She was only five minutes late for the meeting, and luckily for her, some of the others had taken longer to arrive than expected. Haakon was drumming his fingers on the table, staring out through the tent flap with a scowl. When everyone had settled on a chair at last, he brought out a sheaf of photos and spread them over the table. Mia saw that they were aerial views of her property and the surrounding landscape. It gave her a thrill to see it in the light of a prospective site like that and made it sink in that this was real. Next to them lay a large-scale map.

'Right,' Haakon said, 'let's get started. Most of you know each other, but just in case you don't . . .' He began by introducing himself and everyone else, finishing with '. . . and this is Mia Maddox, the lady who owns the cottage. She's a conservator from the British Museum in London, I understand, and she'll be part of the team. That's right, isn't it, Miss Maddox?'

'Please, call me Mia.' She'd forgotten to tell him that earlier and had noticed that no one else was formal here. 'And yes, that's right, but—'

Haakon cut her off, obviously not big on details. 'OK. Now, these photos don't give us much to go on, apart from some mounds on the other side of the road.' He looked at Mia again. 'Presumably that land belongs to a local farmer? Any idea if he'd be amenable to us digging there?'

'Across the road?' Mia bent to look where he was pointing on the photo. 'Oh, no, actually that's my land too, apparently. I had no idea, but the lawyer told me that my grandmother owned part of the forest around here, and some of the fields. I'll, um, try to get hold of an exact map for you.'

'That would be great, thanks. It's probably best if we leave the mounds for when we know where the boundaries lie. For now, let's concentrate on the area around the cottage. I suggest the geophys team should start straight away, while the rest of us get organised. Tomas?' He nodded at a serious-looking young man with short brown hair who had been fiddling with bits of equipment in a corner of the tent. 'Can you get going on the top of the hill? It might mean having to clear some of the vegetation. Anders, Micke, maybe you guys can help him for now.'

'Yep, I'm on it,' Tomas said, and disappeared outside without taking further part in the discussion. Anders and Micke stayed to hear the rest of what Haakon had to say.

Haakon continued as if he was following some unwritten agenda. 'We need to put up our tents, and the ones for cleaning finds and sifting soil. There's a caravan coming later for storage of any valuable finds. Did someone bring all the necessary stuff? Ah, Daniel, great, thanks. And whose turn was it to sort the catering today? I don't suppose anyone brought cinnamon buns?' He looked around and spotted a latecomer, a pretty young girl with platinum-blonde hair, liberally streaked with fuchsia pink, and lots of piercings. She was holding up her hand.

'I did, and I've got the catering covered for today,' the girl said, sounding unnaturally cheerful so early in the morning.

'Excellent, thank you, Isabella. We can draw up a rota later on. Better start everyone off with a cup of coffee, yes? I know I could do with one.'

'No problem.' Isabella smiled and went off to unpack. Mia hoped the coffee would be forthcoming soon, as she could really do with a caffeine injection, having missed out on breakfast.

Haakon was still talking. 'I've got a proper map of the area here, and we need to agree on the likeliest site of any possible dwellings if they're not on that hill, but I think we'd better do some field walking first and meet up again just before lunch to compare notes. I suggest we split into two teams and start down by the lake, then take it from there. Any questions? Right, let's go then.'

'Hold on a minute.' Mia had had enough of being ignored. 'I think you forgot something.'

'I did?' Haakon looked surprised, and glanced down at his papers as if the answer lay there. Obviously it didn't, so Mia pulled a document out of her back pocket and walked round the table to put it in front of him. The contract of agreement between herself and Professor Mattsson. She unfolded it and pointed at a particular paragraph in the text.

She saw him frown as understanding dawned. 'Shit!' he muttered.

'Quite.'

Everyone else had stood up but not left the tent, and they were now staring at Mia and Haakon. He sighed. 'It would seem the professor forgot to tell me about a small detail.'

'Not so small,' Mia muttered.

Haakon sent her an irritated glance.

'Mia here is apparently supposed to be co-director of this dig, so you'll all have to report to both of us.' He took a deep breath, as if he was suppressing a few other things he'd have liked to say on the subject, then turned to Mia. 'Are you in agreement with my suggestions so far?'

She nodded. If she was totally honest, he'd thought of everything. She had no experience whatsoever of leading an archaeological dig, other than in theory. Not wanting to seem completely ignorant, she'd spent some time reading up on the subject before flying to Sweden, but actually putting those theories into practice was different. She would watch and learn, though, and hopefully Haakon wouldn't notice her lack of knowledge. 'Yes, although it would be good if we could discuss strategy before these meetings in future.'

Haakon's mouth tightened. 'Fair enough. Anything else?'

'Not for the moment.'

'Right, let's get started then.' He marched out of the tent, clearly annoyed, but Mia didn't care. It wasn't her fault if his superior hadn't given him clear instructions. This was *her* dig, her property. She would insist on being consulted and involved every step of the way, or it wasn't happening at all.

She followed the others and joined them as they formed a line down by the lakeshore. She found herself next to Haakon somewhere in the middle, and he sent her a quick glance.

'You've done field walking before, I take it?'

'Yes, of course.' She didn't tell him it was at least five years since she'd last done it, but it wasn't rocket science.

'Good, just checking.'

Mia tried not to grind her teeth. She didn't know whether he was insinuating she might not know what she was doing, or if he was just the type of leader who liked to check up on everyone. When she saw an amused glint in his eyes, however, she felt more like punching him. He must have known she'd done this previously. Anyone who'd ever been on a dig would have gone field walking. It was the first step in the process on a new site, picking up any visible archaeological remains before the area was disturbed by all the workers tramping around.

For the next couple of hours she worked alongside him in simmering silence. He really was infuriating, but he obviously knew what he was doing when it came to archaeology, so there was nothing she could say.

'OK, so what do we make of this then? Mia?'

They were once again gathered in the main tent, some sitting, some half standing around the table, looking at the papers spread out in front of them. Haakon had asked someone to gather together the information from the field walking, and the densest concentrations of pottery sherds and other finds had been plotted on a site plan. He wasn't surprised to see that they were almost all on or around the hill, which was after all the likeliest place for a dwelling house.

'Possible longhouse or settlement on the top of that hill,' Mia said. 'It would make sense and it's still close enough to the lake. There was nothing near the cottage itself, and I have to admit I'm grateful for that, as it means you probably won't be digging up my gran's garden.' She smiled to show she was joking, but Haakon had a feeling she really was relieved about that. She'd obviously had a special bond with the woman she had inherited this place from, and having everyone here must be quite disturbing.

Not to mention having him sleep in her grandmother's room. Shit. He hadn't thought about that.

'Yes, there were quite a few possibilities up there.' Tomas, the geophys expert, chipped in. He'd been busy with his instruments all morning, trying to avoid the others as he walked in straight lines following an invisible grid to take readings from the soil in order to detect anything that might be buried under the surface. 'I used both the resistivity meter and the magnetometer and I've had some interesting results. Also, I noticed there's what looks like a mound out on the tip of the little peninsula. I'll move down to that part this afternoon. Best to check it out.'

'Excellent. We'll start by putting in a couple of trenches up on the hill then. Er . . . don't you think, Mia?' Haakon belatedly remembered to consult her. Damn Mattsson – why hadn't he told him about Mia being co-director? The man had never shared that role with anyone before, so it hadn't occurred to Haakon, but he assumed she'd made it a condition for giving them permission to be here. It was a ruddy nuisance though, as he'd have preferred to just do things his way.

'Yep, sounds good to me.'

'I noticed there's a small stream coming down one side of the hill,' he added, pointing at the chart. 'Could be worth investigating, but maybe later during the summer when it's not in full spate. For now, we have a couple of options of where to put a trench – here, here or here.'

He pointed at three places where Tomas's equipment had registered what looked like potential walls, corners of buildings or potholes. They'd probably end up digging all of them, but he thought he'd allow the team to have a say in where to start. He saw Mia watching the animated discussion that followed without contributing anything. Everyone seemed to have a favourite spot, but in the end they all looked to Haakon for the last word. He could feel her resentment that no one asked her opinion, but it was natural. Most of them had worked with him before, but they didn't know Mia at all. And even though it was her property, they had no idea what her credentials were for leading this type of dig. Neither did he, come to think of it.

He could really do without this hassle, but there was nothing to be done now except try to keep things on track.

'Mia, would you mind if we cut down some trees on the hill?' He turned to her and saw her jump, as if she hadn't been paying attention. A slight flush crept across her cheeks, making her seem vulnerable, and Haakon regretted his earlier irritation. This must be difficult for her, being here without her grandmother and with strangers tramping all over the place.

'Oh, er . . . no, go ahead. I could do with some logs for the wood-burning stove in the cottage.'

'I'm not sure if we'll have time to chop firewood for you, but we'll stack the logs somewhere near the house so you can get someone in to do it for you.' Christ, but they weren't here to act as her house slaves. Time was precious on a dig, and just cutting the trees down would take long enough.

Her flush deepened. 'Right. Thank you.'

'Time for lunch, I think,' Haakon said, and there was an instant buzz as everyone scrambled for the tent opening.

He sighed and followed them at a slower pace. Maybe it wasn't going to be such a relaxing summer after all.

Mia left the tent in silence, annoyed with herself and with Haakon for making her seem stupid and selfish. She just hadn't been thinking clearly.

Instead of following the others, she went into the cottage and rummaged in the fridge for the meagre supplies she had brought with her – bread, milk and cheese – to make a sandwich. Haakon had told her earlier that she was welcome to eat with everyone else, but she didn't want to be a drain on the resources. Everything cost money, so if she catered for herself that was at least one mouth less to feed. Besides, she'd told the professor that was what she would do.

'Was it something I said?'

Haakon suddenly appeared behind her, having come in without Mia noticing him. She jumped, her nerve endings tingling at his nearness. He was so close that just one step would have brought her into contact with him, and the mere thought of that had her backing away. She wondered why, as he wasn't threatening her in any way.

'What? No, I'm just having lunch.' She retreated further, ostensibly looking for a knife to cut the bread with.

'You left rather abruptly. I wondered . . . had you agreed with Mattsson that we were to chop up the trees for you? Only, it would take up a lot of valuable time.'

'No, I realise that. I just wasn't thinking straight. It's not a problem, really.'

He didn't look convinced. 'So what's wrong then?'

'Nothing is wrong.'

'I'm sorry about earlier. Mattsson hadn't told me. I guess with everything that happened, he forgot. Understandable when you have all sorts of tubes sticking out of you, I suppose.'

He was trying to make a joke of it, but it wasn't helping. 'It's fine. I . . . feel a bit left out, that's all.' It sounded silly and childish and Mia wished she hadn't said it, but the words had left her mouth before she could stop them. She turned away to hide her embarrassment. He must think her a complete moron. She hoped he would take the hint and go. To her surprise, however, he put a hand on her shoulder and spun her around slowly to face him.

'No, I get it. You don't know anyone yet, but you soon will. We're not a bad bunch. You'll see.' He smiled that heart-stopping smile she had first seen the day he accosted her at the museum, and her breath caught in her throat. 'I suppose it must also feel strange to you to be here without your grandmother. You said she'd just passed away last time we met, right?'

'Yes, yes, she had.' Mia nodded, stunned that he had understood this. Of course she was feeling a bit fragile, being here without Gran and having to share the house with a stranger. And such a disconcerting one at that.

'Just give it time. Will you come and help me open a trench in, say, half an hour? I could do with some assistance.'

'OK, thanks, I'd like that.'

'Good. I'll see you later then.'

He turned to leave, but unaccountably Mia wanted him to stay now. 'Would you like a sandwich?' she blurted out. 'I only have cheese, but it's quite nice dunked in tea.'

He blinked, then his smile returned. 'Dunked in tea? I haven't done that since I was a kid.'

'You mean you've actually tried it? Most people just go "eeeuuuww" when I suggest it. Well, it's about time you did it again then.' She grinned back at him. 'You'll need at least three spoonfuls of sugar and lots of milk in your tea, though, or it won't taste right.'

'I remember. OK, sounds like an offer I can't refuse. Shall I help?'

'No, it's fine.'

He lowered his tall frame into one of Gran's rickety chairs by the old scrubbed-pine kitchen table, and Mia's stomach did a somersault. He looked like he belonged there in a way Charles never had. She quelled this disloyal thought and busied herself with making tea.

Chapter Eleven

As Ceri tried to keep up with Aase, who walked with long strides despite her age, she looked around at the well-ordered settlement that was obviously Haukr's domain. Apart from the longhouse, there were a lot of lesser dwellings, and some smaller huts that looked to have been half dug into the earth and covered with tussocks of grass as a roof. Several goats stood on top of these, chewing away, totally unconcerned that they were not on the ground. Ceri saw a woman come out of one of the huts; from her attire, which was very plain but still adequate – a linen *serk* with a brown woollen tunic on top that had been mended and patched in places – she surmised that she was a thrall.

So that was how she was to live from now on, like an animal in an earthen pit? That was all very well this time of year, but what about when winter came? She shivered, still only wearing her undergown, and pulled the blanket tighter around herself both to protect her from the chilly air and to preserve her modesty – linen could be rather see-through. It was lucky she'd brought a pin to keep the edges together, as she was still carrying Jorun and this hampered her.

Aase frowned and muttered, 'We'll have to find you all some proper clothing. I'll see to it later.' She had stopped in front of one of the smaller houses and indicated that Ceri should wait outside. It seemed to be some kind of food store. 'Here she is. Tyra, are you busy?' An old woman came backing out, carrying a smoked ham. 'Tyra is in charge of cooking, so best do as she tells you,' Aase added.

'Thank you.' Ceri plucked up her courage to ask the question that had been burning on her tongue ever since Haukr's last words to her.

'Excuse me, but could you tell me what ails little Jorun, please? I mean ... I'll be better able to care for her if I know what is wrong.' She didn't want to be thought to question her superiors, but she couldn't make out what was the matter with the girl. Jorun didn't have the vacant look of someone who was simple-minded, but neither did she respond to anything Ceri whispered to her, and she was sure it wasn't a question of the language.

Aase hesitated, putting her head to one side. 'Well, as far as we can tell, the only thing wrong with her is that she can't hear or speak. But who knows? She seems happiest playing by herself, so all you have to do is feed her and follow her around. Most people just ignore her, but she is the jarl's daughter and has to be treated with respect.'

With that, she moved abruptly away and left Ceri to it.

'Yes, what do you want?' Old Tyra had turned around, a grumpy expression on her wrinkled face. She must have been quite tall in her youth, but now she was stooped and probably suffering from pain in her joints, as she had a pronounced limp when she moved. She still cut an impressive figure, though, and obviously no one questioned her authority here.

'I apologise for disturbing you. I'm Ceri, one of the new ... er, newcomers.' She couldn't bear to refer to herself as a thrall. 'I've been told to look after Jorun, and the jarl said to feed her.' She put Jorun down on the ground and waited. The girl buried her face in

Ceri's blanket and made more keening noises.

Tyra sighed and sent the little one an exasperated glance. 'I doubt it's food she needs, but I've some bread and honey in the hall – a real treat. Follow me.' They made their way back into the longhouse, whose beaten earth floor was immaculately swept. With slow but measured movements, Tyra found a piece of flatbread and dipped it in a jar of honey. 'Here, try her with that. Bread. Honey,' she repeated, as if Ceri was deaf too.

Ceri wondered what Tyra had meant by her earlier comment, but she didn't dare ask. 'Here, *cariad*, have some of this.' She held the bread out to Jorun with an encouraging smile, but the girl just frowned.

Ceri knelt in front of her. 'Eat,' she said, pronouncing the word clearly and pointing at the bread, then her own mouth. She took a tiny bite herself, then held it out to Jorun again. 'Eat.'

The girl was watching her intently and finally mumbled something while forming her lips into the shape Ceri's had been. What emerged was merely an incoherent noise, but she took the bread and started to eat it slowly.

'Good.' Ceri gave her another smile and nodded encouragingly.

Tyra waved a hand in the direction of the door. 'Outside, please, so it doesn't drip.'

'Oh, yes, of course. Come, Jorun.' She took one of Jorun's hands in a firm grip and headed for the double doors, which stood open, presumably to give more light to the rooms inside.

'You're wasting your time,' Tyra called after her, the large ham in her grip once more. 'The little one can't hear a thing.'

'I know, but she can see my mouth,' Ceri replied. 'She should be able to learn to recognise some words that way. There was a deaf man in my village who did that.'

Tyra stopped to regard her with a thoughtful look, and Ceri

became self-conscious. What if she wasn't pronouncing the Norse words correctly? When listening to Haukr and his men, she had heard slight differences to the way Eydis had spoken, but put it down to dialect.

'Can . . . can you understand me? I haven't spoken Norse for many years but I had a . . . um, relative from your country.'

A somewhat toothless grin greeted this question. 'Yes, of course. You're doing just fine. And the little one seems to have taken to you – unusual.'

'Thank you.'

Tyra looked at Jorun. 'The man you speak of, he probably wasn't born deaf like her.' She harrumphed and continued with her tasks, shaking her head, but Ceri wasn't daunted. Jorun had definitely been paying attention to her lips. It ought to be possible for the girl to learn to understand at least a few simple words in this manner, as long as she could get her attention. She wondered why no one had ever tried to teach her before, but then there were many things that were strange here at Haukr's manor. No doubt she'd soon learn the answers.

After Jorun had finished the bread, they went down to the lake, where the ship now bobbed up and down in a small secluded bay. Except it wasn't a lake at all, as Ceri soon found out. Finding herself thirsty, she bent to scoop a handful of water into her mouth. She quickly spat it out and made a face. It was salty.

'Urgh!' She licked her lips and frowned, while Jorun shrieked with a strange high-pitched sort of laughter. She obviously thought Ceri's expression of disgust was funny, so to amuse the little girl, Ceri repeated her actions. Jorun imitated her, spluttering saltwater all over the front of her dress, but Ceri didn't reprimand her – it would soon dry.

'You can't drink that,' a man passing by told them. 'If you're thirsty, there's plenty of water in the stream coming down the hill.' He mimed drinking and water gushing, then pointed.

'Thank you, I'll definitely try that instead.'

'Oh, you're Norse? I thought you . . . Never mind.' The man's smile faded. 'I'm from Bretland. Captured many years ago now.'

'So am I, but I learned the Norse language when I was young.' Ceri replied in their own tongue, which instantly made the man's expression turn friendly again. She stared out over the water. 'Why is this salty? We're nowhere near the sea, are we?' She was puzzled. Haukr's ship had negotiated an archipelago of stony islets on its way inland, and these had given way to forested islands and what Ceri had taken to be a lakeshore. Since they had travelled for quite a long while, she had assumed they'd entered the mouth of a river that emanated from a lake, in which case the water should be flowing out to sea and therefore be drink-able. Perhaps they had been rowing in a semicircle and somehow doubled back?

'No. There's a river further inland, but it's a long way off and the sea still reaches us here.' The man gave them another smile and went on his way.

Jorun had turned back to the water and was picking stones up from the beach, and as the man walked off, she threw one after him. Without thinking, Ceri called out, 'No, Jorun, don't do that!' and to her surprise the child turned around and stared at her as if she'd heard the command.

Frowning, Ceri walked around to stand behind Jorun, and when the girl busied herself with picking up stones once more, she called her name softly. No response. She repeated it several times, making her voice louder each time and changing the pitch from high to low. When she spoke in a low but loud voice, Jorun reacted and spun around again.

'You can hear me?' It would seem that Jorun wasn't completely deaf after all; her hearing was only damaged. Ceri smiled. Perhaps this would make things easier. She would have to keep experimenting to see if the girl could learn to communicate somehow.

Tired out, but happy and content, the pair were making their way up to the hall when a bell rang out. Ceri assumed this meant that it was time for food, and since her stomach was by now growling mightily, she set off up the hill with quick strides. She said, 'Eat,' to Jorun, and the child smiled and mimed eating.

'Good girl.' Ceri hugged her briefly before taking her hand again to enter the hall.

⚮

'Excuse me, but who's in charge here?'

Haakon had already headed up to the hill and Mia was just coming out of the cottage to follow him when she heard the question. She looked over towards the gate and saw a man standing there with his arms crossed in a belligerent stance. He was of average height, with closely cropped ash-blond hair and a neatly trimmed beard of the same colour, although slightly darker. She walked over to greet him.

'Hello. I guess you could say I am – I'm Mia Maddox, Elin Hagberg's granddaughter.' She stuck her hand out, but he ignored it and glared at her instead.

'I'm Rolf Thoresson, her nearest neighbour.' He nodded towards the left. 'And what I'd like to know is, what's the meaning of all this palaver?'

Mia felt her eyebrows rise at his hostile tone of voice. 'Er, it's an archaeological dig under the auspices of the Historical Museum in Stockholm. We're taking advantage of the summer months to look for a possible Viking settlement. There's not much to see yet as we've only just started, but you're welcome to come and have a look in a few weeks' time. Hopefully we'll have some exciting finds by then.'

She tried to keep her voice polite and calm, but it was difficult in the face of his rudeness.

'No thanks.' He swept a hand out to indicate the cars parked in the lane. 'And you can tell Mrs Hagberg from me that I'd thank her to clear away this lot as soon as possible. They're in the way.'

'Of what?' Mia looked around. It was a small country road with hardly any traffic, and the cars were all parked up on the verges. There was plenty of room to get past. Even a lorry could manage it easily.

'My enjoyment of the peace and quiet of nature,' Thoresson replied. 'This is a tranquil neighbourhood. If I'd wanted loads of people crawling over the place and a bunch of noisy old bangers coming and going at all hours of the day, I'd have stayed in the city.'

'Well, I'm sorry you feel that way, but we have permission from the police to park here all summer. And for your information, my grandmother passed away back in February. This is now my property and the dig is entirely on my land, so it won't encroach on your privacy in any way. If you have any further complaints, you'll have to take them up with the museum.'

Without saying goodbye, she stalked off, swearing under her breath. What an insufferable man! Who did he think he was?

'What's up? You look like you're about to kill someone.'

Haakon stopped in the middle of removing a square of turf with a sharp spade and looked at Mia. He'd thought he had restored peace between them over lunch, and they'd been getting on quite well. It had felt as if they could work together in harmony as long as he remembered to let her have a say in all the decisions.

But now her eyes were flashing icy shards and she seemed to be fuming.

'Rolf Thoresson, that's what's the matter. What a complete and utter arrogant arse!'

'Rolf who?' Haakon couldn't remember anyone of that name among his team.

'My neighbour, apparently.' Mia pointed west. 'Has his cottage over there somewhere. He had the gall to come and complain about the vehicles parked outside my gate and the fact that there are people "crawling over the place".' She waved her hands around. 'I mean, honestly, it's not like anyone's that noisy, is it?'

To be fair, the guys cutting down trees were making a bit of a racket, but that could happen in any neighbourhood and would soon be finished. Trees needed felling from time to time. As for the rest, they were chatting and laughing, but not in anything other than ordinary voices.

Haakon leaned on his spade. 'He does sound a bit . . . uptight. Had you met him before?'

'No, never. And Gran didn't mention him either. Some neighbour, huh? He didn't even know she'd passed away.'

Ouch. 'Probably just a miserable old git then. We're not doing anything illegal, so he can complain all he likes. Just to make sure, though – you do know where your boundaries are? So we don't stray on to his territory, I mean?'

'Yes, there are fences all around the perimeter. I checked them for Gran last summer, and although some were a bit rickety, none had fallen down. And like I said earlier, I'll get a map from the lawyer to show where the rest of the boundaries lie.'

'OK, good. Forget him then. There are always killjoys.'

She took a deep breath. 'Yes, you're right. It's just . . . No, I shouldn't let him get to me. OK, show me what you want me to start with.'

He grinned and couldn't resist teasing her. 'I thought you were in charge?'

She narrowed her eyes at him, then elbowed him in the ribs. 'Ha ha, very funny. You asked me to help you with a trench, so I'll let you decide. Just for today.'

'Good of you.' He jumped out of the way of another sharp elbow. 'I'm just clearing the top layer of grass off, then we can start removing the earth. According to Tomas's plans, we should be right on top of a possible building. His readings confirmed an anomaly here.'

'Great! Can't wait to get started. I'm ridiculously excited about this and I'm not going to let some old misery-guts spoil it for me.' Mia picked up a trowel.

'Attitude! I like it.'

As he shoved the spade into the mossy grass, Haakon knew he too was very excited about this dig. He couldn't wait to see what they found.

Chapter Twelve

Ceri stopped just inside the wide door that led into the hall, overwhelmed by the sheer number of people as well as the noise that hit her almost like a solid entity. She had forgotten that there was to be feasting to welcome the returning heroes. Not that they were heroes in her mind, but still . . .

Haukr's men were seating themselves on the benches around the walls, together with their women and children. Haukr himself had a special carved chair with armrests at one end of the room, with a couple of free-standing benches either side, presumably for the most important members of the household. The trestle tables were now groaning with dishes of every kind, which sent gentle clouds of steam into the air, filling it with mouth-watering smells. Pork cooked in various ways, hams like the one Tyra had been carrying earlier, glazed with honey, roast venison and chicken, as well as several types of fish and cheese fought for space with barley bread, oatcakes and large slabs of butter. It was easy to see that it was autumn – the only time of year when food was plentiful. Ceri's stomach growled in response.

Jorun hid behind her skirts, but Ceri pulled her forward gently, smiling encouragement. 'You'll be fine. I won't let anyone harm you.' She caught sight of Aase and led the girl over to her. 'Excuse me, but where should I seat the little one?'

'Oh, er . . . she usually just wanders around. She doesn't eat with the rest of them, but perhaps as it's a feast you'd better ask the jarl.'

Ceri took a deep breath and pulled Jorun along towards the table where Haukr sat with Ragnhild at his side. The two of them had ceramic plates and drinking horns set into silver stands, while most other people had to make do with wooden plates and cups. Ceri noticed that Ragnhild was wearing just about every piece of jewellery her husband had brought back as his part of the spoils, but her expression was still one of dissatisfaction and the body language between husband and wife showed clearly that they were not on good terms.

'Excuse me?' She struggled to make herself heard above the general din, but Haukr happened to look up. As he caught sight of her and Jorun, his face broke into the smile that so lit up his features, and for a moment Ceri forgot why she was standing there. Forgot that he was now her master and she his captive. But then his voice broke the spell and she returned to reality.

'Yes? You wished to speak to me?'

Ragnhild glared at Ceri, then at her husband. 'She's a thrall, she speaks when she's spoken to.'

'The lady Ceridwen is not a thrall, she's a hostage,' Haukr said. 'I plan to have her ransomed in the spring. She's to be well treated.'

Ragnhild spluttered into her mead. 'So? She can't just sit around doing nothing until then; she'll have to earn her keep like everyone else.'

'She is. I've put her in charge of Jorun and I'm assuming that is what she's come to speak to me about.' He gave Ragnhild a quelling look and she shot him a dagger one in return.

'Jorun is *my* daughter and my responsibility. Perhaps I don't want her looked after by a foreigner.'

'You haven't taken any notice of our daughter in years, and I believe that as jarl I make the decisions around here, including those concerning Jorun. The lady Ceridwen speaks Norse – not that it makes any difference to the little one, as you well know.' A look passed between the couple that Ceri couldn't interpret, but Ragnhild glanced away, a flush staining her cheeks. Haukr turned back towards Ceri. 'What did you wish to ask?'

'I merely wondered where your daughter should sit to have her meal.' Ceri wished she could simply turn and run out of the hall. She didn't want to be the cause of further contention between the warring couple, and she had a feeling that the lady Ragnhild would not let matters rest despite her husband's words.

'Ah, well Jorun usually doesn't sit anywhere, but she might do so with you next to her. Come here, there's room for both of you.' There was an empty space on the bench beside his chair, and he gestured for the other occupants to shuffle over, making more room. 'You'll have to crawl under the trestle, I'm afraid.' He smiled again, and Ceri had a hard time quelling an answering smile. She didn't want to be charmed by him and she didn't want to sit anywhere near him, but how could she refuse his command? And yet one look at Ragnhild made her wish once more that she'd never approached them.

'You're going to let a thrall sit on your right-hand side?' Ragnhild sounded incredulous.

'I told you, she's not a thrall. She is the daughter of a chieftain in her homeland, not a serving woman. And we must treat her well or the ransom amount will be much smaller.'

Ceri wondered how he had found out about her being a chieftain's daughter. She hadn't been aware that he even knew her name, but perhaps he had asked one of the other captives. It wasn't a secret, after all, and she knew that at least one of the other villagers spoke some Norse.

Quickly she crawled under the table and emerged with Jorun in tow next to him. She made the little girl sit by her father's side and tried to make herself as invisible as possible. Jorun fidgeted, but Ceri took her hand and gave her a smile.

'Eat,' she said, miming the action as well as pronouncing the word with exaggerated care. She handed the little girl a spoon, while keeping the eating knife well out of her reach. Jorun nodded, but put the spoon down and instead helped herself to food with her fingers.

'Have you had a difficult afternoon?' Haukr asked her over Jorun's head, a sympathetic expression in his eyes.

'No, not at all. Jorun is, er . . . enchanting.'

He shook his head sadly. 'She'll never be like other children, but she's my daughter and I just want her to be safe and well fed. You'll see to that?'

'Of course, it will be my pleasure.' And that was the truth – she would enjoy looking after the little girl. It was such an easy task compared to the visions of menial chores and other horrors she'd had during the voyage that she couldn't complain. He was being very kind.

'Good. You must sleep with her here in the hall. She has her place in the far corner. I'll have someone show you later.'

Ceri nodded, amazed at this further gesture of kindness. She understood that he was saving her from sleeping with the thralls, and she was very grateful, even if she felt bad for her fellow villagers and was still resentful that he had the power to decide such matters. She ignored the disbelieving noises and muttered comments coming from Haukr's other side and concentrated on putting some food in front of Jorun.

The little girl had relaxed now that she'd seen her father smiling and tucked into the food, albeit in a rather messy fashion. Ceri watched her and tried to mop up any spillage, while ignoring her own stomach, which was turning itself inside out with hunger. She had no idea when she would be fed, and although Haukr had said she was a hostage, that didn't really help.

'Are you not hungry?'

She looked up to find him frowning at her. 'Well, yes, but . . .'

'Then eat, woman.'

'She's waiting to eat with the thralls,' came Ragnhild's voice from his other side. 'See? Even she has more sense than you.'

Haukr took a deep breath, and Ceri waited for an explosion, but none came. Instead he said in a quiet but deadly voice, 'For the last time, Ceridwen is not to be treated like a thrall. She is different, special. She eats with Jorun, and if Jorun is eating with us, so does Ceridwen. Understood?'

'No sense,' Ragnhild repeated, seemingly unfazed by the menace in his voice, but she didn't argue further, so Ceri tucked in, helping herself to bread, meat and a bowl of stew.

As she ate, she sighed inwardly. She would have to remember to stay well away from the lady Ragnhild.

When Mia came down the stairs that evening, having had a bath and a change of clothes, Haakon was already in the kitchen. He turned, a spoon in one hand, and gestured towards the tiny cooker, which could only fit two pots at a time.

'I'm heating up some soup. Is that OK? I don't know what you were planning on eating, but I've got enough for two here if you want some.'

'Thanks, that would be great. I haven't really had time to buy supplies yet. As I said, I only arrived last night.'

She'd become so caught up in the excitement of starting the dig, she had forgotten all about driving to the nearest super-market. That would have to be first on her list tomorrow morning.

'Well, I think this is hot enough now, so let's eat.'

He had a loaf of sweet rye bread – *limpa* – the soft Swedish kind made with lots of syrup that Mia absolutely adored, and he offered her some of that as well. Together with the soup, it made a perfect meal after a hard day's work, and Mia tucked in with enjoyment.

'This is delicious.' She savoured another spoonful. 'What is it?'

'It's just chicken with noodles. I made it myself.'

'So you're a great cook as well as a Viking expert? Sounds too good to be true.' She smiled to show that she was teasing.

'Nah, I can whip up a few things my mum taught me, but only easy stuff. Do you like cooking?'

'When I have the time for it, which isn't very often. I love baking too, but I rarely get a chance. Too much to do, you know how it is.' She shrugged.

'Yes, takeaways and TV dinners are so much easier. How did our parents ever survive without microwaves?'

They lapsed into an awkward silence. Despite the intimacy of this meal for two in the cottage's tiny kitchen, they were strangers. As if he felt the same, and wanted to break the ice somehow, Haakon gestured towards a tiny CD player that stood on the bench behind him. 'Mind if I put on some music? It helps me relax in the evenings.'

'No, go ahead.'

Mia liked music too, but she almost opened her mouth to protest when he fished what looked like a heavy metal CD out of a bag on the floor next to him. He held up a hand to forestall her, grinning as if he'd known what she was going to say.

'Hold on, I'm not going to blast you with anything noisy. These are just power ballads.'

'Really?' Mia glanced at the cover, which shouted out names like Metallica and Linkin Park. She never listened to stuff like that; she preferred something with a tune and said so.

'Just listen,' he said, and turned the music on. 'I think you'll be surprised.'

He was right. What emerged from the tiny speakers wasn't anything like the noisy guitar riffs she'd been expecting. A man's voice, singing softly of trust and love, vowing that nothing mattered apart from that, held her spellbound until the end. It was a haunting tune, the emotion clear in the singer's voice, and she found herself deeply moved.

'You've never heard that before?' Haakon enquired as another song began, this time belted out by a sultry female voice.

'No, I don't think so. Guess that'll teach me not to have preconceived notions. It was beautiful.'

He nodded. 'Yes, it's the kind of song I think even our ancestors would have liked, because it touches something deep inside you.'

Mia stared at him, very taken with this idea. 'Of course. I suppose people have always loved singing, as it's such an emotional thing to do. The only part that changes is how you do it, not the sentiments themselves.'

'Exactly. Sometimes I close my eyes and imagine I'm in a hall full of Vikings. They're feasting, drinking, joking, laughing raucously, then someone strikes up a tune and a hush falls on the room as the singer holds them spellbound. These fearsome men, who think nothing of killing someone and sending them on their way to Valhalla, are nevertheless moved by the music, which strikes a chord deep within them. It makes them seem more human to me somehow.' He fell silent and looked slightly embarrassed, as if he'd said too much, exposing his thoughts to her like that, but Mia was glad he had.

'I like that. I'm going to try it now.' She leaned back in her chair and closed her eyes, conjuring up the image he had suggested. It came easily. The noise, the cooking smells, the fug of stale air from too many people packed closely into a small space, then suddenly complete silence apart from a lone voice. A man singing about the pain of love, the unbearable yearning for something you couldn't have, and the utter defeat felt when that love was not reciprocated. All eyes turned to the singer, Mia's included, but he was a shadowy figure and she couldn't focus on him properly. Instead her mind reverberated with the emotion in his voice and she allowed herself to feel the hopelessness of love, the despair and loneliness described by the song, and her eyes locked with those of the Viking leader. Clear blue, but far from cold, they gazed into hers and she suddenly wanted to cry because she knew he wasn't for her. His expression turned sad, wistful, and she looked away. She couldn't bear it.

'Mia? Are you all right?'

She blinked in confusion, opening her eyes to stare into Haakon's, so like the fantasy Viking's but not filled with love or yearning, only concern. She shook her head slightly and noticed the song had come to an end. 'That was weird,' she muttered. 'It was so real, I felt like I was there.'

Haakon smiled. 'You have a great imagination, obviously. So you see what I mean?'

'Yes, absolutely.' *Only too well.* She took a deep breath and blurted out, 'Do you believe in reincarnation?'

'Um, actually, I do. At least, I believe some people are re-incarnated; those who have unfinished business perhaps. Why do you ask?'

'Oh, just making conversation.' It sounded like a lame excuse even to her, but he didn't comment.

'Well, I'm for bed. It's been a long day and there will be more hard work tomorrow. Goodnight.'

'Goodnight, and thank you for dinner and, er . . . the music lesson.'

'You're welcome.'

She heard him climb the narrow stairs two at a time and imagined his long legs making easy work of them. A shiver went through her at the memory of those legs in their scruffy, torn jeans – long, lean and well muscled – and she screwed her eyes up tightly to stop thinking about it. So what if he looked great in jeans? She had a fiancé, and Haakon was probably married or in a relationship anyway. A man like him would never be short of female company, of that she was sure. Just because he'd been kind to her today didn't mean he was interested in her in any other way. They had to work together, their relationship purely professional, and he had only tried to put her at ease.

Feeling guilty for even debating the issue with herself, she took her mobile out of her pocket and dialled Charles's number. The UK was an hour behind Sweden, so he ought to be awake still.

'Hello?' He sounded sleepy, and Mia belatedly remembered that he tended to slump in front of the TV every night, which seemed to act as a soporific on him.

'Hey, I just wanted to say goodnight in person. Text messages are so impersonal somehow.'

'Er, right. Apart from all the emojis you always add.' She heard the amusement in his voice.

'Yes, apart from those.' She was very fond of the little hearts and other things one could add, while Charles found them childish. 'You OK? Busy?'

'Oh, yeah, it's been a hell of a week.' He started telling her about some big account he was working on for a famous person, and Mia tried not to become impatient – he knew she wasn't really interested in the details, and she hated name-dropping. He finished with, 'But this weekend is the golf tournament I told you about. My boss asked me to be his partner – ha, take that, Jason bloody Tamworth – and I'm going to play the game of my life.'

Jason was Charles's main rival in the office, the two of them always vying for the next account, the next promotion. 'Congratulations! And good luck, I'm sure you'll do really well.' She just couldn't get excited about golf; it seemed like such a boring game, but what did she know?

'Thanks. I'll let you know how it goes. Better go get some beauty sleep now.' He chuckled. 'Don't suppose that matters where you are – the mozzies and the nerdy archaeology types won't care what you look like.'

'No, I don't suppose they will. Bye! Love you.'

As she hung up, there was a small stirring of irritation inside her. Why did he have to belittle her profession and those who pursued it? An image of Haakon rose in her mind – could you get any further from nerdy if you tried? He definitely didn't fit the stereotypical view of a weedy geek.

But what did it matter?

With a sigh, she stood up and turned off the light. She was tired, that was all, and she did need a good night's sleep.

She only hoped she wouldn't dream of Viking men with blue eyes.

Chapter Thirteen

The feasting continued long into the night, becoming more and more raucous as Haukr and his men partook freely of the ale that flowed in a seemingly never-ending stream. The mead had only been served with the meal, being special, but he didn't mind what he was drinking. He noticed the room becoming blurred around the edges, but he was feeling mellow and content, even though Ragnhild hadn't ceased her constant needling. He ignored her muttered comments and hoped that she'd eventually give up if she didn't receive a response. He'd had enough of her bad moods.

He knew they stemmed from the fact that she'd been barren since Jorun's birth. Something had obviously gone badly wrong, and the wise woman hadn't been able to help her conceive again, giving rise to this endless well of discontent that appeared to fester inside his wife. Ragnhild also seemed to think that Haukr blamed her for giving birth to a defective child, but that wasn't true. He was sad that his daughter would never live a normal life, but he still loved her. Unlike Ragnhild, who had ignored the child since they found out there was something wrong with her.

She should have been caring for her the way Ceridwen was at the moment – sharing smiles, playing games, interacting, heedless of the fact that Jorun couldn't hear her. It looked as though the little girl was enjoying herself, whether she understood or not, and it made him smile. But how different things could have been if his daughter had been born the same as everyone else . . .

He pushed the sad thoughts away and concentrated on the here and now. There was singing and storytelling, with one man in particular holding the audience spellbound while he told a tale about Jörmungandr, the terrifying serpent that he claimed lay in the ocean that encircled Miðgarðr, the world of men.

'Lucky we didn't encounter him as we crossed the sea, eh?' Haukr teased Ceridwen. He'd noticed her eyes grow big as she listened, even though he was sure she followed the Christian god and shouldn't believe in such stories.

'Indeed! And I'm very grateful I hadn't heard about him before setting foot on your ship.' She shuddered delicately. 'It was a perilous enough journey as it was. I definitely didn't need to imagine such a fearsome creature underneath us all the way, even though I doubt its existence for real.'

'Oh, he's real enough, but the gods protected us.' Haukr took another swig of ale and smiled into his cup, waiting to see if she'd rise to his bait.

She didn't reply, though, wisely keeping her beliefs to herself. He noticed that she stayed in her place long after Jorun's eyelids had become heavy and the girl fell asleep with her head in Ceridwen's lap. There was much to observe, and perhaps she was comparing it to the feasts in her homeland?

For a while, Haukr played *hnefatafl* – a board game he loved – with Thorald, but halfway through the evening he was challenged to an arm-wrestling bout by one of his men, who dragged a three-legged stool over to sit on the opposite side of the table. Haukr agreed with a laugh. 'You know you stand no chance of winning until I'm an old man,' he told his opponent, but the man, Ulv by name, was fired up by the ale and remained undaunted.

'I swear I can best anyone tonight,' he shouted. 'By Odin, all that rowing you made me do has given me added strength.'

'We'll see about that.'

Everyone watched as the two men grabbed each other's right hand in a firm grip, then, on a signal from Thorald, the test of strength began. Bulging biceps, gleaming in the firelight from the central hearth, strained against skin tanned by hours in the sun out at sea. Haukr had taken his turn at the oars, so Ulv wasn't alone in having worked hard. But he knew that his challenger was doomed to failure in any case – Haukr had been blessed with a size and strength that was against the other man from the start.

Back and forth they grappled, neither giving way. Haukr was merely humouring his thegn, allowing him time to test his skill in order to spare him humiliation, but he tried to do it subtly. Ulv was far from being a weakling, but no matter how much he strained, he couldn't make Haukr's wrist move more than a fraction. His face became suffused with colour, the veins standing out at the temples, while Haukr hoped the only sign of effort on his part was a clenched jaw. He certainly wasn't straining to the point of bursting a blood vessel. A hush fell on the room as the bout dragged on; then, as suddenly as it had begun, it was over, with Ulv's hand on the table beneath Haukr's. The thump of knuckles on wood startled everyone, but then the cheers broke out and a cry of 'Haukr, Haukr!' went up.

'*Skítr!* I will best you one of these days.' Ulv shook his head, but there was no real aggression. He must have known he'd lose despite his brave words earlier.

Several others tried their luck, but with much the same outcome, and after the third one had gone to console himself with more ale and a willing thrall girl, Haukr turned to Ceridwen with a smile. 'Is this what the men in your country do too?'

'Yes, although none as successfully as you, so far as I know.'

Judging by the way she raised her chin, he gathered that this annoyed her.

'You do not have one man in your village who is better than all the others? The leader, perhaps?'

'My brother Cadoc is strong, but no more so than anyone else. He rules by virtue of inheritance, although he is also the best shot with a bow and arrow in our valley.'

'So it won't matter if that little boy grows up a weakling?' Haukr hadn't forgotten her nephew.

Ceridwen's eyes flashed, but she lowered her gaze. 'Bryn is strong enough normally. He was merely laid low by illness. I pray he is better by now and able to join the other children of the village in their usual rough-and-tumble games. He'll soon be like them again.'

'Unlike my daughter,' Haukr muttered with a sigh.

'About Jorun . . .' Ceridwen started to say, but Ragnhild chose that moment to interrupt, leaning forward to peer past her husband, a scowl marring her lovely features.

'Why is she wearing a gold ring?' she demanded. 'Hostage or not, that can't be allowed. Why, she could escape and buy her passage home with such riches!'

Haukr stared at Ceridwen's ring. He'd forgotten all about it. He shook his head at Ragnhild. 'It's stuck, so I'm letting her keep it for now.'

'Stuck? Surely you didn't fall for such an obvious ruse.' Ragnhild laughed, but it wasn't a happy sound. 'Take it off, girl, and stop pretending. You may be able to fool my husband, but you can't pull the wool over my eyes.'

Ceridwen had a wary expression on her face, as if she was loath to antagonise his wife, but she held her hand out to Haukr. 'Perhaps if you try, jarl, it may come unstuck. No one here can doubt your strength.'

Haukr suppressed a smile. That last sentence was well phrased and very clever. Implied was the fact that Ragnhild must believe her husband, if not his hostage.

He took her small hand in his large one and felt the calluses from all the rowing scrape her soft knuckles. It made him feel big and clumsy, so he tried to be gentle. With one hand around her frail wrist, he pretended to tug on the ring with all his might with the other. It refused to budge despite all manner of wriggling and twisting. He persisted for a while longer, keeping up the pretence of pulling harder than he really was. Then he shrugged in defeat.

'No, it's not budging. That will have to stay. Must have been put on you when you were a child, and then your fingers grew.'

Ragnhild was looking daggers at her again, and Ceridwen nodded. 'Yes, it was my mother's and she died when I was ten. I've worn it ever since. I suppose I ought to have had it enlarged over the years.'

'It'll come off when the winter cold sets in,' Ragnhild said. 'You're to give it to me as soon as it does.'

'No!' The one word hissed out of Haukr in a tone so menacing it surprised even him. He didn't know why he felt so strongly about this, but he did. 'Ceridwen keeps her ring, whether it comes off or not, until I say otherwise. If anyone else is found in possession of it, they'll be beaten to within an inch of their life. Understood?'

For once Ragnhild had the wit to acquiesce, nodding curtly, but Haukr felt sure it wasn't the last they'd heard of this. She turned away, and Ceridwen put her hand under the table, out of sight, in a futile gesture.

Haukr thought he understood her concern – after his raid on her village, that ring would be the only thing she had left of her mother's belongings, as Ragnhild and his men already had the rest. Without thinking, he put his warm hand over her slightly shaking one and squeezed gently under cover of the trestle. She

119

glanced up and he looked into eyes as clear as a beck, shining with what might be gratitude, but also determination.

She wasn't cowed by Ragnhild, this woman, and he would make sure it stayed that way.

Ceri found herself spellbound by Haukr's eyes, the same colour blue as the flowers that carpeted the forests of her homeland in the spring, and with a reassuring twinkle that sent waves of warmth pulsing through her. As long as he was her champion, she was safe. His touch sent a frisson up her arm and straight down to the pit of her stomach, making her want to snatch her hand back again, but she didn't. He gave it one final squeeze before letting go.

Despite everything, she was incredibly aware of him, and even though Jorun was asleep, she was reluctant to leave until she had found out more about him. He intrigued her – fierce marauder one moment, caring man the next. Such a contradiction.

The first thing that had struck her earlier was that he smelled clean. During the afternoon, she and Jorun had walked past a bath house with steam escaping through tiny slits up near the roof, and she assumed Haukr had visited this together with his men. She had noticed that all the Norsemen were very particular about keeping themselves clean. They combed their hair every day, usually wetting it first, and she'd seen many of them using nail picks. Haukr had also changed his clothes, and the fragrance of garments that had been left to dry in a summer meadow wafted past her whenever he moved, as well as the stronger smell of wool from his loose-fitting trousers. He wore only an undershirt of linen – his belted tunic seemed to have been discarded, as it was warm inside the hall. Glancing sideways from time to time, Ceri was afforded glimpses of his throat, not quite as golden as his arms, and his neatly trimmed beard. His hair shone white in the light from the fire, and that too smelled clean. It made her wish she could bathe too.

She had seen some of the other men with their torsos bare earlier, and a couple were without the matting of chest hair she was used to on the men of her village. Not that she had much experience of men, but she'd seen them when they threw off some of their clothing in order to swim in the river. She wondered which group Haukr fell into, then felt her cheeks heat up. She knew she shouldn't even be thinking about that.

He drank his fair share of ale, she noticed, but didn't join in the singing or telling of bawdy jokes. He merely smiled with quiet enjoyment while he watched everyone else, as if he was content when all those around him were.

To Ceri's great surprise, Haukr insisted on carrying Jorun to her sleeping bench when everyone else started heading for bed, and laid her down gently on top of a lustrous wolf pelt. There were two pillows and a pile of soft woollen blankets. Haukr took one and covered his daughter before stroking her cheek.

'There should be room for you to sleep next to her,' he said to Ceri. 'She's not very big.'

Ceri nodded. 'Thank you.' She looked him in the eyes to show him that she was thanking him for all his kindnesses so far, not just this warm, snug sleeping place. He stared back and smiled, his eyes crinkling up at the corners, which made him even more devastatingly attractive than before. Ceri took a deep breath and turned away with a whispered 'Goodnight', determined not to let him affect her equilibrium in this way. He was a married man, firmly out of bounds. And he was her captor, the man who had taken her away from her own people and who now had absolute control over every aspect of her life. That grated no end. She was used to being in charge, not constricted in any way. It was intolerable.

Even as she told herself this sternly, however, she couldn't stop her hand from tingling where he'd held it, nor suppress a tremor as she thought about the way he had looked at her.

'This is madness,' she muttered as she bedded down next to Jorun. 'I must stop thinking about him altogether. He abducted me and stole my brother's wealth!'

But dear Lord, there was no denying she was beginning to like him more than she ought.

Chapter Fourteen

Mia woke to a much warmer room than the previous day, and when she heard movement in the kitchen, she guessed that Haakon must have put some logs in the stove and the heat was spreading upwards. She dressed quickly and went downstairs, where she found her house guest on the veranda with a cup of coffee and some muesli with *filmjölk* and fruit.

'Good morning. That looks disgustingly healthy,' she commented with a smile. *Filmjölk* was a type of sour or fermented milk that resembled yoghurt, or the Icelandic variant *skyr*, which had recently become popular in the UK, and it was a typical Swedish breakfast staple. Mia only liked it with lots of sugar on top, which sort of defeated the purpose. 'Would you mind if I have some of your lovely bread instead? I promise to go and buy you a new loaf later.'

'Morning. No, go ahead, help yourself if you don't want fibre to fill you up.'

'I can eat that in England. Here in Sweden I like to OD on the delicious bread and pastries. Bad, I know.'

'It's fun to be bad sometimes.' He grinned at her, and something fizzed inside her. Had she imagined the double entendre? Yes, he probably hadn't meant it as such. God, what was the matter with her? She was reading things into his words and actions that simply weren't there.

He left the cottage as soon as he'd finished eating. As he was heading out the door, his mobile rang, and she heard him say, 'Hi, sweetie, how's it going?' before he disappeared. She felt even more stupid than before. It was as she'd suspected – he had a partner.

And so do I, she told herself firmly while rinsing her breakfast dishes. So why was she even debating the matter?

After a quick trip to the supermarket, Mia carried on helping Haakon with the trench they'd started. They made good progress, but nothing massively exciting emerged from the soil, at least not in the top layers.

'I think I'm going to open up a deeper test pit over here, just to make sure we're not wasting our time,' he told her. 'What do you think? On the geophys results it looked like it might be the corner of a building, but maybe it's pretty deep down.'

'Sure, good idea.' Mia wondered if she should have been the one to suggest this – being the supposed co-director of the dig and everything – but she tried to look as though she'd been thinking along the same lines.

'OK, I'll get started.' He nodded towards the side of the trench. 'There's a grid over there, and some paper and pencils if you need them.'

'What? Oh.' Mia belatedly remembered that she was supposed to make detailed drawings as she went along in order to record everything about the dig for posterity. 'I . . . um, didn't think it was necessary as we haven't found anything yet.'

He smiled. 'That's fine, just thought I'd mention it.'

She wasn't sure if he was testing her, so she simply nodded and turned to carry on scraping away soil with her trowel. It had been years since she'd last done this, but it was all coming back to her now.

The silence stretched between them, and Mia felt the need to make conversation. 'So how did you end up working in Sweden? I mean, what with you being Norwegian.' Perhaps she was being nosy, but it seemed like a fairly innocuous question.

'My mum is Swedish, so I spent a lot of time in Småland with my grandparents. Mum and Dad are diplomats and I was at boarding school.' He shrugged. 'For shorter holidays there was no point going all the way out to the Far East. Then by the time I was going to start my master's degree, Grandpa had passed away and Grandma had just been moved to a care home. It seemed a good idea to choose the Swedish university of Lund so I could visit her at weekends. And then I met my wife, got the job at the museum and just kind of stayed on.'

'I see.' So it must have been the wife he was speaking to earlier. Mia took a deep breath. Well, good. It was much better having a married man staying in the cottage with her. Less awkward. Wasn't it?

'What about you? You said you had a Swedish mother too, right?'

'Oh, yes, and my dad was English. Well, Welsh really. He . . . died a few years ago. Cancer.'

That had been a terrible blow, and Mia had needed Elin more than ever during that time. Perhaps that was why she was so reluctant to let go of Birch Thorpe now. It was her refuge, her safe haven, the one place where everything seemed bearable.

'I'm sorry, that must have been tough for you.' The look in Haakon's eyes was sincere, and soothed Mia somehow.

She nodded. 'Yes, it was.' But she didn't want to think about that, so she launched into a potted history of the rest of her life while they carried on trowelling.

Just before noon, Haakon gave a shout. 'Hey, what's this? Look what I've just found.'

He picked up a small brush and began to clean the item he was holding between thumb and forefinger. When he held it out to Mia, she almost gasped. 'Oh, how pretty, a gold cross from a necklace!' She took it and turned it this way and that as it winked in sunlight it hadn't seen for nearly a thousand years. As she studied it more closely, excitement bubbled up inside her. 'This isn't Viking, though, it's Celtic. And Christian, obviously. See, a cross with a circle behind it? That's a typically Celtic shape, unmistakable.'

He nodded. 'Yes, I know. Must have been brought back as trading goods, or perhaps from a raid.'

'I wonder how it ended up in here. This doesn't seem like the sort of large house where the inhabitants owned anything that fine. And I can't see that it's broken, so it wouldn't have been dropped by mistake.' Even the loop at the top where a piece of string or leather would have gone was intact. Mia held it up to the light and a strange jolt went through her, almost like fierce longing. She drew in a hasty breath, confused by the sensation. The cross felt familiar, just like the snake ring she wore, and she was extremely reluctant to let go of it. She frowned at such silly thoughts and dumped it unceremoniously into Haakon's palm.

He raised his eyebrows at her. 'What's the matter?'

'Nothing . . . I just . . . Nothing.'

'Tell me.' He pinned her with his blue gaze, and something made her blurt out the truth.

'I felt as if I'd seen it before. Almost like . . . it was mine.' She shook her head. 'No, that sounds ridiculous! It's been buried for a millennium.'

He looked thoughtful. 'Perhaps not. Your family has been associated with this place for who knows how long. Remember we were talking about reincarnation yesterday? Even if there's no such thing, it could be that some deep-rooted memory of owning this has been passed down to you somehow.'

'You really believe that?' Mia was surprised by the idea. She'd never before thought such things were possible.

'Why not? There are lots of things we don't understand. It could be a genetic thing, and one day maybe scientists will be able to explain it, but for now, it's a possibility.'

'I don't know. It was probably just fancy on my part. Let's log it and have a closer look later when it's been cleaned properly.'

'OK. I want you to do it, though, as you're the resident conservation expert.'

'If you say so.' Mia knew she would find it difficult to be near the cross and not covet it. It would be better to send it off to the museum for cleaning.

As some of the other diggers crowded round them to admire the find, chattering excitedly, she had to stop herself from reaching out for it again. *It's mine!* The thought echoed through her brain, but she suppressed it. Even if it had belonged to some long-lost ancestor, she had no right to it now. None whatsoever.

❧

The days passed, and Ceri and the new thralls settled into the routine of Haukr's settlement as if they had always been a part of it. They'd been given over-tunics of coarse woollen material, as well as trousers for the young boys, which although clearly old and used sufficed for now. There was no point in trying to escape – it had been impressed upon them that the punishment if you were caught was so horrendous as to make you wish you had died instead – and everyone appeared to accept their fate with as much equanimity as they could muster. She spoke with the people from her village, and they seemed resigned, stoical, although some of the youths were still looking mulish whenever their new master wasn't around. Their only hope was to be ransomed by Cadoc, but no one expected this to happen before spring at the earliest.

Ceri didn't tell them that Haukr had said she was probably the only one who'd be set free. Time to face that when and if it happened. Besides, she was determined to persuade Cadoc to pay for everyone, even if he had to borrow coin from someone in order to do it.

At least they were all well fed, even if the fare was monotonous – barley porridge for the most part. But they would have eaten more or less the same thing at home, and no one complained. Each thrall was assigned his or her own tasks, and although Haukr had made it clear she was to be treated differently, Ceri made no protest when the lady Ragnhild ordered her to help out with carding, spinning and weaving.

'You should be able to manage that while still watching my daughter,' Ragnhild said in a tone that implied that it was the least Ceri could do. 'She just sits there staring into space most of the time anyway.'

This wasn't true, at least not any longer. Ceri and Jorun had formed a bond, and the little girl followed her everywhere. She seemed more animated, taking an interest in whatever Ceri was doing. The strange noises continued, but she didn't appear to be distressed.

'Who was looking after her before?' Ceri dared to ask Aase as they worked together sorting the wool according to type of fibre and colour, then carding it. The local sheep had a coat of two layers, with the fibres from the outer one longer and coarser, and therefore more suited to making the warp when weaving. The inner layer was much finer and used for the weft. Once carded, the wool had to be spun into a continuous thread. Ceri was used to handling a drop spindle, so this wasn't a problem for her – she was a fast and experienced spinner.

'No one. As I told you, she mostly just wandered round on her own.' Aase's eyes darted about the hut, as if to make sure no one else was listening to their conversation. 'Most people here think the trolls got to her. That she's tainted by *trolldomr* in some way. So they want nothing to do with her.'

Ceri stared at her. 'Do you believe that too?' Surely there was no such thing as trolls? The devil might have had a hand in making Jorun deaf, but Ceri doubted any magic was involved. And either way, it wasn't contagious, was it?

Aase shrugged. 'Probably not, but I have tried to get through to her before and she didn't want to even look at me. She seems to have taken to you, though. You have a way with children, don't you?'

'I like them, certainly.' Ceri thought again about her betrothed who had died, thus depriving her of the children she should have had by now. She would have loved babies of her own, and just before he'd left for the neighbouring village, Cadoc had hinted that he'd found her a new husband. This had made her very happy, as she'd waited much too long already. But now . . . assuming she was ransomed, would that man even want her when she'd been a hostage of the Norsemen? Probably not. Which meant she might never have children at all. She swallowed down the disappointment, determined not to think about that now.

As for Jorun, Ceri guessed that what she had lacked was warmth and someone who really cared about her. It was true that no one touched her, apart from Ceri herself, and now she understood why. Although Haukr had appeared to notice his child occasionally and tried to treat her kindly, he was mostly busy with other things. And it was clear that Jorun was a little bit afraid of him, perhaps because of his size and fearsome scowl. If she was given the chance, Ceri would ask him to try and smile at the girl. That might help.

She continued to teach Jorun new words each day, and the two of them were learning to communicate by miming and hand signs. She also tried to involve Jorun in whatever task she was doing, showing her what to do, and this kept the little girl occupied and happy most of the time.

'She's never wanted to do anything like that before,' Aase commented one afternoon, as Jorun sat on the floor carding wool with an expression of great concentration on her face. 'Whenever we tried to teach her, she would just throw it on the floor and screech at us.'

'I'm glad if I've made a difference to her,' Ceri said. 'I'm sure she would have got there eventually, though. Sooner or later she would have become bored just wandering around aimlessly.'

'Hmm, I'm not so sure.' Aase looked approvingly at Ceri. 'And I see you know your way around a loom, too. That looks nice and even.' They were weaving together, as it took two women working in tandem to use the upright loom.

Ceri smiled and wielded the weaving sword – a blunt implement made of iron, although they could also be made of wood or bone – pushing the threads into a straight line. 'It's a task that has to be done everywhere, I suppose, and I've certainly had enough practice at home.'

The word 'home' still made her feel that sudden pull of sadness in her stomach every time she thought of it, but she clung to the hope of being ransomed and knew it would be foolish to despair until she found out whether that would happen or not. And even though the lady Ragnhild was difficult and demanding, it wasn't all bad here. That this was in no small measure due to the owner of the place, Ceri didn't want to acknowledge even to herself, but she was always supremely aware of him. Although she didn't see him often, whenever their paths crossed Haukr always stopped to enquire how she was faring, and the smile that attracted her so was never far from peeping out. She found herself looking forward to their brief encounters and spent a lot of time day-dreaming about those twinkling blue eyes. It was silly and pointless – and probably insane, given what he'd done to her people – but she couldn't help herself, and where was the harm in dreaming after all?

She bent forward to move one of the loom weights that had shifted slightly to one side. As she did so, a necklace she'd kept concealed fell out of the top of her gown and glinted in the light coming in through the door. By sheer bad luck – or so it seemed to Ceri – Ragnhild chose that moment to arrive in order to inspect their work. Her eyes narrowed.

'What is that you're wearing? Don't tell me you're one of those fools who follow the Christian god?'

Ceri's fingers closed round the small gold cross and she looked back at Haukr's wife. 'Everyone in my country is Christian. Have been for centuries.' The woman must know that – the other thralls made no secret of their beliefs. Ceri had only kept her cross hidden because it was made of precious metal.

Ragnhild held out her hand. 'Give it to me. Such items are not allowed here. And don't try to tell me it's stuck, or I'll pull it off myself.'

There was nothing for it but to give up the cross. Ceri counted herself lucky to have been allowed to at least keep her mother's ring. Although it was costly, the cross had no particular personal significance, and she was sure she could always buy another one when she was back home. Ragnhild took the offending item and went outside. Ceri thought the woman would add it to her kist of valuables, but instead she went straight to the nearby stream and threw it in, spitting after it.

131

A gasp was heard from Aase, but it was quickly stifled. Ceri just sighed.

Was there no end to Ragnhild's spite?

'What a waste,' she muttered. She briefly contemplated trying to look for it, but the stream flowed quickly, and besides, Ragnhild would probably keep an eye on her to make sure she didn't retrieve it. Best to let it go.

Haukr was very busy with threshing, haymaking and all the other autumn chores, most of which he took part in himself. He didn't believe in sitting around watching others do the work, and in any case, he would become bored doing nothing. Sometimes he took a break, though, as he liked to keep an eye on everything happening in his domains. Often he would walk around just observing what went on and giving a helping hand if needed. It was not unusual for him to come across Ceridwen on these walks, and the sight of her always made him smile. She was still a bit reserved in his company, but her shy smile sometimes appeared when he enquired how she was getting on.

Not so today, however.

'Jarl Haukr.' She passed him with a curt nod and continued on her way without so much as a glance.

'Stop!' The word escaped him before he had time to think, and came out much harsher than he had intended. When she halted and slowly turned around, scowling at him, he stepped towards her and said more softly, 'Ceridwen, what ails you? Has something happened?'

'No.'

He didn't believe her; something was clearly amiss. 'Tell me.'

She shook her head. 'It's nothing. Well . . . your wife took something from me and I . . . She had no right. I mean, obviously she does, seeing as I'm a captive, but I feel violated, humiliated. I . . . I hate it here!'

He saw tears hovering on her lashes, but she blinked them away. She was proud, this woman, and courageous, but of course it must be difficult for her to come to terms with captivity when she had been a woman of high rank in charge of her brother's household. Now she was nothing, a nobody. And it was his fault.

He brushed this thought aside and focused on the one thing he could rectify at the moment. 'What did Ragnhild take?'

'A necklace. A golden cross. To be honest, I'd more or less forgotten I was wearing it. But she threw it in the stream and poured scorn on my beliefs.' Ceridwen raised stormy eyes to his. 'I don't belittle your gods, even though they seem cruel to me, with their demands for sacrifice and bloodshed. My god is a peaceful one who brings messages of love and good conduct. Yours can't even agree among themselves, from what I hear.'

Haukr raised his eyebrows. 'I see you've been listening, but perhaps not enough. Personally, I don't understand how a carpenter's son can do anything to help you, but if you wish to believe in him, that is up to you. My gods may be demanding, but have you not noticed that nothing in life is ever free, so why should they help us humans if we don't give them something in return?'

Ceridwen sighed. 'I suppose that makes sense, but the only thing my god demands is trust and belief in him. No unnecessary killing, and we are to turn the other cheek if someone beats us.'

Haukr snorted. 'I'm sorry, but you won't find me doing that. If anyone is stupid enough to hit me, I will certainly hit them back. What good could it possibly do to let them punch me again without retaliation?' He didn't understand that concept at all. It was ridiculous.

'Why does that not surprise me?' she muttered.

He felt his mouth stretch into a smile. 'I think we will have to agree to disagree on this matter. I would gladly add your god to those I pray to, but it would seem foolhardy in the extreme for me to give up on all the others. I can, however, promise you a minimum amount of bloodshed on their behalf. I don't believe in waste and the living need to eat. I'm a practical man, Ceridwen. As for my wife, I don't think she really cares what you believe. She just likes to have the final word on every subject, as I'm sure you've noticed.' No one living here could fail to notice, as Ragnhild made her views known at all times. 'Now, where exactly did she throw your trinket?'

'It doesn't matter. It is probably halfway to the lake by now, or buried at the bottom of the stream. It was the principle of the thing, and it reminded me that I am but a prisoner here.'

He put his hands on her shoulders, which made her look up at him again with those luminous silver eyes. 'No, Ceridwen, you are a hostage. There is a huge difference, believe me. Now go and pray to your god that he can help me find your cross and that your brother is willing to pay for your release. Then all you need is the patience to wait for his arrival.'

It was Ceri's turn to snort. 'I don't think the Lord concerns himself with such trivial matters as my necklace, but I will certainly pray for deliverance. Good day to you, Jarl Haukr.'

He watched her hurry off, then strode towards the stream. Although he could understand her frustration, keeping thralls and taking hostages were universal phenomena, and he was able to ignore any guilt he felt at having taken her and her fellow villagers captive. There was always the chance that someone would do the same to him and his people if they couldn't defend themselves; such was the way of the world. But the anger he felt towards Ragnhild for being unnecessarily spiteful to Ceridwen would keep him looking for that cross until he found it.

Two days after Ceri's confrontation with Ragnhild, Aase came into the weaving hut and took hold of her hand, pressing something into her palm. 'Don't tell anyone,' she hissed. 'Hide it well.'

The shape of the golden cross was unmistakable on her skin, and Ceri gasped as her fingers closed around it. 'Thank you! But . . . how . . . ?'

'Jarl Haukr gave it to me in secret and told me you should have it back. He said he just happened to see it, glinting in the sunlight at the bottom of the stream, when he was washing his hands. But the mistress mustn't find it or we'll all be in trouble, including him.'

'Thank you again, it really is most kind of you. Um, both of you.' Ceri was almost moved to tears by the older woman's kindness. She was risking Ragnhild's wrath for the sake of a hostage, no small thing. And as for the jarl, had he really come upon the necklace by chance? It seemed like too much of a coincidence. Either way, it showed he had compassion beyond what she should expect from someone who had abducted her.

'It wasn't right, what she did,' Aase muttered, and held out some shears. 'Quickly, hide it before someone comes.'

Ceri used the shears to dig a small hole in the dirt floor near the wall, where the soil wasn't packed as tightly. She pushed the cross into the hole and covered it over, then stamped on it. 'There, no one will know.' She wiped the shears on her skirts and gave them back to Aase.

'Good. It will be our secret. Don't retrieve it until you are due to leave here.'

It was sound advice, which Ceri fully intended to follow. And she'd thank the jarl most sincerely next time she saw him. He was her captor, but she was finding it impossible to hate him.

Chapter Fifteen

Halfway through Wednesday afternoon, Haakon thought he saw movement in the forest to his right, but whenever he looked up properly, there was no one there. It could have just been tree branches swaying in the wind, but a prickling at the back of his neck told him they were being watched. For a while, he stared intently into the trees, then he decided to be more furtive. He bent his head to keep on trowelling, but glanced out of the corner of his eye, and this time he saw a face peer out from behind a particularly thick pine trunk.

'Mia,' he whispered. 'Don't look straight away, but I think someone is spying on us. In the forest, to the right of me.' He waited to give her a chance to catch a glimpse of the watcher.

'You're right.' Mia made a face. 'I hope it's not that stupid neighbour again.'

Haakon kept his head down, then stood up abruptly, catching the culprit's frightened gaze peeping out from behind the tree. 'You there, come out,' he ordered sternly. 'Now!'

After a slight hesitation, a teenage boy rounded the tree and ambled towards them, his hands in his pockets. He was dressed in black from head to toe, and wore a sullen expression, part scared, part mutinous, under a long, slanted fringe of dyed raven-black hair. His blue eyes looked incongruous, the only splash of colour in his otherwise monochrome appearance, but somehow the combination was appealing. A young goth in the making, Haakon thought with an inward smile, although the boy didn't look terrifying enough as yet; he was too skinny.

'What are you doing here? This is private property.' Haakon looked him up and down. He didn't really mind if the kid was just interested, but if he had any nefarious purposes in mind, he could think again.

'I was just, like, looking, you know.' The boy's voice did the usual teenage slide up and down the scale, as if it was trying to be manly but not quite succeeding. He had to be around thirteen, fourteen maybe.

'You live around here?'

'Yeah, like, in the next house along.' The boy nodded behind him, and Haakon heard Mia groan, but he pretended not to have noticed. He understood why, though – this was that Rolf guy's son presumably. Had he sent him to spy on them? 'School's out, no one's around, so I was bored,' the teenager continued. 'Sorry. I'll be off now.'

Mia obviously decided it was time to intervene. 'It's OK, don't go yet.' She shook her head at Haakon with a small smile to show she was teasing. 'Stop giving the poor boy the third degree. He hasn't done anything wrong really.'

Not yet, Haakon wanted to say, but he kept quiet for now.

Mia stood up and held out a muddy hand. 'Hi. I'm Mia Maddox, your neighbour. I own this property now, although it used to belong to my gran, Elin Hagberg. Did you know her?'

'Yeah, she was great! Nice old lady. Gave me buns and stuff. I'm Ivar. Ivar Thoresson.' The boy's face brightened at the mention of Elin.

Ivar? Not a very common name for a modern boy, Haakon

thought to himself, but perhaps it was coming back into fashion. He wouldn't know about such things.

'I think I met your dad earlier,' Mia said, not mentioning the altercation. 'Rolf, was it?' Ivar nodded. 'Ah, well I'm afraid I'm not very popular with him.'

'Why's that then?' Ivar still had his hands in the pockets of his jeans, so low-slung Haakon could see the top half of his designer underwear. Calvin Klein, no less. He was scuffing the earth with the toe of one already dirty Converse sneaker.

'He didn't seem to like all the cars parked in the lane. Said we were disturbing his peace or something.' Mia shrugged.

'He's always grumpy. He'll get over it.'

It sounded as though Ivar had learned that from experience. Haakon wondered if this Rolf was always grumpy because his son was a teenager and therefore a pain in the neck, or if he was just a nasty piece of work. From what Mia had said earlier, it sounded like the latter.

Ivar seemed reluctant to leave, and when he glanced up at them from under the fringe once more, Haakon caught his sad expression. He looked so vulnerable, so lost. Why wasn't the kid with his friends? 'Did you say you were bored?' he enquired gently.

'Yup. Dad's working and I finished my latest PlayStation game.'

'What about your friends?'

'No one around.' Ivar wouldn't meet his eye as he said this, and Haakon wondered if perhaps he didn't have any friends, or he was being bullied. Sadly, it seemed to be a common occurrence, and he already worried that it might happen to Linnea in the future. He'd have to teach her to stand up for herself.

'How would you like to help out here for a bit then? We can always do with an extra pair of hands.' He looked at Mia with raised eyebrows to make sure she didn't mind, and was rewarded by a big smile. A smile that for some reason hit him right in the gut.

Sure, she'd smiled at him before, but not with such obvious pleasure. It lit up her whole face and made those silvery eyes sparkle, beautiful in the afternoon sun. He turned back to Ivar. Mia was wearing an engagement ring – a big ugly diamond that had to be in the way when she was digging in the dirt – and he had no business standing there admiring the woman.

'Really? You sure?' Ivar's face was suddenly transformed from sulky teenager to something quite angelic by an equally huge smile, and Haakon found himself smiling back. 'What do you want me to do?'

'Well, if you don't mind getting dirty, I have plenty of jobs for you. Come with me.'

He put Ivar to work shovelling soil and transporting it to the archaeologist in charge of sieving for tiny finds, and the boy set to without complaining. Soon, Haakon saw other people finding him odd jobs, and he was pleased that they accepted him so readily.

'That was nice of you,' Mia commented when he returned to his place next to her.

'I think he was lonely, poor kid. Maybe he's being bullied. Teenagers can be such little sods.'

'Yes, dreadful. They tried to bully me at school because I was something of a swot.'

Haakon laughed. 'Me too – they didn't like the fact that I actually enjoyed reading, but luckily I was too big to be intimidated. Ivar is a bit on the small side, though. And is it just me, or is that an unusual name? Could be enough for someone to be picking on him. We'd better keep an eye out, though; there's no saying what mischief he could cause.'

'No, and I wouldn't put it past his dad to have sent him.' Mia frowned.

'My thoughts exactly. Let's see how it goes. I think he'll be fine.'

Ivar certainly seemed happy enough, and Haakon was pleased to catch sight of his wide smile more and more frequently as the afternoon wore on. Poor kid. Being a teenager was horrible.

But then being grown-up and a parent wasn't always much better.

Haakon's test pit had shown them that they were on the right track, and the further down the layers of soil they went, the more interesting it became. Two days later, their hard work finally started to pay off.

'I think I've definitely got a stone wall here.' Haakon scraped the trowel against something hard, and Mia winced.

'Aargh, that noise hurts my teeth!'

He laughed, but he was proved right, and slowly, painstakingly, a small house began to emerge. It had probably been dug into the ground and had a couple of feet of stone wall at the bottom, then possibly some sort of wooden upper structure with a thatched or turf roof.

'Such a shame the timber has rotted away – we can only guess what this would have looked like from the post holes.' Although strangely enough, Mia could picture it perfectly in her mind, complete with smoke drifting out of the roof and a goat standing on the top, munching away . . . *A goat? What the hell?* She blinked and the vision was gone.

Haakon was replying and she made herself concentrate on him rather than her over-fertile imagination. 'Yes, although there have been quite a few attempted reconstructions, of course, so we know what works and what doesn't.' He frowned. 'I can picture it quite clearly.' He shook his head, as if sweeping the images away. 'Any finds over there yet?'

Mia was working on the opposite side of the house – though 'hut' was probably a more apt description, as it wasn't huge – and held up a tray with a dirt-encrusted object. 'Just prised this out of the soil. It will have to be cleaned properly later, but it looks like it's a broken comb. Made of bone or antler judging by the colour.'

'Excellent! And I have what I think is a loom weight over here. Need to record it before I lever it out.'

Mia looked at the item on her tray again and felt a small pull of . . . what? Attraction? That sounded weird, but she had a strange urge to study the comb in more detail, as if it was egging her on to look at it. 'I wish I could start cleaning this straight away.'

She didn't realise she'd said that out loud until Haakon replied. 'Why don't you? The second caravan arrived yesterday, and I had them rig up a sort of mobile lab for cleaning and restoring objects in there – a workbench, a microscope and all the tools you need. You're an expert on that sort of thing, aren't you?'

'Really? How did I miss that?' She'd noticed the caravan being parked the day before, but she'd been busy at the time and later forgot to ask why they needed another. 'I've never heard of having a mobile restoration unit.'

Haakon shrugged. 'We don't usually have one, but for some reason I thought it might be a good idea. Sorry, I probably should have mentioned it.'

'No problem. OK, I'll go and have a closer look at this now then, if you don't mind?'

'Fine with me. Maybe you can clean that cross too, if you have the time.'

Mia nodded, but didn't promise anything.

There was no one else in the caravan, so she helped herself to the tools of her trade. It was great to feel on more familiar ground – this was what she was used to doing, and she knew she was good at it.

Bent over the workbench and the microscope, she didn't notice the hours passing until her back told her it was almost time to stop. What was emerging from beneath the soil was fascinating, though, and she really wanted to carry on until she was done. An ivory comb – possibly made from an elk antler – it was constructed out of a rectangular piece with 'teeth', wedged in between two smaller top parts with elaborate carving and a runic inscription, all riveted together and of superb workmanship.

A knock on the door startled her, but when she saw that it was Haakon, she smiled. 'Hey, you're just in time!'

'For what?' He stepped inside and grabbed a chair to sit down next to her, his cornflower-blue eyes sparkling with anticipation. 'Something good?'

Mia nodded and tried not to notice how close he was. She could smell the shampoo he'd used that morning – something exotic – as well as the more earthy scents of soil and dirt. 'I think so. Exciting anyway. Have a look at this.' She took the newly cleaned comb from under the microscope and held it out to him on a small tray. 'See the writing?'

'Oh, wow! K . . . E . . . R and . . . I – Keri?' Their eyes met and they grinned at each other. 'So this belonged to someone called Keri. But hang on, that's not a very Viking-sounding name, is it?'

'Nope. Sounds Celtic to me. Welsh, in fact. I'd guess it's meant to be Ceri with a C, but the Norse alphabet doesn't use a "c" for the "k" sound, of course.'

'Makes sense.' They exchanged another glance. 'So we have a Celtic woman, presumably a thrall, who is allowed to have her own comb and maybe even keep her Christian gold cross? Interesting scenario.'

Mia considered the possibilities. 'We don't know who owned the cross – I haven't looked at it yet, remember? And it could be that the comb had been stolen from someone called Ceri, though since the writing is runic, that would tend to point to it having been carved in Sweden for someone of that name. A Celt who had somehow ended up here, a long way from home. I'd say either she had worked long enough to buy her freedom, or she was, er . . . someone's favoured mistress.'

Haakon laughed. 'I like the second option, but I suppose the first is more likely.'

'You really think the cross belonged to the same person?' Mia had a deep-rooted conviction that this was true, but she couldn't have explained why.

Haakon shrugged. 'Seems likely, don't you think? We found them in the same building, and how many Celtic women owning nice things could there have been here at any one time? Unless some Viking guy had a whole harem of foreign concubines.'

'Always possible, but no, I shouldn't think so.'

'It's definitely intriguing, though, and how wonderful to know the name of at least one person who lived here!'

'Yes, fantastic.' They beamed at each other, and a warm feeling snaked through Mia. It was awesome to share this special moment with someone who really understood the thrill of it. An adrenalin rush like no other.

'Let's go and show the team. This calls for a small celebration – beer round a campfire tonight, I think. And maybe even grilled hot dogs!'

'Gosh, you know how to live around here,' Mia joked. When Haakon pretended to look offended, she added with a laugh, 'But it sounds great to me.'

As they headed up the hill towards the rest of the team, she decided not to tell him how her feelings of ownership had increased as that name on the comb emerged from the soil. She'd had an almost irresistible urge to pick it up and try to run it through her hair. She'd resisted, of course, but whoever Ceri was, her possessions were calling to Mia for some reason. That thought scared her, and she'd rather keep it to herself. She was probably just imagining it anyway.

Chapter Sixteen

In between chores, Ceri took Jorun for walks to stop the little girl from getting bored. In her experience, you had to keep children stimulated and interested in order to get the best out of them. They simply weren't capable of sitting still all day long. At least, that was certainly true of her nephew Bryn and the other village children she had known and looked after.

One afternoon she took Jorun's hand and led her down to the water's edge. They were both barefoot, since Ceri hadn't had time to put on any shoes before leaving her home with Haukr. Jorun presumably didn't wear any during the summer months, and the weather was still relatively mild, although the evenings were growing colder. Ceri lifted her skirts and waded into the water; the little girl happily followed suit. They stood still for a moment, letting the water settle while they became accustomed to the chill of it on their legs and feet. Then Ceri bent over and looked into the calm surface. Jorun was doing the same, and their two mirror images smiled at each other.

Ceri made a face, stretching her mouth out with her fingers so she looked like a frog. Jorun's strange laughter rang out, then she did the same. Ceri put a finger on the tip of her nose and pushed it up, forming a pig's snout, which seemed to amuse the little girl even more. Again she copied her, and so they went on for a while, laughing together and each trying to outdo the other with terrible grimaces.

When they'd run out of ideas, they stood still again and just enjoyed the feel of the water on their legs and the softness of the mud squishing beneath their feet. As she stared at herself in the glassy surface, it occurred to Ceri that this might be a way of teaching Jorun not just to read her lips, but to try to copy her better. She pointed at Jorun's reflection, then at the girl's chest and said 'Jorun' loudly, making the child watch her lips in between glancing at her image. Then she pointed at herself and said 'Ceri' several times, exaggerating the movement of her mouth. She tried to use the tone of voice the little girl could hear.

Jorun stared at her but said nothing. She'd stopped laughing and seemed to be paying attention, so Ceri repeated the exercise over and over again. To reinforce the fact that she wanted Jorun to make a sound, she took the girl's hand and placed it on her throat, where she could hopefully feel the vibration. Finally, to her delight, Jorun pointed at herself and said 'Go-uhn', then to Ceri, followed by what sounded like 'Ce-ih'.

'Yes, that's it!'

It wasn't perfect by any means, but it was a start. Ceri picked the little girl up and hugged her tight, swinging her round while smiling. Jorun smiled too and bounced up and down in Ceri's arms, repeating the two words and pointing to one or the other of them according to which name she was uttering. Ceri put her down, very pleased to have made a breakthrough.

During the next few days, they continued the lessons, with Ceri pointing to various things around them and telling the girl what they were called. Now that she had caught on, Jorun learned quickly, although she refused to do it when there were other people around. Ceri found that there were certain sounds

Jorun couldn't make and others she changed, such as turning an 's' into a 'k' and a 'j' into a 'g', but all in all, she did very well. And once Ceri became used to the substitutions, she had no trouble recognising what Jorun was saying. She also managed to teach her the words for some actions, such as walking, eating and sleeping, by miming them for her first. It wasn't long before Jorun was miming things herself, obviously wanting to know what they were called.

It was a joy to see her so animated, and very far from simple-minded.

'Trolls, eh?' Ceri muttered to herself. 'We'll see about that!'

She knew it might never be possible for Jorun to hold a conversation with anyone, but the main point, as far as she was concerned, was for her to be able to communicate. It freed her from the isolation she must have been living in, that silent, empty world where everyone ignored her. As long as they both understood what was meant, the words didn't need to be perfect.

Haukr entered the weaving hut one afternoon, looking for Aase, and found Ceridwen and Jorun there alone.

'I'm sorry, she's just this moment gone to speak to Tyra,' Ceridwen told him.

'Thank you, I'll seek her elsewhere then.' He hesitated, wanting to linger for a while. It wasn't often he had an opportunity to talk to Ceridwen without Ragnhild glaring at him, and although he knew it shouldn't matter, he felt a need to make sure his captive was not unhappy. Her declaration that she hated it here had disturbed him, and he sincerely hoped it wasn't true.

'Are you well, Ceridwen?' He loved saying her name; it was beautiful. As was she, although she was so small and delicate he feared she would break at the slightest touch.

'Yes, thank you, Jarl Haukr.'

'Just Haukr is enough when we are alone.' He smiled at her and was pleased when her cheeks turned slightly pink, but she smiled back.

'And I'm usually called Ceri, not by my full name.'

He nodded and was about to reply when, tearing his eyes away from her for a moment, he registered the fact that Jorun was helping her to wind a ball of yarn. He stared, blinking in surprise. 'By Odin's ravens, am I seeing things?'

'No, how so?' Ceri gently touched the little girl, who was concentrating hard on making the ball round and even and therefore hadn't noticed the newcomer. She made her look at her mouth, said 'Father' and pointed behind her. Jorun turned around and jumped visibly, her eyes widening. Ceri put her hand on the child's shoulder and gave it a reassuring squeeze while whispering to Haukr, 'Smile at her, please, then she might not be so afraid.'

He stretched his mouth into as wide a smile as he could muster. Jorun relaxed, then looked back at Ceri.

'Father,' Ceri repeated loudly with an encouraging nod. Obediently, Jorun faced Haukr once more and said something that sounded like 'Va-eh'. He felt his eyes grow round.

'Now I know I'm dreaming.' Nonetheless, he moved forward to squat before her, staring into her eyes. 'Jorun?'

'Exaggerate the movement of your mouth and say it a little louder,' Ceri instructed from behind him. He did as she asked and was rewarded by a smile from his daughter.

'Go-uhn,' she replied, and pointed at herself. 'Va-eh.' She pointed at him.

A lump lodged itself in Haukr's throat as he glanced at Ceri. 'She's talking. She understood what I said?'

'She recognises a few simple words now, although she needs to see your mouth when you say them. I believe she has some hearing, but not enough. If you exaggerate your speech a little, that makes it easier for her.'

'We have tried talking to her before, but she wouldn't respond.' Haukr was shaking his head in disbelief. 'How did you manage to make her listen?'

Ceri shrugged. 'It happened when we were down by the water. I used it as a mirror to show her an image of herself and of me, then said her name until she understood. It worked.'

Haukr was sure his smile was positively beaming now. 'But this is wonderful! So everyone was wrong to say that she's simple. And you are teaching her weaving?'

'Well, we're starting with easy tasks first, like winding wool and carding, but there is no reason why she shouldn't learn to weave in time. I don't think she is stupid at all. It's just that she has lived in isolation for so long, inside her own head, and we have to be patient.'

He laughed out loud and picked Jorun up, swinging her round until she laughed with him. 'Jorun, good girl,' he said, making sure she could see his lips. 'Do you think she understands that concept, Ceri?'

'I believe she knows the difference between good and bad. And, um, she likes being hugged.' With an uncertain glance, as if she wasn't sure whether he'd be offended, Ceri added, 'She doesn't seem afraid of you now.'

'No. I never meant to scare her, but I suppose I'm not always in the best of moods, so she's often seen me scowling.'

Jorun repeated his words in her own way, whether she understood or not, and he was just pleased to be interacting with her. This was something he had given up hope of ever doing, and the joy of it was making the blood sing in his veins.

Still holding his daughter, he went over to Ceri and bent to kiss her soundly on the mouth, still beaming. 'I can't thank you enough. You have given me the most precious gift, Ceridwen. You are a wonder, you truly are!'

A fiery colour spread across Ceri's cheeks and down her neck. Perhaps he had acted inappropriately, but he had kissed her out of gratitude, and if his arms hadn't been full of Jorun, he would have lifted Ceri up to hug her as well.

'You're very welcome,' she mumbled. 'I'm glad you're pleased. Hopefully she will learn more words every day.'

'You must teach me whatever she's learning,' he said. 'I want to be able to communicate with my daughter.'

'Of course. I'll let you know of any progress.'

'Good. I will seek you out whenever I can.' He thought of telling Ragnhild, but knew instinctively she would belittle Jorun's achievement until the girl learned to speak better. 'Would you mind if we keep this between us for now? There are those who . . . might hinder Jorun rather than help her. Better to wait and show them when she is more confident, perhaps?'

'Yes, good idea. She will only do it when we are on our own in any case. Aase knows, but I will speak to her and tell her to keep it to herself.'

'Thank you again. You have no idea how much this means to me. Goodbye, Jorun.' He waved at his daughter, who waved back.

As he left, he couldn't help but smile broadly at everyone he met. Quite a few people stopped to stare at him, obviously wondering if he was quite sane. Well, let them think him mad – he didn't care.

Chapter Seventeen

Haakon went to Stockholm for the weekend, leaving Mia in charge. 'I've got some stuff to do, sorry. You can cope, right?'

'Of course.' She hadn't expected him to work weekends, but the thought of him going home to whoever he'd been talking to on the phone made her feel unaccountably lonely and depressed. She really ought to go back to London and see Charles soon. Perhaps spending the whole summer here hadn't been such a great idea after all. But she was enjoying the dig immensely.

She tried not to let on that the thought of directing operations without his presence scared the living daylights out of her, and in fact, everything went well. The rest of the team knew what they were doing and there were no dramas or major finds. When Haakon returned, he seemed to bring summer with him, as the weather turned almost overnight into scorching hot sunshine and blue skies.

'This makes a nice change,' he commented, and pulled off his T-shirt. 'We'll soon look like we've been on a holiday abroad if this carries on.'

'Er, not me, I'm afraid.' Mia tried not to stare at the nicely defined abs and chest displayed in front of her. 'I don't tan much. My freckles just kind of merge.'

Haakon laughed. 'Sounds interesting.'

'Not how I would describe it. I'd better go find some sunscreen before I burn.' *And get away from the awesome sight that is Haakon in just combat trousers and work boots.* She looked around and saw that all the other guys had followed suit and the girls were in bikini tops or sports bras, but although there were some fairly impressive torsos on display – archaeology was hard work – Haakon's was the only one she had the urge to stare at. She headed for the cottage and tried to think about Charles instead. He worked out and played football and rugby with his mates all the time, so he had a nice body too, or so she'd always thought. Just not so . . . yes, awesome.

But he was her fiancé and Haakon was not. She gave herself a stern talking-to and went back to the dig.

'I'm loving these loom weights,' Mia commented when they laid out their finds from the weaving hut, as they were now calling it. 'And this stone spindle whorl. Wonder how hard it was to use a drop spindle?'

'Should think it took years of practice, but it was a necessary skill, of course. I watched some YouTube tutorials once; it was very interesting.' Haakon smiled. 'I got the feeling I'd be really clumsy if I tried, though.' He had a vague memory of his grandmother trying to teach him how to knit once during a rainy day when he'd been bored, and him giving up fairly quickly. Handicrafts of any kind took ages to learn and a lot of patience.

'I really want to try the type of weaving done here with an upright loom. I believe there are places where you can go and learn.'

Mia's face shone with enthusiasm and Haakon found himself grinning at her. He loved how passionate she became about things – it exactly mirrored his own feelings about his job – and after a day in the sunshine, she was looking flushed and, he couldn't help but notice, seriously cute. Her skin glowed with health and vitality, and the freckles across her nose and cheeks were definitely merging. As were those on her chest above the dipping line of her bikini top . . . Haakon shook himself mentally. He shouldn't be noticing; that was inappropriate. Sexist. Besides, they were just work colleagues and she was taken.

'My gran taught me to weave on a modern loom,' she continued. 'Well, modern relative to what the Vikings used anyway. I think my mum has it stored somewhere in her garage. I'll have to find it, as I'd like to have another go sometime. I'll check out those spindle tutorials too; could be fun.'

'I had a go at weaving on an upright loom once. It was . . . interesting.'

'You mean you were rubbish at it?' Mia laughed. 'It's OK, you can admit it. I don't think I'd be any better.'

'Yeah, OK, I was terrible. But it *was* fun to try, like you said.'

He was pleased that she dared to tease him now, her grey eyes twinkling with humour. She'd been a bit reserved at the beginning, uptight even, but now they were like old friends, joking around. And she'd relaxed around the others as well, part of the team. Even Ivar joined in, and it was great to see him happy and animated instead of just grunting the way most teenage boys seemed to. He'd turned up every afternoon, eager to help out in any way, and was learning fast. So far he'd proved to be an asset rather than a liability, even though Haakon had explained that they couldn't afford to pay him.

'I don't need paying. My dad gives me more than enough pocket money, so I'm OK.'

That made Haakon wonder about Ivar's relationship with his parents. In his experience, no teenager ever claimed to have enough money, but perhaps things had changed since he was young. Either that, or the parents were giving their son loads of money in lieu of spending time with him, which was a sad state of affairs if it was true.

He focused on the present and the animated woman next to him. 'You into experimental archaeology then?' he asked. 'Living history, that kind of thing?'

'Whenever I have the time, which isn't often enough. It's fascinating, don't you think? We should try cooking some Viking food while we're here.'

'Absolutely! I've got a Viking cookbook somewhere. I'll dig it out next time I'm at home.'

'Excellent! I'll look forward to trying the results. Should be easier than spinning yarn anyway.'

'Hmm, I wouldn't be too sure about that . . .'

By Tuesday lunchtime they had reached the bottom of their trench, where it was clearly just natural soil and there was nothing more to find, and after taking photographs and making detailed notes, they closed it up. They'd had a few more non-weaving-related finds – a small brooch of bronze with the pin missing; a couple of needles made of antler or bone; a large hairpin, also of bone, possibly from an elk; and some potsherds – but nothing as spectacular as the gold cross, which was still awaiting Mia's attention. Haakon had noticed that so far she'd avoided cleaning it, but he knew she couldn't put it off indefinitely.

He wondered if the cross had disturbed her because it had belonged to one of her ancestors. But then he knew from experience that some objects just spoke to you and there didn't have to be a specific reason. He had, in fact, brought the gold ring from the museum out to this dig – with Professor Mattsson's permission this time – because he'd had such a strong feeling that it belonged here. The reason he'd given was that he needed to study it in conjunction with Mia's, which was partly true. It was ridiculous really, but he was convinced the snake rings could help them find things here. That they had been at Birch Thorpe before, even. How fanciful was that?

A couple of times he'd taken the ring out at night and tried it on again, and each time he'd had weird dreams about Vikings afterwards. Of course that had to be coincidence, and, having been staring at a Viking ring just before bedtime, his mind would be thinking about such things. That was all there was to it. Had to be.

'Right, that's this trench done then.' He indicated the site of the weaving hut. They hadn't excavated the entire house, as it was always good to leave some parts for future archaeologists who might have even better methods to use, but he didn't think they'd missed anything vital.

'Yep. Should we help out with the possible longhouse now?'

The team had been in luck so far, finding substantial post holes as well as the base of a huge hearth up on the top of the hill, which indicated a very large dwelling. A broken axe head of the right period – early to mid ninth century – had been buried just outside, as if it had been discarded during the building work. And inside, near the hearth, a ninth-century Islamic silver *dirham* – extremely common in Viking-age Scandinavia and usually acquired through trade – had been discovered, as well as numerous potsherds. It was all very encouraging.

'Yes, let's go and see what needs doing.'

The weather grew even hotter as the week progressed, and soon they were positively sweltering. By the time work finished for the day, a couple of days later, Mia was hot and exhausted, but she was happier than she'd been for a long time. Being out in the open air, doing something physical that didn't require infinite patience, listening to the friendly banter and camaraderie between the other members of the team – it was all a far cry from the stress of recent months with a sullen Charles. She felt guilty for thinking this way, but she couldn't help it. She was glad he wasn't there.

'So are you up for a swim?'

Haakon walked next to her towards the caravan where the equipment and finds were kept locked up at night, carrying most of it even though she'd protested that she was quite capable of doing her fair share of hauling things around. She stared at him.

'A swim? Are you mad? The water must be freezing!' Although the air was very warm, Lake Mälaren was enormous and probably deep, so it wouldn't heat up much before July or August, as she knew from previous years.

He laughed. 'Yes, but we're all hot and sweaty, so if we run straight in, we'll be fine. Come on, show us there's at least a little bit of Viking left in you, or have you gone soft living in the mild English weather?'

The amusement in his blue gaze spurred her on to accept the challenge, even though she knew she'd regret it. 'If you can do it, so can I.'

They put everything away in the caravan, and Haakon locked the door and pocketed the key, then shouted, 'To the lake! The last one in has to buy us all beer.' There was an instant stampede, accompanied by whoops of delight and challenges issued.

'But don't we need to change?' Mia protested. She was wearing a T-shirt today to protect her back from the fierce sun. Haakon shook his head and grabbed her wrist, beginning to run in the direction of the water.

'No point. We'll all have to change our clothes anyway, so we're just going to swim in our underwear. Hope you didn't put on your oldest ones this morning,' he added with a teasing smile, pulling her along at breakneck speed. She had trouble keeping up with his long legs, and almost stumbled a couple of times.

'What if I didn't put any on at all?' she shouted, some devil prompting her to tease him back.

It was his turn to almost stumble as he glanced at her in surprise. Then he grinned. 'Even better. Come on.'

Down by the small jetty, which Gran had had built many years before, there was a mad scramble as everyone tried to pull their clothing off as fast as they could. The run down to the lake had made them even hotter, but they knew that if they didn't get into the water quickly, they'd lose their nerve. Mia hurried and got her kit off in record time – she was, thankfully, wearing some fairly respectable-looking underwear – finishing just as Haakon kicked out of his jeans. She was already regretting her decision to agree to this madness, but he gave her no time to think about it. Again he took hold of her wrist, a wicked glint in his eyes.

'Ah-ah, no chickening out.'

He propelled her into the freezing waves before she had time to think about it. She screamed as the icy water hit her warm skin, and so did the rest of the group.

'Ah, shit, it's like ice!'

'Damn it all, whose idea was this? Aaargh . . .'

But there was laughter too, and everyone's good spirits were infectious. Mia felt herself grinning from ear to ear and resisted the urge to rush back to shore.

Tomas, minus his gadgets for once, began a water fight, and someone else produced a ball. At first Mia thought she would never be able to move her limbs again, so cold were they, but she forced them into action and soon her body adjusted to the temperature of the water and she was able to join in. She had always been a good swimmer, and she began to enjoy herself. She'd only ever swum here in the little bay alone, or with Gran and very occasionally her mother, so it made a nice change to have so much company. Charles had refused point blank to even try it.

'I'm not a masochist, even if you are,' he'd told her, after dipping one toe in and recoiling.

One by one people began to drift back to shore, and eventually Mia stood up too and made her way towards dry land. She shivered when the evening breeze hit her and goose bumps broke out all over her body. She'd forgotten that the worst part was actually coming out of the water, not going in.

'*I helvete*, Haakon, we don't even have a towel!' she said to him as he stood beside her. 'We really didn't think this through, huh?'

'*Ja, faen*, it's cold! I'll race you to the cottage, that'll keep us warm.' He bent down to pick up his clothes. 'Are you ready? Let's go.'

He shot off, and this time he didn't wait for her. He made it to the cottage way ahead of her and had the door open already by the time she arrived. He knew by now where she hid the key, under a particular paving stone.

'You know, that's a pretty obvious hiding place,' he commented. 'You might want to rethink that one.'

'I only l-leave it th-there while we're ar-round.' Her teeth were chattering so much she could hardly speak.

'Hold on, I'll get some towels. Jump up and down.' He took the stairs two at a time and returned with towels and the old dressing gown, which he draped round her before rubbing her arms vigorously. 'There, is that better?'

'Mm-hmm, th-thank you. Aren't you cold?' He seemed impervious, although there were goose bumps on his chest and arms. She averted her gaze, not wanting to stare at his near-nakedness, although the sight was imprinted on her brain in any case after a week of working next to him shirtless. The sinewy muscles of someone used to physical work, smooth skin with a glowing tan, and long, loose-limbed legs covered in golden hairs . . .

He interrupted her thoughts. 'Not as cold as you. Let's get the stove going. I think we'll need it tonight.'

Neither of them moved, however. Instead, they stared at each other, standing close enough to touch, yet still apart, and Mia felt as if some invisible current passed between them, keeping them rooted to the spot. Their surroundings became indistinct, almost blurry, and she heard nothing other than the pumping beat of her heart, still working overtime from swimming and running. For a crazy moment, she imagined she saw him with longer hair, dressed in the outfit of a Viking, his fierce blue gaze holding hers captive, but then Haakon the real man returned and his look was more one of surprise.

Abruptly he turned away and headed into the kitchen. 'Right, fire,' he muttered, his voice slightly gruff. He wrapped his towel securely round his middle as he went, and Mia watched the play of muscles across his broad back. He really was magnificent; it was no wonder she'd seen him in the guise of a Viking warrior. With the right clothes, he'd fit the role perfectly.

Vikings were to be treated warily, though, she reminded herself. They took what they wanted and left. She couldn't deny that there was chemistry between herself and Haakon, but she knew nothing about him and it would be unwise to let herself be drawn in by his charm. She had a feeling she'd only be burned.

Besides, there was Charles, she added almost as an after-thought, then felt guilty all over again. They'd spoken or texted most nights, but the messages were getting shorter each day, as if neither of them could be bothered. Mia decided she should make more of an effort. It was, after all, her fault they were spending the summer apart.

As if on cue, her mobile rang. She fished it out of her jeans pocket before dropping her clothes on a chair. 'Hello?'

'There you are! I've been calling for ages.' Charles, not sounding best pleased.

'Sorry, I was swimming so I didn't hear the phone.'

'Swimming? Are you insane? It must be below zero. This is Sweden we're talking about.'

'Yes, but Sweden in June, and it's been baking here today. So not quite zero, but it wasn't warm, that's for sure. I've been working hard all day, though, and it felt good, but now I've got to try and get warm again. Can I ring you later?'

She glanced through the door into the kitchen, where Haakon was just shutting the door to the stove. He stood up and made his way to the archway that led to the glass veranda, and stopped to stare out at the garden. Mia had a sudden urge to go over to him and wrap her arms around him from behind. He looked so strong, but vulnerable at the same time, as if he was carrying a heavy burden of sadness. It was unbelievably tempting to try and find out what it was and lessen his worries. Charles's irate voice brought her back to her senses.

'Mia? Are you still there?'

'Yes, yes, I am. Bad connection out here in the sticks. What were you saying?'

'I said I'm going out later, some work thing, but I just wanted to check if you're still coming back this weekend. Only I've got this five-a-side football tournament, so I might not be around as much as I'd hoped. It's for charity and my boss especially wanted us all there. I can't really get out of it.'

'Oh, OK. Yes, I'm coming, but no worries, I can always meet up with friends, and I'll see you in the evenings, right?' It would be good to have a chance to catch up with Alun, for one.

'Sure. Unless . . . No, it should be fine. There'll probably be

160

drinks at the pub afterwards, but I'll make sure I only have one. Or you can come and join us.'

'Right.' That was the last thing Mia wanted. Charles's boss Rory had wandering hands that often seemed to find their way to her backside, and the rest of his workmates were forever talking shop. But never mind, she'd go for Charles's sake as she knew it was important to him. 'I'll see you on Saturday then. Bye for now!'

She glanced at Haakon, who was busy drying himself now, and suppressed a sigh.

The only problem was, she didn't want to leave.

Chapter Eighteen

Autumn arrived with a vengeance and the days became shorter and colder. It happened much faster than it would have done at home, and Ceri couldn't help but wonder how severe the coming winter would be. She feared for herself and her fellow countrymen in their threadbare summer clothes, but she need not have worried. Haukr's right-hand man, Thorald, gathered them all together one morning and Aase distributed warm clothes and footwear. They were obviously cast-offs, as most were worn and mended, but the material was good and there were many years of wear left in the garments.

As well as woollen trousers, long-sleeved over-tunics and socks, the men and boys were given cloaks of thick wool with small iron pins to fasten them. The women also received socks and large shawls with simple brooches, plus thicker woollen gowns to wear over their linen under-tunics. The shoes were of soft leather, with fur on the inside to keep their feet warm, and laced around the ankles.

'Look after these clothes,' Thorald warned them, 'for they must last you as long as possible.'

'Any tears are to be darned immediately,' Aase added. 'I have a supply of needles and thread for anyone who needs it.'

There were murmurings of thanks and looks of gratitude as everyone put on their new outfits. 'Whoever heard of giving thralls new clothes?' one woman muttered to Ceri under her breath. 'Not that I'm complaining, mind.'

Ceri was as astonished as everyone else, but she surmised that Haukr was just being careful with his property. After all, it wouldn't be to his benefit if his servants froze to death, and everyone would surely work harder if they were warm enough. She was sure that logic rather than kindness was behind this.

In return, they were all made to work hard throughout the autumn months, as there was much to do to prepare for the coming winter. Animals had to be slaughtered and the meat preserved, either by drying, smoking or being immersed in barrels of whey, which was a great preservative. Other meat products, such as *blothmor*, or blood pudding, had to be produced and stored; vegetables and fruits were to be dried or placed in the cold cellar dug deep into the ground, and there were berries, nuts and mushrooms to pick and take care of as well. Large quantities of fish and game added to the workload, and many of the women toiled long hours making dairy products such as *skyr*, cheese and butter, while others brewed ale in large quantities, as well as some mead.

Ragnhild directed operations with fierce determination and threats, whereas Haukr appeared to rule his side of things with smiles and praise. Ceri noticed that even the sullen youths from her village began to do his bidding without complaint, while she and the other women often grumbled about their mistress. Haukr seemed to be a good man in many respects, and she found it difficult to relate this to the fierce marauder who had so ruthlessly plundered her village. Which persona was the real man?

One evening in late autumn, he proved once again that he was more benevolent than most masters. After the meal, he asked for silence, and when a hush fell on the room, he stood up. 'I understand that a child was born yesterday, and I must determine its fate. Bring it in, please.'

Everyone craned their necks as the door was opened to reveal a thrall woman by the name of Eira carrying a small bundle.

'What's happening?' Ceri whispered to Aase, who happened to be next to her.

'The jarl has to decide whether the poor mite is to live or die.'

'What?' Ceri couldn't keep the horror out of her voice. 'He has the power to choose life or death for babies born to thralls?'

'Yes, didn't you know?' Aase seemed surprised, as if this was entirely normal. 'If he decides the baby is too small or sickly, or that he has enough mouths to feed already, it will be put out into the forest.'

Ceri shuddered at the thought, even though freezing to death was a kind way to dispose of someone. Unless wild animals reached the child first, of course . . . But taking anyone's life was a grave sin.

Aase continued, still whispering, 'Ordinarily, such babies are left to die, so that they won't become a burden on the settlement. But the jarl – unlike his father – has never condemned a child to death in such a way. At least, not yet. It is my belief that, having spared the life of his own child, he can't in all conscience have others killed. Although, to be sure, it wasn't immediately clear that little Jorun wasn't like other children . . .'

Ceri relaxed slightly. She should have known Haukr was different to most men. She waited in silence to see what would happen this time.

'Another of yours?' Ragnhild sneered in a whisper loud enough to carry throughout the room. 'Can't keep your hands off the thrall women, can you?'

Haukr frowned at her but made no reply. Most people knew that her words were patently untrue. Unlike some of his men, he never sought out the serving women, despite the fact that it was rumoured Ragnhild was denying him her bed. He had also decreed that no woman was to be forced; she had to be willing, thrall or not, and his men had learned to adhere to this rule. Ceri had heard many of the women thank the Lord for this mercy, although she had also noticed that a few of them had already given in to the charms of their captors.

Haukr turned towards Eira now and beckoned her forward. 'Show me the child.'

The woman pushed the folds of the shawl away from the baby, her hands trembling as she exposed a scrawny scrap that looked as if it would blow away in a gust of wind. To everyone's horror, judging by the collective intake of breath, the baby appeared to have one leg shorter than the other. Ceri felt her stomach muscles tighten. Surely Haukr would have to condemn such a poor specimen to death; it would never grow up to be of any use as a worker.

Eira obviously thought so too, for there were tears already coursing down her cheeks as she gazed sadly at her child. Ceri noticed that one of the male thralls standing nearby was looking supremely anxious. She gathered he must be the baby's father.

'Hmm, do you think she will thrive?' Haukr asked gently, and Eira looked up, blinking at him. He reached out a finger, and the baby gripped it in her tiny fist.

'I-I . . . With care, yes.'

'Perhaps if you feed her well, she'll grow strong enough to overcome her difficulties,' he mused.

The mother grasped this straw, nodding almost too enthusiastically. 'Yes! Yes, indeed. She's a little fighter, I'm sure of it. She has a good pair of lungs and eats well already.'

Haukr nodded as if this confirmed his own thoughts. 'She may live.'

'What? Are you mad?' It was Ragnhild who expressed what everyone was thinking. 'How is she going to walk with that affliction?'

Eira quickly wrapped the child up in her blanket and hugged her to her chest protectively while staring wide-eyed at Ragnhild. She'd just been given hope, but was it now to be snatched away again?

'She may never walk very well, but there's nothing wrong with her hands,' Haukr retorted. 'Her grip was strong on my finger. She can be put to work indoors with spinning and such like. We can't all be perfect.' He fixed Ragnhild with his gaze and she subsided, understanding the message. Their own child was far from perfect and she knew it.

He turned back to Eira, who was now staring at him in stunned silence. 'You may go. Tend the little one well, do you hear? I want the rest of her strong.'

Eira nodded and smiled, then scurried off, closely followed by the relieved father, while everyone else in the room broke into excited murmuring. The warring couple at the centre of the room were forgotten, but Ceri, who went to sit next to them with Jorun, heard them continue their acrimonious exchange in a hissing undertone.

'You're too soft for your own good,' Ragnhild was saying. 'How will anyone ever respect you if you cannot even take a simple decision like ending a useless thrall's life? Honestly, you were the only person in this hall who thought she should live.'

'No, I believe there were at least three of us eager for that outcome – as I'm sure you saw, the child wasn't mine. I haven't noticed anyone being disrespectful to me apart from yourself, and as a mother, you ought to have had some sympathy with Eira. I'm telling you, Ragnhild, you'd better curb that waspish tongue of yours or I'll have to do something about that instead.'

Ceri wished they would stop bickering. She had learned by now that Haukr's wife had her reasons for the bitterness that seemed to spew out of her at every turn, and she did feel sorry for her. Being barren must be hard to bear, especially on occasions like this, when babies were brought to her attention, but Ceri still couldn't condone such behaviour towards a husband. It would never have been tolerated in her homeland.

'I suppose you wish the child had been yours, deformed leg or not,' Ragnhild muttered.

Haukr sighed. 'The gods decide our fates and there is more to married life than children. I only wish you could see that. Besides, we have a child. Perhaps you should spend some time with her occasionally.'

Ragnhild sent a look of despair Jorun's way. 'And constantly be reminded of my shortcomings? No thank you.' She stood up abruptly and stalked off towards their bedroom.

Haukr sighed again and glanced at his daughter. 'I'm sorry you have to witness these, er ... exchanges between my wife and myself, Ceri,' he whispered, 'but at least Jorun doesn't have to hear them. Perhaps when we tell Ragnhild of her progress, she'll change her mind.'

'Should we let her know sooner rather than later?' Ceri felt as if it was a guilty secret between the two of them, although to be fair, Ragnhild could have discovered it for herself if she'd paid the slightest attention to her child.

'Soon, but not yet. Let the little one become better at speaking first, then she'll be sure to astonish her mother all the more.'

It made sense, and Ceri hoped he was right.

*

Haukr gazed at nothing in particular, his thoughts turned inward. 'There is more to married life than children,' he'd said to Ragnhild, but at the moment there wasn't, as they lay next to each other every night without touching. She hadn't refused to lie with him, the few times he'd attempted it, but neither had she participated the way she used to that first year of their marriage. It was as though she was just waiting for him to finish what he had to do and wanted no pleasure out of it for herself.

Or she just didn't want him.

Either way, it was unbearable.

He'd tried to tell her that it didn't matter if their lovemaking didn't lead to pregnancy. 'I just want you for yourself, *ást mín*.'

But she'd refused to believe him and he came to realise that a part of her had become locked inside. Or perhaps it had withered and died. Ragnhild was a changed woman and he had no idea how to bring back the version of her that he had loved. Now, he no longer even wanted to try.

Because she wasn't his love any more. She had killed his feelings as well as her own.

This insight hit him hard – it meant he would be spending the rest of his life in a loveless union. One that would not give happiness to either of them. And that was a very sad state of affairs.

'Can't you make her divorce you?' his friend Thorald had said, the one and only time they'd discussed the matter.

'She won't. She's too proud to return to her father and brothers, and what would be the point? Ragnhild can never marry again because any future husband would want a wife who can give him children. At least here she has a household to rule, duties to fulfil. If she left, she would be at best a hanger-on, having no say in any decisions made by her oldest brother's wife.'

Haukr also didn't want to offend Ragnhild's relatives; his

hands were tied if he wanted to keep the peace with his neighbours, and alliances were important. Blood ties.

He could have sons with someone else – an unattached woman or even a thrall. Children born outside of marriage were accepted, as were multiple wives on occasion, but he hadn't even attempted it because he knew Ragnhild would make their life a misery. How could he knowingly subject anyone to that? And he wouldn't be around every moment of every day to protect them.

'What if we adopt a motherless baby?' he'd suggested to her once, but her expression had said it all.

'It's not the same; it won't be mine. And it will just remind me of little Olaf.' The son they'd lost.

And that, it seemed, was the end of the matter.

During the last few years, Haukr had found himself wishing Ragnhild would be selfless enough to divorce him anyway. Set him free. That wasn't fair on her, but he had the future of his settlement to think of. He needed someone to inherit his holdings. And he needed someone in his bed who actually welcomed his advances. He found his gaze straying to Ceridwen. There was no denying he was attracted to her – whenever he had the chance, he drank in the sight of her small but womanly figure. He wanted to drown in her sparkling gaze and bury his fingers in those incredible long curls that glinted with flashes of copper in the firelight. He wished . . . but no, he couldn't act on those wishes, no matter how tempting he found her. And being so small, she'd probably think him a big oaf of a man. And yet . . .

'Va-eh? Eat.'

The little voice beside him interrupted his thoughts, and he smiled at Jorun and nodded. 'Yes, I should, shouldn't I?'

She held out a piece of bread to him and he opened his mouth like a baby bird, which seemed to amuse her. Joy coursed through him. What was he doing sitting here being so gloomy? There was no need. The gods had solved his problem another way – they had sent him Ceridwen, who had shown him his daughter wasn't as damaged as he'd thought. There was hope now; hope that Jorun would grow up to be as beautiful as her mother and able to communicate enough to rule a household. Then with a dowry consisting of Haukr's entire domain, and excellent family connections, what man wouldn't want to marry her?

All he had to do was make sure to choose a truly good man for her who could one day take over and provide him with grandchildren. He would be content with that.

Chapter Nineteen

On Friday morning, Mia collected her post from the little mailbox by the gate while waiting for the kettle to boil. She took her mug of tea and went to sit on the veranda to sip it while she slit open a large brown envelope.

'Oh!' A fat sheaf of documents emerged, some of them very old by the looks of it.

'Anything good?' Haakon had followed her, bringing with him the aroma of coffee. He claimed the rocking chair and somehow looked as though he belonged there, his long legs stretched out and crossed at the ankles. Mia was becoming used to having him around now, and they'd fallen into a morning routine that felt familiar and almost comforting. Before coming over to Sweden this time, she had tried not to think too much about the fact that the cottage would be so empty without Gran, but with Haakon there she'd hardly noticed in the end.

'It's from my solicitor,' she told him. 'Hopefully he's sent the plan of the property with the boundaries clearly marked. And I think I'll be able to show you that will at last. Let me see . . .' She leafed through the papers and located a very fragile-looking document that had been slotted into a clear plastic cover, presumably to protect it from damage. 'Oh wow, this really is old!

Here, look, the ring is mentioned somewhere. I remember Gran showing it to me once.'

Haakon came over to sit down next to her, and the two of them peered at the old will, which was dated 1604. The handwriting was surprisingly legible, if a bit spindly, and Mia traced the lines with her finger as they deciphered it together.

'*I, Johannes Hageberg, being of sound mind and body . . . hereby bequeath to my wife Margareta* . . . blah blah . . . Wait, here it is! *And the gold serpent ringe that was worne bye my mother & my father's mother before her, to be gifted to my sonne's wif & bye her to her sonne's wif & so on in perpetuity . . .*'

'Dreadful spelling!' Haakon smiled. 'But OK, you've proved your point. I believe you. Although . . . how come it's yours now? You're no one's wife yet. I mean . . .' He glanced at her engagement ring. 'You won't be a Hagberg wife anyway.'

'Oh, that's because my grandmother never had a son and her only brother died childless. I know she was very sad about that, as it broke the chain, but she made me promise to give it to *my* son's wife, if I ever have a boy. If not, it's to continue down the line of daughters. Strictly speaking it should have gone to my mother's older son – my half-brother – for now, but as I told you, she and Gran didn't get on well. Obviously my children won't have the surname Hagberg, but I don't think it matters these days. It's the bloodline that counts.'

'I see. Nice tradition. I like it.'

'Yes.' Mia glanced at some of the other documents, then handed Haakon the map of the property and started to read the letter from the solicitor. As she reached the final paragraphs, she almost choked on her tea. 'No! Bloody hell!'

'What's the matter?' Haakon put down his bowl of muesli, looking concerned.

'It's that damned Thoresson guy! He's disputing my ownership of the little island out there.' She pointed at the island just opposite the peninsula that jutted out next to the bay. 'How dare he? It's been in Gran's family for as long as this ring, I swear!'

'Well in that case, you should be able to prove it quite easily, shouldn't you?'

'No, that's the thing – the papers relating to it are missing.' Mia stabbed the solicitor's letter with her finger. 'Mr Almquist says they can't find them "at present".'

'Hmm, I don't think much of their filing system then.'

'Says the guy whose office is a tip,' Mia joked, remembering the piles of stuff he'd had to move just so she could have a seat.

Haakon laughed. 'Point taken, but I'll have you know I call it organised chaos and I know precisely where every single thing is. This Almquist guy obviously doesn't. What's he going to do about it?'

Mia sighed. 'He just says they're going to look again and he's sure they'll turn up soon. They'd better, because I'm not giving up my island to that annoying man.'

'Special, is it?' Haakon stood up and stared out at the small speck of land. 'Doesn't seem to have any buildings on it.'

'No, and it never will. I promised Gran it would remain unspoiled. It's where we used to go for picnics and it's just so peaceful, you know? It would be a terrible shame to ruin it.' There was more to it than that, she could feel it in her bones, as Gran would have said, but she couldn't explain it. The island had to be protected at all costs, though.

'It would. I'd like to go out there sometime, if you wouldn't mind? But hang on, you don't have a boat, do you?'

Mia had gone to stand next to him, and together they looked at the empty bay, its little jetty bathed in sunlight. She pointed to a shed over to one side. 'There's a rowing boat in there, but it will probably need to be repaired and varnished. And who has time for that?'

'Hmm, well maybe on one of our days off, I can help you. If you want it done, that is?' Haakon glanced at her and Mia had to suppress the urge to step closer to him. It was weird how she felt so at ease with him now, wanting to just lean into him for no reason. It must be because he was so big; it made her feel small and protected in his presence. She turned away and went back to collect her mug and the pile of post.

'Thanks, that would be very kind of you. Do we get days off? I had the impression we'd be working non-stop all summer in order to get as much done as possible. I hear you're a slave driver.' She was joking again, as he'd been away the previous weekend and she was going to London the following day.

'Ha ha, very funny. But seriously, I'll . . . no, *we* should make up a rota tonight, make sure everyone gets some down time. Agreed, co-director?' There was a teasing note in his voice that made Mia laugh.

'OK. Good idea. For now, we have a meeting to go to.'

A plan of the longhouse – or hall – was slowly emerging, and it must have been an impressive building; about thirty-five metres long and seven wide, with a double row of timber posts supporting the roof on either side. There was something confusing about the way the post holes were positioned, though, until Haakon realised what had happened.

'Guys, I think there must have been at least two buildings here in more or less the same place, and one of them burned down at some point,' he told the others at their morning site meeting. 'As you've seen, some of the post holes we've found have charred bits of wood in them, and I've plotted that type separately on this plan – look. They form a slightly different rectangle to the others. It's as if they reused some holes, but not all of them, or at least not exactly.'

'Of course, that makes sense,' Anders said. 'Fires must have been a constant hazard in those days, no matter how careful you were. Wooden houses, turf roofs, mattresses stuffed with hay . . .' Some of the others nodded. 'Would have been gutting for them, though, having to rebuild something that big.'

'Yes. I'll have another look at the hearth to see if that was changed at all or if they just built a new hall around it. We've only found the one, right?' Haakon looked around at his team.

'Yep. No sign of a second one.'

Everyone went off to continue with their various trenches and Haakon followed with the plan. He walked around the perimeter of the two longhouses, then stopped by the hearth, which had been partly excavated by now. Built of stone and raised to about knee height, it was as impressive as the hall itself and the only tangible remains, as everything around it had rotted away. He put out a hand to feel the contours of the stone and could picture it clearly, back in the Viking age, blazing merrily and adding warmth to the crowded room . . .

Two iron cauldrons, giving off enticing aromas, hung from a metal frame above the fire, and one even larger pot was suspended by a chain from the rafters. Meanwhile the smoke escaped upwards, making its way out through the thatch or the two holes either end of the gables high up near the roof – the vindauga. *The air inside the room was still a bit smoky, but you got used to it after a while . . .*

Haakon shook his head and frowned. The images had been almost too precise, as if he'd been there and seen the hall in its heyday for himself. A tingling sensation crawled through him and he moved, too restless to stay still. What had just happened? Was it possible to have flashbacks to a bygone era just by touching something old? Or was this site haunted somehow, the ghosts of the past trying to reach out to him to show him what had happened here? Because he was convinced something *had* happened, although he didn't know why. It was just a very strong hunch, an almost visceral knowledge seeping into him the longer he spent here.

His hand was still resting on the stone surround and something flashed in the sunlight – the snake ring. *Faen!* He'd taken to wearing it at night so that he wouldn't lose it, and he must have forgotten to remove it this morning. Normally he hid it in his room during the day. The tingling sensation returned, and it seemed to be emanating from the snake. Haakon shivered. He really must return it to the museum, but perhaps not yet . . .

What was it the ghosts – or restless souls perhaps? – were trying to tell him?

They'd have to keep digging to find out.

***

One of Ragnhild's brothers arrived one morning with the news that their father lay on his deathbed. The old man had asked to see Ragnhild in order to say his farewells, and she immediately prepared herself for the short journey inland to the family holdings.

It was as if the entire farmstead breathed a sigh of relief after their mistress had gone, sitting regally in the prow of her brother's small ship surrounded by baskets of provisions.

'Does she not think they'll feed her?' Aase had muttered, huffing and puffing as she ran to and fro trying to organise everything for Ragnhild's departure. 'Honestly, you'd think she was travelling to Garðaríki or Gríkkland.'

There was almost an atmosphere of feasting during the days that followed, and even thralls were heard to go about their work singing or humming to themselves. It was remarkable how one person's absence could change things, and the difference was especially noticeable in Haukr, who was seen to smile frequently and spent the evenings laughing and joking with his men.

Ceri felt happy and almost content for the first time in months, but on the third night she was woken up by a fretful Jorun, who was tossing and turning.

'What's the matter?' Ceri whispered, but she knew the child couldn't hear her so she stroked her head instead, trying to soothe her back to sleep. Jorun was burning hot to the touch, so Ceri left the warm blankets and furs and went to fetch some water.

The little girl settled down temporarily, but was soon whimpering in her sleep, and Ceri knew she had to do something. The only thing that helped against a fever was to bathe the sick person's forehead with cool water, but in order to do this she needed to see what she was doing. She wondered if she dared to put wood on the hearth to give her more light, or whether she'd be reprimanded for this. In the end, there was only one thing she could do – she went in search of Haukr.

Quietly pushing past the heavy curtain that separated his sleeping quarters from the rest of the hall, she stepped inside and stopped to get her bearings. She knew that Haukr's bed was in the far corner, and she took a few hesitant steps in the dark. Before she had gone even halfway, a voice hissed out of the darkness. 'Who goes there?'

'It's only me, Ceri. I'm sorry to disturb you, but your daughter is ill.'

'Jorun? What ails her? Wait.'

Ceri heard movement as he walked past her into the main hall. In the next moment he was back carrying an oil lamp. As he stood in front of her wearing nothing but his trousers, the light reflected off his massive torso, which had a dusting of golden hairs tapering down towards his waistband. She looked away, embarrassed.

'Jorun has a fever. I need to bathe her with cold water, but I couldn't see out there in the hall.'

He seemed to understand immediately, without her explaining further. 'I'll bring her in here. You go and fetch water.'

It wasn't long before Jorun was installed in Haukr's bed, and Ceri sat down next to her, sponging her forehead, neck and arms with ice-cold water that she had fetched from the stream. The little girl whimpered and tried to move away, but her father held her still. 'Shh, Jorun *mín*, let us help you.'

The hours passed. Ceri was very aware of the big man sitting so close to her but tried to ignore the feeling of intimacy. She caught herself wishing that this was her child, her husband, and that she had a right to be here, but such thoughts could not be allowed. No good would come of it. Unconsciously, she sighed.

'Are you tired? Shall I take over so you can go back to bed?' Haukr misunderstood the reason for her sigh.

'No, no, I'm fine. Why don't you lie down instead? You're going hunting in the morning, are you not? You'll need to rest.'

'My daughter is more important. Hunting can wait,' Haukr replied. 'Here, let me.' He gently prised the cloth from her fingers. 'You lie down and rest for a moment. Go on.' He patted the bed and nodded encouragement.

'H-here? But . . .'

'Only for a little while. I won't take advantage of you, if that is what you fear. I gave you my word, did I not?'

'Your word?' Ceri's brain seemed to have ceased to function. All she knew was that lying down in Haukr's bed was surely not a good idea, no matter what he said.

'That I would allow your brother to ransom you in the spring. You're safe until then, unless you wish it otherwise?'

He stared into her eyes and she understood what he was

asking. The thought that he wanted her but wouldn't force her was a heady one, giving her the power to decide. Power over him. She opened her mouth to tell him yes, but the words refused to emerge. Could not be allowed to emerge. He was married and she would be leaving in the spring. Lying with this man while his wife was away would be a sin, and she would be damned for all eternity.

Instead of nodding as she wished to do, she looked away. Her mind was screaming at her to confess to him that she wasn't sure she wanted to be ransomed, that perhaps she wanted to stay here with him and Jorun, but she knew it wasn't possible. It was a grave sin even to want him in her dreams.

'Ceri?' He turned her face to his with a gentle hand on her cheek. 'You're tired. Just lie down and rest. Everything will be well, trust me.'

She nodded, unable to speak. She was sure that nothing would ever be well again, because she had a suspicion she'd fallen in love with this gentle giant, and she couldn't have him.

She lay down next to Jorun and drifted in and out of sleep until the little girl became less fretful. Then Haukr stretched out on the other side of his daughter and put an arm across her and Ceri, gathering them both close. It felt so right, so safe, Ceri made no protest. This was where she wanted to be.

For ever.

Haukr didn't sleep at all that night. Instead, he lay awake watching over the two people in his bed, revelling in the sensation of holding them close. They were both precious, and as the hours crawled by, he came to the realisation that it was more than that. Much more. He knew now that he'd never loved Ragnhild at all – he'd felt lust for her, certainly, but they didn't have the much deeper connection he felt with Ceri. It was as though his mind and Ceri's were alike, their outlook on life the same. He wanted her in a way he'd never wanted Ragnhild, but as he could not marry her, he would never bed her unless it was her wish.

He respected her and her beliefs, and he also knew that neither of them would ever be happy seeing her merely as his mistress, with Ragnhild ruling the roost. It was a recipe for disaster and he couldn't do that to her. To either of them.

He sighed. Ceri would go back to Bretland in the spring or summer – as late as possible, if the gods were willing to grant him more time with her – but he had to resign himself to the fact that she would leave. For now, though, she was here and he could enjoy the sight of her; even, as tonight, hold her – a precious gift he hadn't expected. Although Jorun was lying between them, she was so tiny he barely noticed her. His whole focus was on Ceri, also small, but perfect within the circle of his arms.

One night, and it would be imprinted on his memory for ever.

Chapter Twenty

It felt very strange to be back in London after spending so much time in the Swedish countryside. Mia caught herself noticing the dirt and the pollution much more, as well as the frenetic pace of life, but she knew she'd soon get used to it again. She'd always loved the British capital and felt at home there, just as she did in Sweden. It was as if she was split in half and neither side of her was more right than the other.

'Hello? Anyone home?' She dragged her small suitcase in through the front door of the flat and looked around, spotting a note on the coffee table.

Gone to the football tournament. Will text you later to say which pub we're in. Expect to meet us around 6-ish. C x

She ought to have arrived on Friday night, but the plane tickets had been a lot more expensive than first thing Saturday morning. Now she wouldn't see Charles until this evening. She sighed. Maybe their reunion would be all the sweeter for waiting a bit longer. In the meantime, she'd see if Alun was free for lunch.

'I'm always up for a bite to eat, you know that.' Alun had been working overtime and was happy to meet up in Soho for a Chinese meal. 'Tell me about the dig – anything interesting?'

Mia filled him in on all the exciting finds – the longhouse, the weaving hut and the Celtic cross. 'I wish I knew if it was trade goods or if the owner of the settlement went on a raid and stole it. Either way, someone was very careless with it, as we found it buried in the floor of the weaving hut.'

'Unless they put it there on purpose.' Alun grinned and helped himself to more dim sum, wielding his chopsticks expertly. 'Maybe one of the thralls stole it from his master and intended to retrieve it at some point and make a run for it?'

Mia laughed. 'Well, if he did, he obviously never made it. Oh, I almost forgot – I found a comb as well, made of bone, and it had the owner's name written in runes: Ceri, but spelled with a K.'

'Really? Seems like there were a lot of Celts in that settlement of yours.'

'It's not *my* settlement. Well, OK, technically I own it now, but you know what I mean. Anyway, that's only two items, so not that many really.'

Alun was staring into space, deep in thought. 'Ceri as in . . . Ceridwen, perhaps? Quite a common name in Wales. In fact, that old tale I was telling you about a while back has a Ceridwen as the heroine.' He made a face. 'I'm still working on the text. Parts of it are pretty much indecipherable due to its age.'

'Yes, could be there was a Celtic thrall girl called that. Haakon – that's the guy in charge of the dig – and I were speculating that she might have been a favoured mistress or something.'

'Ooh-er! You Vikings and your sexual antics, eh?'

Mia elbowed him. 'Nothing to do with me, and I'm sure it was exactly the same over here at the time, so don't give me that. Everyone owned slaves.'

Something about the way Alun had pronounced the name Ceri – his lovely Welsh lilt almost caressing it – stirred a memory inside Mia: Haakon during their first meeting, reading out the inscription inside her ring. *It looks like it could be E and R, and the last letter might be an I, but it's not clear.* Could it be that these were preceded by a K? No, that would be too fantastic, surely? She'd have to check it out as soon as she had access to a magnifying glass.

They parted company after a good two hours of chatting, and Mia felt cheerful as she did a bit of shopping before heading off to the pub to meet up with Charles. She and Alun were always on the same wavelength and there was never any need to watch what she said so as not to bore him about archaeological stuff. A thought flashed through her mind that she and Haakon had the same connection, the same interests. Unlike her and Charles. What did they actually have in common? She struggled to think of a single thing.

It hadn't mattered much at first, when everything was new and exciting between them. Although they had different tastes in music, films and even restaurants, they'd been happy to compromise, taking turns to decide where to go. Mia thought that was what a relationship was all about, but lately it felt as though she'd been the one giving in most of the time. Charles always had a reason why his choice was better or had to come first – his boss had told him he just *had* to try out this par-ticular restaurant, or someone at work had seen this film and it was *amazing*, so of course they had to see it. The boundless energy and enthusiasm that had so enthralled her in the beginning, when all his focus was on her, was now deployed only at work or for things like golf tournaments and corporate events. In fact, everything revolved around his job and his career. By the time he got home, he was always tired and grumpy, and Mia had become used to humouring him so as not to start an argument. She wasn't quite sure when the change had begun, but it had happened gradually and she hadn't really thought about it much until now. When had he stopped taking her wishes into account? When had their relationship become so one-sided? And why should she be the one making all the effort?

As she entered the pub where, judging by the loud voices and flushed faces, Charles and his mates were already several rounds in, she felt guilty for even thinking that. His work was important, high-powered, and of course he was tired, working such long hours. He was doing it for them; for their future. Besides, she was in love with him and hadn't hesitated when he'd asked her to marry him. If you loved someone, you put up with their little foibles. But now that she had started thinking about it, the little voice inside her head refused to be silenced. *I work hard too! What about when I'm tired?* Charles never noticed these days. Tonight it was as though she was looking at him with fresh eyes. And she didn't like what she saw.

'Mia, at last! Was beginning to think you weren't coming.' He enveloped her in a bear hug and kissed her a bit too enthusiastically, making his mates whoop with glee and shout out rude comments.

'It's dead on six, Charles,' she protested, and extricated herself from his arms, but he wasn't paying attention. He'd turned away to listen to some anecdote about the game earlier.

She took a deep breath. Maybe she was just tired. It had been a long day, getting up at the crack of dawn to drive to the airport, and she owed it to Charles to be supportive. These company get-togethers weren't just for fun; they were part of his career, something he had to do. But when his boss, Rory, was the next person to greet her, attempting to put his arm round her shoulders, she ducked out of the way with a muttered excuse about going to the ladies.

There was only so much she was prepared to put up with, and she had some serious thinking to do.

Haakon sat on the veranda of Mia's cottage and stared out over the lake. He'd offered to stay here at the weekend as it wasn't his turn to have Linnea. He and some of the others had worked all day, but now everyone else had gone off for a meal somewhere. They'd asked him to come, but he couldn't leave the dig site unattended, so he'd declined. Now he felt lonely.

It was mid June, which meant it hardly became dark all night. He watched the beautiful scenery around him – a sweeping vista of lake, island and forest – and felt something shift inside him. This was the sort of place he wanted to live, not in a cramped flat in the city. It called to him, Birch Thorpe, on a primeval level, and the thought of having to leave at the end of the summer was gut-wrenching. But that was just silly. He could always rent a cottage next summer, or even buy one – he had a decent salary and some money inherited from his grandparents.

It wouldn't be the same, though. There was something about this particular place that . . . No. He shook his head. He was being fanciful again. Perhaps there were spirits here, or ghosts, and they were enticing him to stay, but they couldn't make him.

A knock on the window made him jump, and for a moment he really thought one of those ghosts had come to haunt him. There was a pale face outside, surrounded by darkness, and it took him a while to recognise Ivar. He got up to open the door.

'God, you scared the shit out of me! What are you doing here?'

The teenager shrugged and came inside, slouching into the nearest chair. 'Nothing to do. Thought I'd come see if anything was happening. Wanted to get away from my aunt for a bit.' There was a strained look on the kid's face.

'Your aunt?'

185

'Yeah, Ingegerd. My dad's gone on a business trip to the Far East and he didn't want me to be alone for that long, so he asked her to come and stay. She's a major pain in the arse. Always fussing about stuff.'

Haakon hid a smile. 'That bad, eh?'

'You have no idea. She's much older than Dad and she's a doctor, so she's used to bossing people around.' Ivar scowled. 'I'd had enough of it. Told her I was out of there.'

'Well, nothing much is happening here, as you can see. I was just sitting thinking about Mia's ancestors. They were so lucky to own all this.' He gestured towards the shadow-filled garden.

'It's sick, isn't it?' Ivar said, and Haakon gathered he meant 'sick' as a good thing. 'Hey, they could be my ancestors too, you know. Maybe we're related?'

'You think?'

'Yeah, my family's been here, like, for ever, Dad says. He's really into that kind of stuff. Genealogy, he calls it. And he's got this old book with lots of names in. One of the earliest ones is Thorald, so he gave me that as a middle name. I mean, come on! As if Ivar Thoresson isn't bad enough. So lame.'

Haakon suppressed another smile. Ivar Thorald Thoresson? The kid had a point. 'Hey, no one ever likes the names their parents choose for them. I'm not exactly enamoured of Haakon. Besides, old names are in right now. My daughter is called Linnea after my great-grandmother.'

'You have a daughter?' Ivar was temporarily distracted, then returned to the subject of his father. 'My dad is, like, obsessed with the past. You should see his collection of old rubbish.' He snorted. 'He's forever telling me I've got pure Viking blood or some such crap. Not that I give a shit. You wouldn't believe the fuss he made when I dyed my hair black. Went on and on about how I should be grateful to be blond. I mean, seriously?

What the actual fuck . . . Sorry, but, you know . . .'

Haakon was a bit taken aback. Ivar's father sounded like a complete nutter, but he didn't want to say so. 'Er, I'd love to see his collection sometime. What sort of things does he have?'

'Viking swords, old brooches, knives . . . all sorts of stuff. I think he gets it on eBay and he goes to auctions a lot. Oh, and there's, like, secret bidding wars online. Encrypted. I know, 'cos he gets very angry if I come into the room when he's in the middle of one.'

'Viking swords?' Haakon frowned. 'You mean replica ones, right?'

'I dunno.' Ivar shrugged. 'He says they're real.'

'They can't be. People aren't allowed to own Viking artefacts; they have to be in a museum.'

'Maybe he doesn't know that. Anyway, I'll show you sometime when he's out. He got some new stuff just the other day. Said there's more coming soon.'

'Thanks, I'd like that.' In fact, Haakon would be extremely interested to see this collection so he could tell the authorities if anything illegal was going on. He decided not to mention that to Ivar, though, as it wasn't the kid's fault what his father was up to. It was time to steer the conversation in a different direction. 'So what does your mum think about it all? The, um, collection and stuff?'

'I don't have a mum. She died when I was little.'

'Oh, I'm so sorry. I didn't mean to . . .' He should have realised. There wouldn't have been any need for Aunt Ingegerd to come and stay if Ivar's mother had been around.

Ivar held up a hand, looking much more mature than his years for an instant. 'It's OK, don't worry. I'm used to it now. It was a long time ago. And no, I don't have a wicked stepmum either.' He grinned. 'Dad's had a couple of girlfriends, but they never last.'

Haakon laughed, relieved the boy could joke about it. 'A shame. I hear wicked stepmums can be a lot of fun.' Again, time to change the subject. 'So have you eaten? I was just about to have some pasta, but there's enough for two. And then maybe watch a film?'

Ivar's face lit up. 'Yes please! What film have you got?'

'*The Matrix*. I'm just catching up on some recent movies.'

'Awesome!'

Haakon smiled as he got up and made his way into the kitchen. He was glad Ivar had stopped by – he'd definitely livened things up. And the ghosts from the past had gone. For now.

Jorun had a streaming cold for a few days, but thankfully the fever didn't return. Ceri told herself she was pleased not to have to spend any more nights in Haukr's bed. He was able to go off on his hunting expeditions, while she stayed indoors trying to amuse the little girl at the same time as weaving with Aase. It was hard work, but it took her mind off the thoughts that she knew she ought not to be having. In quiet moments, however, she couldn't stop the images in her mind – of Haukr half naked in the faint light, Haukr tenderly bathing his daughter's face with water and whispering endearments to her, and of his arms around the two of them in that big bed, so solid, so strong, so wonderful . . .

But it was stupid to dream and she prayed to her god for forgiveness and for help in resisting the feelings Haukr stirred up. Nothing good could come of them.

The nights grew ever darker and the winter months Ceri had dreaded arrived with a vengeance. Snow, so much snow – piles and piles of it. And frost, which coated everything, making the surrounding forest look enchanted. To her astonishment, the huge lake – or sea inlet – also froze, and people were able to walk on the ice without fear of falling through. She refused to go on it at first, fearful despite everyone's assurances, but when Jorun ventured out into the bay, slipping and sliding, she had no option but to follow.

It was great fun and she soon forgot her fears. Holding hands, the two of them skidded across the smooth, shiny surface, sometimes bumping into some of the other children who had been given permission to play on the ice, sometimes falling over amid much laughter.

The happy interlude came to an abrupt halt, however, when Ragnhild arrived back, escorted by two of her brothers. They were tall and blond, like their sister, but had none of her beauty. One had a flat nose, as if he'd been punched repeatedly, and the other sported a scar that ran from one temple down towards his mouth, making him look slightly lopsided. It wasn't their lack of good looks that made Ceri shudder at the sight of them, however; it was the hostility in their eyes as they scanned the group on the ice.

'What is going on here?' Ragnhild demanded. 'Why are you not all working? Do you think that just because there is ice on the bay, we need not eat? Go on, everyone, back to your tasks.'

The children scattered like a flock of birds startled by a cat, even the smallest ones, who had no particular chores to perform as yet, running to seek the sanctuary of their mothers' skirts. Ceri took Jorun by the hand and led her towards the shoreline, very aware of Ragnhild's angry glare on her back, but the other woman said nothing, merely climbed out of the sled her brothers' servants had been pushing her in and stalked up the hill.

Ceri sighed. It would seem that life was back to normal.

A few days after Ragnhild's return, it was Haukr's turn to leave. He and his men had gathered together all the food, furs and other goods they had to sell and were going to Birka, the main trading centre on an island further out towards the sea. They had spare venison and elk meat to trade, on top of that from domestic animals, and they were hoping to exchange these for salt, as stocks were running low after the autumn slaughter, as well as a few other items.

'We may be gone a day or two, depending on how long it takes us,' Haukr told Ragnhild. 'As your brothers have decided to stay for a while, you'll have congenial company at least.' Not that he found them congenial, but he assumed she did.

And, he added silently to himself, hopefully they would keep her occupied so that she didn't harass everyone else.

'Don't let them drink all the ale, will you?' he joked, but this elicited only a very small smile and a nod. He wasn't worried, though – whatever else she was, Ragnhild was good at running the household, and she kept a tight rein on stocks. And he was leaving Thorald behind to keep an eye on things – he'd trust his right-hand man with his life.

As he strapped on his bone ice skates and pushed his arms into a long harness fastened to one of the sleds carrying the goods, he saw Ceri watching. She looked to be in awe and he gathered she'd never seen ice skating before. He'd have to show her how it was done when they returned. It was essentially just a fast way of travelling across the ice, but it could be great fun as well. Perhaps Jorun would enjoy it too.

He waved to the people gathered by the shore as he set off with Steinn and Ulv, each of them pulling a sled and propelling themselves forward with the help of a wooden stave that had a sharp metal spike at one end. There was a special way of moving your feet and arms, and once they had a rhythm going, they travelled quite quickly. Haukr soon began to feel warm, despite the freezing temperatures. He was well wrapped up in layers of clothing, with a sheepskin hat covering his head and ears and sheepskin mittens on his hands. The frostbite wouldn't harm him this day.

It felt good to leave the farmstead behind for a while, and he hoped Ragnhild would be in a better mood when he returned. Perhaps he ought to buy her a trinket? Yes, he'd find something he knew she'd like. Silver this time, obviously.

Upon his return the next day, however, he forgot all about the little arm ring nestled in an inside pocket, as the first thing he heard was the shrill but indistinct yelling of his daughter. They'd made good time and arrived before dark, but dusk was falling now and Jorun ought to be indoors.

'What on earth . . . ?' He exchanged glances with Steinn and Ulv, and quickly unlaced his skates, setting off up the hill at a run.

Jorun was being hauled away from the thralls' huts, kicking and screaming, by Svein, one of her uncles. 'Stop that, you little cat. Come now, we're going into the hall and then—'

'Let go of her this instant!' Haukr strode up to Svein, who obviously hadn't heard him coming.

'What? Oh, but . . .'

Haukr pulled his daughter out of the man's grip and picked her up, hugging her close. 'What's the matter, Jorun *mín*? What is going on?'

'She's being disobedient. Ragnhild said to fetch her inside.' Svein glared at him, but when Haukr scowled back, the man held up his hands, palms out. 'Very well, you can deal with her.' He shot Jorun a look of acute dislike and set off for the hall with angry strides.

Jorun was still agitated and seemed to want to be put down. Haukr complied, and the little girl immediately ran back towards one of the huts, which he now saw was closed from the outside with a bar. Someone had locked the thralls inside.

'Ce-ih,' she said. 'Ce-ih!'

'What? Ceri is in there?' Haukr lifted the plank and opened the door. 'Hello? Someone tell me what is going on!'

'Haukr?' The voice was faint, but he'd recognise it anywhere – Ceridwen.

He ducked his head and rushed in through the low opening. There was barely any light in there, but he could make out several shapes. 'Ceri? Where are you?'

'H-here.' One of the shapes detached itself from the others and stood up, swaying slightly.

Haukr grabbed hold of her shoulders to steady her and led her towards the door. No one else said anything, and he could almost taste the fear in the air. 'Is everyone all right?' he asked. 'Tell me what's happened; you won't be punished.'

'We're all well, master,' a voice told him. 'But Ceridwen . . .'

'I'll see to her.' He hustled her out of the door and drew in a sharp breath at the sight of her in the fading light. '*Skítr!* What on earth . . . ?'

She had a black eye and bruising on her arms, where the sleeves of her gown had been pushed up. Her hair was in disarray and there was no sign of her shawl. Understandably, she was shivering with cold and shock. It was obvious that she was feeling dizzy, as her eyes weren't focusing properly. He guessed the blow to her face had been quite hard, if indeed it had only been the one. She was holding on to one hand with the other, as if protecting it, and as he gently untangled her fingers, he swore under his breath. The middle finger on her right hand was bloody and quite clearly broken, and the rest of the hand was red and bruised. The skin was mottled as if it had come close to frostbite, and Haukr began to guess what had happened. He swore again, loudly this time.

'Ce-ih!' Jorun threw her arms around Ceri, and Haukr felt her wince.

192

'Jorun! Careful!' He grabbed his daughter's arm and grimaced to try and show her that Ceri was in pain. The girl seemed to understand. Then he looked again at Ceri. 'Who did this? No, actually, you don't need to tell me. Come, let us find Aase – we'll need her to dress that hand.'

And after that, there was going to be a reckoning.

Chapter Twenty-One

'So what do you think? I don't like the sound of it, not one bit.'

Haakon had just been telling Mia about his conversation with Ivar, and what the boy had said about his dad and his collection of artefacts. She had returned from London looking tired and drawn, and he didn't really want to add to whatever burdens she carried, but this was serious. Potentially criminal.

'Hmm, yes, really weird. But it's not like we can just march into the guy's house and demand to see what he's got, is it? And we can't tell the police without proof, either.' Mia's quicksilver gaze was troubled, and Haakon had a sudden urge to pull her in for a hug and ask what was bothering her. Apart from her arse of a neighbour, of course.

He resisted.

'You're right, but it bugs the hell out of me. I hate that there's a black market in ancient finds. They should be available for everyone to see. It's like those bastards who steal famous paintings and hide them away for their own enjoyment. Just beyond selfish, if you ask me.' At Mia's raised eyebrows, he kicked sheepishly at the ground. 'Sorry, I know, I get a bit carried away on the subject.'

She smiled, for the first time since her return, and put a hand on his arm. 'It's OK. Rant all you like. I'm with you on this one.'

Then she grew solemn again. 'But I'm not sure what to do, so let's think about it for a while, OK?'

'Sure.' Her soft touch sent a jolt up his arm, and he had to make a conscious effort not to put his own hand on top of hers. He tried to concentrate on more immediate things. 'Right, time to get back to work.'

Halfway through the morning, there was a commotion over by the gate as a car pulled up and a woman got out and started to shout at a passing archaeologist. Haakon, who recognised the voice only too well, dropped his trowel and sprinted over.

'Sofia! What are you doing here?' At a distance, she looked like a model – tall, beautiful, blonde and willowy – but close up her eyes were bloodshot and the bags underneath them practically had bags of their own. Her face was pale beneath a slight tan, and as he approached, she pulled her sunglasses down from the top of her head, wincing at the strong sunlight. Haakon's heart sank. She must have had one hell of a weekend. When was she going to grow up and stop partying so hard?

'There you are! Jeez, this place is the back of beyond, isn't it? Took me ages to find.'

Haakon wasn't quite sure how to answer that, so he didn't. Sofia opened the back door of the car and Linnea came shooting out, throwing her arms around his legs. 'Daddeeeee!'

'Hey, sweetie! How lovely to see you!' And it was, although the visit wasn't exactly scheduled. He lifted her up and hugged her tight. It looked as though Sofia hadn't had the time – or energy – to do Linnea's hair, which hung in messy rat's tails down her back. It was a darker shade of blonde compared to his own, more golden, and very pretty if it was brushed, but it took a lot of effort to keep it neat. He swallowed a sigh. Not brushing a kid's hair wasn't exactly mistreatment, but at the same time it was just one thing among many other such oversights.

Sofia was now busy opening the boot of the car and dumping bags on the ground by his feet. 'Here. I'm afraid you'll have to have Linnea for a couple of weeks. My parents decided to go to the South of France, so she couldn't stay with them as I'd planned. Honestly, they could have said they were going away!'

'Er, right.' This was all news to Haakon. He hadn't known Linnea was due a holiday with her grandparents, and since when did Sofia plan anything in advance? 'And where are *you* going?'

'India. There's this retreat where they teach you meditation, life skills, that sort of thing. It's in the most wonderful palace – well, it's not a palace now, obviously, but it used to be – and there's a spa and pool and everything. I'm seriously stressed. Can't cope at all at the moment. My friend Angelica said she'd been there recently and it was just amaaaazing. She's going back, so I decided to tag along. How was I to know Mum and Dad had arranged to visit friends in Nice? Anyway, it's all booked and paid for now; I can't *not* go.' At his raised eyebrows, she added. 'Oh, Daddy paid, of course.'

Of course. Sofia's salary would never stretch to a spa holiday in India. He suppressed a sigh. Her parents had always supported her in every way. Too much so, never encouraging her to stand on her own two feet. Somehow they'd always been there to pick up the pieces. Although they meant well, Haakon had a suspicion their daughter could have done with a reality check. How could one possibly get stressed from too much partying and shopping? But it wasn't his problem. Or not usually.

'So you're saying you want me to drop everything and look after Linnea for . . . how long?' He tried to keep the sarcasm out of his voice, but didn't quite succeed.

'Two, three weeks? Four max.' Sofia shrugged. 'I've been under so much pressure, I don't really know how long I'll need.'

'Pressure. Right. And it didn't occur to you that this might be

196

a bit inconvenient for me?' Haakon gestured towards the dig. 'We're in the middle of an archaeological excavation here. One that I'm in charge of, so I can't just leave. And I'm staying here during the week, not at home.'

Sofia's eyes flashed. 'Well, it's about time you did your fair share of looking after her. Daddy offered to pay for a temporary nanny, but I don't see why he should when Linnea has two parents. You hardly ever have her, so no, it didn't occur to me that it would be "inconvenient" for you to see your daughter for a while. It's summer, for Christ's sake. Most people have holidays this time of year.'

Haakon's jaw clenched and he bit down hard so as not to start a proper argument in front of Linnea. He'd have to sort this somehow, but it wouldn't be easy. His own parents weren't coming back on annual leave until August, and he assumed Linnea wasn't enrolled at any day-care centres for kids of working parents. 'Fine. Whatever. But when you're back from India, expect to find a letter from my solicitors. I'll be asking for a different custody arrangement from now on. So I can do my "fair share".'

Sofia's eyes went from angry to little-girl-sad-and-hurt in an instant, tears gathering at the corners. 'God, you're such a shit sometimes. But fine, we can talk about it then.'

She turned to open the car door and Haakon cleared his throat. 'Um, aren't you forgetting something?' He nodded surreptitiously towards Linnea, who'd stayed quiet during their exchange.

'Oh, silly me!' Sofia pretended consternation and pulled their daughter out of his arms and into hers for a big hug. 'Bye, sweetheart! Have fun with Daddy, won't you? I'll see you soon, and then Mummy will be feeling much better and we can do lots of things together, all right?'

'OK. Bye, Mummy.' Already at the age of six Linnea had a very adult look in her eyes that told Haakon she wasn't buying it. She'd heard too many promises and excuses from her mother in her young life.

The thought made him sad, and he was determined to protect her better in future. Now all he had to do was figure out how to look after her and an important dig at the same time.

Mia was intrigued as Haakon took off for the gate. She followed him with her eyes and was surprised to see a woman emerge from the car, followed by a small girl, whom he picked up and hugged. Raised voices could be heard, and soon afterwards, car doors slammed and the woman sped off in a cloud of dust. Left standing in the road was Haakon, and next to him the little girl and a couple of bags.

'What the hell?' Ivar had joined Mia in staring at the scene and expressed her feelings exactly. 'Oh, that must be his daughter. He told me he had a kid but he didn't say she was coming here.'

'I didn't know he had one!' The realisation that Haakon was a father hit her right in the chest, and for a moment she was short of breath. He and the little girl looked so perfect together. And the woman in the car must be his wife or partner – she'd looked stunning too, the ideal match for Haakon. Mia swallowed down a spurt of annoyance she had no business feeling. What was it to her? She did her best to sound normal as she commented, 'I think we're about to be introduced.'

Haakon had taken the girl by the hand and was walking towards them. He dumped the bags outside the cottage and strode on, the little girl struggling to keep up with his long strides. The expression on his face was ostensibly happy, but Mia could see a muscle jumping in his jaw as if he was biting his teeth together hard. What was going on?

As he drew level with Mia and Ivar, he stopped. 'This is my daughter, Linnea. She's apparently come to stay for a while as her mum has had to go away for a few weeks. Hope that's all right? It was a bit . . . um, sudden, so I wasn't expecting her. Linnea, say hello to Mia and Ivar.'

'Hello.' Linnea's eyes were huge blue pools in a small heart-shaped face. 'I'm six, how old are you?'

'Linnea! You don't ask people that, especially not ladies,' Haakon reprimanded, but Mia laughed.

'It's OK. I'm twenty-nine and Ivar here is fourteen. It's nice to meet you.'

Linnea smiled, showing a huge gap where her front teeth should have been, which was very endearing. The rest of her was so thin, Mia wondered if she had been fed properly, but she knew that some girls were naturally like that, and judging by the girl's mother, the tall and skinny gene ran in the family.

Haakon sighed and ran a hand through his hair, which was as usual already standing up. He only succeeded in adding a streak of mud to it. 'How I'm supposed to keep an eye on Linnea and perform my job at the same time is anyone's guess. Still, we'll have to make the best of it, eh, squirt? You'll have to help Daddy dig.' He smiled at his daughter, clearly doing his best to sound positive about the situation. 'Are you hungry? It's almost lunchtime, I think.'

'Yes, I'm starving. Mummy didn't have any food at home this morning, so she said I had to wait until we got here.'

'Did she indeed?' Mia saw that muscle twitch again as Haakon's jaw clenched. 'Well then, we'd better find you something straight away. You two coming?' He looked at Mia and Ivar, and he was so obviously in need of support that Mia didn't have the heart to refuse.

'Sure, we can have an early lunch today, don't you think, Ivar?'

'I'm always hungry.' Ivar grinned. 'Must be growing or something. About time, too.'

'Yes, you're eating me out of house and home,' Mia joked. 'No, only kidding. It's a joy to see you tuck in, honestly.' And it was. She loved watching him eat as if every morsel she gave him tasted wonderful simply because someone else had prepared it for him. It made her want to give his father a good kicking, since according to Ivar they only ever ate takeaways or TV dinners, most of which he had to get for himself. Now that she knew the boy didn't have a mother, she felt especially protective of him.

'OK, let's go then.'

Mia followed Haakon and his small daughter. She couldn't help but wonder about his relationship with Linnea's mother, but she didn't want to pry. If he wanted them to know, no doubt he'd tell them.

'Do you mind if Linnea sleeps in my room?' he whispered as they stood side by side preparing sandwiches in the cottage kitchen. 'That bed is big enough for two and she doesn't take up much space anyway.'

'No, that's fine. There should be an extra duvet and pillow in the cupboard if you need them.'

'Thanks, that would be great. Really sorry about this. It would have been nice if Sofia had given me a little more warning, but that's not her style. In fact, she's incapable of being organised in any way. It drives me bonkers sometimes.' He clenched his jaw again as if he was tamping down some fairly strong emotions.

'It's not a problem. I'm sure it'll be fine.'

'I hope so. Sofia has a tendency to act on impulse, and now she seems to have booked some sort of holiday in India with a friend to learn meditation and stuff. Would have been nice if she'd checked with me first, but I don't think she quite understands that being on a dig isn't the same thing as a holiday.' He shrugged. 'Probably my fault, actually, as I always enjoy it so much it doesn't feel like hard work, and I've told her that. Still . . .'

'I see.' Mia didn't want to comment, since she didn't know Sofia, but it did seem a rather haphazard thing to do without consulting him first. They must have a very odd relationship. She could understand Haakon's frustration at having his daughter dumped on him in this fashion. 'Never mind. We'll have to try and occupy her as best we can.'

This proved to be less of a problem than Mia had thought. The little girl was apparently used to being left to her own devices and was quite happy to sit in a small tent that Haakon erected for her near the trenches, drawing or playing with her Barbie dolls and Game Boy. When she got bored, she chatted to Mia for ages, then took to following Ivar around, asking him endless questions. To everyone's surprise, the boy didn't seem to mind.

'She's all right,' he muttered when Mia enquired if Linnea was bothering him. 'Just lonely, I expect.'

Mia thought to herself that perhaps it took one to know one. She was pleased that he had the maturity and patience to put up with the little girl, instead of telling her to push off the way most boys of his age would have done. Although he was still absorbed in the excavation, he wasn't averse to taking time off, and Haakon happily gave him permission to take Linnea swimming in the lake.

'Just watch her at all times, please,' he said. 'I trust you to look after her.'

'Course I will. She's only little,' Ivar replied, as if that explained everything. And perhaps to him it did.

Haakon stared at the TV screen – only a fraction the size of the one he had at home, but still perfectly adequate – and tried not to move so much as a muscle. He and Mia had been sitting watching the news together on the two-seater sofa after Linnea had finally gone to bed, and sometime after the third news item Mia had fallen asleep leaning against him. Murmuring something, she'd wrapped one arm around his waist and made herself comfortable. He assumed she was dreaming of her fiancé and didn't want to disturb her.

No, stop kidding yourself. The truth was, he liked the sensation of having her snuggled against him.

It had been a long day and they'd worked hard, plus the hot sun made you extra tired. No wonder she was exhausted. Add to that having to cope with Linnea's chatter all afternoon. His daughter had taken to Mia straight away and had stayed in her vicinity, talking about everything under the sun. Haakon thought it was a wonder Mia's patience hadn't snapped after the first hour, let alone four or five.

She deserved to rest. And he didn't want her to let go of him yet.

The news had finished now and he should change the channel. There was a documentary on TV4 he'd prefer to watch, rather than the crime series just starting. Slowly he reached for the remote, but he wasn't stealthy enough. Mia stirred, then sat bolt upright and blinked.

'Oh! I'm so sorry, I . . . Did I nod off?'

Haakon smiled. 'Yep. You looked so angelic, I didn't have the heart to wake you. Besides, I owed you for entertaining my daughter all afternoon.'

'But I was . . .' She gestured at his stomach as if she couldn't even say the words.

'Cuddling me?' He grinned, in the mood to tease her a little. 'Yeah, I noticed.'

Her cheeks turned bright red. 'I didn't mean to. You should have shoved me away.' She pushed a strand of hair out of her eyes and behind her ear. 'God, how embarrassing. I hope I wasn't drooling, at least.'

'Nah, just snoring.'

Mia narrowed her eyes at him, then punched him lightly on the arm. 'Thanks a bunch.'

He laughed. 'Hey, just kidding. You didn't do anything other than breathe deeply, and I figured you needed the rest. No big deal.'

'Huh, well . . . thanks, I guess.'

'Feel free to hug me any time.'

He'd meant the words as a joke, but for a moment their eyes locked and Haakon held his breath. He could so easily have pulled her back and kissed her then. She did look eminently kissable, with her hair slightly mussed and her cheeks still tinged pink. But he didn't have the right to touch her. They were just friends and colleagues, and that was how it had to stay. She was engaged and she had a life in England. Her visit here was only temporary.

But when she scooted further away from him on the sofa, and soon afterwards fled upstairs, he couldn't help but feel bereft, and he wished she'd stayed asleep just a little bit longer.

Chapter Twenty-Two

Ceri had watched Haukr's departure with mixed feelings. Relief because she wouldn't be tormented by seeing him every day, and sadness for the same reason. She wondered if she was going mad and told herself not to be so ridiculous. He'd soon be back but he still wasn't for her.

It quickly dawned on her, however, that with him gone, she was decidedly vulnerable. The speculative looks Ragnhild sent her way made her uncomfortable, but she hoped the woman wouldn't make trouble for her in Haukr's absence. She also noticed Thorald watching both of them, which was a relief. Hopefully he would keep the peace at the farmstead in Haukr's absence.

But her misgivings proved well founded.

'Is the thrall Ceridwen in there?'

Ragnhild's cold voice could be heard loud and clear outside the weaving hut on the morning of the day after Haukr's departure, and Ceri stopped what she was doing, a frisson of fear snaking down her spine. Taking a deep breath, she squared her shoulders and went to the door. 'I'm here, lady.' She forbore to remind Ragnhild that she was not a thrall. No good could come of sparring with her, she was sure.

'Good. Then come to the stream with me, please.'

'The stream? But—'

'Just do as you're told for once,' Ragnhild snapped, grabbing Ceri's arm and marching her outside.

Jorun, who had been in the weaving hut with Ceri and Aase, started to follow them, but Ragnhild ordered Aase to keep the child out of the way. Ceri saw Aase hold on to Jorun, despite the girl's protests, but neither of them went back inside the hut.

When they reached the stream, Ragnhild's brothers were waiting for them, and Ceri's stomach began to churn uncomfortably. She looked around. Where was Thorald? Come to think of it, she hadn't seen him at all that morning. What had become of him?

'Now, take off that ring or we'll have to do it for you,' Ragnhild commanded.

'What?' Ceri blinked and returned her gaze to Haukr's wife.

'The gold ring, you stupid girl.' Ragnhild dealt Ceri a ringing blow to the cheek and pointed at her finger. 'It's winter now, so it should come off easily.'

Her brothers stood silently watching, arms crossed over powerful chests. Their eyes glinted with amusement and something else . . . Anticipation? Ceri shivered.

'Honestly, it doesn't come off. I told you, and even your husband tried, but—'

The blow to the side of her head came out of nowhere, or so it seemed. For a moment she saw double, and there were two Sveins in front of her eyes, but they soon merged into one smirking one. 'My sister gave you an order, thrall. Now obey her or it will be the worse for you.'

Ceri felt nausea rise in the back of her throat and a hammering inside her head, while one eye was rapidly closing up. Pain sliced through her, but she tried not to show it. She gritted her teeth and started tugging at the wretched ring. If she'd known it was going to cause so much trouble, she would have asked Haukr's blacksmith to cut it off for her. It still didn't budge.

'The water,' she heard Ragnhild order.

In the next instant, she was lifted off her feet and suspended over the edge of the stream, while one of the brothers pushed her hand into a small opening in the ice where the water still flowed. Ceri's fingers went numb almost instantly, and a strange pain spread up into her arm, as if the marrow inside her bone was freezing too. Just as her skin was turning a bluey-white colour and she thought the entire hand would surely fall off, she was pulled back out, but her tormentors weren't finished.

Svein took hold of the ring and tried to lever it off her finger. He was far from gentle, however, and it felt as though he was pulling the entire finger away from the rest of her hand. Ceri cried out as he twisted and turned, jiggled and pushed until the ring moved a little bit.

'Go on, you almost have it,' Ragnhild encouraged him.

'Can't you ask the smith to just cut it off?' Ceri hissed, gritting her teeth. 'It would be faster.'

'And ruin the shape of it? I think not.' Ragnhild's smile was not a nice one.

Ceri's hand felt as though it was on fire now, and she tried to fight Svein off, but the other brother had her in a firm grip and kept her virtually immobile. Svein carried on, and she knew he wasn't going to stop until he had that ring. She began to pray, in her head at first, then out loud. The priest at home had told them stories about martyrs who endured much worse than this; surely if she prayed to God, he would help her through this suffering?

'Þegi þú!' Another slap from Ragnhild, but Ceri refused to shut up and continued muttering prayers.

She vaguely noticed people watching from a distance, but no one came to her aid. Where was Thorald? Had they bribed him to turn a blind eye? Or perhaps he just didn't care. Ceri was no one after all, even if Haukr claimed she would bring them a large ransom sum.

After what seemed like an eternity, and several more dips in the stream, Svein finally succeeded in scraping the ring off her finger, taking a goodly amount of skin and flesh with it at the same time. But she was past caring, happy to be rid of it. As a final act of malice, he broke her finger with a loud snap, but her hand was so cold and numb from the repeated dunkings that she hardly noticed.

'Lock her in one of the thralls' huts,' Ragnhild ordered. Ceri saw the woman put the gold ring on her smallest finger after her brother had washed off the blood. 'And make sure she stays there.'

Ceri was dragged away, and before she was shoved into a hut, Svein hit her again, on the same side as before. 'That'll teach you to do as you're told,' he snarled. Looking at the frightened faces inside the hut, he added, 'Don't even think about helping her in any way, or you'll receive worse yourselves.'

The door was slammed shut and everything went dark.

Svein's words notwithstanding, Ceri felt hands reaching out to help her to a straw mattress. Her legs gave way and she lay down, allowing darkness to claim her.

At least that way she couldn't feel any pain as the blood rushed back into her numb hand.

'Did I not make myself clear? I believe I told you that Ceridwen was to keep her ring until I said otherwise. Give it to me.'

Haukr was so angry, it was as if the flames of Hel were burning him up from inside, but he managed to keep his voice calm and deadly. Ragnhild jumped and looked up. She obviously hadn't expected him back so soon; indeed, he was a whole day early by normal standards. But he'd been eager to return, and although he'd told himself it was only because he wanted to be back in his own home, he knew now that he'd been spurred on by a niggling feeling that something bad would happen. And it had.

She was lounging in Haukr's carved chair – usually reserved for his exclusive use – looking relaxed and happy, with her brothers on either side of her. The three of them had been murmuring together and laughing while sipping ale from the finest drinking horns, which were normally only brought out for special occasions. There was a dish of little honey cakes to go with it – a rare treat, as honey was hard to come by. Ragnhild straightened up and swallowed visibly, then made a fist, concealing the ring on her little finger, but Haukr had already seen it.

'Now, *víf*!'

Presumably she'd intended to hide it before he came back, and now he had surprised her in possession of it. Not one to back down, however, she tossed her head.

'And I told you that it was dangerous to allow a thrall . . .' at his intense glare, she amended her words, 'very well, a hostage, to keep such a thing. Why, she could skate to Birka at any time under cover of darkness and buy passage home.'

Haukr ignored her protest and the dark looks of the two brothers flanking her. 'I believe I also told you that if anyone other than Ceridwen was found in possession of that ring, they would be flogged to within an inch of their life. Come outside, please.'

'What? You can't be serious!' Ragnhild went pale, but then smiled when she remembered her brothers. 'No, of course not.'

'I assure you, I am perfectly serious. And whoever it was that harmed my hostage will also feel the force of my wrath.' He looked from one brother to the other. 'This is my domain and I am the only one who raises a hand to my thralls, servants or hostages here.'

'Haukr, be reasonable. The woman was disrespectful. She

needed to be taught a lesson. If you're too weak to administer justice, like Ragnhild told us—'

Haukr interrupted his brother-in-law with a roar of fury and surged forward to grab the front of the man's tunic in his fist. Almost nose to nose, he shouted, 'I. Am. Not. WEAK! Understand? Come outside and I will show you!'

Svein held up his hands. 'Very well. I take it back and I apologise if I did anything wrong. It was my belief that my sister was in charge here in your absence, and my duty was to follow her orders.'

Haukr let go of him and stepped back, trying to calm his breathing. He looked Ragnhild in the eye and held out his hand. Glaring back, she tugged the ring off her finger and slapped it into his palm. 'Such an overreaction for a silly little trinket. I hope she's worth it.'

'Ragnhild, I want you to swear a blood oath that you will not touch Ceridwen again. It's that or the flogging. Which is it to be?'

She gasped as if outraged, but he held his hand up to forestall any arguments. 'I don't care what the circumstances are. Even if she kills someone and I'm not here, I wish to be the one sitting in judgement of her, is that clear? It is my right as head of this household.'

'This is ridiculous. She is a captive, a nobody, and I am your wife. I'm in charge whenever you are away and—'

'*Enough!*' Haukr slammed his fist into the table, making the plate of delicate cakes tip into her lap. She exclaimed in disgust but kept her eyes on him. 'You will do as I say or I swear on Thor's hammer that you will be the one punished. I have had enough of your little games, do you understand? You have your duties and I have mine. Mistreating my hostage is not within your remit. Now let's go outside to the sacred ash grove. Where's Thorald? I want him to act as witness, make sure it's done properly.'

'Thorald is . . . indisposed.' Svein smirked and nodded towards one of the benches in a corner of the hall, where Haukr now saw his right-hand man slumped in a stupor. That was most unlike him, but he would deal with it later.

'Very well. Steinn! Ulv! To me.'

He allowed Ragnhild to put on a warm cloak, then led her away, holding her arm in a grip that was none too gentle. He heard her muttering under her breath, but he was past caring. This had to stop. Ragnhild had to be made to see that she had gone too far and that his authority could not be challenged. Once she'd sworn the oath, he could rest easy, because even she wouldn't dare break that. It was sacred to the gods and binding.

As, unfortunately, were his marriage vows.

Ceri woke to the sound of a door opening. She blinked against the light from a small oil lamp but didn't immediately recognise her surroundings. It didn't matter, though. She was on a narrow bench in a small hut, with a straw mattress underneath her and surrounded by warm soft furs, and her hand wasn't throbbing quite as much as before. Neither was her head; there was just a dull ache somewhere below her left eye. It was bearable. And she was safe.

'Ceridwen? Are you awake?' To her surprise Haukr sank down beside her and took her good hand. 'Forgive me. That was incredibly stupid of me.'

'What was? Making your wife swear a blood oath?' Now she vaguely recalled waking earlier and Aase telling her what had happened in the hall. Apparently Ragnhild had been in a foul mood afterwards, but she'd had the sense not to voice her anger for once.

Haukr smiled gently and touched her bruised cheek with soft fingers. 'No, I meant that I shouldn't have left you here without supervision. I should have known Ragnhild would try something.'

'But Thorald . . . ?'

'Was given a sleeping potion. At least that is my guess. Svein claimed they'd all been drinking too much last night, but I have never known my friend to have a sore head for an entire day. Not to the point that he couldn't wake up, at any rate.' He frowned. 'Ragnhild must have known he would stop her and her brothers from harming you.'

'She really doesn't like me, does she?' Ceri sighed. 'The sooner I'm ransomed, the better.' And yet, despite what had happened this day, she was not looking forward to the spring as much as she ought to . . .

'Ragnhild doesn't like anyone who stands up to her, and you did, on your very first day here.' Haukr shook his head. 'She also accused me of having slept with you when she was visiting her father. She said you'd been seen in my bed. I have no idea who told her, but I informed her that Jorun was with us and it was entirely innocent.' He shrugged. 'I'm not sure she believed me, though.'

Ceri felt her cheeks heat up. 'Well, that won't happen again.'

He smiled once more, but teasingly this time. 'Ah, but I was hoping it would.'

Ceri couldn't tell him that she did too, so she kept quiet.

He must have taken her silence as a reprimand, because he held up a hand. 'I know, I know, I shouldn't even mention that. It is not to be, but a man can dream. And no matter what, I will always dream of you, Ceri. If that is wrong of me, so be it.'

Ceri closed her eyes as he took her hand again and squeezed it gently. A woman could dream too, but he had a wife and there was nothing they could do about it. Not that he had mentioned anything about marriage. He probably just wanted to bed her, but he had said the choice was hers and she refused to be any man's plaything. 'Haukr, don't—'

'Shh, I won't mention it again, I swear. But . . . when I was in Birka, I bought a silver arm ring I'd intended for Ragnhild, and one for you as well. She doesn't deserve hers now and I want you to have them both. Will you accept them as a gift from me?' He dipped his head as if he was unsure, which seemed most unlike him, then held out his hand, palm up. Two slim bands made of plaited silver strands lay there. It was good craftsmanship, she could see that. 'It might sound stupid, but perhaps you'll remember me in future when you look at these, as I will always remember you. Here, let's see if they fit.'

'No, I shouldn't. It's not right . . .'

She tried to pull away, but he took her good hand and threaded the arm rings on to her wrist. 'They are mere trinkets. There, perfect.' He held on to her hand, lingering slightly longer than he should before letting go. 'Oh, and here's your gold ring. I took it back from Ragnhild.'

The arm rings looked new and shiny, unlike her mother's ring, which was now somewhat mangled from Svein's clumsy attempts to remove it. Ceri took it and put it on her little finger so that it could easily be removed in future if necessary. It seemed wrong to accept gifts from Haukr, but they weren't very costly and it would be all she had to remember him by. Besides, he had taken much more from her family – she could look at them as part repayment perhaps. Yes, he definitely owed her, both for that and for Ragnhild's mistreatment of her. She looked up at him. 'Thank you, they're beautiful.' She didn't tell him they would always make her think of him. That was best left unsaid. 'But if you don't mind, I'll hide them for now, just in case . . .' She didn't want to put her fear into words, but he nodded his understanding.

'Of course. Rest now. You are in Aase's hut and I want you to stay here until you are fully healed. Just one thing . . . Would you mind if Jorun joins you? She's been frantic with worry and wants to be with you.'

'Yes, I would love to have her here.'

When, sometime later, the small body of Haukr's daughter snuggled down beside her, Ceri told herself to be content with that and the beautiful arm rings. Anything else was impossible.

Chapter Twenty-Three

'You're going where?' Mia almost did that classic thing of removing the phone from her ear to look at it in disbelief, but caught herself in time. 'Ayia Napa? Seriously?'

'What's wrong with that? It's cheap and lots of fun, or so I'm told. The lads went there year before last. Had a ball.' Charles sounded defensive but determinedly upbeat. 'You said I should go on holiday with my mates, and now I am.'

'Yes. Right.' Mia wasn't sure what to say. He hadn't mentioned it two days ago when they were together, but then he'd had a massive hangover the entire Sunday and hadn't really done much more than grunt for most of it. But . . . Ayia Napa? On an 18–30 holiday? He was turning thirty in less than two months, so wasn't he a bit old for that? But she had a feeling he was just trying to punish her, and to be fair, she had gone to Sweden without really consulting him. Perhaps she owed him this. 'Well, I hope you have fun. I'm surprised you got time off work when you're so busy at the moment.'

'Oh, I booked it ages ago. Didn't I say?'

'No. No, you didn't.' But did it matter? 'When are you leaving?'

'Weekend after next.'

'OK, well, I'll talk to you before you go then. Bye for now.'

As she hung up, she had much food for thought. The fact that she didn't really care this time about him going on a lads' holiday was yet another sign that something was very wrong with their relationship. She needed to mull this over.

Slightly later than usual, she headed out of the cottage, and as she closed the door, her ring caught her attention. She remembered her intention to check out the inscription again – with everything that had been happening since her return, she'd forgotten. She'd have a look at it now.

'Haakon, I'm just going to check something out,' she called to him as he passed with a wheelbarrow and a bunch of equipment. 'I'll be with you shortly.'

Inside the little caravan, she took off the ring and held it under the microscope to study the inscription. Definitely an E and an R, and at the end, that could be an I. Unless it was just part of another letter with something missing? There were plenty of runes that had a single line as part of their configuration, but as far as Mia could see, there was no indication that anything else had been etched in next to it here.

So ERI for sure.

Taking a deep breath, she turned her attention to the beginning of the word, trying to make out the first letter. The ring was worn smooth there, and the inscription was very faint, but she'd swear it was a K. The K rune was the shape of a V but turned clockwise on its side. A couple of other runes had that as part of their make-up, but again, she couldn't see any trace of anything else around this one.

KERI.

The name reverberated inside her and Mia shivered, sitting back in the chair. Out of nowhere, some images flashed through her mind . . . *a large hand pushing the snake ring on to the fourth finger of her left hand, blue eyes gazing at her with desire burning in their depths, soft wolf pelts surrounding her and a small fire crackling nearby . . .*

She drew in a sharp breath. Bloody hell.

Grabbing the ring, she sprinted out of the caravan and went in search of Haakon. When she found him, she grabbed his arm. 'Haakon, can you come and look at something under the microscope, please?'

'What? Now?' He was covered in dust and his hands were dirty, but he must have seen the urgency in her expression. 'Oh, OK. Coming.'

When she told him what she could see and asked for his opinion, he took the ring and studied it the same way she had done. Then he looked up and nodded. 'Yep, I think you're right. So this could have belonged to the woman who owned the comb? Extraordinary!'

'Yes. Maybe there's something to your theory after all. She must have been highly valued for . . . well, whatever.' She saw those blue eyes again, burning with lust. Had he been trying to buy this Ceri's favours and she was refusing? Did she succumb after receiving such a magnificent gift? They'd never know.

Haakon handed back the ring and she slid it on to her own finger again, triggering the familiar frisson of awareness. Ceri, whoever she'd been, was trying to tell her something, but she wasn't sure she wanted to know.

'Come on, time to get some fresh air, I think.' Haakon ushered her out of the caravan. 'You're so pale you look like you've seen a ghost.'

Well, maybe she had.

As Haakon led the way outside, Tomas came running from across the road. Although part of the team were still working on the longhouse trenches and some of the other, lesser, buildings on and around the hill, a couple of archaeologists had also opened up a trench to check out the two mounds they'd seen on the aerial photos. Now that Mia's solicitor had confirmed the area was part of her property, there was no problem about digging there.

'Hey, guys, you need to come and see this!' Tomas's face shone with excitement, and he was out of breath, as if he'd been running the whole way. 'I think we're really on to something.'

'Oh yeah? What have you found?'

But Tomas refused to say; he just smiled.

Haakon and Mia followed him into the forest on the other side of the road, a dense area of trees that covered most of the rest of the property. The two mounds were situated in a natural clearing, with a small stream nearby. It was the same waterway as the one that passed the settlement, which made sense, and Haakon had noticed there was an old bridge where the road crossed the water.

'We started with the larger one, like you guys said,' Tomas began. They'd had a site meeting where Mia and Haakon had both agreed that would be best. 'And we've already come across some very interesting things, even though we're only halfway in. Come and look.'

Isabella and Anders were busy scraping away soil, but they both stood up and beamed as Tomas pointed to an item lying in a box, half hidden by bubble wrap. Haakon drew in a sharp breath. 'A sword? Seriously?'

He bent to study it in more detail, and although it was massively corroded, there was no mistaking the Viking-style hilt and the sheer length of the weapon, which made it so distinctive. 'Wow, this is amazing! So this is the grave of a warrior or someone high-born?'

'We think so, although we've only come across animal bones so far. A horse by the look of it. The sword may have been dislodged slightly. We'll keep digging, though.' Tomas was still grinning and Haakon smiled back. This was fantastic, exactly what he'd hoped for.

He touched the sword hilt with reverence and something tingled inside him. Closing his eyes, it felt as though he was transported back to the time of its owner. *He watched as the dead man was carried to his final resting place, then heard chanting and the loud neighing of the man's horse as it was killed in order to follow its master to the afterlife. He breathed in sharply and smelled the iron tang of blood in the air, the smoke from torches held aloft and the musty aroma of wet wool from people's clothing. The torches touched the funeral pyre and the flames took hold, soaring into the sky. He heard weeping but felt no sorrow himself, only relief . . .* He opened his eyes, disorientated for a second, before pulling his hand away. Now why hadn't he been sad? He shook his head. *Duh!* It wasn't real, just his imagination, obviously. He hadn't slept very well since Linnea arrived, so he must be tired.

He stood up and tried to concentrate on the here and now. 'Any dating materials?'

'Yes, actually. An Anglo-Saxon coin from the reign of Æthelwulf of Wessex, so the 840s or 50s maybe? Although I suppose the grave, if that's what it is, could be later.'

'OK, great! Well, keep digging and let us know what else you find. Do you need our help?'

'No, the three of us is enough, I think. It would be too crowded otherwise.'

Tomas joined the others in the trench and continued where he'd left off as Haakon and Mia walked back towards the cottage. 'So a possible grave from the early or middle part of the ninth century,' he commented. 'Now we're really getting somewhere.'

'Yes, that's wonderful! I've no idea why we never realised it was there. Gran and I used to go picking mushrooms in that forest, but I guess those mounds never stood out much. Either that, or she didn't point them out to me. She was very protective of the past.'

'I suppose one could easily walk past them and think nothing of it.' Haakon was pleased they were making such good progress, but at the same time he felt weirdly restless.

'Are we continuing up on the hill?' Mia's face had by now returned to its normal colour – slightly tanned, with an ever-growing number of freckles across her nose and cheeks. They were almost irresistible, it had to be said, but Haakon tried not to notice.

'We could, but I'm happy to leave that to the others. I . . . OK, this is going to sound weird, but I just have this feeling we're meant to be looking somewhere else. That we're missing something.' He shook his head. 'I know, I've probably been out in the sun too much, and I'm not sleeping well, but there's this niggling at the back of my mind . . .'

Mia put a hand on his arm to stop him. 'No, I don't think you're crazy, because I feel the same. It's like I'm restless. Have ants in my pants. Well, not literally, but you know what I mean.'

'Yeah, that's it exactly! Phew, I'm glad it's not just me.' He smiled. 'OK, let's say we go with our gut reaction – where to?'

'Let's close our eyes and listen. I don't know about you, but I'm getting some sort of vibes from this place and maybe they'll tell us where to dig. Back there at the mound . . .' She shook her head. 'No, it was probably nothing. We should go and have a look at the site map and geophys results and—'

But Haakon interrupted her. 'Chanting? The sounds of a horse being killed? And weird smells?' He stared at Mia and her head snapped up.

'You heard it too? Oh my God . . . What's going on here?'

'I don't know, but I think we have to just go with it for now. Not that we seem to have a choice, but still . . .'

They stopped at the back of the house, facing the lake, and Haakon hesitated for a moment, then reached out to take Mia's hand. She didn't resist, her fingers closing around his. 'Let's see if it happens again.' He closed his eyes and breathed deeply, calming his heartbeat while he strained to listen. Was he mad? But it felt so right.

At first he heard nothing but the sighing of the wind in the nearby trees and the little waves lapping at the shore and jetty. There were distant voices from the hill, bursts of laughter, sounds of scraping. Surreal. Faint, as though his ears were stuffed with cotton wool. Then, subtly, the sounds changed, became indistinct, then clearer. Inside Haakon's head, images exploded into his brain. *A gathering by the shore, a group of men grunting and heaving, trying to pull a huge stone into a hole that would keep it upright. Women and children chattering and commenting, pointing at the fabulous carving on the front of the stone, painted dark red and black. A snake drawn around the perimeter with a message written in runes . . .*

Abruptly he opened his eyes. It was as if someone had smacked him on the back of the head, and he blinked at Mia. Her eyes, an extraordinary clear grey in the bright sunlight, were enormous.

'Did . . . did you see that?' she asked.

He felt her hand shaking in his and squeezed her fingers. 'A rune stone? Yes.'

She nodded. 'Bloody hell.' Pulling her hand away, she ran her fingers through her unruly hair. 'What is happening? I'm a bit scared, to be honest. It's like we're being haunted. I mean, I don't even know why I suggested we should try this. That thought just sort of came to me, as if . . .' She swallowed visibly.

'As if someone else put it in your head?' Haakon nodded. 'I know. But if there really are spirits here, then they're helping us, so I don't think we need to be afraid.' He pointed towards the shore. 'What we should be doing is digging down there. Didn't Tomas identify a huge anomaly under that little grassy hill? Let's see if it's the stone.'

'OK, but if it is, I might just freak out totally – you've been warned.'

Haakon laughed. 'I'll happily deal with that for the sake of finding a previously unknown rune stone.'

That would just be incredible.

Chapter Twenty-Four

The *völva* Gudrun – a wise woman or seeress of some sort – arrived in the middle of January, just before the midwinter *blōt*, or Yule, as it was also called. Aase told Ceri that there was usually feasting at this time of year, together with sacrificial offerings to the gods in the sacred grove in the forest near the farmstead. The Norse people also put out food for their ancestors, as well as to appease magical creatures that Aase called wights and gnomes. Ceri crossed herself at the thought of such strange practices, which made the older woman smile.

'You might need to call on their help one day, so I would add something if I were you,' she advised.

Ceri reluctantly placed an oatcake on one of the plates – it probably wouldn't hurt to be on the safe side, even if it went against her own beliefs. And someone – whether it was her own god or theirs – had been looking out for her that time her finger was broken, because it had healed well and was back to normal again.

She assumed Gudrun had come to conduct the proceedings in the grove, but as she didn't want anything to do with heathen rituals, she stayed well away from the woman.

Gudrun was old and bent, but with an agility that belied her age and a surprisingly sharp gaze that appeared to miss nothing. Her eyes were a watery blue that darkened noticeably when she stared at you, something Ceri found disconcerting. It was as if those orbs could see straight into her soul and discover her innermost secrets, then hold her to account for her sinful thoughts.

It made her shudder and cross herself again surreptitiously.

Haukr was out ice-fishing with some of his men when Gudrun came shuffling up the hill, having arrived on foot and alone, and therefore presumably didn't notice the newcomer until the evening meal. From her usual position one seat away from him, Ceri heard him draw in a breath of surprise as he caught sight of the old woman entering his hall.

'What is she doing here?' he hissed at his wife, which seemed to indicate he hadn't been the one to invite Gudrun. He and Ragnhild had stopped bickering at the table and mostly ignored each other since the ring incident, so Ceri was surprised to hear them talk at all.

'Oh, she was at my father's side when he passed away in the autumn, and I spoke with her at length about . . . well, about our situation. I asked her to come here if she was free to help with the midwinter *blót*.'

'We don't need assistance. Old Tyra has always managed well enough.'

'Ah, but that's just it – she is getting too old. Her legs barely carry her when the weather is so cold, and her memory is fading. We need someone who can really invoke the gods' help on our behalf. I don't think they can hear Tyra any more, and I have waited long enough for another child.'

'There's nothing wrong with either Tyra's memory or her voice,' Haukr protested, 'and unlike her, Gudrun will need to be paid for her services. Dearly.'

But Ragnhild carried on as if she hadn't heard him. 'Gudrun

has advised us to sacrifice one animal of each kind, especially a horse and a pig, and then add a male thrall to make sure the gods really take notice. We've been too lax in the past few years – no wonder I haven't conceived again.'

There was a curious mixture of pain and patience in Haukr's voice when he replied. 'Ragnhild, you know as well as I do that it was something to do with Jorun's birth. Tyra said so and—'

'It's been five years. More than enough time for my body to heal.' Ragnhild's voice was waspish, with a hint of desperation, and Ceri couldn't help but feel for the woman. Her longing for another child was obviously strong to the point of obsession. Being barren was a terrible blow for any woman, and especially so for the wife of a jarl who needed heirs. Enough for her to contemplate sacrificing precious animals . . . and a thrall? Dear God, no, that couldn't be right.

'I can't spare any of the horses.' Haukr's tone was brusque. 'And we are certainly not sacrificing any humans, thrall or not. We need them to work the land.'

Out of the corner of her eye, Ceri saw Ragnhild turn towards her husband, a pleading look in her eyes. 'Haukr, please, it may be the only way! We have to try, don't you see? If we can just make the gods listen . . .'

'No.' Haukr put his hand over Ragnhild's, which was lying on the table. 'I'm sorry, but I don't believe it will help. The gods have already made their decision, else you would have conceived before now. We have to accept that there is nothing to be done.'

'You just don't want it enough.' Ragnhild's eyes flashed accusingly as she pulled her hand away. 'Are you really going to be satisfied with one daughter who is tainted by *trolldomr*? Witless? Or are you planning to have children with someone other than me?'

Haukr sighed. 'Ragnhild, can we talk about this in private?'

'No!' She slapped the palm of her hand on the table. 'I don't care if the entire world is listening, I want your agreement to Gudrun's suggestions now or I'll let everyone know you care nothing for me or for the future of your holdings.'

'That is not true. The future is secure. Jorun will marry well and give us grandchildren, I'm sure. Just look at her – she is already pretty and will grow into a beauty like her mother.'

The child's mother ignored the compliment and considered her with disparaging eyes. Ceri looked away, sad on Jorun's behalf. 'What does it matter how she looks if she's a halfwit?'

'She's not! Listen, Ceri has been teaching Jorun to speak. She can say a few words already and will learn more as time goes on.' Haukr smiled at his daughter, who had paused in her eating and was staring wide-eyed at her parents, obviously aware that something was going on. 'We were going to wait a little longer to tell you, make it a surprise, but you may as well know now.'

'A likely tale,' Ragnhild scoffed.

'No, it's true,' Haukr insisted. 'Jorun *mín*, say Mother.'

Ceri and Haukr had taught Jorun to call Ragnhild 'Mother', although Ceri had a suspicion the child didn't understand the concept of motherhood and just thought it was Ragnhild's name.

Jorun looked away and didn't reply. Haukr touched her shoulder and tried an even bigger smile on her. 'Please? Say Mother.' He pointed at Ragnhild and repeated the word several times, but Jorun – for reasons only known to herself – refused to even acknowledge that she'd understood.

'See? You're wrong. She's as stupid as she's always been.' Ragnhild's frown made Jorun bury her head in Ceri's lap while making some incoherent noise.

'Perhaps if you smile at her?' Ceri suggested. 'She's intimidated by, er . . . fierce expressions.'

But Ragnhild wasn't listening. She had turned back to Haukr

and resumed their earlier conversation as if Jorun was unimportant. Poking him in the chest, she demanded, 'One horse, one bullock, one pig and a male thrall, as well as five other animals. That is what I need. Nine sacrificial offerings, worthy of the gods. It's what is required if you want sons. Now, are you coming with me to greet Gudrun and treat her with the reverence she is entitled to?'

Haukr threw one last despairing look at his daughter, as if wishing Jorun hadn't decided to be disobedient at this particular time, then stood up and followed Ragnhild to the door. Gudrun was led to a seat at a table opposite Haukr's and shown every courtesy. Ceri gathered she was considered powerful and special, and even Haukr, who didn't seem to want the woman here, didn't dare be impolite.

But would he allow the sacrifices to go ahead?

Haukr would happily have sacrificed whatever it took in order for his wife to bear him more children, but he had known and trusted Old Tyra since childhood and believed what she'd told him – something had gone seriously wrong during Jorun's birth and there was no way Ragnhild could ever conceive again. She'd been lucky to even survive. It was therefore madness to encourage her to think that Gudrun was right and all they needed to do was appeal more strongly to the gods. Even deities couldn't help someone who was broken on the inside.

It would be like asking them to heal a scar – an impossibility.

Troubled, he sought out Ceri and Jorun the next day in the weaving hut; Aase tactfully scurried off on some errand to leave them alone. 'Would your god be able to heal something that was irreversibly broken?' he asked. He and Ceri had spoken a few more times about her beliefs, and although he was convinced his own gods were stronger, he didn't mind her praying to the

Christian one. It was just one more; what could it hurt?

'Well, the Lord's son did miraculously raise someone from the dead, or so I was told, but only the once. And I assume you would need God or his son to actually be present, but . . . perhaps it's not entirely impossible.'

Haukr sighed. 'I don't think there's any hope, but Ragnhild won't let it go.' He rubbed his face, closing his eyes. The strife was wearing him down, eating him up from inside. He just wanted peace. A quiet life.

'Does that mean you'll allow her to go ahead with the sacrifices?' Ceri's expression told him she was appalled, her grey gaze troubled, and although he didn't see anything wrong with such rituals, he'd met enough Christians to know they didn't condone killing of any kind.

'Some of them. It is our custom, after all, and I will let her and Gudrun slaughter the largest pig and a bullock, but no horses and definitely not any of the thralls. It would be in vain, a waste.'

'You mean you would have allowed it if you could spare them? That is . . . that is despicable!' Ceri's eyes were shooting angry sparks at him.

At times like this, Haukr realised that there were profound differences between them, and he had no idea how to bridge the gap. 'You don't understand . . .'

'Oh, believe me, I do. Your gods demand bloodshed and you think nothing of killing any creature, be it animal or human. How many of my fellow villagers were murdered the night you took the rest of us captive?'

'None, I swear. They might have been injured while resisting us, but no one died. I do not kill for the joy of it, Ceri, the way some men are wont to do.'

She bent over her carding, refusing to look at him.

'Ceridwen, what do you want me to say? I am but following my ancestors' ways. Is that so wrong?'

'It is when it involves taking someone's life.'

'I told you, no one is to die apart from the animals. They would have been slaughtered at some point anyway, and it may as well be now. It'll save on fodder.'

'Thank the Lord . . .' The words were a mere whisper, but Haukr heard them.

'No, thank *me*,' he tried to joke, then held up both hands. 'Yes, yes, I know, it's just an expression. Will you attend our ritual? Perhaps our gods will help you return to your homeland more quickly.' Although to tell the truth, he didn't want her to leave. He would miss her terribly, and so would Jorun.

Ceri shook her head. 'No, thank you. I will trust to my own god for that. He looks after his flock. Perhaps if you were to pray to him as well, he might help you.'

'I suppose it wouldn't hurt.'

He was disappointed, as he'd wanted her to be present for the midwinter *blót*, but he would never force her.

That afternoon, most of the inhabitants of the farmstead gathered in the sacred grove. It was a clearing surrounded by huge trees – some ash, some oak, as well as fir and pine. Gudrun was dressed in a black cloak that shimmered with some sort of crystals sewn into it, and she held an iron staff in one hand to show her importance. Haukr held back a grimace. He didn't like her, but he had tried not to show it, as it wouldn't do to offend anyone who had the ear of the gods. It had taken him ages to placate Old Tyra, whose nose was firmly out of joint at being usurped in this manner, by saying he'd make sure Gudrun didn't come back next year, and he fully intended to keep that promise.

The midwinter *blót* ritual involved killing the selected animals, splashing everyone with their blood, and then stringing up the carcasses in an ash tree while chanting incantations to the gods. Later they would be taken down and the meat eaten. It was a messy business, but everyone was used to the autumn slaughter so no one batted an eyelid. Besides, it was necessary for the continued prosperity of the farm.

'I call upon you, mighty Odin, Freyr, Thor and Freyja, to help the people of this place – protect them, increase their crops, keep them and their animals healthy . . .' Gudrun went on at some length in the same vein, finishing with, 'And I especially entreat you to look favourably upon Ragnhild, mistress of this household. Make her fruitful and happy. Help her to conceive, we beg of you.'

Ragnhild was splashed with extra amounts of sacrificial blood and Haukr watched the expression on his wife's face – determination, desperation and an iron will. But none of those things would help her, and a great sadness welled up inside him. Their lives could have been so different if only little Olaf had survived and Jorun was like other children . . . But what was the use of repining? If he had learned one thing, it was that you made the best of what you had. Unfortunately, that was not Ragnhild's way.

'To the feast!' The cry was taken up by everyone as the ritual came to an end.

As jarl, Haukr led the way back to the hall. Having spotted Jorun lurking at the edge of the crowd, he picked her up and settled her on his shoulders, prancing like a horse. She laughed out loud, seemingly unfazed by the slaughter she must have witnessed. As they reached their seats at the trestles, however, she wriggled out of his grip and rushed to join Ceri as soon as he put her down. Haukr saw the two of them having some sort of strange conversation by means of a combination of words and gestures, but when Ragnhild and the others arrived, Jorun grew silent.

Would she ever speak to her mother?

And Ceri, had she accepted that he was only doing what was best for everyone? If they had not held the *blōt*, he would have been shirking his duties. He was responsible for the well-being of every single person here, and they needed the protection of the gods. Surely she must understand that?

He threw her an uncertain glance and raised his eyebrows in an unspoken question. In return, he received a shrug and a small smile, by which he surmised she was not angry at least. Perhaps that was the best he could hope for, even if he wanted so much more.

Chapter Twenty-Five

'This little hillock gave off quite a strong signal when Tomas surveyed it. There was definitely something inside. Could just be natural bedrock, but I'd bet my last *krona* it's the jarl's rune stone.'

They were standing on the promontory that pointed towards the island, and Mia laughed. 'The jarl's? I think your imagination is running away with you.'

Haakon grinned. 'I like to think of the owner of all this as a jarl, someone with authority striding about the place. And if he died or had done something heroic, they'd definitely raise a rune stone down here in his honour. It's the most prominent place. Let's go and get our equipment. Ivar can come too. He must be bored with looking after Linnea by now.'

Ivar had very kindly offered to occupy the little girl for a while, but he did look relieved when they found him and asked him to come and help open a trench. He and Linnea followed them to the promontory, and Haakon set to work, using a strimmer at first to remove the long grass that grew on top of the small mound. That done, he picked up a spade and positioned it to cut through the turf, but when he pushed with his boot, there was a clang as if the metal had struck something hard, and he pulled it out again.

'There's something in the way. Sounded like stone.' He grinned at Mia, and she felt an answering smile stretch her mouth. This was insane. No normal archaeologist ever dug somewhere because some sort of spirit had told him to. But so far they seemed to be on the right track.

Haakon managed to remove the top layer of grass. 'Right, now we'll have to do the rest the hard way, on our hands and knees.'

The three of them knelt down with small trowels and began to scrape away the soil. Linnea danced around nearby, picking flowers and singing to herself. She seemed content just to watch them, which was just as well. Ivar had by now been taught the correct technique for excavating – though Haakon still kept an eye on him to make sure he did it right – but Mia wouldn't have wanted a six year old to have a go.

It soon became clear that there was indeed stone not far underneath the surface, but it wasn't natural bedrock. Instead it seemed curiously smooth and flat. Mia's stomach did a somersault of anticipation. Could it really be ... ?

'Hmm, interesting,' Haakon muttered.

They kept on trowelling until they had exposed a section about two feet in diameter, then Haakon brushed the stone with a large soft brush. Mia and Ivar stopped working and watched him.

'You're sure that's not just an ordinary stone that's ended up with soil on top of it?' Mia peered at it, but Haakon pointed to the surface of the rock.

'Nope. Look, those are chisel marks. This stone has been cut or dressed somehow, although I can't see why, as there are no carvings or anything. Unless ...' He stood up and looked at it with his head to one side. 'What if this is the back?'

'You mean it's a stone that's fallen over? Like a monument or something?' Ivar's face lit up. They hadn't told him of their weird vision; for him, this came as a surprise. 'Awesome! We need to see what's on the other side.' He rushed forward, ready to dig around the edges.

'Whoa, take it easy! We can't rush this, and there's a special way of doing it.' Haakon smiled. 'I'll go and get some of the others – this needs a lot more manpower. Besides, it could be exciting, and the longhouse can wait.'

An hour later, through joint effort, a large stone had been exposed, about eight feet high by four wide. It was flattish and tilted forward as if it had fallen face down. 'Right, we need to turn this over,' Haakon said. 'I'm dying to see what's on the other side.'

Mia had a tingling feeling in her veins and was sure Haakon did too. She could still picture the stone in her mind. But it was proof they needed, not imagination.

'Can anyone see any cracks?' he continued. 'I don't want it breaking into pieces.'

They all studied it, but it appeared to be intact. 'No cracks.' Daniel, an archaeology student with a blond ponytail, looked up at Haakon. 'Shall I fetch some planks to put underneath?'

'Yes, and some of the other timber we brought, please. We need to excavate tunnels at intervals and insert planks as support, then build a sort of wooden cage around it before moving it.' Haakon glanced at Mia, who was entranced. 'Do you agree? Or is it too risky?'

'Huh? No, it looks fine to me. As good as new, almost.' She could see the excitement in his eyes and it fuelled her own.

'OK, let's do this.'

It seemed to take for ever, but eventually a frame had been built around the stone so that it would be supported in every way. All the other members of the team were called down to help, and on the count of three, they slowly turned it over, inch by inch, all the time checking for possible cracking or damage.

'It's doing fine, isn't it?' Mia didn't want to be responsible for breaking whatever this turned out to be. It must have been buried for a long time.

'Yes, can't see anything wrong with it.'

'Nearly there, watch your feet, everyone!'

The stone was carefully lowered to the ground again, face up, and there were cheers, clapping and even some wolf whistles. This was an amazing find, no doubt about it.

'Whoa, would you look at that!'

There was soil clinging to the face of the stone, but in places a pattern etched into the surface was clearly visible.

'Runes! Yessss!' There were delighted exclamations, with people jumping up and down and slapping each other on the back.

Mia was sure she was grinning from ear to ear. She couldn't believe this had been found on her land and that it had been here for so long. She must have stood on this spot hundreds of times without realising what was beneath her feet.

They removed the planks from the top, while keeping the rest of the frame just in case. Haakon used a brush to remove some loose soil, and what looked like a piece of a snake emerged at the top, filled in with runic writing. It was only a tiny section, as soil still clung to the rest, but Mia couldn't believe their vision had been right – there really was a serpent on there. This was just incredible.

'This has to be restored back at the museum. We'd better not touch it any more.' Haakon sounded wistful, and Mia shared his feelings. She so wanted to know what it said, but they'd have to be patient.

'Is that a snake?' Ivar was peering over someone's shoulder. Mia could hear the awe in his voice and was sure they had an archaeologist in the making – the boy had been bitten by the bug. She didn't want to tell him that this sort of thing happened very rarely and that most of the work was mundane. It was still worth it for moments like these.

'Looks like it. We'll have to wait and see what else there is.' Without thinking, she put her hands on Haakon's shoulders and studied the small part of the inscription that was visible. 'What does that say? I think it's . . . "*Jorun let ræisa*". Yes. "Jorun had this erected", or "raised".'

'Sick!' Ivar's eyes shone and his expression was reflected on other people's faces too.

'We should be able to read the whole message when it's been cleaned, then hopefully all will become clear.' Haakon smiled at the boy. 'Although sometimes the carvings on rune stones are just depictions of tales about the gods. We'll see.'

'This is absolutely brilliant, much better than I'd ever hoped for!' Mia leaned in next to him and they shared another smile. 'Now we know that someone called Jorun lived here, and there may be other names mentioned further down.'

'Let's hope so. I'll go and call the museum, ask them to send some people to transfer this back to town immediately.'

From the little they could see, the stone was in pretty good condition. It seemed as though it had simply fallen down and then been forgotten, nature covering it with soil and grass, reclaiming it. There were traces of colour inside the carvings, and while they waited, Haakon explained to Ivar that these giant markers had often been painted, but the colour hardly ever survived. 'It would have been magnificent when it was new.'

He knew it had been, because he'd seen it, but that was too freaky to share with anyone other than Mia.

The rest of the team dispersed, but Haakon refused to leave the rune stone until he knew it was in safe hands. He, Mia, Ivar and Linnea decided to have *fika* on a blanket nearby so they could keep an eye on it. *Fika* was the Swedish word for coffee and cake, or whatever you consumed during a break or in a café. Linnea was all for it and wolfed down the shop-bought cinnamon buns that Mia fetched from the cottage as if she hadn't been fed for days.

Haakon noticed that Mia herself wasn't eating much. She had a pensive, almost sad look in her eyes and kept gazing into the distance. He nudged her with his shoulder. 'What's up? Aren't you pleased we found this?'

'Huh? Oh yes, of course. It's just . . . for some reason the name on the stone makes me feel like crying.' She took a deep breath and tried to smile. 'I don't know what's the matter with me. These people have been dead for centuries.'

'At least we have a name to associate with this place – we can call it Jorun's farm now.'

Mia frowned. 'No, that doesn't sound right. Let's wait and see what the rest of the inscription says.'

'Fair enough.'

'Hey, what's this?' Ivar had gone over to stare at the stone again, and had been sitting near the base of it, absently pulling at tufts of grass. Now he started scrabbling in the soil and then held something up, an object that sparkled in the sunlight. 'Look! How cool is that? A ring! Is that, like . . . gold? No way!'

'Ivar, haven't I told you context is everything?' Haakon knew he sounded stern, and Ivar's expression dimmed a little, but they needed to be sure of the ring's exact location in the soil in order to use it as proof of its age. The teenager was so obviously excited, though, Haakon didn't have the heart to spoil the moment totally. He smiled and held out his hand. 'But well spotted. Let's see, then.'

Ivar relaxed and muttered, 'Sorry, got a bit carried away,' as he handed over his find. 'I can show you exactly where it was lying.' He picked up a light-coloured stone. 'I'll put this in as a marker.'

'OK, great.' Haakon held the ring on the palm of his hand as he and Mia bent to inspect it. They both drew in a sharp breath and then looked at each other. Haakon was sure there was a strange buzzing in his brain, and his stomach went into free fall. 'It can't be . . .'

'It is,' Mia whispered.

'*Faen i helvete!*' His heart was beating triple time now, or possibly doing somersaults. He couldn't believe what he was seeing – yet another ring identical to the one Mia owned. 'But it's so tiny, as if it's . . .'

'. . . for a child. Amazing!'

Haakon's arm brushed hers, and he could feel her shaking with excitement, just as he was.

'What's going on? Is it a Viking ring?' Ivar brought Haakon back to earth.

'Yes, I think we can safely say it is. It's, um, very similar to this one.' He grabbed Mia's hand and her ring flashed as if in response. Haakon didn't mention the museum one for now; Ivar didn't need to know about that. Besides, he and Mia would have to really study the three of them together in order to make sense of this.

A his, hers and child's. Incredible! Was it even possible?

'Whoa! Cool!' Ivar exclaimed. 'Linnea, come see what I found!'

'We should have a proper look round the base to see if we can come up with any more dating material after the stone has been taken away.' Haakon stood up, the ring safely back in his possession. 'For now, I'll keep this safe. I want to take it inside to clean it up a bit and look at it with a magnifying glass. Ivar, could you go and get me a plastic bag to put it in, please?'

'Sure, I'm on it.'

The rune stone was collected an hour later by some museum personnel, which was a relief. Haakon knew it was in good hands now. Mia looked pleased too.

'I wouldn't feel comfortable having something so precious on my property. But perhaps I can have a replica made so that the original can stay at the museum,' she said to Haakon as they watched the van drive away. 'It would be nice for there to be a stone here as Jorun intended.'

The four of them went to have a closer look at the ring, and after Ivar had cleaned it with Mia's help – not difficult, as gold never rusted – Haakon checked the inside. He began to smile as he looked through the microscope. 'Surprise, surprise. It says "Jorun". The runes are clear, as if this ring hasn't been worn as much. I suppose if it was made for a child, she would have grown out of it and maybe kept it on a string round her neck later instead.'

'Sounds plausible.' Mia studied the inscription for herself, then nodded. 'Yep, no doubt about it. Good work finding it, Ivar! You obviously have eagle eyes.'

The boy's cheeks went red and he ducked down, hiding behind his black fringe, but Haakon could tell he was pleased to be praised. He was obviously bright. He was learning so fast, seeming to absorb every detail like a voracious sponge, and Haakon wondered if Rolf Thoresson ever paid him any attention at all. It was as if Ivar was starved for company and stimulation, and his mind had only been waiting for something to catch his interest before the hunger to learn gripped him. It was very rewarding when he was so attentive.

It wasn't Haakon's problem, though – he had his own.

Chapter Twenty-Six

The feasting continued long into the night, but to Ceri's surprise, Ragnhild retired early.

'Gudrun has advised me to rest more. It will make it easier for the gods to help me,' she heard the woman say to Haukr.

He just grunted in reply, as if he didn't much care what his wife decided. It was a sad state of affairs, but it was none of Ceri's business, so she turned away and concentrated on a song someone was singing.

She was growing tired and a bit drowsy when Jorun tugged on her sleeve and indicated she wanted to go outside to use the privy. It seemed like a good idea for both of them before bedding down for the night, so Ceri wrapped the little girl up in shawls and took her out. As they traversed the yard on the way back to the hall, muffled shrieks could be heard in the distance, and Ceri stopped to listen. The noise seemed to be coming from one of the thralls' huts.

'Jorun, wait!' Ceri showed her she was listening to something and pointed. 'I want to go and look.' Jorun knew the word for 'look', and there was just enough light from the moon reflected on the snow for her to see Ceri's mouth.

The two of them hurried over to the huts and found one

barred, just as it had been when Ceri herself was shut in. She quickly lifted the wood and opened the door. 'What's going on? Who's there?' She'd thought everyone was inside the hall, including the thralls.

'Oh lady, it's my Toki, they've taken him!' A wild-eyed Eira emerged into the night clutching her wailing baby. 'They're going to kill him! Please, you must help me.' She clung to Ceri's arm, sobbing, her fingers desperate claws.

'Who has? What do you mean?'

'The mistress and that old crone. Took him to the grove. Said . . . said he had to be sacrificed!'

'What? But I thought . . .' Ceri clenched her fists. 'Wait here, and don't let Jorun out of your sight. I'll fetch the jarl.'

She ran back to the hall, slipping and sliding on the snow and ice, then through the doors and along the trestles like one demented, coming to a halt before him. 'Haukr, quick, you must come. Now! The grove. Eira's man is being sacrificed. There's no time to lose.'

Everyone else had gone silent, and her words echoed round the room. Her frantic expression must have alerted Haukr to the urgency of the situation, and he wasted no time. Vaulting the table without regard for tumbling plates and drinking horns, he set off towards the doors at a run, shouting for Thorald, Steinn and Ulv. The men staggered after him, clearly inebriated but fast nonetheless, and Ceri brought up the rear. She heard others begin to follow but didn't stop to look.

Haukr might be big, but he was fast and his long legs made short work of the distance to the sacred grove. 'STOP! Stop, I say! I forbid it, do you hear me?'

Ceri heard his voice raised in a fearsome roar long before she herself reached the grove, and the commotion that broke out as a result. When she finally arrived, her lungs fit to burst with the effort, she took in the scene before her. Haukr's favourite horse lay on the ground, its lifeblood pulsing into the snow, and Toki, Eira's man, stood naked in the moonlight, his skin tinged blue with cold and his hands bound in front of him. Ragnhild was holding on to the rope, and Dagmaer, one of her serving women – an older lady who had apparently been with her since childhood – was frozen in the act of putting a noose around the man's neck.

Kneeling by the horse was Gudrun, a vessel at the ready to catch the last of the animal's blood. She threw a look of acute dislike over her shoulder at Haukr but didn't stop what she was doing or cease muttering under her breath.

'Ragnhild, what is the meaning of this? Did I not expressly forbid you to sacrifice any of my horses or thralls?' Haukr's voice was low and menacing, and colder than the snowdrifts all around them. He walked over and ripped his wife's cloak off her shoulders, covering Toki with it before slashing the ropes that bound the man's hands with his knife. 'Get that off him,' he ordered Dagmaer, gesticulating at the noose, but she seemed unable to move, so he pushed her out of the way and did it himself. 'Can you walk, Toki?' The man nodded. 'Ulv, please take him back to the hall and get someone to warm him up. Hot water, pelts, whatever it takes.'

'Will do.' Ulv led the man away, supporting him as best he could.

Ragnhild put her arms around herself, shivering without her cloak, but her chin went up and she stared at her husband defiantly. 'I did what had to be done, because as usual you're too soft.'

'Soft, is it? We'll see about that. Come with me.' He took hold of her upper arm and started to drag her back towards the hall. To his remaining men he said, 'Make sure that horse really is dead and not suffering unnecessarily. Then bring it to the stores.'

Ceri shuddered. She knew the horsemeat would have to be eaten now – it would be a waste otherwise – but she was sure it would pain Haukr to partake of any of it.

'As for you, Gudrun, I will pay you your dues in the morning, then I hope you have other farmsteads to visit,' Haukr added to the old woman.

Gudrun stood up slowly and regally, those frightening eyes narrowed. '*Já*, I'm sure they'll make me more welcome. You'll come to regret this night, mark my words.'

Ceri shuddered once again. That sounded ominous, and she feared for Haukr, but he had already started walking and didn't seem to hear. Perhaps that was for the best.

'You deliberately defied me, in front of everyone. You killed my favourite horse against my wishes, and you were about to sacrifice a valuable thrall. Toki is the blacksmith's apprentice, an essential workman. In the name of Odin, what were you thinking?'

'I told you, it was necessary. Why can't you see that?' Ragnhild was sitting on the edge of their bed, back ramrod straight, while Haukr paced in front of her. Her mouth was set, her chin still jutting in defiance. 'If you don't sacrifice that which you value, then why should the gods listen to you? It's not a sacrifice unless it's precious. And who cares about a horse anyway? It's just an animal like all the others.'

'But it would not have served any purpose. Why can you not accept that? We will never have any more children, Ragnhild, face it!'

She stood up, fists clenched at her sides and blue eyes flashing. 'You don't know that for sure. Have you no faith in the gods? What kind of man gives up without trying everything?'

'The kind of man who doesn't delude himself that there is hope when there is none.' Haukr glared at her. 'And now, in order to show everyone I'm not as soft as you think, I will have to punish you for disobeying my express orders. I should have done it when you took that ring from our hostage, but I thought you'd learned your lesson by having to swear that oath. I can't have a wife who acts against my will on purpose, doing things behind my back. You will give me the keys you carry to show that you are no longer in charge. I'll let Tyra have them until I can trust you again.'

Ragnhild walked up to him and glared back, her dark blue eyes almost black with anger and frustration. 'I will not be humiliated in such a way. Holding the keys to this place is my right.'

'A right you have forfeited by acting contrary to my wishes. You want me to be a strong leader, but you undermine me at every turn. I can't allow that to continue.'

'The trolls take your wishes! I'd rather leave than be treated in this way. By tomorrow you will no longer have a wife.'

Haukr stared at her, this woman whom he had once wanted with a passion, and found that the only emotion running through him was one of sudden hope. He swallowed hard. 'What are you saying?' Wary now, sure that he'd heard her wrong.

'I'm saying I'll divorce you tomorrow in front of witnesses and then your men may take me back to my brother's hall. I'll not stay here where I'm not wanted.' Her mouth twisted into a travesty of a smile. 'I wish you luck with your next wife. I'm sure you'll be eager to find one. But she will have to bring you a large dowry, as I'm taking mine back, and I want every item of value you own in recompense – you owe me that.'

Haukr was almost light-headed with relief, but he knew that he mustn't show it or all would be lost. 'I owe you nothing. You've not exactly been the ideal wife and I should reclaim the bride price I paid your family. But you may take items equal to the value of the dowry you brought yourself.' Something else occurred to him. 'And Jorun stays here. She may be the only heir I ever have.'

'As if I'd take her! What use is she to me?' Ragnhild turned and headed back towards the bed. 'Now I'd be grateful if you would allow me a peaceful night's sleep, without your snores to keep me awake. I'm sure you'll find plenty of willing women out in the hall to share a bed with.'

Haukr ignored this dig and left the room, but not to sleep. He would sit outside the curtain all night to make sure Ragnhild didn't try to sneak off with everything he owned. He wouldn't put it past her.

'What do you mean, Ragnhild is gone?' Ceri blinked at Haukr as he stamped the snow off his boots just inside the door of the weaving hut. She'd retreated there with Jorun first thing that morning, guessing that Haukr and his wife would not be in the best of moods after what had happened the night before. It had seemed a good idea to keep the little girl out of the way until the matter had been resolved, one way or another.

'She divorced me in front of all my men. Three times she repeated the words in three separate locations – by the bed in my chamber, by my seat in the hall and on the threshold of the house itself. That is how it is done and now there is no going back. We are no longer married. She's gone back to her brother's home by sled with some of my men as an escort and more valuables than she deserved, but that's a price I was willing to pay.'

Haukr was beaming, making Jorun stare at him and ask, 'Va-eh? Abby?'

He picked her up and swung her around. 'Yes, little one, I'm happy. The gods forgive me, but I am so relieved to be rid of your mother. Perhaps one day you'll understand.' Jorun shrieked with laughter and touched his neatly clipped beard, which glistened with snowflakes. It was a dark gold and perfectly complemented his white-blond hair and blue eyes. Ceri thought she'd never seen anyone look as handsome as he did in that moment. But had she heard him right?

'But . . . is that legal and binding? Divorce, I mean?' She still didn't quite comprehend. She'd been told that in Norse society a marriage could be undone in this way, if the wife so wished, but it went against everything she had been taught in her homeland.

'Yes. Our marriage is over. Ragnhild left with more valuable objects than she arrived with, so there can be no dispute.' He winced. 'In fact, she probably took most of the things from your village. I'm sorry.'

'It doesn't matter.' Ceri had come to realise that they were merely objects. Apart from her mother's ring, which Haukr had given back to her, she didn't much care about the rest now.

'It does to me. In recompense, I will not make your brother pay a ransom for you. In fact, from now on you are a free woman and I'll make sure everyone here knows it. You are no longer my hostage.'

'Truly?' Ceri felt her spirits rise. 'I can leave any time?'

Haukr's smile faded a little. 'If that is your wish, certainly, but I would advise you to wait until the spring at least.'

'Of course. But . . .' She wanted to tell him she didn't really want to leave at all, but he hadn't said anything about hoping she would stay. And why would he? Haukr would need to remarry now, to a woman who was his equal in social status. There must be other near neighbours with whom he would be keen to form an alliance. Ceri had learned by now that blood ties were very important to him and his people, and he was a jarl after all. 'We can discuss it nearer the time. Perhaps my brother will even come to fetch me home.'

'Certainly.' Haukr drew in a deep breath and turned for the

door. 'Now I have much to do and I need to speak to Old Tyra. I'll see you later.'

Ceri was happy for him, really she was, but his new status as an unmarried man made no difference to her. He was still out of bounds and would remain so for ever unless she wanted to live in sin for the rest of her life. And that she was determined not to do.

Chapter Twenty-Seven

Haakon sat up in bed and pulled the Viking ring off his finger. It clattered on to the bedside table, but thankfully Linnea didn't stir. She was a deep sleeper, once you persuaded her to actually go to bed – not always an easy task – whereas Haakon's nights had grown increasingly disturbed.

He'd been dreaming again. Vivid dreams, terrifying, visceral. He was fairly sure that what he'd seen was a *blót*, a sacrificial ritual to appease the gods and ask for their favour for the coming season. The one in his dream had taken place during winter, because he couldn't shake the images of scarlet blood spraying on to pure snow. The sight was etched into his retinas; the smell clogged the back of his nose. He grabbed his water bottle and drank deeply, trying to eradicate the metallic taste.

Glancing at the ring, he knew he ought to take it back to the museum, but it was as though the golden snake resisted. It had more to tell him; it wasn't done yet. He shoved his fingers through his hair and leaned his forehead into his hands. This was seriously crazy. He'd never experienced anything like it before and he didn't want to believe it was happening now. But it was.

Perhaps he should contact a shrink. Was he cracking up? But in that case, so was Mia, and surely two people couldn't be going insane in the exact same way simultaneously? That made no sense. A hypnotherapist might be better. At least then he might get some answers.

He lay down again and tried to get comfortable, but the lonely hours of dawn stretched before him, and sleep was a long time coming.

'Doing anything nice this weekend, Ivar?'

It was Thursday afternoon and the following day was Midsummer Eve. Swedes tended to celebrate this more than British people, with get-togethers and *Smörgåsbord* that always included pickled herring. For children there was dancing round a maypole, which was called a midsummer pole here. Mia was looking forward to it.

'Nah. Dad's back but he's gone to some auction up north for the weekend. Asked if I wanted to come, but I said I'd rather stay here. Got a new PlayStation game to try out. And now my aunt has gone, I can do what I want.' Ivar was shovelling soil into a wheelbarrow, and Mia thought he was starting to look strong and healthy. Must be all the hard work he'd been doing these last few weeks. And having a tan helped no end – the goth pallor was long gone, and his blond roots were growing out, giving him what Mia thought was quite a cool look.

'So you'll be all alone in the house? Maybe you'd better camp out on my sofa while he's away.' Although Mia knew the boy was perfectly capable of looking after himself, it still seemed irresponsible to her that his father should leave him without supervision for days on end. He should have asked the aunt to stay on, but perhaps she wasn't able to.

Ivar shrugged. 'I'll be fine. I'm used to it, doesn't bother me – we have a burglar alarm. Besides, he's left me his shotgun, in case anyone breaks in. I know how to use it.'

Mia glanced at Haakon and saw her own alarm mirrored in his eyes, but neither of them said anything. However, she became more determined than ever to persuade Ivar to stay at the cottage for the weekend.

'Hey, maybe you guys can come over to my house this evening? You know, so I can show you Dad's stuff? I mean, since he's away and everything this might be a good time. He texted me to say he won't be back till Sunday.'

'I'd better stay here with Linnea,' Haakon said, 'but perhaps Mia would like a quick peek?'

'Um, sure.' She didn't feel right about sneaking around someone's house while they were away, but at the same time it would be good to find out what Thoresson was up to.

'Excellent! I'll take you over later then.'

After dinner, she set off with Ivar through an unexpected rain shower. The soft droplets whispered on the leaves of the bushes and trees all around them, which sent out a heady perfume of oxygen-rich scent. Mia breathed in deeply and savoured the sweet tang of pine resin from the nearby forest, and the various flowery smells mixed with the occasional whiff of mushrooms and cow manure coming from the fields.

'Mmm, this is why I love Sweden in the summer,' she said, more to herself than to Ivar. 'The air is so fresh and clean, there isn't a high-rise building for miles and I feel free.'

'So why don't you live here?' Ivar huddled into his black hoodie.

'Good question. Mostly because my work is in London and I enjoy that. It's what I was trained to do.'

'Can't you do it over here?'

'I suppose. The thing is . . . well, my mum lives in Sweden with her second husband and my two stepbrothers. We don't get on all that well and I've always kind of felt more English.' And yet now she was torn. Could she really face going back to London and that awful commute every day? Or would she give in and sell Birch Thorpe like Charles wanted her to?

Ivar jolted her out of her thoughts. 'We're nearly there; my house is just round this bend.' And as they walked a bit further, his home came into sight. Mia stopped dead and just stared.

'Bloody hell! That's not a house, it's practically a castle! You didn't tell me your dad was *that* rich.'

'Er, well, does it matter?' Ivar squirmed and scuffed at the road with the toe of his sneaker. 'It's just a house.'

Mia disagreed, but thought she'd better not tell him that. She had exaggerated after all – his home wasn't a castle, but it was big. A classic Swedish manor house, timber-clad and painted yellow with white window frames, it had identical wings attached to either side. It was set on a slight hill overlooking the lake, and the views were spectacular.

'Wow,' she said. 'It's lovely.'

'Come on, let's go inside.' Ivar obviously didn't want to discuss the merits of the place and led the way to the front door, which was approached via a wide timbered porch decorated with intricate latticework. This looked to have been fashioned by a true craftsman, perhaps as early as the beginning of the nineteenth century. Mia silently admired it before following the boy into a huge hallway.

A staircase rose in a semicircle to one side, but the hall itself was open to the roof, where an enormous chandelier was suspended, its prisms reflecting the light from a round window above the door. The floors were of wide pine boards that looked well worn, the patina of age and much polishing giving them a brilliant sheen. Oriental carpets were everywhere, seemingly laid down at random but giving a sense of opulence that had to be calculated. Mia glimpsed a huge reception room straight ahead, with a row of windows overlooking the lake and antique furniture befitting the style of the house. She wanted to have a closer look, but Ivar beckoned her towards one of the side doors and she reluctantly turned away.

'Dad keeps his collection in one of the wings, in here.' He led the way through a room that must be his father's office, the huge desk piled with paperwork attesting to his workload. 'He keeps the door locked, but I watched him open it and memorised the code.' The boy grinned. 'He didn't notice me looking because he was a bit drunk that day. Anyway, I could've probably guessed it 'cos it's just his date of birth.' He shook his head as if that was the stupidest combination code anyone could possibly use.

The door into the wing looked sturdier than the others and much more modern. Definitely fireproof too, Mia thought to herself. There was a keypad to the right, and when Ivar keyed in a sequence of numbers, the lock on the door sprang open, allowing them to pass through. Just inside the threshold was another control panel, and again he pushed some buttons. 'Burglar alarm and CCTV,' he explained. 'Dad says you can't be too careful, even though hardly anyone knows he's got all this stuff.'

He turned on the lights and Mia gasped.

'*Vad i helvete . . . ?*'

She stood stock still and just stared around the large room that housed Thoresson's 'collection'. She had never seen anything like it outside of a museum vault, and wondered for a moment if she was imagining things. Slowly she began to walk around the room, stopping to examine several of the items, but she didn't really need to study them too closely – it was obvious that they were all genuine antiques. And not just antiques, but ancient artefacts in many cases.

She picked up a sword, almost three feet long, that had been casually placed on top of a cabinet. There was a polishing cloth next to it, as if someone had been busy cleaning it and been called away halfway through the task. She blinked as the light bounced off the intricately decorated gold filigree handle, so delicately wrought it was a piece of art in itself. 'I don't believe it, this is a Viking sword! A real Viking sword and it's hardly rusty at all.' She turned to Ivar. 'Where the hell did he get it?' She didn't add that Thoresson probably had no right to own it, or if he did, he certainly had a duty to lend it to the nearest museum. It was incredibly rare.

'Oh, that one's a family heirloom, Dad says. It's his favourite and it's even got "Thoresson" written on the blade or something. He showed it to me, but I can't read runes like you can. I want to learn, though. I'm going to study to be an archaeologist, I've decided.'

Mia barely registered his words as she slid her gaze along the double-edged blade, which, although it had a few patches of rust, still looked fairly lethal. It was decorated with engraved motifs, and on one side she found the writing Ivar was talking about. '*I am Man-Slayer, Thorald carries me,*' she read out, translating from Old Norse.

'What?'

'That's what it says; it means it was owned by a man called Thorald and he named his sword Man-Slayer.'

'Their swords had names? That's, like, a bit Disney, isn't it? You know, Excalibur-type stuff.'

Mia laughed. 'I guess so, but maybe that's where Merlin got the idea, or vice versa.'

'So it doesn't say anything about Thoresson, then? Dad seemed so sure.'

'Afraid not, although your name could still derive from Thorald. "Thorald's son" would easily turn into Thoresson if you say it fast, don't you think?'

Mia put the sword back and walked along the many glass

cabinets, frowning at the contents. There were a lot of Viking items, mostly weapons: rusty old axe heads, knife blades and more swords – the corroded kind Haakon's team had found in the burial mound. But there was also jewellery and everyday necessities such as combs, keys and cooking utensils. Finally she came to a halt in front of a case that seemed to have nothing to do with Vikings whatsoever, and which made her eyes widen and her stomach muscles clench involuntarily. It contained numerous Nazi items – a flag, some armbands, a pistol and what looked like a signed copy of Hitler's book *Mein Kampf*. She frowned and glanced at Ivar, who had been following her.

'I know,' he said, as if he'd expected her to comment on this. 'I don't like it either, but Dad is, like, obsessed with pure genes. He calls them Aryan and says that Hitler guy was right, even though he went about things the wrong way. Dad wants pure Scandinavian genes to be preserved and not "diluted", or whatever.' He made a face when he said the word. 'Something about blonde people becoming extinct in, like, two hundred years? Although not with gassing people and stuff; he just doesn't think we should intermarry with all the foreigners they're letting into the country these days. Doesn't want me even talking to the immigrant kids at my school.'

'Are you serious?' Mia stared at him. 'That's . . .' She was lost for words.

Ivar didn't seem offended. Instead he gave a small smile and shrugged. 'Pretty crazy, yeah, but what can I do? I can't tell anyone, 'cos then he might get in trouble and I'd probably be sent to some foster home or something. Anyway, soon I'll be grown up and can live by myself. Then Dad can take his money and shove it. If I marry, I'll marry whoever I like; I'm not going to choose a girl just because she's got blonde hair and blue eyes. I mean, that's just stupid. Plus, I looked it up on the internet and it's a hoax. Blondes are not disappearing at all. I tried to tell him, but he got very angry so I shut up.'

Mia was still stunned. 'Where did he get these ideas?' she ventured to ask.

'His grandma was German. Dad said she was something called a Bundmädel before she married a Swedish guy.'

'Ah, I see.' The BMD, Bund Deutscher Mädel – or Band of German Maidens – had been the girls' wing of the Nazi party youth movement, the Hitler Youth or Jugend. Mia had heard about them. The woman had obviously brought her beliefs with her when she moved to Sweden, later indoctrinating her grandson. *Good grief.*

No wonder Ivar didn't have any friends; he was probably scared to bring them home in case his dad said something weird.

'Come over here.' He beckoned her towards another display case. 'This was what I wanted to show you really.'

Mia walked over to see what he was pointing at. A silver brooch, round with a pin through the middle. Most definitely Celtic in style. She exhaled sharply. Ivar opened the case and took the brooch out. 'Isn't it great?'

'Where did it come from?' She almost didn't dare to ask, but she had to know.

'Oh, Dad found it around here somewhere.' Ivar didn't quite look her in the eye, and Mia suddenly wondered whether Thoresson had been illicitly digging on her property while it stood empty. The thought made her furious. 'It's got writing on the back, but Dad wouldn't tell me what it said. You can read it though, right?'

Mia could and did, although she had to swallow hard before she could get the words out in a somewhat strangled voice. '*Keri owned me.*'

There it was again, that name. A Celtic woman in a Viking

settlement, owning things as precious as a silver brooch and a gold ring. *And a gold cross necklace?* Mia had almost forgotten about that, but her subconscious reminded her.

'Neat! Like the comb, huh?' Ivar commented. 'I was hoping that was what it would say.'

'Yes. This is amazing!' Mia reluctantly handed the brooch back. 'But . . . you know that if your dad found this somewhere around here, he should have reported his find to the authorities, right? You've been around our team for weeks now. I'm sure you must have heard that rule more than once.'

Ivar nodded. 'Yeah, but . . .'

'What? Is there something you're not telling me? I won't get angry, I promise you, and I can't report anything to the authorities because strictly speaking I shouldn't be in here without your dad's permission. We both know that.'

Ivar took a deep breath. 'OK. You probably will get pissed off, though, because . . . and I didn't know until last week, I swear, but now I do . . . Dad found the brooch on the little island, the one you say is yours. Just before he went on that trip to the Far East.'

'No way! So that's why he wants possession of it. Does he think there's more out there?'

'Yeah. He's sure of it. Said he's going to dig some more, and he mentioned finding a human bone.'

'Oh my God . . . a grave? But I've never noticed any mounds out there. Gran and I had picnics by the shore . . . Actually, come to think of it, we never really went anywhere else. Always stayed by the water. Hmm . . . I guess it would be a fitting resting place for someone, peaceful and undisturbed.' Had Gran known? And was that why she was so anxious that no one should build on the island? Possibly.

'Can we go out and take a look?' Ivar seemed to be fizzing with excitement.

'Yes, soon, but I still have to prove I own it. My lawyer is working on that.' At least she damn well hoped he was. 'I don't believe your dad has any right to it.'

'Probably not, but I think he's stalling just long enough so he can go and dig there. He hasn't had a chance since he came back, as he's been busy with work and stuff, and now he's away.'

'Yes. Well, we'll have to stop him.' Mia clenched her fists. *The utter bastard!* Thoresson obviously had complete disregard for proper archaeological practices. He'd dig willy-nilly without recording anything, and artefacts would disappear into his little 'collection' and never be seen again. No, unthinkable. 'Seriously, he'll ruin the site, you understand that now, right?'

'Sure, but what can we do?'

'I don't know, but I'll think of something. Round-the-clock surveillance perhaps? Yes, all the members of the team will have to take turns sitting at the tip of the peninsula, and if they see any boats, they can shine a powerful torch at whoever it is and tell them to leave. Your dad can't dig there in daylight, and neither he nor I are allowed to go there until the dispute has been settled, so if he tries anything, it will be at night.'

She put her arms round the boy's skinny frame and pulled him close for a fierce hug. 'Thank you, Ivar, I really appreciate it. I understand that this can't be easy for you and I hope you won't get into trouble with your dad, but you did the right thing in telling me. We have to fix this somehow.'

Ivar returned the hug awkwardly, but he didn't completely shrug her off so she knew he was pleased really. 'I can handle my dad. He thinks I'm really stupid, so I'll just act like I don't know what he's talking about if he says anything.'

Mia stared at him. 'Why does he think you're stupid? Anyone can see you're very clever.'

Ivar's cheeks turned bright red and he looked away. 'I never do any work at school and I only sort of mumble when he asks me questions, so he thinks I'm a hopeless case.' He glanced up under his long fringe. 'But I'll try harder at school now, 'cos Haakon said I had to if I want to be an archaeologist.'

'You do that. Show them what you're made of.' Mia gestured at the brooch. 'Would you mind if I took some photos of that? Just to show Haakon, no one else, I promise.'

'OK.' He held it out while she snapped pictures of both sides with her mobile.

'Come on, we'd better get out of here. Can you make sure nothing looks as if it's been touched? And we're not being filmed by the CCTV cameras, are we?'

'No, I turned them off. Chill, Mia.'

It was almost a relief to leave the room, and Mia waited in Thoresson's study while Ivar switched the alarms and cameras back on. She happened to glance at the massive antique desk and froze when something caught her eye – a familiar logo. Checking to see that Ivar was still busy, she went over to look more closely.

'I don't bloody well believe it . . .' She swore under her breath. There was a folder in the top filing tray with her lawyer's company name stamped on the outside. Flipping it open, she saw that it contained the missing documents about the island. So that was where they'd got to. *Damn Thoresson!*

Well, he wasn't going to get away with it. There was a printer nearby and she quickly grabbed a sheaf of copying paper more or less equal to what was in the folder. Then she substituted them for the island documents and stuffed those inside her jacket before closing the folder. Hopefully Thoresson wouldn't be looking at them for a while and therefore wouldn't notice they were missing. She folded her arms across her stomach to make sure the pages didn't slide out. She felt bad for not telling Ivar, but the less he knew about it, the better.

Anyway, Thoresson had no right to have that folder in his possession in the first place – he was the thief, not her.

Outside, the rain was still coming down in a steady stream, and Mia breathed deeply once more. There had been something unwholesome about Thoresson's collection, and it was a relief to be out in the fresh air. As they walked back towards the lane, she turned to Ivar.

'I'm going to have to tell Haakon about this, you realise that? I know he represents the authorities in a way, but if we tell him in confidence, I think he'll keep shtum for now. Without him we can't organise a surveillance team. What do you say?'

Ivar bit his lip and hesitated. 'I guess. Yeah, we'd better. You do it, OK?'

'Let's do it together. Tonight, after Linnea's gone to bed. And please, I would really like it if you stayed with us. I know you're fine on your own, but I'd worry.'

'Sure, whatever.'

Chapter Twenty-Eight

The weeks passed and everyone adjusted to the fact that Haukr's domain had no mistress. He'd given the keys to Old Tyra for the time being, as he had no sisters or aunts who could assume the reins, but they all knew this was a temporary arrangement. Although capable, Tyra was well past her youth, and anyone could see she would not want to be in charge for too long.

Ceri went in daily expectation of hearing an announcement about a betrothal, a new wife to replace Ragnhild. Haukr had gone to Birka several times, and she assumed he also visited his neighbours along the way. Nothing was said on his return and she wondered if perhaps marriage negotiations took a long time here, but she didn't want to ask. It was not her place and she was wary of showing too much interest in the matter.

He still spoke to her whenever he had the time, and continued to be involved with little Jorun's progress, but not once did he mention the attraction between them. He was polite, he was kind and concerned about her welfare, but there was no more talk of him dreaming about her or anything of that sort. Ceri wasn't sure if this was because he didn't want to give her any false expectations, or if he genuinely didn't desire her any longer. Either way, she found it difficult to cope with and longed for spring, when she could hopefully escape the whole situation.

On a sunny morning in late April, when the snow had finally melted away and the bushes and trees were starting to bud, a messenger arrived. Ceri happened to be on her way to the main hall and saw the man first. A feeling of foreboding washed over her – this had to be it, the reply he had been waiting for. Tonight Haukr would announce his impending nuptials to some well-born lady of his acquaintance, and Ceri knew it would be one of the worst moments of her life.

'Can I help you?' She walked forward, aware that as there was no mistress, it was now up to all of them to look after guests, whether welcome or not.

'I need to speak to Haukr Erlendrsson. I have an urgent message for him.'

'Very well. I will take you to him directly.' Ceri didn't like the anxiety she saw in the man's eyes. His gaze kept sliding away from hers, as if he was hiding something. It boded ill. Was Haukr about to receive unwelcome news? Had his proposal been turned down? It seemed unlikely, but still, something was amiss.

They found Haukr in the smithy, where he and the smith, and Toki, the apprentice, were fashioning some new axe heads. With his immense strength, he often helped out and claimed to enjoy the work.

'You are needed by the king,' the messenger announced as soon as Haukr had greeted him. 'He is in Gotland and there is to be a council there. As one of his trusted advisers, your presence is required.'

Ceri blinked and stared at the man. This was not at all the sort of message she'd been expecting, and for a moment she thought she had misheard.

Haukr seemed less surprised and frowned instead. 'In Gotland?

What is he doing there? That's very far from his usual domain at Adelsey.'

The messenger shrugged. 'I believe that is where the threat is, to the safety of his kingdom and us all. I'm afraid I was not entrusted with the whys or wherefores.'

'No, of course. Very well, I will begin preparations for the journey immediately. Ceri, perhaps you can ask Tyra to see to refreshments. Rest, eat and drink, man, then we will be on our way.'

'Thank you, but I will go in the opposite direction with messages for other jarls. You go ahead without me; we will catch you up.'

Haukr strode off, shouting for his men and some of the servants, and a mad flurry of packing began. Ceri served the messenger herself, then watched him leave before helping Tyra to pack some clothing and other essentials for the jarl, while Aase oversaw the loading of food and drink into the ship.

Just as they were finishing, Haukr came into his room and began to change his tunic. Ceri hesitated, but stayed behind when Tyra hurried back into the main part of the hall. She was worried and needed some answers. 'Does this happen often?' she blurted out. 'The king summoning you, I mean.' Something about the whole situation seemed off to her, but then she had only a hazy idea of how much power a king had in this country, and what might be required of his vassals.

'From time to time, if there is a threat as now, for example.' Haukr pushed the lid of his travelling kist shut and looked at her. 'Why?'

'And you know this messenger?'

'Egil? Yes, he's been here once or twice.' He came over and put his hands on her shoulders. 'Are you worried about me, Ceridwen? Or about your own safety? Don't be. I'll try not to be away for too long. A month at the most. And half my men will be staying behind to make sure everything runs smoothly here.' He smiled, hesitated as if he was debating with himself, then bent to give her a soft kiss on the mouth, adding in a whisper, 'Wild horses can't keep me away from here a moment longer than I absolutely must.'

'What? But Haukr . . .' Ceri put up a hand to touch her lips, which were tingling from his kiss. Warmth spread through her and she wanted to reach up and twine her arms round his neck, demanding that he do it again, only more thoroughly. But he was clearly in a hurry.

'When I come back, there is something I want to ask you. In the meantime, look after yourself and Jorun, promise? I'm leaving Steinn and Ulv to guard you this time – poor Thorald still feels bad about letting you down before. You should be perfectly safe, but just in case, remember to carry a sharp knife at all times, yes?'

'Of course, and . . . may the gods be with you. All of them.'

He laughed at that. 'Ah, well said! We'll make a heathen of you yet, Ceridwen.'

She wasn't so sure about that, but dear Lord, she'd miss him and she would be waiting for his return with impatience. What had he meant by that kiss? And what did he want to ask her? She yearned to find out, but knew this wasn't the time. Instead she watched as he picked up the heavy kist and hefted it on his shoulder as though it weighed nothing.

Soon afterwards, she held Jorun's hand as they waved the men off. They stood on the promontory for a long time, watching the familiar shape of his ship disappear into the distance. A hollow feeling settled in the pit of her stomach, but she told herself he would be fine and she couldn't mope around. She had things to do, and Old Tyra had asked to cast the runes for her – a heathen practice, but well meant, so she didn't like to refuse. Besides, it would take her mind off worrying and secretly she had begun to believe in some of the rituals here despite herself.

'Right, Jorun, let's go and continue your lessons.' She fixed a smile on her face as they headed up the hill. 'What is that?' She pointed at a tree.

Jorun grinned. 'Dee.'

'Good!' The little girl was making progress, talking more and more every day, and they were able to have entire conversations now. It wasn't always easy to understand her, but it was progress. Perhaps if they worked really hard during Haukr's absence, he'd be pleased with what they could achieve.

But sleep was impossible that night, and she went to sit on the outermost tip of the peninsula. She waited and watched through the lonely hours of dawn, scanning the water as far as the eye could see for a glimpse of the familiar snake's-head carving at the prow of his ship, but of course it was much too soon.

He would come back, she knew it. The runes had told her so, and Tyra said they were never wrong.

He would come back.

And she would be waiting.

Ceri thought afterwards that she ought to have listened to her instincts and told Haukr not to leave without finding out more about the supposed gathering, or perhaps checking whether his neighbours were going too – because it all turned out to be a ruse.

She knew it as soon as the hand came out of the darkness and covered her mouth. It was exactly as the night Haukr had abducted her, but this time there was no chance of a positive outcome. This time it was deathly serious.

Haukr had only been gone for a day and a night, showing

clearly that the attackers had known when to strike. Egil, the messenger, must have been bribed, hence the anxious glances, and then gone straight back to whoever had hired him to report that Haukr had left. And although Ceri fumbled for the knife she kept next to her on the bench where she and Jorun slept, she didn't stand a chance. The blow to the head felt familiar and made her woozy. 'Don't try anything. Just come with me now, or you die.'

Her heart almost stopped at the sound of those words; she recognised the voice all too well – Svein. *Hateful man!* Would she ever be rid of him and his sister? For she was sure Ragnhild had to be behind this. Who else would hold a grudge against Haukr? He had no other enemies as far as Ceri was aware.

Panicking now, she tried to fight him off, but fear was making her limbs uncooperative, and he was too strong anyway. Terror gave her a momentary surge of energy, and she managed to at least claw his hand away from her mouth, letting out the scream that had been steadily building in her throat. She knew it probably wouldn't help – he must have brought accomplices, which meant no one would come to her rescue – but it felt good to give vent to her despair and fury. *Why couldn't they just leave us alone?* But Ragnhild wasn't the type of woman to let a slight go unpunished, and she'd clearly felt wronged.

Ceri suddenly remembered that Jorun was sleeping next to her as always. Would Svein hurt the little girl too? She reached out a hand and shoved at her, then shouted, 'Run, Jorun, RUN!'

She heard Svein laugh in the darkness. 'She can't hear you, can she, you halfwit.' Then, 'Ouch! Why, you little cat . . .'

He seemed to be trying to hold on to Ceri while grabbing for Jorun at the same time, but it sounded as though Jorun had evaded him somehow – perhaps bitten his hand? Good. 'Run, Jorun!' Ceri repeated as loudly as possible. She knew the child ought to be able to hear her if she screamed at the top of her voice, and the word was a familiar one, often used while they played games outside.

'Come. I'll deal with her later.' Svein pulled her off the bed by her hair, and Ceri had no choice but to follow. She was only wearing her under-tunic – it seemed to be her lot in life to be forever abducted in her *serk* – but at least she wasn't naked. She continued to struggle against Svein's hold, kicking out and flailing her arms as the dread built to a crescendo inside her again, but he was much bigger and stronger and she stood no chance.

'Haukr will get you for this,' she hissed, digging in her heels, but her feet found no purchase against the hard earthen floor.

Svein just laughed again. 'No, he won't, because he'll think you dead, and if the man is even half as soft as my sister tells me, he'll crumble with grief.' He chuckled. 'This'll serve him right.'

'He cares nothing for me. I am but a hostage,' Ceri protested.

'That's not what I hear. Now *þegi þú*!'

All around them in the main hall, pandemonium had broken out. Svein's men appeared to be fighting with the men and servants Haukr had left behind, and even the women were joining in. But Ceri knew his people didn't stand a chance. She could see they were vastly outnumbered, and they'd obviously been taken by surprise. She could only assume that whoever had been on guard outside had been killed.

As she was dragged towards the doors, she looked around for Jorun but couldn't spot her anywhere. She finally caught sight of her just outside the building, hiding behind a clump of bushes. She motioned for her to stay silent and invisible. Jorun nodded as if she understood, and Ceri tried to make sure Svein didn't see the little girl by choosing that moment to struggle further.

Another clout round the head made her legs wobbly, and he

half dragged, half carried her down to the jetty, where two ships waited. She was picked up and dumped like a sack of grain into the bottom of one of them, and as her head hit the wood, everything went black.

Chapter Twenty-Nine

'I don't believe it! I mean, obviously I know there's a black market in antiques and artefacts, but for someone to be able to build up a collection like that, well . . .' Haakon was stunned by the things Mia had seen, but he rallied quickly. 'Sorry, no offence, Ivar, but you know it's illegal.'

'Not all of it,' Mia interjected. 'The Thoressons obviously go way back, just like my family, and some of those items were heirlooms. I'd be willing to swear that sword has never been in the ground. What little rust was on the blade has come from normal ageing, and there's no way it would be that intact if it had ever been buried anywhere. Plus, it said it belonged to someone called Thorald – the name Thoresson could easily derive from that.'

'A real, complete Viking sword in near pristine condition . . .' Just the thought of that made Haakon want to jump up and down with excitement. He really hoped he could get to see it at some point, hold it, examine it closely. 'But seriously, Mia's right. We'll need a round-the-clock guard on that island. I'm not letting anyone dig there, whether he owns the place or not. No way.'

'I'm with you.' Ivar seemed unfazed, but Haakon suspected he must feel strange, caught in the middle like this.

'I'll have a word with some of the other people on the team, those I trust, and this won't go any further. Your dad's coming back Sunday night, you say?'

'Yep.'

'Then we'd better start after dark on Saturday, just in case.' He looked at Mia, who was gazing at the screen of her mobile, which showed one of the photos of the Celtic brooch. Another 'Ceri' item – it couldn't be coincidence. 'Mia, would you mind if Linnea and I stay here for the weekend? I was going to take her back to Stockholm so you could have some peace and quiet, but I'd better take my turn watching the island.'

'Sure, no problem. Although I need to go into Stockholm myself tomorrow, to see my solicitor. I've, um . . . got something to talk to him about.' Mia looked a bit furtive, and from the way she quickly glanced towards Ivar, Haakon gathered she didn't want to discuss it in front of the boy.

'Why don't we all go?' he suggested. 'How about a trip to Birka after your meeting? We can show Ivar and Linnea how the Vikings lived and traded there.'

'Great idea! Haven't been for ages. Ivar?'

'Totally! I'm in.' The PlayStation game appeared to have been forgotten – the archaeology bug had definitely bitten the kid.

'OK, we'll take tomorrow off and Tomas can be in charge. Better have an early night then. Let's get you a sleeping bag and a pillow, Ivar.'

As they headed upstairs, Mia motioned for Haakon to come into her bedroom for a moment. To his surprise, she pulled a large sheaf of documents out from under her sweater. 'What on earth . . . ?'

'Shh. I found these on Thoresson's desk. Ivar doesn't know I took them. Look – it's the missing papers about the island!'

'What? No! The absolute bastard . . .' The implications sank in and a spurt of anger shot through Haakon. '*Dette er jævlig!* He took them so we couldn't go to the island.'

'Yes, that was my thinking too. I'll give them back to Almquist, then we can stop Thoresson legally.'

Haakon shook his head. 'We can't afford to wait. We have to go out there soon to have a look.'

Mia chewed her lip, drawing his attention to the fact that she had a very inviting mouth and he was standing far too close to her. In her bedroom. Oh hell . . . He turned away, fighting down the attraction he'd been suppressing for weeks.

'OK,' she said. 'How about on Saturday? If Thoresson is away, we can go in daylight.'

'Right. Yes. OK, let's do that. I'd better . . .' He gestured towards the door and fled, throwing a whispered 'Goodnight' over his shoulder.

If he'd stayed in there another moment, he would have had to kiss her.

'You really think that sword has been handed down through your family for a thousand years? I mean, what are the odds of that happening? It's incredible.'

They were in Haakon's jeep on their way to Stockholm, and Mia couldn't stop thinking about all the things she'd seen the night before.

'I dunno, but that's what Dad says. He's got some kind of old book to prove it, I think.'

'What sort of book?' Mia saw that Haakon was all ears and knew he must be wishing he'd gone with them to Ivar's house.

'You know, written on cow skin . . .'

'Vellum.'

'. . . whatever, with weird writing. I could make out some of the letters, but not all, and I've only ever seen it a couple times 'cos

269

he keeps it in the safe. But he did say it proves the sword belonged to one of our ancestors.'

'I would love to see that,' Haakon commented.

Ivar mumbled something else, which the others didn't catch.

'What was that? Ivar?' Mia, who was in the front seat, turned to look at the boy.

'Nothing.' Ivar scowled from under his fringe. 'Well, all right, it was about that stupid Aryan thing again. Dad said the book proves how pure our blood is, but it's all bollocks.'

'It's OK,' Haakon said. 'People are allowed to hold beliefs, you know, even if they seem strange to others, as long as they're not doing anything illegal or violent. I mean, most religions only make sense to those who believe in them, right?' Ivar's expression brightened a little as this message hit home, and he nodded.

'I s'pose.'

'No supposing about it, that's how it is. There will always be fanatics of one kind or another, and the fact that your dad is one of them isn't your fault.'

'That's not what the kids at school say.'

'They know about it?' Mia was aghast that Thoresson should have broadcast his views to that extent.

'Not exactly, but they know Dad's a member of a very right-wing party. There was something in the paper about it last year and some guys in the year above me started saying I was the son of a fascist pig and stuff like that.' Ivar's face had turned red and he muttered, 'Stupid bastards. Doesn't matter, though. I wasn't exactly Mr Popular anyway. Everyone was always jealous because Dad's rich and I get given whatever I want.'

'That's plain stupid.' But Mia knew that kids didn't need more of a reason than that for bullying. There wasn't anything she could do about it, other than try to be there for Ivar somehow.

After she'd dropped off the documents to an astonished and

somewhat shamefaced Almquist – 'How on earth was that man able to get hold of our folder?' – they went to catch a ferry to Birka.

Birka – or Björkö as it was called in modern Swedish – had been a trading town for over two hundred years during the Viking age. It was situated on an island in Lake Mälaren and the only way to reach it was by boat. The ferries departed from Stadshusbron, a quay right in the centre of Stockholm, and the journey took over an hour and a half, as there were stops at other islands along the way. But Mia didn't mind, as it was a very pleasant trip. And Linnea was mega excited, having never been on a ship that big before.

'Daddy, Daddy, look! We're going really fast now!'

That was an exaggeration, but they did pick up speed eventually, the ferry sending up lots of spray along the sides. The waters were slightly choppy, but not enough to make them seasick. And the views were spectacular – the high-rise buildings of Stockholm on the left and its famous Stadshus – the City Hall – on the right, with other ferries moored nearby. This soon gave way to a vista of seemingly hundreds of islands. Most were heavily wooded, with rocky outcrops along their shores, and fringed with reeds, just like Mia's own island. Some were inhabited; others had sheer cliff faces, thirty to fifty metres high.

'Daddy, I'm hungry!'

Mia wasn't surprised, as the smell of cinnamon buns and cooking coming from inside the main cabin had been wafting past them since they came on board.

'OK, early lunch everyone?' Haakon led the way inside, where there was a spacious dining area.

Later, as they approached Birka, the water became more open and a lot choppier, the noisy engine having to work that much harder. They disembarked on a large pier and joined a walking tour, the guide showing them fields full of graves.

'There are about three thousand here in total, many of them children's burials, as only half of children reached the age of ten, but we haven't excavated them all yet. And there are lots of different types – stone circles, single stones and mounds. About fifty per cent were cremations, and the richest graves were the ones we found inside the city's wall . . .'

He went on to tell them about some of the finds. Because of the trading connections, these ranged from locally produced items to Arabic silver, Russian pearls and other exotic artefacts, but elk-horn combs and bronze oval brooches were the most common grave goods, sometimes with a string of beads in between.

'Vikings liked having clean hair,' Haakon told Linnea. 'I bet they didn't make a fuss when someone tried to untangle their ponytail,' he teased.

'Bet they did.' Linnea danced away with a laugh, then came back and demanded a ride on her father's shoulders. Mia smiled at the sight; he was such a great dad.

Birka had been home to a thousand people, pagans and Christians apparently living side by side, and quite a few of them were foreigners. Merchants, artisans, farmers and slaves, all in tightly packed houses that fanned out in three semicircles around the bay, which formed a natural harbour. Mia stopped to look out over that bay, and for a moment it was as if she could picture the scene. *Wooden houses, some with walls made of wattle and daub, the smoke steaming gently out of the roof thatch, boats bobbing up and down at anchor in the harbour, a constant breeze, sun shining on the lake, and activity everywhere, people going about their busy lives . . .*

'Mia? Are you coming to the museum?'

'Huh?' She jumped as Haakon touched her arm. 'Oh, yes, sure.'

'It all feels very familiar, doesn't it?' he whispered. 'I can almost smell the woodsmoke and the middens . . . creepy.'

Mia shivered and hugged herself. 'Yes. Uncanny.'

She followed the others into the museum, where there was a small-scale model of the town as it would have looked in Viking times. It was exactly the way Mia had already imagined it, which made her shiver again. Ivar and Linnea rushed around, checking out the other exhibits, but Mia and Haakon remained standing next to the model, staring at it for ages. Haakon sighed and pointed at one of the houses. 'That one there is where the rings were made. A goldsmith, Asbjörn, brilliant at his work. I just . . . know. It's like I remember going there, ordering them.'

'How is that possible?' But she didn't doubt him.

He looked at her, his blue eyes troubled. 'I'm not sure I like this, Mia. It's getting out of control and I feel like we're building up to something. Something . . . we may not like.'

She nodded. 'Yeah, me too. But what can we do? I mean, how do you stop supernatural things from happening? Contact a medium?' A slightly hysterical giggle escaped her. 'We'd be locked up for sure. No one would believe us.'

He smiled. 'No, probably not.' His fingers closed around hers in a gesture that felt so right she didn't even consider pulling her hand away. 'And it seems we're in this together, so at least we know we're both crazy, right?'

'Totally, as Ivar would say. I guess we'll just have to go with the flow, or whatever.'

What else *could* they do, after all?

They returned to Birch Thorpe, tired but happy, just after dinner time. Linnea was still chattering about the fact that she'd been allowed to help a woman make Viking bread – which had tasted pretty good, actually – and even grind the flour beforehand, while Ivar was discussing Viking weapons with Haakon.

'And I loooove my elk!' Linnea was cuddling a stuffed toy with the lugubrious face of a Swedish moose.

'I'm surprised you didn't want one, Ivar,' Mia joked.

'Nope, but I got this. Cool, huh? It's elk sh— . . . I mean poo.' Ivar glanced at Linnea, who hadn't noticed his use of what she would term a bad word, and held up a key ring made of fossilised moose droppings. It was dangling off a long chain attached to his low-slung jeans.

'Yuck.' Haakon shook his head but grinned nonetheless. 'I'm surprised Linnea didn't want one too.'

Ivar waved it at the little girl, who squealed and shouted, 'No, gross!' so he repeated the action umpteen times, while both of them laughed.

Haakon rolled his eyes at Mia. 'Kids, eh?'

Mia smiled back. She almost felt like they were a normal family – mother, father, teenage son and young daughter – and the thought sent an ache of longing through her that took her by surprise. She hadn't even thought about wanting children except in the distant future; now suddenly she was swamped by maternal feelings. It was very disconcerting.

She was just trying to analyse this when they drew up in front of the cottage and she caught sight of a gleaming Volvo that hadn't been there when they'd left. 'Who on earth . . . ?' she began, then almost groaned out loud.

Sitting on the steps was Charles, wearing a suit and an expression of acute annoyance.

Chapter Thirty

Haukr heaved a sigh of relief as his home finally hove into view, but the sense of doom knotting his stomach did not abate. Rather, it intensified. Standing in the prow of his ship, holding on to the snake's-head carving, he could soon make out every detail, and it wasn't the peaceful scene he'd been hoping for, with everyone going about their duties. Instead, all he saw was devastation.

He'd believed the summons by the king to be genuine, since Egil had delivered such messages before. And as he and his men left, they'd met up with a few other ships also bound for the supposed council, which had laid to rest any niggling feelings of doubt. But they'd all been duped – Egil had been very thorough. Now more than two weeks had passed and his impatience had had to be reined in tightly while he and his men battled contrary winds.

Upon reaching Gotland, he'd found out that he had been tricked – the king wasn't even there – and fear had coursed through him, almost freezing the blood in his veins as he realised the implications. Someone had wanted him out of the way for a reason, and he could only think of one. Because although the other shipowners were equally angry at being fooled in this way,

Haukr was sure the entire subterfuge was aimed at him. He could feel it in his bones.

As the ship came to rest next to the jetty, he was the first man to jump out, and he threw the thick rope to Thorald, who was gazing with horror at the scene before them. With long strides, Haukr climbed the hill to the blackened remains of his great hall. Where once the beautiful building had stood, there was now only ash and charred timber. Some of the other huts had also been destroyed, but about half remained, and as he called out, a few people emerged cautiously, their expressions turning to relief when they caught sight of him.

'Jarl Haukr! Thank the gods . . .'

His heartbeat quickened as he tried to pick out the one he was longing to see above all others, but he'd known instinctively that she wouldn't be there.

'What happened here? Where's Ceri?' he asked as Aase and a thrall named Tanwen hurried towards him. Belatedly he remembered his daughter. 'And Jorun? Where are they?' he barked.

'Jorun is well, but . . .' Aase shook her head, tears running silently down her cheeks, while Tanwen whispered two words. 'The grove.'

The massive fists of the god Thor seemed to grip his lungs and squeeze until he thought he'd never be able to breathe again. A large hand came to rest on his shoulder and he found Thorald behind him, trying to imbue him with his strength and support. Haukr nodded to show that he appreciated it, then the two of them set off as one, heading for the sacred grove.

Even though he didn't really want to see what that grisly place had to reveal, he began to run. Thorald's feet pounded behind him, but he was only vaguely aware of the man's presence. His focus was entirely on what was in front of him, coming into view. He ran faster than he'd ever run before in his life, heart pounding, lungs bursting, and didn't stop until he was standing right before the enormous ash tree.

He hadn't allowed any human sacrifices for years, only animal ones, and it had been months since the last *blōt*. The tree was therefore normally fairly bare this time of year, but not today. He sensed the shadowy form that adorned it before he even saw it, the smell of slaughter lingering in the air, making him gag. Slowly he raised his eyes, inch by inch, forcing himself to keep them open even though every fibre of his being screamed out to him not to look.

'Oh no, please, no!'

The words tore out of him in the form of a wail, and he drew in a sharp hiss of breath that turned into a dry sob. Although he'd known what he would see, his gaze still recoiled at the gruesome figure hanging from one of the branches.

A human shape.

Long, dark curling tresses blowing in the wind.

Plaid shawl, also flapping in the breeze, pinned round the shoulders with the plain brooch Ceri had been given on arrival here.

One shoe dangling from the end of the left foot.

And flesh in the process of being picked clean by birds and other creatures, but one hand . . . one hand with a gold ring still glinting on its finger. Ceri's mother's ring.

Haukr felt his entire body grow cold. He emitted another strangled cry, then sank to his knees, gasping for air. He became aware of a strange keening noise and realised that he was the one making it, but he couldn't stop and nor could he seem to breathe properly, no matter how much his lungs struggled to draw in air. He wanted nothing more than to lie down and die himself, because what was there to live for now? Without Ceri, there was no meaning in anything. Without Ceri, all joy had gone from the world.

Without Ceri . . .

He had no idea how long he sat there, staring with unseeing eyes into the forest around him. On some level he was aware of Thorald standing frozen at the edge of the clearing as if guarding him, but he couldn't speak to him. Not yet.

Perhaps not ever.

When Ceri came to, she was shivering with cold and her head throbbed fit to burst. She opened her eyes slowly, but there was no light and she couldn't see her surroundings. Despite the pounding inside her skull, she managed to raise herself into a sitting position and her hands encountered a cold earth floor. There seemed to be no blanket or anything else within reach, and when she attempted to crawl in a circle, she could find nothing but bare walls.

Where in the name of all the gods was she?

Some sort of earth cellar, like the ones at Haukr's settlement where they kept vegetables over the winter? Yes, her questing fingers found a couple of sacks now, one still bulging with what might be turnips. Terror took hold of her and the shivering turned into uncontrollable tremors, but she hugged herself for warmth and clamped her teeth together, drawing in deep breaths to stem the rising panic. When she managed to think more clearly, she gathered together all the sacks she could find, and fashioned a sort of bed from them – a few underneath her, the rest wrapped around her body. That helped, and her shivering subsided.

'Stay strong,' she admonished herself. If they hadn't killed her yet, they must want her alive, and knowing Ragnhild, she'd want revenge of some sort. The woman had been humiliated – or so she'd said – and she obviously blamed Ceri, since she was the one who had alerted Haukr to what was going on in the sacred grove. Therefore she would wish to humiliate Ceri in return. 'She wants

278

me to be afraid, so I mustn't give in to it,' Ceri muttered. 'Haukr will come for me, I know he will.'

But she remembered Svein's words – that Haukr would think her dead. How would they persuade him? Show him charred remains with her jewellery on it? Because her fingers were bare, her mother's ring gone once again. She shuddered at the horrible image conjured up by her mind. Hopefully he wouldn't believe them, but what if he did?

She gritted her teeth. She mustn't think like that or else she'd go mad. And whatever happened, she was determined not to give Ragnhild the satisfaction of seeing her cowed.

Chapter Thirty-One

'You could have let me know you were coming.' Mia tried to keep her voice even while she preceded Charles up the stairs and into her bedroom. Their bedroom. She would have to share with him – he would expect it, of course, and it wasn't as if there was anywhere else for him to sleep, especially since Ivar had declared that he'd stay another night on the sofa.

She tried to rationalise her feelings, telling herself she'd only been thrown by his sudden appearance, and that as soon as she became used to him being there, everything would be fine. But she knew deep down she was just kidding herself.

'I wanted to surprise you.' Charles looked hurt and still cross about the long wait he'd had. Mia had taken the key with her instead of hiding it, following Haakon's comments on that subject. 'I thought it would be nice to spend the weekend with you since I'm going to Ayia Napa next week. How was I supposed to know you'd be off having fun in Stockholm with other men?' Charles thumped his suitcase down on the bed with jerky movements.

'Other men?' Mia glared at him, but a dart of guilt pierced her as she remembered holding hands with Haakon at the museum. 'Haakon is in charge of this dig and we both had business in Stockholm today, so we decided to save on petrol and share a car, that's all. Also, we needed to do some research at Birka.' Neither of those things was true, but probably better to tell him a white lie.

'Taking his kids with you?'

'They couldn't be left behind, so they had to come. Actually, Ivar is my neighbour's son, not Haakon's. I'm sort of looking after him for the weekend.' And she was, even if Thoresson hadn't asked her to.

'Right. But what's he doing living here? You never said anything about having a lodger.'

'I had agreed to let the project leader stay at the cottage – someone has to be on site at all times. I didn't know who it was going to be. And he brought his daughter; she's been staying here too.'

Charles grunted something, but still looked unhappy.

'I'd almost forgotten, it's midsummer.' Mia attempted to sound cheerful when they rejoined the others downstairs. 'Linnea, do you want to come and pick flowers with me? It won't take long.' She had to get out of the house for a bit, have a breather.

'What, now? But it's dark.' The little girl looked adorably confused, and Mia laughed.

'Not really, just a bit dim. Girls have to pick flowers at midsummer and put them under their pillow so they'll dream about the man they're going to marry.' She deliberately didn't glance at any of the males in the room. Charles had turned on Gran's tiny television, which Mia had bought her only a year ago, and Haakon had his nose buried in some archaeology paperwork, while Ivar was absorbed in a handheld games console.

'Oh, OK.' Linnea grinned.

They headed for the far reaches of the back garden, which was more or less a wildflower meadow. 'Tonight is Midsummer Eve, which is one of the special nights of the year, when there's magic about,' Mia told Linnea. The little girl's eyes shone; she loved stories of magic. 'You and I have to collect seven different types of flower, without saying a word. Got that? You have to be absolutely silent, or the magic won't work. But that's not all – you need to be able to name those flowers quietly inside your head while you pick them. Do you remember the names I taught you the other day?' They'd had an impromptu mini botanical lesson one afternoon.

'I think so.'

'Shall we run through them again before we start?'

'Yes please. I don't want to ruin the magic.'

'All right.' They walked around and Mia pointed to the various flowers and made sure Linnea had memorised their names. For most of them she only knew what they were called in Swedish, since she'd been taught by her grandmother, although similar flowers grew in England too. '*Smörblomma, hundkex, mormors glasögon, ängaboll, blåklocka, prästkrage, midsommarblomster.*' She could almost hear Gran's voice inside her head, chanting the names, and it made her feel as if the old lady was still with her somehow. She turned to Linnea. 'Are you ready then? OK, let's go.'

Together they each collected their seven flowers, without saying a word. Mia had secretly doubted that Linnea could ever be quiet for that length of time, since she normally chattered non-stop, but the sense of occasion seemed to keep her spellbound and she managed it.

They returned to the cottage, where Haakon was getting a couple of beers out of the fridge, presumably for himself and Charles. Mia was relieved, as it must mean Charles was being polite. 'Hello, what have you got there?' He hunkered down next to his daughter, who was holding out her little bunch of flowers.

'Seven flowers, Daddy. I'm going to put them under my pillow, and tonight I'll dream of the boy I'm going to marry.'

'Wow, really? Actually, I think I've heard of that. My granny told me about something similar. Do you think it will work?' Haakon pretended to take it seriously, and Mia gave him an approving smile from behind Linnea's back.

'Of course. It's magic.'

Haakon glanced at Mia. 'And will you be doing this too?' His eyes held a teasing glint, which made her catch her breath.

'Yes, I always do it when I'm here. My gran insisted.'

'Has it worked?'

'Of course,' Mia said, crossing her fingers behind her back. The truth was, she'd never dreamed about anyone, but she didn't want to spoil things for Linnea, whose eyes were shining with excitement again.

'I hope I dream of Ash,' the little girl said. 'That'd be so cool, even if I can't tell anyone until he asks me to marry him.'

'Who?' Mia was confused and not a little surprised that a six year old should be in love already. 'Is he your boyfriend at school?'

Linnea went into gales of laughter, and Haakon grinned. 'No, he's the hero of Pokémon – Ash Ketchum. Linnea loves those cartoons.'

'Cartoons?' Mia had heard of Pokémon from her half-brothers, who were into collecting cards from the series, but for Linnea to think that the characters were real enough to marry seemed weird. Still, she was only little and clearly had a great imagination.

'Oh, right, well let's hope you do dream of him then.'

'You'd better get ready for bed. The sooner you go to sleep, the sooner you'll start dreaming,' Haakon said, and for once Linnea didn't argue, just skipped up the stairs after giving Mia a goodnight hug.

Later that evening, Mia lay on her side of the bed, staring out of the window at the Swedish summer night. This time of year, it never really became fully dark. Instead the landscape was bathed in a soft glow, making it seem ethereal and unearthly. It must have looked the same to the Vikings, and she wondered whether they had appreciated its beauty the way she did. Her garden was a place full of shadows and whispered sounds, imaginary or otherwise, and she had a sudden urge to go out there.

'Did you miss me?' The voice coming from behind her wasn't imaginary, however, and sadly, it wasn't one she wanted to hear. Although she longed for contact with another human being with a yearning that took her by surprise in its ferocity, she knew that the last person on earth she wanted touching her was Charles.

This certainty had grown throughout the evening, as every little thing he said or did irritated her. Where before she would have made allowances, thinking it endearing that he held such strong opinions on everything under the sun, now it only annoyed her. He'd held forth at length to Haakon about the famous people his firm represented, and bored Ivar silly with his opinions on the latest *Star Wars* film. And then he'd started talking about how he hoped Mia was soon going to sell this place. When Haakon asked quietly whether this was what Mia wanted, Charles's face had darkened.

'It is if she has our best interests in mind,' he'd said, his cheeks rosy from having consumed several more bottles of strong beer. 'I mean, what's the point of owning something we can't use? Who wants to spend every summer in this godforsaken place?'

'Er, me?' Ivar muttered, but Charles hadn't heard him.

Mia had seen Haakon's mouth twitch, but he remained serious when he replied. 'Well, believe it or not, there are actually people who enjoy spending time here.'

Charles didn't notice the slightly sarcastic tone and went on blithely. 'Yes, yes, but they're Swedes, they're used to it. And if it rains or whatever, they can pack up and go home to town. If we come here, we can't exactly get in the car and go back to London in a jiffy. Besides, if it's summers in the rain you want, there's always my parents' house in Devon.'

Mia had kept silent, knowing that she would only anger him further if she voiced her views.

His whispered question hung in the air now, although whisper wasn't quite the right word, since his voice had sounded very loud in the stillness of the night. Mia didn't know how to reply; the truth was, she hadn't missed him at all. Charles didn't seem to notice her silence. His hand reached out under the duvet and started a slow ascent from her belly upwards, but she halted it before it got very far, pushing it away and shifting further towards her side of the bed.

'Don't, please, the walls are really thin in this cottage. Remember how you complained about Gran snoring?'

A year ago it wouldn't have bothered her whether anyone listened in on their lovemaking, but the thought of Haakon so close by with little Linnea, not to mention Ivar downstairs, was enough to cool any ardour on her part. Not that she had experienced any – quite the opposite.

This had to end, but not like this, in the middle of the night. She clenched her fists around the covers and swallowed the words that longed to escape. She would tell him tomorrow.

With an angry grunt, he rolled over on his side, apparently accepting her rebuff, although with ill grace, and she breathed a sigh of relief when she heard him begin to snore.

Yes, tomorrow. Definitely.

She slipped her hand under her pillow to fluff it up and found the flowers she'd put there. *Oh Lord*. Would she dream about anyone this time? Not likely.

But the dreams, when they came, turned out to be nightmares, and she woke towards dawn with a hammering heart, fighting her way out from under the duvet. *She'd been locked in, complete darkness, cold, damp and with a hard earth floor and no hope of escape . . .*

She sat up and waited for dawn. She wasn't going back to her prison.

Haakon made himself scarce the next morning; judging by the twin scowls on Mia and Charles's faces, there was about to be a big bust-up. He wasn't quite sure what was going on, but he'd sensed an atmosphere between them the night before, and Mia hadn't looked particularly pleased to see her fiancé. Poor guy. Charles had seemed quite crestfallen for a while, before the beer helped him rally. Then he'd become talkative – too much so. And oh boy, did the guy have opinions. It could have been the alcohol, of course, but Haakon had found Charles much too arrogant, as if no one else's thoughts mattered, only his. The few times Mia commented, her views had been swept aside, especially when it concerned the future of the cottage. Haakon hadn't even known that she'd been thinking of selling it – she hadn't given the slightest indication of that – and he could understand her reluctance, especially as she seemed to have had a very strong bond with her grandmother. Something Charles clearly failed to grasp. What was the matter with the man? Insensitive didn't even begin to describe it.

But it wasn't Haakon's problem. 'Linnea, Ivar, let's go and see if Mia's boat is seaworthy. If not, we need to do something about it.'

The little rowing boat, when they got it out into the sunshine, wasn't too bad; with the application of some sealant or similar it would probably be OK. At least as far as the island, which was all they needed. He got the kids to help him scrape off old paint and set about making the hull watertight.

About an hour later, he heard doors slamming and the squeal of tyres as a car sped away. It would seem that Mia's fiancé had gone off in a huff.

He gave it another half-hour, then went back to the cottage to see if Mia was OK. He found her sitting on the veranda, nursing a cup of tea that had to be fairly cold, judging by the state of the milk in it.

'You all right?' He hunkered down in front of her and noticed immediately that she wasn't wearing the ugly diamond engagement ring any longer.

'Yes, fine.' She inhaled slowly. 'It's over. Charles isn't the right man for me. I . . . He was a bit upset, as you can imagine.' She made a face. 'These things are never easy.'

Haakon didn't much care about Charles right then. He was sure the guy would get over it; he hadn't seemed to care much about the feelings of anyone other than himself. 'And you? Are you upset?' He gazed into Mia's eyes, which glittered like shards of ice in the morning sun slanting through the windows. They were suspiciously moist.

She nodded. 'A bit, but I'll be fine. I just feel so . . . guilty. I hate hurting anyone. You know?'

He did know. Sofia had made him go through a massive guilt trip when he'd asked for a divorce, blaming it all on him. But it was never just one person's fault if a relationship failed. 'He'll be OK. As long as you're sure it's what you wanted.'

He took her hand, the one with the snake ring, and realised that he was wearing the museum one again. *Faen!* He'd forgotten to remove it. Luckily Mia didn't seem to notice.

'Yes. I didn't love him any more. Maybe I never did, who knows?' She sighed. 'I'll have to go to London and pack up my stuff, put it into storage, but it can wait a week or two. Maybe Charles can go and visit his parents for a weekend so we don't have to see each other. And we'll either have to sell the flat or he can buy me out, I don't care which.' She took another deep breath. 'Anyway . . . what's happening outside?'

'We're fixing the boat so we can go to the island this afternoon. It'll take a while before the sealant is dry.'

'Oh good. I can't wait to see what Thoresson has done. I just hope he hasn't ruined everything.'

'Amen to that.'

Mia followed him outside, and as they walked side by side, Haakon sensed a new lightness in her step that was matched by an answering joy in his. Perhaps there was a chance after all that something could develop between them. He'd have to give her time, obviously, as it took a while to get over a break-up, but at least he now had hope.

Chapter Thirty-Two

Haukr was eventually startled out of his trance by the sound of footsteps and angry voices. As he slowly lifted his gaze and tried to focus, a group of armed men burst into the clearing and headed straight towards him. He frowned at the foremost one, who looked familiar even though he was sure he'd never met him before.

'Where is she?' the man demanded, his speech heavily accented. 'Where is my sister? You will tell me, or so help me God, I'll run you through this instant.'

Haukr stared at the sword raised high in menace, but it was as if he was seeing it from a distance. The man's words made no sense at first, but slowly their meaning seeped into his muddled brain and he frowned. 'Sister?' he repeated dully.

'Yes. Ceridwen. My sister. You abducted her and some of my villagers. She told my son your name and I've been searching for you for weeks. Now I've come to ransom her – well, all of them. I'll pay whatever you want, even though you already took most of my possessions, you swine. I demand you tell me where she is, or else . . .'

Haukr closed his eyes and shook his head. He couldn't believe this was happening, didn't want to believe any of it. Hysterical

289

laughter bubbled up inside him, but he pushed it down. It might be ironic that her brother should arrive today of all days to claim her, but it was no laughing matter. Unable to form coherent words, he simply pointed to the tree behind him.

Cadoc – Haukr remembered the brother's name now, since Ceri had been speaking of him not long before he went to see the king – cried out in much the same manner as Haukr had earlier, his face turning ashen, and there were further cries of disbelief from the men who accompanied him.

'How ...? Why ...? No! It cannot be.'

Cadoc's face turned slowly red, and he lunged for Haukr, shouting something in his own language. For an instant, Haukr contemplated allowing the other man to kill him, but in his fury, Cadoc had forgotten his weapon, and he tried to take Haukr on with his bare hands. Instinctively, the jarl defended himself, and although Cadoc's strength was multiplied by his emotions, he was no match for the much bigger man and soon lay sprawled in the dirt.

Cadoc's followers surged forward, but Haukr turned to them and bellowed, 'Halt!' so loudly that they stopped in their tracks and stared at him. 'Cadoc, translate, please. This is not my doing, I swear by whatever god or gods you believe in. Your kinswoman was very dear to me, too dear, some would say, and this ... this tragedy occurred while I was away. I will gladly take you to the person who is responsible, but it will not give you ... us ... Ceridwen back.'

His voice broke on the final words, and at last his genuine grief seemed to penetrate Cadoc's fog of rage. The latter stood up and dusted himself off, while frowning at Haukr. 'Ceri was dear to you, you say? You mean she went with you willingly?'

'Not at first, no, but we ... I believe we came to care for each other. Had she still been with us, I would have asked for her hand in marriage.' He stared at the ground and added in a hoarse whisper, 'I swear I am telling the truth.'

'You wanted to marry her?'

Haukr looked up again and held Cadoc's gaze firmly. 'I loved your sister, more than my own life. I would never have harmed a single hair on her head, ever. I had not yet asked her if she would have me, but I was going to. I just wanted to give her more time to get used to being here first.'

Cadoc appeared to consider this for a moment, then he nodded. 'I believe you. I see now that you share my grief. So who is to blame for this? Another man? An enemy of yours?'

'My former wife.'

'What? You had a wife already? But I thought you said . . .'

'It is a long story and I wish to tell you everything from the beginning. Let us go back to . . . well, not to my hall, as it seems to have been destroyed, but perhaps to one of the other buildings.' He sighed at the thought, but found he didn't care right now. A hall could be rebuilt, whereas a human life once taken . . . 'I give you my word no harm will come to either you or your men. You can put away your weapons. We will settle the rest of your grievances later.'

Cadoc nodded again. 'Very well.' He spoke to his men in their own tongue, and they followed Haukr back to the settlement.

When everyone was seated in the weaving hut, which had miraculously survived, and had been offered some ale by a silent Aase, Haukr told them truthfully all that had occurred, leaving nothing out.

'Dear Lord, and all this because of one woman's greed?' Cadoc was incredulous. 'My poor sister . . .'

Haukr was trying not to think about Ceri, but the family resemblance between her and Cadoc was strong, and every time the man spoke or looked at him with his silvery eyes, so like hers, he felt as if someone twisted a sword in his guts. He hoped the foreigners would accept his offer of compensation and leave as soon as possible. He couldn't bear to be near them, truth to tell.

'Va-eh? *Va-eh!*'

Haukr looked up to see Jorun rushing into the hut, her little face looking pinched with worry but lighting up at the sight of him. She was clutching a wooden horse that he'd carved for her a few weeks before he left, and her grip on the toy was so tight, her knuckles were white.

'Jorun, by all the gods! How could I have forgotten about you? Come here, daughter *mín*, and greet your father.' He opened his arms and tried to smile at her, even though it was the last thing he felt like doing at the moment, and she threw herself into his embrace.

'Va-eh,' she said happily, and smiled back, although there was a wariness in her eyes that he hadn't seen for a long time now.

He hugged her close and turned to Cadoc, who had been watching them. 'This is my daughter Jorun. She can't hear very well, but your sister taught her to speak a little. She was very patient with her.'

'I see.' Cadoc smiled at Jorun when she turned to gaze at him, and said, 'Hello, Jorun.'

She answered, 'Eh-oh,' then tilted her head slightly to one side and studied him in more detail. 'Ce-ih?' she asked her father, turning back to him.

He winced inwardly, but managed to reply, 'Yes, Ceri's brother.' He pronounced the words clearly and she nodded her understanding. Then, after drawing in a steadying breath, he added, 'But Ceri gone. Ceri's brother sad. Father sad.' He made a sad face in case she didn't recognise the word, but she nodded and repeated her version of it, before frowning.

'Ce-ih it.' She mimed a punch. 'Go.' She pointed vaguely towards the jetty.

'Yes, gone away. Into the tree. Tree.' Haukr pointed in the other direction, to the grove. He knew that she was familiar with this word and was therefore surprised when she shook her head vehemently.

'No. No dee. Go Mu-eh bwu-eh.'

'What? What did you say?' Haukr regarded her intently. 'Ceri gone where?'

'Mu-eh bwu-eh ay,' Jorun repeated. She mimed someone putting their arms around her, pulling her hair and dragging her away, while pretending to fight against this, and Haukr suddenly understood what she was saying.

'Mother's brother took Ceri? By Odin's ravens, I don't believe it!'

'What is she saying?' Cadoc was watching them intently now. 'It wasn't your wife who killed Ceri, but her brother?'

'Yes, yes, that's it, but hold on.' He faced Jorun again, speaking slowly and clearly. 'Mother's brother hang Ceri?' As he mimed hanging by the neck, the action made him seize up inside, but he knew it was the only way of making Jorun understand what he was asking. The girl shook her head again.

'Oma ang. Ce-ih go. Ip.'

'Woman? Another woman was hanged while Ceri left on a ship?' Haukr felt a glimmer of hope but tamped it down. He couldn't bear it if he was mistaken. Just to make doubly sure, he went through the whole miming sequence again, asking Jorun questions that could only have specific answers, but he still reached the same conclusion. He turned to stare at Cadoc. 'I think she's definitely saying that another woman was killed and hanged in the tree, not Ceri, and that Ceri was taken away by my wife's brothers. If that is so, we must go in search of her. Their home is further along the lakeshore. Will you come with me and my men? I'll not rest until I know for certain.'

'Of course. Nothing would stop me!' Cadoc exclaimed. 'But can this really be? How come no one else knows of this? And who is the woman in the tree?'

'I don't know. Perhaps Jorun was the only witness, and as my former wife won't acknowledge that her daughter isn't a halfwit, she won't have realised that she can tell anyone. Ragnhild has never tried to talk to her. Or maybe she was hiding while watching them.'

Aase came into the hut carrying more ale, and Haukr asked for her opinion. 'Could the woman in the grove be someone other than Ceri? Did you see her being killed?'

'No, none of us saw. We were locked in for an entire day until Jorun freed us. We assumed she'd been hiding outside somewhere but didn't dare let us out until she was sure all the attackers were gone. And then . . . We didn't think to go and look in the grove. We had enough to do here, trying to salvage what was left. It was only by chance that someone went past the tree while hunting for the pigs that had escaped into the forest.'

'So it is possible.' Haukr felt the tiny flame of hope flash inside him again, but he tried not to put too much faith in it. Better to be prepared for the worst. He turned to Cadoc and Thorald, who'd stayed next to him throughout. 'Well, what are we waiting for? Let us go.'

'Indeed.'

Haukr grabbed Jorun by the hand. 'We go to find Ceri, understand? Ceri. You wait here with Aase. Jorun wait.'

Jorun beamed at him. 'Ce-ih,' she reiterated happily.

If only they weren't too late.

Chapter Thirty-Three

'We're having a picnic? Yeah!'

Linnea skipped all the way down to the shore, closely followed by Ivar. Mia was carrying blankets and a cool box, while Haakon brought up the rear with a small array of archaeological tools.

The rowing boat seemed watertight and held their combined weight, even if it wobbled precariously as they climbed in. Mia, who'd been rowing since she was a child, took the oars.

'Hey, I can row too, you know,' Haakon protested with a smile.

'Yes, but it's my boat.' Mia grinned back. She felt carefree and happy now, having decided that there was no point brooding about the past. Charles hadn't been in touch to ask her to reconsider, so maybe he'd realised she was right and they weren't suited. Either way, it was done and no use repining, as Gran had always said.

There was a tiny bit of sandy beach on the inner side of the island, and they left the boat there, tied to a nearby tree. 'You can see it from the mainland, but hopefully it won't matter today,' Mia commented quietly to Haakon. She hoped Thoresson wouldn't come back early and spot them from his house, which was clearly visible from this part of the island.

'Let's leave our stuff for now and reconnoitre.' Haakon set off along the shore.

'Reco-what, Daddy?' Linnea took his hand and hopped on one leg for a bit.

'We're looking for treasure.'

'Ooh! Goody.'

'But we'll let Mia go first, because this is her island.'

Mia knew he had another reason, but kept that to herself. He wouldn't want Linnea to see any skeletons, if there should happen to be one.

They walked all the way around the perimeter but didn't find anything. 'Shall we look among the trees?' she suggested.

She headed towards the middle of the island, where she'd never been before. The land sloped upwards to form a small hill, and at the top of it, she stopped abruptly. 'Uh-oh.'

'What? Oh, sh— . . . I mean, blast!' Haakon had come up behind her and looked over her shoulder.

There were two piles of rocks on top of the hill – tumuli or cairns, oblong in shape and clearly man-made – and one of them had been disturbed, with a hole dug into the soil on the right-hand side. A small mound of earth was heaped beside it. It looked as though someone had been in a hurry, as a couple of random bones stuck out of the soil heap. There were others in the hole itself, and at one end, the top of a skull could be glimpsed.

'Is that the treasure, Daddy?'

Linnea's question made them both jump. 'Er, maybe, sweetie.' Haakon turned to block her line of sight. 'But it looks like someone got here before us, so we'll have to search somewhere else.'

'Oh, bummer.'

That was one way of putting it.

Mia took the girl's hand. 'Why don't we go and unpack the

picnic while your daddy takes a closer look? Just to make sure there's nothing left here.'

'Yes, good idea. You guys start without me, I'll catch you up.' Haakon's eyes met Mia's over the top of Linnea's head. This was about damage limitation now. They had to find out if the skeleton had been disturbed completely or if some of it was still intact. Then they'd need an osteoarchaeologist, as well as the police – any bodies found in the ground had to be investigated to make sure they weren't a recent murder victim.

'Ivar, are you coming?' Mia nudged the boy, who was staring at the hole in the ground with an expression of grief.

'Huh? Yeah.'

As he followed Mia and Linnea back to the boat, he said quietly, 'Dad did that, didn't he? He has no idea . . .'

Mia turned and put a hand on his arm. 'No, but then he's not an archaeologist. He probably doesn't understand. But we'll make sure that no more damage is done, so it'll be fine.'

It wasn't really, but she couldn't stand the boy's sad expression.

Haakon had brought some of the tools and started to brush away any loose soil. Miraculously, it seemed that Thoresson – if indeed this was his handiwork – had stopped digging when he found what he'd come for.

Had there been more items apart from the brooch? Probably. If a woman was high-status enough to be buried with such a beautiful object, she'd have had other grave goods too, like a sewing kit perhaps, some beads or other jewellery, a spindle and an eating knife. There was nothing here but bones, though, as far as Haakon could see, but the second stone cairn had been left untouched. Another grave? It had to be.

Thoresson must have been short of time or he'd have dug there as well. Hadn't Ivar said his father had only just found the brooch before he went off to the Far East? That would explain why he hadn't been back yet; he'd obviously been too busy since.

Bastard.

Haakon felt bad for thinking this way. He'd come to like Ivar a lot in just a few short weeks. But the kid's father was another thing altogether. He had to be stopped.

Giving up on the woman's grave for now, he went to join the others. This place merited a full-scale excavation, and he needed to get the rest of the team over here so they could do it properly.

He tried to act normal as the four of them consumed their picnic sitting on a flattish rocky outcrop, but his thoughts were elsewhere. In his mind's eye, he could see a Viking boat, complete with snake's-head prow, come to rest on the little sandy beach. *A woman, carried high on a bed of wolf pelts, people chanting, crying, whispering . . . a small procession snaking up the hill, the bier laid down with care and reverence next to a hole in the ground. The woman herself, covered in a plaid blanket with that magnificent brooch holding it in place . . .*

'Daddy, look! I found treasure. Ivar says!'

Linnea threw herself on to his lap, jolting Haakon back to the present. 'What?'

'Isn't it pretty?' She held out a tiny round object with a hole through the middle. 'We washed it in the lake.'

'Oh, an amber bead. You have indeed found something precious.' Haakon smiled at his daughter. 'Show Mia.'

'Yes, that is gorgeous, Linnea. I love how the sun shines through it, don't you?'

'I found this.' Ivar held up something wet and floppy, a piece of material by the look of it, and made a face. 'We were digging on the beach and it was buried there, near the water's edge. Looks like your picnic blanket, Mia. Guess your gran must have dropped it one time.'

'Can I see?' Haakon took the piece of material and noticed the dull colours and coarse weaving. 'Bloody hell,' he muttered.

'Daddy! You said a bad word!' Linnea laughed and poked him in the ribs.

'Sorry, but . . . Mia, take a look at this, will you? I'm going to get a Tupperware box.'

'It's definitely plaid.' Mia placed the material in the box. 'Do you really think it could be old?' Her eyes held an expression of awe. 'That would just be . . . wow!'

'We'll have to have it carbon-dated, but yes. I think it's possible.' Haakon looked up. 'Well done, Ivar, I think you found treasure too. If this is what I think it is, the people back at the museum are going to get mega excited.'

'Really? Awesome!'

Eventually they returned to the mainland and sent Ivar home, despite his protests.

'But I want to help guard the island,' he grumbled. 'It would be great, staying up all night and stuff.'

'Think about it,' Mia told him sternly. 'We can't let your dad find out you've been helping us, or that we're on to him. He might do something stupid, like hide that fantastic collection before we've figured out a way of making him allow us to study it. And if you're the one who catches him going to the island, what do you think he'll say? You'd be in big trouble.'

'Well, yes, I know, but . . .'

'Come on, we've got to outsmart him. You have to make him think you've just been hanging around at home all weekend playing PlayStation or whatever. If he finds out you've been working with us, he'll be livid.' A thought seemed to strike Mia. 'Has he ever been, you know, violent towards you? Or shown any such tendencies?'

'No, he mostly just ignores me. We don't talk much.'

'Oh, OK. Just checking. Still, be careful, eh? It's probably best if you cultivate your mumbling teenager act.' She smiled at him and he grinned back. Haakon wondered what she meant, but it was obviously a private joke between them.

'OK, I'll do my best. If he asks where I've been, I'll just say "out".'

'Excellent. And Ivar, please don't come over here tomorrow until you know he's gone out or whatever. You have to be extra careful from now on. Deal?'

'Deal.'

Haakon went back to the island on his own to rig up a tarpaulin over the opened grave, weighting it down with some of the cairn stones. Whatever was left here had to be protected now at all costs. As he worked, he heard the voices whispering all around him again – the sorrow, the entreaties to the gods to look after the dead woman, the wish that they would be reunited with her in the afterlife . . .

He swallowed down the tsunami of grief that threatened to engulf him. She was nothing to do with him.

And yet he knew that somehow she was.

Chapter Thirty-Four

Ceri had no idea how long she had been kept in the stinking little root cellar, but her captors didn't intend to starve her to death at any rate, since she was fed at least once a day. The fare wasn't the best, but it kept her alive, and she spent a lot of time jumping up and down to keep warm so she didn't become too stiff or immobile. With nothing else to do, she also tried to think of a way out, and she finally came up with a plan.

Since the hut was mostly underground, the lower part of the walls consisted entirely of earth that had hardened over time. Scrabbling around in the dark, she found a sharp stone sticking out, which she managed to prise free, and then she began to hack at the wall in various places to see what else she could find.

She was hoping to discover a larger stone, small enough to fit comfortably in her hand, but still heavy. Whenever her food was delivered, it was brought by only one man, who obviously considered her too weak to challenge him in any way. She encouraged that belief by appearing listless and unresponsive, and she reasoned that she might be able to surprise him by hitting him over the head. For that she needed a weapon.

Days passed – she lost count of how many – and none of her little excavations yielded any suitable stones. She made sure she put the soil back afterwards, patting it into place in case anyone came to shine a light around the place, but it proved unnecessary. No one seemed even remotely interested in her. Not yet, at any rate, but she couldn't take any chances.

She continued her explorations, and at last she came across the perfect stone. The right size, heavy and with a sharp bit sticking out at one end. She wanted to dance around with joy, but instead she cleaned it as best she could with the bottom of her now filthy under-tunic, and prepared herself to attack.

The food arrived at different times each day, so she had to stay vigilant. Not that she had any way of measuring time, but she tried to judge it by the way her stomach was reacting – if too long had passed, it would feel as though it was turning itself inside out for want of sustenance, whereas other times she was merely ravenous. Waiting in the pitch black, it seemed like an eternity, but at last she heard muffled footsteps approaching and went to stand to one side of the door. Luck was with her. Darkness was descending outside, which meant that her gaoler couldn't see much more than she could. He grunted something that sounded like 'Here y'are', and bent to place a bowl on the floor just inside the door.

Ceri struck, bringing down the stone, sharp side out, on the back of his head with as much force as she could muster, grunting with the effort. There was a muffled thud as stone connected with flesh and bone, which quite turned her stomach, but she forced down the bile that rose in her throat. To her relief, he crumpled without a sound, pitching forward into the hut, and she threw the stone to one side and dragged him in as fast as she could. Peering round the door frame, she scanned the surrounding area but could see nothing threatening. She hurried outside, closed and barred the door, then crept away to the right and ran towards a stand of trees that seemed to afford some protection.

Just as she reached cover, she suddenly heard what sounded like a Celtic war cry, mingled with a dozen other voices yelling in anger or threat. She stopped behind a tree trunk and leaned against it, catching her breath and shaking her head. Was she going mad? There were no Celts here.

No, her brain must have been addled by spending such a long time in the dark. Or perhaps she was still suffering the after-effects of that blow to the head. Svein hit hard, as she knew to her cost.

Listening intently, she became aware of the sounds of fighting – screams cut off in mid sound as if the person's throat had been slit, strangled cries as of someone horribly maimed, and the terrified high-pitched shrieks of women and children scared witless. Her legs began to shake, and however much she wanted to, she couldn't run away.

Another cry rang out, and this time she was absolutely certain it was in her own language. What was more, she recognised the voice that had uttered it, and with a sob of relief, she stumbled towards it.

'Cadoc!' she shouted. 'Cadoc, over here!' Her heart filled with joy and the knowledge that someone had come to find her. Why or how her brother had turned up here, of all places, she had no idea and cared even less. All she knew was that she would be safe with him.

If only she could reach him.

Chapter Thirty-Five

Mia couldn't go to sleep that evening. She knew Haakon was taking his turn to sit down by the shore, watching the island, and the thought of him out there in the semi-darkness was driving her crazy. She wanted to be with him.

She wanted him, she could admit it now.

The longing inside her was almost unbearable. She'd been suppressing it for weeks, knowing it was wrong when she was still engaged to Charles, but now she was free and there was nothing to stop her acknowledging her feelings. Except for the fact that Haakon was married. From the way he avoided talking about Sofia, however, she'd gathered things were a bit strained between them at the moment. Did that mean there was a chance he might leave her? And might he consider getting together with Mia instead? She doubted it, but she couldn't stop fantasising about such a scenario, and it was unbearable.

She glanced at the snake ring on her finger, which seemed to be sending little electric shocks up her arm, as if to say, *Go and find out! What are you waiting for?* But that was just her imagination. The tingling inside her had nothing to do with the snake; it was pure anticipation. Or nerves. Maybe both.

Throwing off the covers, she stepped into a pair of flip-flops.

She had to talk to him or she would go mad.

The fresh scents of the garden at night surrounded her as she walked through the grass down towards the jetty. Haakon was sitting next to it, at the water's edge, on a waterproof picnic rug, hidden from sight. He was dressed in dark jogging trousers and a hoodie, and he had his arms wrapped round his knees.

'Hey, seen anything suspicious?' Mia whispered, sinking down next to him.

'Hello! Can't sleep?' He was whispering too, although sound carried in the still night air so it was probably louder than they thought.

'No. I wasn't sure if it was OK for me to leave Linnea alone in the cottage, though. I locked the front door and we can see the back from here, but should I go back?'

'Nah, she's fine. If she wakes up, the entire neighbourhood will hear her, trust me. The window is open.' Haakon chuckled. 'And to answer your question, I haven't noticed anything so far. We've got a spotlight set up at the end of the jetty, so I'll be able to light up a large part of the bay if anyone tries to row out to the island. Should be a good deterrent, I hope.'

'Sounds great. I really hope Ivar's dad doesn't try anything, though.'

'It's best to be prepared anyway. We just can't let it happen.'

They sat in silence for a while, and Mia began to feel awkward. What was she doing here? She should leave him to it. Just because she was attracted to him – OK, massively attracted to him, be honest – didn't mean he would feel the same way. Why would he want her when his taste ran to tall, slim blondes? And he probably wouldn't leave Sofia anyway – she was the mother of his child. She opened her mouth to say that she'd better be off, but he spoke first.

'So come on, tell me who you dreamed of. I'm dying to know.'

'Dreamed of? Oh, that.' Mia smiled. 'No one that night. In fact, don't tell Linnea, but I don't think that flower thing works. I've only ever had one dream at midsummer, and that was about my dog. Gran laughed so much I thought she was going to have a heart attack.'

Haakon laughed quietly. 'Oh well, there's always next year.'

'I do dream most other nights, though, about a Viking, would you believe? It's getting kind of tiresome.'

Haakon gave her a searching look. 'I have strange dreams too. Whenever I wear this.' He held out his hand, and she saw the museum's snake ring on his finger. 'And yes, I know I shouldn't be wearing it, but it seems the safest place for it to be.'

'Are your dreams about one particular person?' Mia held her breath, waiting for his answer.

'Mostly. A beautiful woman with long, dark curly hair, just like yours. She isn't you, but . . . at the same time, she is.'

Mia drew in a sharp breath. Had he meant to imply that she was beautiful? No, he'd been talking about the other woman. She looked down and pulled at a nearby clump of grass before whispering, 'It's the same with my Viking – he has your eyes. Haakon, what are we going to do?'

She shouldn't have come. It was all the golden snake's doing. Somehow he was influencing her thinking and she should have resisted. It was wrong. And yet, looking at Haakon, she wanted to stay right where she was.

It was dark down by the lake's edge, but Haakon could see Mia's face clearly and he knew exactly what he wanted to do. But he mustn't. It was too soon.

'How about a midnight swim?'

'What?' She blinked in surprise. 'Now? Are you crazy?'

'No, it's the perfect time. We'll still hear Linnea if we don't splash too much, and we can see the bay just as well from the water. Better, in fact. Come on. I haven't gone skinny-dipping for years.'

'Skinny d— What? Haakon!'

He tried not to laugh out loud at the incredulity in her voice. It had been worth a shot. 'OK, fine, keep your underwear on then.' He took off his hoodie and jogging bottoms, then pulled his T-shirt over his head.

'I'm not wearing any.'

Her words froze his movements. 'Huh?'

'So if you're serious, it's going to have to be the skinny option.'

He stared at her, arrested by those luminous grey eyes, which he could still see clearly in the half-light. A bolt of pure, unadulterated lust shot through him and he swallowed hard. 'Mia, I . . .'

'It's fine. I can go back to the house if you'd rather swim alone.'

'What? No! I just . . . I was joking.' He hesitated, but had to ask. 'You wouldn't mind swimming naked with me?'

She smiled. 'I'd love to. If you're sure you're OK with that.' Then her smile dimmed. 'But what about Sofia? I'm not sure she'd approve of you skinny-dipping with other women.'

'Sofia? What's she got to do with . . . Hell, you don't know, do you?'

'Know what?' Mia's eyes were huge, fixed on him as if his answer was incredibly important.

'I'm divorced, Mia. Sofia is my ex.'

'Really? Well, in that case . . .' She grinned and pulled off what he now realised were pyjama bottoms, then reached for the oversized T-shirt that seemed to serve as her nightdress.

'Wait! Can I help you?' He knew he was asking something else really, and hoped she understood. She nodded, and he leaned forward to pull the T-shirt off with one swift tug, smiling when he saw that she'd been telling the truth. Her breasts were pale in the half-light, the scattering of freckles on the expanse of skin above them enhancing their beauty. Her nipples were taut and he was sure it wasn't from cold. Desire clawed at him again with near-unbearable intensity, and he had to stop himself from touching her. 'Jesus, but you're so beautiful it hurts.' Literally, because he was so hard he thought he'd explode any second.

'I am? But . . .'

'You have no idea.' Haakon couldn't resist any longer. They were both on their knees, facing each other, and he buried his fingers in that glorious hair before pulling her face to his for a kiss. She tasted of toothpaste and smelled like the summer evening – fresh and intoxicating. He tried to be gentle, but when she nipped his lower lip with her teeth and rubbed up against him, he knew she wanted this as much as he did. 'Mia,' he breathed, deepening the kiss. 'Oh God, I . . .' His arms went around her, stroking the soft skin on her back, his hands moving down to encircle her waist and up between them to stroke the underside of her breasts. 'I want you so much!'

He'd wanted her from the first moment he saw her, and the fact that she seemed to want him too was amazing. Was there such a thing as soulmates? Because he was convinced he'd found his.

He really wants me! And he did find her beautiful. Mia had trouble believing it, but she couldn't doubt what his body was telling her. She felt her bare breasts pushed close to his broad chest, where the slight friction of his warm skin on hers made her breathless. He'd been tentative at first, but now the urgency of his kisses hinted at a passion that had been kept under control for far too long. They were ruthless, heady, firing her blood. When she came up for air at last, she protested half-heartedly, 'Haakon, this is probably not a good idea. What if someone sees us?' But at the same time, she knew that if he stopped, she would be devastated.

'Oh yes, it is. The best one I've had for years,' he murmured, and blazed a trail of kisses along her throat and shoulder, moving down to cover one nipple with his mouth. Mia gasped and gave herself up to the enjoyment. Who was she kidding? She wanted this and she didn't care if the entire world watched them.

She raised her hand to push her fingers through his hair and caught a glimpse of the snake ring out of the corner of her eye. Its two faces appeared to be grinning at her and she stopped for a moment. 'Haakon?'

'Hmm?'

'Take off your ring.'

He was breathing heavily but stopped kissing her. 'What?'

'I don't know about you, but I have a horrible feeling we're being manipulated here. Let's take the rings off and do this without their help. Whoever "they" are.' Mia was serious now. It seemed important to make love to Haakon because she wanted to, not because some long-dead spirits were egging them on.

He nodded. 'You're right. Here, give me yours and we'll put them under a stone for now.' They found a suitably large one and he shoved the two golden serpents underneath. 'OK?'

Mia nodded and put her arms round his neck, pulling his mouth towards hers with a smile. 'Yes. Now, where were we?'

He kissed her again, and it didn't feel any different. She was still consumed with lust, and it had nothing to do with any long-ago Vikings, she was sure. She stopped thinking about it and gave herself up to the wonderful sensations Haakon's mouth and hands were sparking inside her.

His big hands cupped her behind and he groaned. 'You're so perfect.'

'Not as perfect as you.' She drew her nails lightly down his back, and he shuddered. 'What was that you said about a swim?'

'Sod swimming! Christ, woman, you're going to drive me mad,' he whispered hoarsely, then stilled for a moment and leaned his forehead on her shoulder. 'Sorry, I'm going too fast, aren't I? You really want to go swimming?'

Mia laughed. 'No, I was just teasing. Don't stop what you were doing. Just . . . don't stop at all.'

She pushed him down on to the rug and straddled him, leaning forward to kiss him. She couldn't get enough of his mouth; it was beautiful, sensuous and felt so good under hers. 'I seem to be the only one who's naked here. Are you going to take these off?' She played with the waistband of his boxers, her touch making him shiver.

He grinned. 'You do it.' He didn't have to ask twice.

Mia half expected him to turn the tables on her and throw her to the ground, like a marauder from the past, but he allowed her to explore and take her time, at least for a while.

'You're killing me here,' he whispered hoarsely, inserting a finger between them and finding exactly the right place to drive her wild. 'Take me inside you, please, Mia. Now! Unless we need a . . . Damn, my wallet is in my room.'

'No, it's fine, I've got it covered.'

She couldn't wait another second, and slid the length of him into her warmth. He was a perfect fit, tight, hot and unbelievably hard. She began to move, and he joined in with her rhythm until they both exploded with muffled cries. As she collapsed on to his warm chest, she felt blissfully sated as never before. *This* was what lovemaking was supposed to feel like.

And she was definitely in love.

Chapter Thirty-Six

The scene before her was one of carnage, the evening sky lit up by flames that made quick work of several houses, as well as any nearby vegetation. Ceri stumbled on, as if in a dream, but just as she caught sight of her brother's face, an arm encircled her neck from behind and she was yanked back against a hard body.

'Haukr? Show yourself! Is this what you've come for?' her captor shouted defiantly. 'If it is, you're too late.'

She recognised Svein's voice yet again – it haunted her nightmares and she loathed it with a vengeance. She'd had ample time in the hut to remember every last detail of her capture, and she knew that this man had been responsible for the deaths of Steinn and Ulv, whose lifeless bodies she had glimpsed on the way to the jetty. The thought of that made her so angry, she twisted in his grasp and tried to attack him with her fingernails. Ragged and torn after weeks of scrabbling in the soil, they tore the skin of his cheeks, but he was a hardened warrior and such minor pain was as nothing to him. He laughed and captured her hands with one of his.

'Don't think you can escape,' he snarled at her. 'I should have killed you earlier, but my sister wanted you to stew for a few weeks first. Too bad. I'll do it now.'

He lifted his knife, and Ceri tried to put up her hands to shield herself, but before the blow came, another voice sounded behind them.

'I don't think so, *aumingi*. You're the one who will join the goddess of death in her domain!'

She heard the heavy thump of a blow to Svein's head and fell out of the man's arms just as he stumbled sideways, dropping the knife. She watched in a daze as Haukr picked Svein up by the front of his tunic and proceeded to pummel him black and blue. Finally he put his hands round the man's throat and squeezed until Svein's eyes bulged and a strangled gurgle erupted from his throat.

'*Niðingr!* I should kill you, but I'm not a murderer like you,' Haukr hissed, throwing Svein to the ground and spitting after him. 'We'll let the *þing* decide your fate.'

Svein got to his knees and attempted to stand, but he was unsteady on his feet, and as he backed away from Haukr with fear in his eyes, he stumbled over something and fell again heavily.

Ceri heard a crack and blinked, while Haukr frowned and went to haul Svein up again. 'Don't think you can get away . . . *Skítr!* He's broken his skull on a stone.'

'Well, that's . . . that's good, isn't it? Is he dead?' Ceri whispered.

'Yes, more's the pity. I was going to bring him to the king and have him judged for his misdemeanours. Now he's escaped that ignominy.'

But Ceri didn't care. 'Haukr? Is it really you? I thought I'd never see you again.' A sob of relief escaped her as she rushed towards him.

He seemed to come out of his haze of rage and focus on her, as if seeing her properly for the first time. 'Ceri, *ást mín*.' He crushed her to him, enveloping her in an embrace so fierce she could barely breathe. And he'd called her 'my love'.

'But how . . . why . . . is Cadoc really here? I thought I heard him,' she stammered.

'We came together. I'll explain it all later, but you don't need to worry. He knows I mean you no harm, and he hasn't killed me yet.' He grinned ruefully, and Ceri began to cry in earnest with mingled relief and happiness. Haukr stroked her cheek and held on to her. 'Are you unharmed? Did they . . . misuse you?'

'No. I've been locked up for ages in a root cellar, weeks maybe, and no one has come near me since I arrived, although I dreaded it daily. I think that was the point, to terrorise me into madness. The darkness and cold. And he . . .' she nodded in Svein's direction without actually looking at him, 'said something about Ragnhild wanting me to suffer before he—'

'She is going to pay, I'll see to that if your brother doesn't beat me to it.'

'Is Jorun all right?' Ceri had been so worried about the little girl and had prayed to any god she could think of to keep her safe.

'Yes, she's well. As a matter of fact, you have her to thank for this rescue. She told me what happened.'

'She told you?'

Haukr laughed. 'Yes, the way you taught her, using a few words and miming. It took me a while before I understood, but that was mostly my fault because I was so sunk in misery. I thought you were dead, you see – but I'll explain about that later.'

'Well, thank God you came. Although I had actually just managed to break free, I really had no idea which direction to go in order to return to you. I would have been completely lost.'

'Come, let us go and find your brother. He'll be very happy to see you. I just hope . . . But we'll discuss that later.'

'Are we all agreed that Ragnhild is guilty as charged?'

Haukr stood solemnly at one end of his former brother-in-

313

law's hall, where everyone, including Cadoc and his men, had gathered. Ragnhild's four older brothers were all dead, as were a large proportion of their men, but her youngest sibling Leif had surrendered and brought the fighting to a halt.

'I swear I had no part in this; I didn't even know this woman was being held here,' he'd said, indicating Ceri. 'Svein brought a number of thralls here a couple of weeks back and I thought he'd purchased them. It wasn't my place to question him in any case. Please, let us settle this in a less violent manner.'

As the youngest son, he was lucky not to have been sent out into the world to fend for himself. Haukr had met Leif before, and he was the only one of Ragnhild's brothers he actually liked. The pleasant youth had grown into a man since he'd last seen him, and the look in his eyes was sincere and regretful. Now they both regarded Ragnhild, who stood in front of them with her hands bound.

'I, for one, agree,' Leif said, staring at his sister dispassionately. 'Ragnhild has done nothing but cause trouble here since she divorced you, and I'll be glad to be rid of her. She's no sister of mine any longer.'

'Coward,' she spat. 'Svein should have sent you away. You were never one of us.'

Haukr decided to cut their bickering short. 'Nevertheless, Leif is now the owner of this domain and head of your household. He will be the one to decide your fate and what is owed to me in compensation for the damage you wrought to my property.'

'Your hall was burned, you say?' Leif frowned. 'And half your people killed. Not to mention livestock and supplies destroyed . . .'

Haukr nodded. 'Then there is my . . . er, guest, Ceridwen, who was mistreated by your kinsmen.' He glowered at Ragnhild, but managed to stay calm even though he'd have liked to tear her limb from limb for what she'd done to Ceri. Not to mention giving him the shock of his life with that sacrificial body in the ash tree.

'Then I'd say I owe you half my thralls, all the treasure Ragnhild brought back as returned dowry, plus some livestock and food supplies. Perhaps if we tally all that is left between our two holdings, then divide everything in half ... Does that sound reasonable?'

Ragnhild gasped. 'I take it back – Svein should have killed you at birth, you little *aumingi!*'

'*Þegi þú!*' Leif walked over and slapped his sister. 'This is all your fault, and you have brought shame on our family. The least I can do is try to repair the damage. This way both our settlements have a chance to survive and prosper again. As for you, I think a fitting punishment would be . . .' He turned towards Cadoc, who had kept silent throughout. 'Ceridwen's brother, how would you like to acquire a very difficult thrall and take her back to your homeland?' He indicated Ragnhild, whose eyes narrowed in fury.

Cadoc smiled and looked Ragnhild up and down with a glance that boded ill for her. 'Oh, I think I can tame even the most recalcitrant of thralls. Thank you, yes, I'll gladly have her.'

'Good, that's settled then. Haukr, what do you say to my proposal?'

'It is more than generous, and I accept.'

Neither man spared another glance at Ragnhild as she was led out of the hall by Cadoc, shouting and swearing. Haukr had no doubt she'd soon be made to change her tune, and it was no more than she deserved. She had made so many people's lives a misery; it was her turn to suffer now.

Ceri sat at the back of Haukr's ship, huddled inside a woollen blanket, but she wasn't really cold any longer. Haukr was right next to her, steering while his men rowed and holding her hand in a firm grip as though he'd never again let go. The touch of his callused fingers warmed her like nothing else could, inside and out.

Cadoc's ship was alongside theirs. It looked like a Norse one and she assumed he must have bought or borrowed it in Dyflin, where he had trading connections. His own boat wouldn't have been large enough to go sailing across the seas. She hadn't had a chance to speak to him properly yet, but she was looking forward to it and to hearing about everyone in their village.

'When I draw up the list of thralls for the purpose of sharing with Leif, I will omit the ones from your village.' Haukr's fingers tightened around hers.

Ceri looked up into his blue eyes and saw them crinkle at the corners, while his mouth turned up in a smile that seemed to be just for her. She wasn't sure what this meant, but at the moment it was enough just to be with him. 'Thank you. I'm sure Cadoc would have paid you for them, but . . .'

'He doesn't have enough, I know.' Haukr sighed. 'I shouldn't have taken them captive in the first place, but then again, if I hadn't, I would never have met you, so I have no regrets.'

'Really? But . . .'

He was about to reply, but they were interrupted by a commotion on board Cadoc's ship that made them turn and look that way. 'What's going on?' Ceri sat up straighter so she could see over the side. 'Oh no . . .'

Ragnhild was screaming at the top of her voice, seemingly going berserk, and two of Cadoc's men were trying to subdue her. It was like fighting an eel, by the looks of it, as she threw herself this way and that, wriggling, kicking, spitting and head-butting.

'By Odin, I feel sorry for your brother,' Haukr muttered. 'He'll have his work cut out for him.'

But in the next instant, Ragnhild suddenly flung herself

sideways, catching Cadoc's men by surprise. There was a splash as she hit the water, lots of shouting while the men stopped rowing to stare into the lake and gesticulate, then someone jumped in after her.

'Dive, man, dive!'

'She jumped in further to the left. No, left, I said!'

'Over there!'

Ceri drew in a sharp breath. 'Can you see her? What's happening?' She craned her neck but couldn't see any sign of Ragnhild.

'Stupid woman.' Haukr swore. 'She must be trying to swim to freedom, but her hands were fettered with iron chains.'

'She could still keep afloat, couldn't she?' Ceri had never liked Ragnhild, but she didn't wish her to drown.

'Perhaps.'

But it soon became clear that Ragnhild hadn't made any attempt to save herself, as she was nowhere to be seen. It was only after a long while that her body surfaced further along the lake, and by then it was too late.

'Oh, dear Lord! She couldn't face the thought of being anyone's thrall.' Ceri could understand that, but at the same time, Ragnhild's suicide seemed extreme.

Haukr closed his eyes. 'May the gods receive her,' he whispered. 'It is for them to judge her now.'

Chapter Thirty-Seven

They'd had their midnight swim and then Haakon had made love to her again, hard and fast, exactly as she'd imagined he might. Mia still had a silly grin on her face the following morning, when he stole a kiss in the kitchen behind Linnea's back. He was looking a bit bleary-eyed, and winced when Linnea started using a skipping rope out on the veranda, singing loudly.

'God, where does she get all that energy?' he groaned.

Mia sent him a teasing glance. 'Maybe she didn't have a long night, like her father? Perhaps you should have gone to bed instead of . . . hanging out by the lake.'

Haakon pulled her round the corner and up against a wall, giving her another fierce kiss. 'I'll put up with any number of sleepless nights if I can spend them with you,' he whispered.

Mia kissed him back, then reluctantly pushed out of his arms. 'Did he turn up, Thoresson?' She'd gone back to the house while Haakon finished his shift.

'No, which is probably just as well. I'd rather not have to take on a madman single-handed.'

'You really think he'd resist? I mean, if you shouted that the police were on their way or something, don't you think he'd just turn back and go home?'

'Who knows? If he's hell-bent on taking something, it might not be enough. But I've decided that from tonight onwards, there will be at least two people on guard at all times. Should be safer.'

As Mia made breakfast for them all – a full English because she was in such a good mood – Haakon checked his emails. Halfway through, he called her over. 'Hey, Mia, come and look at this. It's from the museum – they've finished cleaning up the rune stone at last.'

'Oh yes?' She slid the frying pan off the stove and hurried over. 'What does it say?'

'See for yourself.'

She peered over his shoulder and read the words out loud. *'Jorun let ræisa stæin þenna æftir Haukr inn hvíti, faður sinn . . .'* she began, then started on the translation underneath instead. *'Jorun had this stone erected in memory of Haukr the White – or the White Hawk – her father. He went to Bretland – ooh, Wales! – and brought back the greatest gift. Now he is gone to join his dearest. May the gods keep them safe and together.'*

For some reason the words caught in her throat and she suddenly felt like crying. Grief welled up inside her, and she blinked rapidly to clear her eyes. What was the matter with her? These people had been dead for centuries and they were nothing to do with her, but she felt an affinity with them and she could sense Jorun's sorrow as she decided what the carver should write on the stone.

'I wonder what that means.' Haakon looked puzzled. *'Brought back the greatest gift.* What would he have brought her from Wales?'

'A mother.' Mia heard herself say the words, but she had no idea where they'd come from.

'Huh? You think?'

The snake ring reflected the sun into her eyes and she stared at

319

it. They'd both put the rings on again before she'd gone back to the house last night, and now she was sure it was communicating with her once more. She nodded. 'That's what *he* thinks.' She held out her hand.

Anyone else would have told her not to be so silly, but Haakon just nodded too. Then his eyes lit up. 'Haukr!' He pulled off his ring and ran off, returning with a magnifying glass, which he used to peer at the inscription. 'I swear this has to say Haukr. Look!'

Mia did, and although the writing was as indistinct as before, she could see it now. 'Yes, I think you're right. Haukr and Ceri, and little Jorun – perhaps motherless until Ceri's arrival? The rings bound them together. It would make sense.'

They smiled at each other, and Mia sensed the pieces of the puzzle slotting into place with a satisfactory click.

'I called the police forensics guys and they should be here this afternoon. Do you think we ought to go out to the island, just quickly, and open up the second tumulus? If, as I suspect, it's another grave, it will save them a journey if they can look at both of them today.' Haakon didn't know why, but he was itching to go back. It was almost as though the island was calling him.

Mia nodded. 'Sure, that would be logical. What about Linnea?'

'I've asked Isabella to look after her for a while. She's happily washing potsherds with a toothbrush at the moment.'

'Excellent. Let's go then.'

It didn't take them long to row out to the island. Haakon wondered whether to tether the boat on the other side this time, just in case Thoresson was watching and got any ideas, but it was broad daylight. What was the guy going to do, for goodness' sake?

He hefted a bag of equipment on to his shoulder and Mia had a rucksack with everything else they needed. It wasn't long before

320

they had started removing the stones at the head end of the second cairn.

'If the skull of the woman was at this end of her grave, it makes sense the second one will be laid out the same way,' Haakon commented. Viking graves weren't usually in any set orientation, unlike Christian burials, but as these two were side by side, he figured they'd be more or less equal.

The heavy rocks shifted to one side, they began to carefully scrape away the soil, and it wasn't long before the bleached dome of a cranium emerged. 'Yep, there he is.' Haakon dusted it off with a brush and they sat back on their haunches to stare at it for a moment.

'He?' Mia glanced at him.

'I think so.' He put a hand over his heart. 'I feel it here. Don't you?'

She nodded, blinking back tears. 'This is nuts,' she muttered. 'We should have left the damned rings at home.'

'Maybe.' And yet it felt as though it had been the right thing to wear them.

Haakon pulled out another tarpaulin and together they unfolded it and covered the head end of the grave. 'No need to excavate the rest. We'll leave that for the forensics guys.'

They worked in tandem to weight the material with rocks, and then gathered up their tools. 'Let's go back to the—'

'Not so fast. Stay right where you are, or I'll shoot.'

Haakon and Mia both swivelled round to find Thoresson standing on the other side of the first grave, a shotgun raised and pointed straight at them. 'What the . . . ? Are you insane?' Haakon couldn't believe the guy could be this stupid. The archaeology team knew he and Mia were out here. If they heard shots, they'd come running. Or swimming. Whatever . . . they'd fetch help anyway.

'Get off my land.' Mia's voice was vibrating with anger, her clear eyes shooting sparks. 'My solicitor has confirmed that this island belongs to me and so does anything that is found on it.'

'Yes, well that's where you're wrong. Finders keepers is my motto.' Thoresson smirked. 'And right now, I believe I'm the one holding a gun, so how about you just come over here now, or I shoot your precious boyfriend, OK?'

'How did you . . . ?'

'Oh, come on, the caveman look in his eyes.' Thoresson nodded in Haakon's direction. 'It's a dead giveaway. Any minute now he'll thump his chest and go "my woman" like bloody Tarzan. Ha ha! Now get the hell over here! I'm not joking.'

'Don't, Mia.' Haakon knew he'd rather die than have her in that maniac's power, but at the same time he was aware she probably wouldn't listen.

He was right. Mia threw him an anguished glance, then stepped slowly forward. 'What are you going to do?' she asked.

Thoresson grabbed her and swung her so he had one arm round her neck in a stranglehold. 'I'm going to tie the two of you up, take whatever is in that second grave and get the hell out of here, that's what,' he snarled. 'And then my son and I are going to emigrate under new names. Fake IDs aren't as hard to come by as you might think. Maybe we'll go to South America – a vast continent that would easily swallow us up. Some of my ancestors went there after the Second World War, I think. Or perhaps to Iceland, a nice country with very little immigration and lots of pretty blonde girls. Not Celtic scum like you.' He gave Mia's hair a vicious yank.

'Ow! You stupid bastard! You won't get away with this.'

'Shut up!' Thoresson squeezed her neck until she started turning red in the face.

'Stop it!' Haakon held up a hand. 'Come on, there's got to be a way to make a deal here.'

Thoresson relaxed his hold, allowing Mia to wheeze some much-needed air into her lungs, but he shook his head. 'No deal. You, start digging. I want you to put whatever is in that grave in my bag.' He nudged a sports bag with one foot, kicking it over to Haakon. 'Do as I say, or I shoot Ms Hagberg right this minute. I won't kill her, but I can sure as hell do some damage, and if you can't get her to a hospital fast enough . . . well, not my problem.'

Haakon didn't bother to correct the man. What did it matter if he got Mia's name wrong?

He started moving rocks again, picking up a slightly smaller one surreptitiously. If he could throw it at Thoresson and catch the man off guard, perhaps Mia could duck out of his grip. It was worth a try. He tensed, ready to make his move, when suddenly another voice rang out behind Thoresson.

'No! Dad, what are you doing? Let Mia go!' Ivar. A very wet Ivar, who must have either fallen overboard when rowing to the island on his own or swum out here. By the way he was panting and red-faced, Haakon guessed the latter. Wow, the kid had courage, and stamina.

Thoresson's head turned. He obviously hadn't expected his son to turn up. 'Ivar? What the hell do you think you're—'

Haakon didn't hesitate. He threw the stone as hard as he could, hitting the hand Thoresson was gripping his shotgun with. The weapon fell to the ground, and at the same time Mia half turned and kneed the guy in the groin. He shrieked in agony and doubled over, then dived for the gun.

Haakon was already there, though, and kicked the weapon out of the way before grabbing the man in a deadlock from behind. 'Don't even think about it,' he hissed.

'You'll pay for this!' Thoresson was thrashing around, trying to wrestle himself free. 'I'll rid the country of scum like you once and for all. Bloody immigrants!' He sent his son a death glare. 'As for you, you had no business sticking your nose into my affairs. I suppose it was you who told them I'd been digging out here, huh? Did you? Well, you're no son of mine, you hear! Little bastard with your stupid black hair . . .'

Haakon had had enough. He could see the shock on Ivar's face and he couldn't stand it. In such a short time, the boy had become very dear to him, and it was obvious that he was hurting now. Haakon did the only thing he could and hit Thoresson with his fist on the side of the head. The man slumped forward, unconscious.

Mia had been on the phone, calling the police and the rest of the archaeology team. Now she rushed over to Ivar, taking him in her arms before persuading him to undress so she could wrap him in Haakon's hoodie. Haakon kept an eye on Thoresson until a police boat showed up, two sturdy officers escorting the groggy man down to the shore.

The others followed, standing on the rocky outcrop to watch as the boat sped off. It hadn't gone very far, however, when someone was seen to jump into the water. Ivar cried out. '*No! Dad!*' He ran down to the shore, as though preparing to swim out to his father's rescue, but Haakon held him back.

'Wait! They're too far out. You'll never make it, and I'm pretty sure those police guys can swim.'

They watched the flurry of activity that followed, but as far as Haakon could see, only two people climbed back into the boat. After what seemed like hours, it came back towards them and the only dry member of the police team jumped on to the shore. They ran to meet him, but from his sombre expression Haakon knew it wasn't good news. He put his arms round Ivar from behind, trying to give him strength.

'I'm really sorry,' the policeman said, 'but Mr Thoresson

jumped and . . . I'm afraid he had no intention of surfacing again. We couldn't find him, so he must have swum deep, then just . . . stayed there. Young man, please accept my sincere condolences.'

He put a hand on Ivar's shoulder, and the boy nodded, then turned into Haakon's chest and began to sob. All Haakon could do was hold him tight.

Chapter Thirty-Eight

Ceri was appalled at the state of Haukr's settlement, but she was whisked off to the bath house by Aase almost as soon as they arrived and did not have a chance to look too closely.

'You poor thing! The state of you! But I'm so pleased you are alive. We thought . . . but never mind that now.' Aase was clearly delighted and Ceri was equally happy to see her.

'It was a close-run thing, but the jarl and my brother arrived just in time.'

'Thank the gods! Now, let us see about making you more presentable. And I'll fetch some salve for your wounds.'

'They are merely scratches, nothing major.'

At that point, Jorun came rushing in for another joyous reunion. Ceri had to assure the little girl that she was fine and calm her down. Eventually Jorun insisted on helping with Ceri's bath. It took quite a lot of scrubbing to get her clean, but Ceri did not mind. It was wonderful to wash the stench of the root cellar off her skin, and if it glowed a bit more than usual afterwards, so much the better. Aase found her some clean clothes, and it was bliss to be wearing more than just an under-tunic. 'And shoes! My poor feet have been so cold.' She hugged Aase in gratitude, making the older woman laugh.

'The jarl is wishing to speak to you. Do you feel up to seeing him, or would you prefer to rest first?'

'I rested on the ship. Take me to him now, please.'

Haukr was waiting in the weaving hut, and Aase tactfully left them alone, taking Jorun away with her, but did not close the door. 'Are you well, Ceridwen?' He peered at her intently, those blue eyes of his sparkling in the light from outside.

'Yes, thank you, quite well. You and Cadoc came in time. I'm in your debt for rescuing me.'

He shook his head, his gaze troubled. 'Let us not speak of debts. If I hadn't brought you here in the first place, you would never have been in danger.' He sighed. 'I don't want your gratitude. I want ... Ceri, is there any chance I can persuade you to stay here with me rather than returning home with your brother?'

Her heart made a somersault. 'S-stay?'

'Yes. I can't bear to let you go. I ... When I thought you had been killed, something inside me died too. What do you say? Must you leave?'

'But when you marry again ...' She swallowed hard, not wanting to even think about that, and shook her head. 'I can't be your mistress. It simply wouldn't work and—'

He leaned forward and gripped her hands as he interrupted her. 'Ceri! Do you really think there is anyone I'd want for a wife other than you? Surely you must have gathered how I feel by now, even if I've not been able to put it into words properly?'

'I ... No.' Her cheeks burned and she shook her head. 'You can't want to marry me. I mean, I would bring you nothing. The ransom, perhaps, but you said—'

He let go of her hands and put his arms around her instead, pulling her up hard against him. 'The trolls take the ransom! I don't need it, I only need you. From the moment I first saw you,

I knew I couldn't leave you behind. It was our fate to be together and I have dreamed of it constantly. Just seeing you every day was wonderful, but for you to be my wife would be the ultimate joy. It is all I could ever wish for. Please, tell me you can bear to remain here. Will you stay with me, for ever, *ást mín*?'

'Oh Haukr, of course I will. If you're sure?'

'I've never been more sure of anything in my entire life.'

He leaned forward. His big, strong hands came up to cup her cheeks on either side, and Ceri stared at him as his mouth descended towards hers. She knew she ought to stop him, especially in view of the fact that Aase could return at any moment, but she couldn't tear herself away. When his lips touched hers, she almost sobbed, it was such a sweet moment. For months now she had longed for him to do precisely that, had wanted him to look at her just so, and wild horses wouldn't drag her away now.

'Oh, Ceri,' he whispered against her cheek. 'Will you marry me soon? Please? We could do it while your brother is here to help us celebrate.'

'That would be wonderful. I just hope he won't become angry all over again.'

'Go and speak to him. I'm sure he will understand. He strikes me as a reasonable man.'

'I will.'

She and Haukr belonged with one another, she knew that now, and nothing and no one could change that. She gave herself up to the enjoyment of his embrace.

'Are you sure you wish to stay here? You've not been coerced in any way, *cariad*?'

Ceri and her brother were sitting on the jetty while his men went to and fro, readying his ship for departure. Little wavelets lapped the shore and the evening breeze brought the scents of early summer. It was peaceful, beautiful and, she realised, it was now her home.

'No, no force has been applied whatsoever. I love him, Cadoc, he's a good man. The best. And I want to share the rest of my life with him.' Ceri felt her love for Haukr swell inside her chest until she thought she might burst with it.

'Then I'm pleased for you and give you my blessing.' Cadoc kissed her cheek and hugged her to him. 'I'm only sorry I won't be taking your tormentor back with me to receive a fitting punishment. I would have enjoyed that.'

Ceri nodded, but secretly she felt it was better for God to judge Ragnhild, rather than her fellow men.

'Perhaps it was for the best, though,' she said now. 'She would have caused no end of trouble for you, and maybe even harmed Bryn.' She shuddered at the thought. 'I'm so glad he's well. You must send him my love and bring him for a visit sometime. Promise?'

'I will, I swear.'

Ceri left Cadoc to oversee his men while she went in search of Haukr. She found him in the little hut they shared – alone, as Aase had tactfully persuaded Jorun to stay with her until the hall was rebuilt – and he was pacing.

Her stomach flipped over. 'What's the matter? Has something else happened?'

'What? Oh, no, it's just . . . You haven't changed your mind, have you?' He stopped in front of her and peered at her intently. His eyes were very blue, despite the gloomy interior of the hut, and Ceri felt herself drowning in his gaze.

'No, of course not. Why, did you think I would?'

'I thought your brother might try to persuade you by remind-ing you of all you've left behind, but I'll make it up to you, I promise. Although . . . well, I did bring you here against your will.'

Ceri stepped close to him and stood on tiptoe to twine her arms around his neck. 'Maybe so, but now I've chosen to remain here for ever. Cadoc will come back, and we can also visit him and the rest of my family. Thanks to you, he's taking all the other villagers home with him – those that don't want to stay here as freemen – and there is no ill feeling on either side. All is well.'

'Thank the gods! I was so afraid . . . Oh, Ceri, *ek ann þér*. I love you more than I can ever say!'

'And I love you, my white hawk. I'll never leave you again.'

'Good. Then we'll be together for all eternity,' Haukr whispered, kissing her with a passion that lit an answering flame in her veins. 'I'll not allow anyone else to tear us apart, I swear.'

Ceri smiled at him between kisses. 'Me neither, by Odin. Just let them try!'

Nothing ruined the marriage ceremony a few days later, and no one seemed to mind that the hall had no roof or walls as yet. A lot of hard work was still needed to restore all the damage done, even though Cadoc and his men had stayed to help with some of the rebuilding. Leif had sent some of his people as well, once he'd finished clearing up his own settlement. There was much to do, but none of it was necessary for the wedding feast, as the weather stayed warm and dry.

Trestle tables were placed on either side of the space that would soon be the main room of the hall, with the high table at one end. There were carved chairs for both Haukr and Ceri, with a special smaller one for Jorun placed to Haukr's right. Colourful woven runners covered each table, and there was every imaginable dish of food, including some prepared by the women from Ceri's homeland. Carved wooden platters were heaped with roasted pork, lamb, venison and elk, as well as game birds and fish of every kind. Various types of bread – rye, barley and oat-cakes – were set out next to cheeses of different kinds, dried fruit, nuts and honey. Drinking horns jostled for space with ale tankards of pewter and wood, and there were even two exquisite glass vessels brought by a neighbour as a present, together with some imported wine.

Ceri and Jorun both wore beautiful red over-gowns with panels of silk appliquéd to the front and sleeves, and edged with matching woven bands. A plaid shawl covered Ceri's shoulders, fastened with a lovely Celtic brooch that was Cadoc's gift to her. Haukr was just as resplendent, his tunic embroidered around the hem and cuffs.

'Marriage is normally a long-drawn-out process,' he had explained, 'with negotiations about dowry and bride price, as well as rituals to determine the most auspicious date. But none of those things matter this time. I just want it to be done quickly, if you're in agreement?'

Ceri was.

The wedding feast was to last three days, even though there were no special guests invited. Many of their neighbours turned up anyway, as word had obviously spread, and they were all made welcome. Haukr and Ceri shared the wedding mead, participated in various rituals and swore the marriage oaths. Cadoc seemed as happy as everyone else. He and his men cheered loudly when the oaths had been sworn and Haukr kissed his new wife for much longer than was seemly. Ceri was sure that her cheeks must be on fire, but at the same time she had never been happier.

Then Haukr held out his hand, revealing three exquisite gold rings in the shape of little snakes. 'I bought these for us to exchange.

331

Let me put one on your finger and then you can do the same for me.'

'Gladly!' Ceri watched as he threaded the medium-sized ring on to the fourth finger of her left hand, then she put the largest one on his finger. 'But why three?'

Haukr smiled and beckoned to his daughter. 'I thought Jorun should have one too, as you are marrying both of us, as it were. Here, Jorun *mín*, hold out your hand.' He mimed the action and she complied, allowing him to put the tiniest ring on her finger. The glittering gold appeared to mesmerise her as she turned it this way and that to catch the light. It was clear that she liked it very much.

They had tried to explain to her that they were in love and getting married, and although Ceri wasn't sure Jorun quite understood, the little girl seemed happy enough. There was no need for her to call Ceri 'Mother' – she felt as though she was her parent in every other way, and a name made no difference to the way she loved Jorun.

When the exchange of rings was done, Jorun was led away by Aase, while Thorald and the rest of Haukr's men, together with Cadoc and his warriors, came to escort the newly married couple to their bed. Ceri felt her cheeks heat up once more, but Haukr just laughed when she protested.

'There must be no doubt that this marriage is valid, which is why we need witnesses. And I've arranged for a priest from Birka to come tomorrow and perform his own kind of ritual as well, even if it is a little after the event. I hope you don't mind. He couldn't come any earlier.'

'A priest? Really? Oh, thank you, that will be wonderful!' Although Ceri had been prepared to sacrifice everything for this man, she would feel much better knowing their union was sanctified by God.

'For now, though, I want to take my wife to bed. Thorald, lead on!'

Thankfully, the men didn't stay to watch beyond them getting into the bed, and Ceri was very grateful for that. She wanted Haukr all to herself.

Chapter Thirty-Nine

'Hi, Mia, it's Alun. How's things? Sounds like you're having a lot of fun with the Vikings!'

Mia smiled and looked out over the lake. She'd emailed Alun their latest findings in confidence, as she was so excited about them, and also told him all about Thoresson and the amazing things the police had confiscated at his house. Being the good friend he was, he'd called straight away.

'Yes, the excitement never ends here,' she quipped. 'But I could have done without the shotgun incident, for sure.'

'Yeah, scary. I'm glad you're all right. I mean, you are, aren't you?' Alun sounded a bit worried now, and she hastened to reassure him.

'I'm fine, but poor Ivar, Thoresson's son . . . Well, I guess it takes a while before you get over something like that. He's staying with us for now, though. The social services said that was OK. We're doing our best to give him as much support as we can.'

'Good. Poor kid. Anyway, listen, I think I've got something interesting to tell you as well.'

'Oh yeah? What's that then?'

'Remember that story I was working on? The one I told you about back in the spring?' Alun's voice was bubbling with excitement and Mia almost sighed. He was like this every time he came across some new manuscript, and they always turned out to contain something he couldn't prove in the end.

'Yes, what of it? Don't tell me – it proves that King Arthur really existed and there were dragons in Wales?'

'Ha ha, very funny. No, actually, it's better than that – it's about that *hebog*, your hawk.'

'My what?' Mia wondered if he'd been out in the sun too much.

'*Hebog – haukr* – means hawk. As in your White Hawk. Didn't you say that was the name of the man in the grave you found? And his wife was Ceridwen? Well, those are the main characters in my story. Not *my* story, but you know what I mean.'

'You're kidding!' Mia's heart beat faster. 'Tell me. Please.'

'OK, so it's all about how this Haukr guy kidnaps a Welsh girl called Ceridwen and takes her to a land far to the north. She manages to tell someone his name is the White Hawk – I guess he must've been really blond or always wore white clothing or something. Anyway, her brother Cadoc goes in search of her, trying all the known trading towns where slaves are sold: Dyflin – that's Dublin to you and me – Hedeby, Kaupang, then finally Birka in Sweden. Or the land of the Svíar, as I think Beowulf would've called it. He finally finds his sister, but by then she's fallen in love with the Hawk and wants to stay. There's a whole bunch of other drama, but bottom line is Haukr's former wife kills herself, Ceridwen marries him and they all live happily ever after. How's that for a great yarn?'

Mia was stunned. 'I . . . That's incredible. You really think they're the same people as the ones we've found here?'

'Who knows? But it sounds like more than mere coincidence, don't you think?'

'Yes, it does. Wow. That's . . . awesome!' Mia laughed. 'I can't believe it – you finally found a story where you can almost prove the characters were actually real people. Congratulations!'

'Oh ye of little faith,' Alun muttered. 'I'm going to take it as definite proof, and maybe the Stockholm Historical Museum will agree to a joint exhibition on the subject. I'll suggest it to them anyway.'

'You do that. We'll back you all the way. Thanks, Alun! Talk to you soon.'

As she hung up and went to find Haakon to tell him this extraordinary tale, she almost laughed out loud. What were the chances of someone writing down that particular story and Alun finding it just as she and Haakon dug up the protagonists' remains? She glanced at her snake ring.

'You, my friend, have a lot to answer for, huh?'

Haakon found Mia sitting at the end of the jetty, staring out over the lake. It was the middle of August and the dig was nearly finished, at least for this year, although the museum had indicated they might want them to continue the following summer.

'There you are! Did you read the email from Professor Mattsson?' He lowered himself on to the jetty next to her and dangled his bare feet in the cool water while putting an arm around her shoulders. 'Some very exciting carbon-dating results, and also that report from the osteoarchaeologist.'

She nodded, but he thought she felt a bit stiff, not leaning into him the way she normally would. 'Yes, wonderful! I can't believe that piece of plaid really was ninth century – it must have been Ceri's, or perhaps a thrall's. And if that was her and Haukr in those graves on the island, it's good to know that they lived to a reasonable age and were buried next to each other.'

The bone specialist had confirmed the skeletons were those of a man and a woman of between fifty and seventy years of age –

fairly old for the Vikings. And neither Haakon nor Mia really doubted the identity of those buried, knowing in their hearts who they were. As for the man in the grave found near the forest clearing, DNA had shown him to be Haukr's father.

'And now that he's feeling better, Mattsson's agreed to us doing a special exhibition about their lives. With the brooch and other items from Thoresson's house that belonged to Ceri, plus all the grave goods we found buried with Haukr and his father, it should make for a fascinating display. And the three rings, now that you've agreed to lend yours to the museum for a while. Oh yes, not to mention your friend's manuscript.' Haakon shook his head. 'I still can't believe that – what are the odds, honestly?'

Mia smiled. 'Indeed.' She sighed. 'I guess I'll be seeing Alun soon. I have to go back to London next week. My leave of absence is almost at an end.'

'About that . . .' Haakon let go of her shoulders and took her hand in both of his instead. 'I was wondering . . . how would you feel about looking for a new job?'

She raised her eyes to his, a questioning look in their depths. 'Here, you mean?'

'To begin with, yes. I'm sure Mattsson could find you something temporary, if you wouldn't mind a slight pay cut.' She opened her mouth to protest, but he forestalled her. 'Hang on, let me finish. I . . . well, Linnea and I . . . would really like you to stay with us. And no, not just because I need help with childminding.' He grinned and leaned forward to kiss the tip of her nose. 'Although that would be very welcome, obviously, now that I'll have full custody of the little madam for the foreseeable future.'

Sofia had decided to stay in India indefinitely to do charity work and further courses in meditation, and had agreed to let Haakon have Linnea. Sofia's parents, surprisingly, had helped persuade her, perhaps realising it was the best thing for their granddaughter. 'As long as we can still see her,' they'd said, and Haakon was very happy to allow that.

'So you're saying you want me to move in with you guys?' Mia's gaze was still searching his, as if she was looking for something more.

Haakon smiled. 'Sort of.' He swung his legs up and got on to one knee next to her. 'This is probably the most awkward place ever for this, but is there any chance you would like to marry me? Or us, rather? I can only speak for myself, obviously, but I am totally and utterly in love with you, and I think I can safely say Linnea likes you a lot too.'

'M-marry you?' Mia's eyes opened wide, the brilliance of the clear grey shimmering like diamonds. 'Oh, Haakon, I'd love to!' She threw her arms around his neck and almost propelled him off the jetty. 'But are you sure? I mean, you've already tried it once and, well . . .'

'I'm sure. This feels completely different and I know you're the only woman for me, *elskede* Mia.' He kissed her, then pulled away to smile at her while digging something out of his pocket. 'You might like to wear this then. It's a one-off replica of one of the other Viking rings in the museum's collection. I got special permission to have it copied. I'll also be allowed to copy Haukr and Jorun's rings for myself and Linnea, for when we marry. That way we'll have matching ones, just like them, even if yours will be the only original. What do you think?'

'Oh, how wonderful! I love this one too, it's gorgeous. Thank you! And it will be great for us to have a set, like the people from the past.' Mia allowed him to put the new ring on the fourth finger of her left hand, where it fitted perfectly. 'I kind of feel the old ones should stay together, though, don't you? Now they've found each other again after so long. Could we have a new one made for me too, and then I'll lend mine to the museum indefinitely? I think my gran would have been OK with that.'

'Sounds like an excellent idea. I'll talk to Mattsson about it, but I'm sure he'll be thrilled. I have a few other things to discuss with you too – for instance, I've heard there are a couple of jobs coming up in York next year, so maybe we could all move over there for a while. So much Viking stuff to find there still, and it would be great if we could work together.'

'Sounds amazing.' Mia grinned. 'You're full of surprises today! Lovely ones, I hasten to add.'

'One last thing – I've just come off the phone with the social worker and with Ivar's aunt Ingegerd, who as you know is now his guardian. I sort of hinted to them that we were about to get married – sorry, had to jump the gun a bit there and take a chance that you'd say yes – and they've both agreed Ivar can live with us as our foster son. Ingegerd said she's too old to cope with a teenager – she's never had kids herself and likes her well-ordered life, apparently – plus she works long hours as a doctor. And the social worker has seen him with us and knows we love him and will look after him well. He seems to like us too. What do you say? Can you cope with not just one, but two kids?'

They'd both come to love Ivar, who had matured so much over the summer. Although he still had moments of grief, for the most part he was happy and relaxed, and he'd fit into their family perfectly as he and Linnea got on so well. He'd also done a complete about-turn and was now embracing what he called his 'inner Viking' – his hair was returning to its original blond and he was determined to study archaeology, specialising in the Viking era.

'If they're ours, I think I could handle at least two more.' Mia smiled.

'Are you saying . . . ?' Haakon felt a thrill race through him at the thought of having lots of children, his and Mia's.

'Yes, I am. I want you, Linnea, Ivar and as many kids as we can afford. Oh, and at least one dog.'

Haakon laughed and pulled her in for another kiss. 'As long as you stay with me, you can have whatever you want, *ást mín*, as the Vikings would say.'

She was, and always would be, his love.

Epilogue

Birch Thorpe, AD 871

On the outermost tip of the peninsula, Ceri waited and watched through the lonely hours of dawn, scanning the water as far as the eye could see.

Just as the faint tinge of pink in the sky turned to pearly grey, a pair of strong arms came around her from behind, surprising a small squeak out of her as she hadn't heard anyone approaching. 'Haukr!' she protested, but they both knew she didn't mind one bit. The sensation of having his solid bulk pressed up against her back was something she'd never tire of, and she half turned her head so he could give her a kiss.

He pulled her close, squeezing gently just below her bust. 'Is she keeping you awake again, the little one?' His voice was tender, and he stroked her distended stomach with a gentleness that filled her already overflowing heart with love.

'He,' she corrected him. 'The runes told Old Tyra it's a boy, and you know they are never wrong. Besides, he kicks something fierce – no girl would be so violent.'

He chuckled, the sound making her shiver as she felt it right to her core. 'We will see – it matters not. Whatever it is, this child will be more than welcome, you know that.'

She did, and she also knew there would be many more – again the runes had spoken. She was so grateful to all the gods – including her own – for giving her these precious gifts. She sent up prayers of thanks daily, and had left a small gift for the goddess Freyja in the sacred grove, just to be on the safe side. Best of all, she no longer needed to scan the horizon for a glimpse of the familiar snake's-head carving at the prow of Haukr's ship, because he had promised they would never again be parted. From now on, wherever he went, she would go too.

They'd sworn to spend eternity together.

'You weren't standing here pining for your homeland, were you? It was just the child keeping you awake?' Haukr leaned his cheek on the top of her head as he waited for her reply.

She put her hands over his and squeezed tight. 'Just the child. I've told you – wherever you are is my home; always will be. It doesn't matter what country we are in. You are my world.'

'As you are mine.' She felt him smile against her hair.

She still had a lot to discover about Norse ways and being mistress of such a large settlement, but she was enjoying learning and there were always people willing to help guide her. They had fully accepted her into their community and she didn't feel like an outsider any more. This was definitely her home, every day a new adventure.

The first rays of sunlight appeared on the horizon, heralding another spectacular morning, the iridescent colours mirrored in the still waters of the lake. Most of the settlement's inhabitants would be waking soon, but Haukr had other ideas.

'Do you think you might like to come back to bed now, *ást mín*? Perhaps I can make you forget the little one for a while?' His hand moved lower, knowing exactly how to entice her after nearly a year of being married. The spark between them was as strong now as the very first time, and she could never resist him.

'Mmm, I think I can be persuaded.' She turned around within the circle of his arms and, smiling, put her own around his neck. 'Take me back to the hall, my love.'

She didn't have to ask twice. He swung her off her feet, lifting her easily despite the added burden of their unborn child, and headed up the hill towards the newly built hall, which was even more splendid than the former one. He had made sure they had a private chamber at one end with a proper door for extra privacy rather than just a flimsy hanging, and soon his blue eyes were gazing at her with desire burning in their depths, while soft wolf pelts surrounded them in their bed and the dawn chorus started up outside. As Haukr made love to her, slowly and carefully to take account of the baby, Ceri was happier than she'd ever thought she would be.

She had been waiting for this man all her life.

And now he was hers.

Acknowledgements

I have dedicated this book to my mother as a thank you for her unstinting love and support – we don't live very close to each other unfortunately, but we are always together in our hearts. And thank you so much, Mamma, for accompanying me to all those Viking museums – best road trip ever!

To the lovely Kate Byrne and her team at Headline for taking a chance on my Viking story and for the fantastic job they've done on this book – a massive thank you!

Thank you to Lina Langlee, my brilliant agent and fellow Swede, for encouraging me to embrace our ancestors and write more about Vikings – I am so grateful for everything you do!

A huge thank you to Dr Rebecca Merkelbach for patiently answering all my questions regarding Old Norse words and phrases, and Viking customs in general – any grammatical/ vocabulary mistakes are entirely my own.

Thank you to Anne-Marie Ugland for helping me with modern Norwegian words for my hero Haakon; to Elanor Stanley for help with archaeological dig details; and to Sam and Mark Grayshon – Viking reenactors with the Ormsheim group (http://ormsheim. org.uk/) – who very kindly answered my many questions about their clothing, equipment, food and experiences. Also to Anne

Katrine Jybaek at the Viking Ship Museum in Roskilde for taking the time to show me around and give me some extra information about sailing a longboat – I really appreciated that!

When things are looking bleak and you're ready to give up writing altogether, there's nothing you need more than really good friends. I am truly blessed by having some of the very best and want to thank (in no particular order) Sue Moorcroft, Myra Kersner (aka Maggie Sullivan), Henriette Gyland and Gill Stewart for always being there and keeping me going. I can't tell you how much that has meant to me! An extra thank you to Myra for advice and information regarding people who have hearing problems.

Thanks are also due to my Swedish friends Gun-Britt Lager and Chicki Jonsson – always ready to meet up for *fika*, chat and moral support – can't believe we've been together since the age of six!; to Caroline Dahlén-Fräjdin, lovely friend and fellow booklover, always positive, always supportive; to Anna Belfrage, Swedish author extraordinaire, who encouraged me to write fantasy and who truly understands about time slip and time travel; to Anna Rambäck for good times and for being my go-to person for questions regarding Stockholm; to my amazing niece and nephew, Lea and Anthony Tapper, for all the love and help you give; and to all my friends in the Romantic Novelists' Association (RNA) who are the most supportive group of people I've ever come across – thank you!

Last but not least, thank you as always to my faithful canine writing companions Fu-Tsi, Fudge (now sadly gone and greatly missed!) and Shennie; and to my lovely family – Richard, Josceline and Jessamy – you mean the world to me!

Echoes
of the
Runes

Bonus material

Redeeming the Vikings

For as long as I can remember, I've been a 'history buff' – I loved hearing my grandmother talking about her childhood when there were still wolves roaming the forests outside the small Swedish town where we lived, and how things were in the old days. When I had learned to read, I devoured everything to do with history, including stories about Tutankhamun, the Greek gods and all the Norse sagas. Because I was half Swedish, the stories about the Vikings in particular captured my imagination and ever since, I've been fascinated by them and their culture.

When I turned thirty, my parents wanted to give me a very special gift to mark this milestone and they came across the most perfect thing – a gold ring that was an exact replica of a Viking ring kept at the Historical Museum in Stockholm. I absolutely loved it, and I wear it a lot. During a visit to Stockholm some years later, I was of course curious to see the original for myself, and visited the museum's so-called Gold Room. Mia's description in my story of this underground vault is accurate – it's the most amazing place full of treasure – and I was thrilled to find 'my' ring on display with a lot of others.

As I stood there looking at it, the idea for *Echoes of the Runes* came to me and, like all authors are wont to do, I started to ask myself 'what if' questions. What if the ring I was wearing wasn't a copy at all but the real thing? What if it had some sort of power? What if it gave me dreams of the time when it was made? And so the story was born.

I didn't write it immediately. I often have ideas like this and usually a single scene comes into my mind at first, not the whole book. I write that scene down and eventually others join it until the entire story becomes clear. In the meantime, I started to do some more in-depth research about the Vikings in order to be able to accurately portray that era. I took my mother and daughters on a trip to Birka, the trading town west of Stockholm which was a busy place in Viking times. I read everything I could find on the subject, visited more museums and watched TV programmes and films. Although they are very much fantasy (albeit based on the Norse sagas and myths), Marvel's *Thor* films also inspired me to hurry up and write.

There was a lot of serendipity involved and at times I almost felt as if someone or something was trying to make me write this book. There just happened to be a TV series where archaeologist Neil Oliver followed in the Vikings' footsteps. There just happened to be a huge exhibition about Vikings at the British Museum in London. I was unexpectedly taken on a trip to the island of Gotland in the Baltic Sea, where there is a museum full of rune stones. And those Marvel films came along just when I needed a push. Who knows how these things work – perhaps it was just that I became hyper aware of any mention of Vikings because they were on my mind anyway? – but it all conspired to make me finish the story.

At the British Museum exhibition, there had been a recording of people speaking Old Norse and for me, that was thrilling to hear. I speak Swedish, which is one of the languages descended from Old Norse, but it has evolved quite substantially. Although it sounds very similar, yet I only understood some of the words. (I've since listened to a lot of Icelandic and the same thing applies.) On a visceral level, though, the language resonated with me and I decided I wanted to add some authentic words and phrases to my manuscript. I believe that helps the reader to feel as though they are really there, listening to the characters. I therefore needed more expert help and wrote to Cambridge University, where someone kindly put me in touch with Dr Merkelbach, who was able to translate my phrases into Old Norse. Using these made my characters come to life even more in my mind.

The more I read about the Vikings, the more I became annoyed that they've had such bad press throughout the ages. Sure, some of them were marauders who thought nothing of killing people for the sake of plunder, but the vast majority by far were peaceful farmers and traders who didn't go raiding. Instead they created an amazing culture where all free men had a voice and free women had rights, including divorce. (There were slaves, but that was the norm in every society of that time and didn't make the Vikings more cruel than anyone else.) Unfortunately, they didn't write anything down about their own society until much later (centuries afterwards) so any accounts written about them were from the point of view of those who were defeated by them in some way. That makes for some rather one-sided descriptions! I wanted to show them from a different perspective and I hope I've done them justice in *Echoes of the Runes*.

The thing with Vikings is that they were not afraid to die – only to die dishonourably. That made them fearless and perhaps, in the eyes of others, ruthless. It also led them to achieve amazing things and their adventuring spirit took them to what they probably thought of as the ends of the earth. From Scandinavia they travelled in every direction, as far as America in the west and Baghdad in the east. All this without proper navigational tools and with only sheer determination and curiosity to drive them. I find that awesome and I hope you've enjoyed spending time with my Vikings as much as I have!

Christina x

Read on for an exclusive early preview of
Christina's next enthralling novel

THE RUNES OF DESTINY

Coming soon from

REVIEW

Chapter One

Kneeling in a muddy trench in the middle of an archaeological dig might be considered a dirty and boring job by some, but it was just what Linnea Berger needed right now. The rhythmic scraping of a trowel on soil was soothing, mind-numbing, creating an inner peace she had been craving for weeks. And who cared about a bit of mud?

'Finding anything, Linnea?'

She looked up into the kindly face of Uncle Lars. He wasn't her uncle really, but the grandfather of her best friend Sara, as well as her dad's boss. Lars and his family had been a huge part of her life for as long as Linnea could remember, hence the honorary title.

'Nothing much.' Although to be honest she hadn't really been paying attention. *Oops!* She glanced quickly at the heap of soil behind her, hoping she hadn't missed anything vital. It was a good thing her dad wasn't here or he'd have told her off for sure.

'Well, what's that then?' Lars pointed at a cream-coloured patch that was just emerging from the soil in front of her. He hunkered down and smiled, the grooves around his eyes deepening. 'Keep trowelling. I think this could be good.'

'Oh, right.' Linnea refrained from making a face. She'd learned by now that the finds an archaeologist considered 'good' usually proved to be something extremely mundane and boring, like a glass bead or a rusted piece of metal that resembled nothing more than a pitted lump. But then she didn't have their expertise in the minutiae of Viking life, which was what they were exposing in this field. Lars' enthusiasm was infectious though and she always enjoyed watching him at work.

Lars and Haakon, Linnea's father, oversaw archaeological digs every summer. Since around the age of six, Linnea had been dragged along, even though she'd never been all that keen. It was just an inevitable part of her summer holidays and as Lars usually brought his granddaughter Sara, who was the same age as Linnea, at least they'd had fun when the hard work stopped each day. The two girls had hit it off right from the start and they'd been best friends ever since. Although Linnea normally lived in the UK these days, while Sara had stayed in Sweden, their bond remained strong.

The archaeology bug had never bitten Linnea, or at least not in the practical sense. Instead she'd become fascinated by runes and the Viking language – Old Norse – to the extent that she was now a PhD student in that subject at the University of York. It required a certain amount of knowledge about the culture, of course, and a love of all things Viking which she'd acquired through her parents. But she'd always preferred to read about the period rather than dig up the evidence first-hand.

That all changed with the accident . . .

She continued to scrape and Lars joined in, pulling his own trowel out of a back pocket. What began to protrude from the dark earth was ivory in colour and slightly domed. Linnea swallowed hard and hesitated. It couldn't be … could it? Tense now, she levered off a large piece of soil and was suddenly face to face with a gaping eye socket, its dark, mournful stare directed straight at her. She jumped and emitted a small shriek.

Lars didn't seem to notice. 'Well, hello! What have we here? I do believe it's the first grave of the site. Excellent! Just what I was hoping for.'

Linnea wasn't listening. Confronted with the reality of death and the remains of an actual body, she'd tuned out. The only word that registered was 'grave', which sent her mind into a spin. It was far too close to home. Her surroundings disappeared and instead she was in the back of a car again, travelling at way over the speed limit, and then everything imploded. *The screech of tyres breaking too late, the vicious crunch of metal being compressed, the tinkling of shattering glass, and the screams of people who knew they were on an unstoppable path to destruction, taking their last breath . . .*

How did you forget? Was it even possible to make your brain delete something like that, once experienced? Linnea closed her eyes and tried to stem the rising tide of panic that assailed her every time she relived those moments, but it didn't work. *Breathe, Linnea, breathe. In slowly, hold it, then push the air out through half-closed lips, making a weird rasping noise.* The therapist's instructions were clear, but she couldn't do it. It was impossible. A cold sweat broke out between her shoulder blades and her hands started shaking. Her heart fluttered against her ribs in a frantic dance and somehow her lungs weren't big enough for any amount of air to get through . . .

'Hey, Linnea, are you OK?'

She blinked and returned to reality – a field in the wilds of the Swedish countryside. Sunshine on her face, a soft breeze caressing her hair and cheeks, and Uncle Lars peering at her with concern written all over his face. At last, she managed to suck in the much-needed breath, but her heart was still going ballistic. Was she OK? No, not really. The fact that she'd escaped almost unscathed while Sara's parents hadn't . . . It made her feel worse, not better. Survivor's guilt, even though she'd only been a passenger, the accident not her fault. She tried to focus on Lars, putting up a hand to push against her ribcage as if she could calm down her heart from the outside. *At least Sara is going to be OK, focus on that. Breathe!*

'Um, yes. Yes, I'm fine, thanks. Just ... you know, remembering. He ... it ...' She nodded in the direction of the trench but couldn't bring herself to look a second time at that baleful eye.

'Oh, sweetheart, I'm so sorry! I should have realised. Come on, let's get you away from here. You've gone as white as ...' He glanced at the skull in the ground, then quickly looked away. 'I mean, we don't want you fainting now, do we?'

'I'm OK,' she repeated, but didn't resist when he pulled her out of the trench and tucked her arm into the crook of his elbow, steering her towards the food tent.

Linnea was grateful. She didn't think her legs would carry her away from the horrible sight of the skeleton – she shuddered at the mere thought of the word – but Lars supported her. His kindness made her want to cry, but she'd run out of tears ages ago. The well was dry.

'Let's get you some coffee and a chocolate bar. You've had a shock. Entirely my fault. I get too carried away. Poor girl ...' He patted her arm and found her a seat at a camping table while he went in search of coffee.

If only she could be stronger, like him. It was his son and daughter-in-law who had died in that car, after all, and his granddaughter seriously injured. But he seemed to be coping with the grief much better by burying himself in his work. The only outward sign was the profusion of new wrinkles on his brow, and the occasional sombre, contemplative expression.

For Linnea, however, it wasn't that easy. It had become impossible for her to concentrate on translating obscure old texts or memorising syntax and grammar of Old Norse and related languages. Her brain seemed unable to function the way she wanted it to, preferring to dwell on the terrible waste of two lives cut short far too early, and giving her no peace. And her anxiety attacks had grown worse – every time she stepped out into the York traffic and heard car brakes screeching or horns blaring, her breathing became laboured and her heart rate went into overdrive.

It was unbearable and she'd just had to get away for a while. Joining this dig was a godsend. Or at least, it had been until just now . . .

Lars returned with a mug, a bowl of sugar lumps and a chocolate bar. 'Here you go. Put lots of sugar in that coffee, best thing for shock, or so I've been told.' He made a face. 'I really am sorry, my dear. I'm a thoughtless old man. When I'm working, I don't let real life intrude. I mean, of course I'm just as sad as you are, but I simply don't allow myself to think about it during the day. And digging up skeletons is part of my job, always has been.'

'Don't worry about it. Not your fault.' And it wasn't. He didn't mean to be insensitive and Linnea had to toughen up, stop associating everything with what had happened. She'd been doing better this week, forgetting about it for several hours at a time, but that creepy, empty eye socket had brought it all back in technicolour detail.

She still had no idea how she'd escaped the accident with only minor injuries, but she knew one thing – if Sara's dad hadn't been driving too fast as usual, he and his wife might have been alive now. Linnea was still angry with him for being such a speed freak. For never listening. Hadn't Sara and her mum told him over and over again it would end in tears? Although they'd never imagined it would be something this awful . . .

'Earth to Linnea?'

'Huh? Oh, sorry, I was miles away.' Linnea blinked away the

images, willing them to stay buried in her subconscious. She had to let it go. *Had to*. Especially now that Sara was finally getting better and might be out of hospital soon. She would need Linnea's support to recover fully and not to have to deal with someone else's depression. 'What were you saying?'

'I said, how about I let you loose with a metal detector instead? Then you don't have to do more than indicate to others where to dig and you won't get any nasty surprises.'

'Sure.' Linnea had to admit that sounded better.

'Come on then, finish that coffee and I'll show you what to do.'

She swallowed the last of the hot drink and shoved the remaining pieces of chocolate in her mouth as she followed Lars out of the tent and over to a stash of implements. He picked up a metal detector and showed her how to use it. 'And if you get a strong signal, put one of these plastic markers for now.' He handed her a bag of those as well.

'OK. Where do you want me to start? Or am I part of a team?'

'No, it's just you today. Try over in the next field, behind that hedge. The geo-phys guys haven't even been in there yet so it's virgin territory.'

'Right.' She hesitated, then reached up to give him a quick hug. 'Thanks for having me here, Uncle Lars, you're the best.'

His cheeks turned a bit ruddy. 'It was the least I could do in the circumstances. It was my son who nearly . . . But anyway, glad I could help, if only in a small way.'

But Linnea knew he would have helped out, whatever the reason. He was that kind of man. When he'd heard that her dad's summer project had been delayed, Lars hadn't hesitated in offering her a place on his own dig with immediate effect, allowing her to get away from everything when she needed it the most. And it was working. Just not when faced with . . . skulls. She suppressed a shudder.

As she set off towards the field, she knew she was very lucky to have him in her life.

Starting on the other side of the hedge, Linnea began to methodically scan the ground with the detector. Every now and then it gave off beeps, signalling something of interest. Without thinking too much about it, she marked the spots and carried on. As she walked, she tried to steer her mind in a happier direction – the beautiful bird song coming from all around her, the soft caress of the wind on her face, the wonderful scents of burgeoning leaves and flowers. It was peaceful, she couldn't deny that, and her therapist was right – it was time to start enjoying life again.

'She means that you need a man,' had been Sara's comment when Linnea told her about this advice. Happily settled in a relationship herself, Sara seemed to think that having a boyfriend was the answer to everything, but Linnea wasn't so sure.

'No, I think she was trying to tell me that moping won't bring your mum and dad back. That me being miserable isn't helping anyone, least of all myself. Besides, there aren't exactly a whole bunch of guys queuing up to date me.'

That wasn't quite true. She'd had offers – fellow PhD students and guys hitting on her in pubs or clubs – but she wasn't interested. There was only one man she wanted – her tutor, Daniel. Ten years older than her, she'd had a crush on him since the first time they met. With their shared interest in Old Norse, history and an academic career, he'd seemed perfect for her. It didn't hurt that he was tall, dark and handsome – such a cliché – although Sara didn't agree.

'He's too intense. The archetypal nerd,' was her verdict, the one and only time she'd met him.

'Is not! I'd rather have him than some rugby-playing type, all muscles and no brain.' Linnea hotly defended her crush. And she

361

wasn't the only one who had noticed Daniel – he always seemed to have a gaggle of starry-eyed female students around him. 'But it's all academic anyway, as he never seems to notice me except as someone who can take on some of his research workload and do his filing.'

Not that she minded helping him. It was a great excuse to talk to him. Her mobile pinged and she stopped halfway along the field to fish it out of her pocket. Speak of the devil . . .

Hi Linnea, Haven't you had enough of the archaeology malarkey? We're all missing you at the department, especially me ☺ *D x*

It was the weirdest thing, but when she'd told Daniel she was taking time off to go to Sweden, it was as if he'd suddenly realised that he was about to lose her and couldn't bear it. Ever since she arrived, he'd been texting her and the tone was growing warmer. Today's message actually made her blush. There was a smiley face and that x – a kiss? Linnea stared at the screen, her heart hammering in her chest for a different reason now.

What should she reply?